The O. Henry Prize Stories 2013

SERIES EDITORS

2003–	Laura Furman
1997–2002	Larry Dark
1967–1996	William Abrahams
1961–1966	Richard Poirier
1960	Mary Stegner
1954–1959	Paul Engle
1941–1951	Herschel Bricknell
1933–1940	Harry Hansen
1919–1932	Blanche Colton Williams

PAST JURORS

2012	Mary Gaitskill, Daniyal Mueenuddin, Ron Rash
2011	A. M. Homes, Manuel Muñoz, Christine Schutt
2010	Junot Díaz, Paula Fox, Yiyun Li
2009	A. S. Byatt, Anthony Doerr, Tim O'Brien
2008	Chimamanda Ngozi Adichie, David Leavitt, David Means
2007	Charles D'Ambrosio, Ursula K. Le Guin, Lily Tuck
2006	Kevin Brockmeier, Francine Prose, Colm Tóibín
2005	Cristina García, Ann Patchett, Richard Russo
2003	Jennifer Egan, David Guterson, Diane Johnson
2002	Dave Eggers, Joyce Carol Oates, Colson Whitehead
2001	Michael Chabon, Mary Gordon, Mona Simpson
2000	Michael Cunningham, Pam Houston, George Saunders
1999	Sherman Alexie, Stephen King, Lorrie Moore
1998	Andrea Barrett, Mary Gaitskill, Rick Moody
1997	Louise Erdrich, Thom Jones, David Foster Wallace

The O. Henry Prize Stories 2013

Chosen and with an Introduction by
Laura Furman

With Essays by Jurors
Lauren Groff
Edith Pearlman
Jim Shepard
on the Stories They Admire Most

Anchor Books
A Division of Random House LLC
New York

AN ANCHOR BOOKS ORIGINAL, SEPTEMBER 2013

Copyright © 2013 by Vintage Anchor Publishing, a division of Random House LLC
Introduction copyright © 2013 by Laura Furman

All rights reserved. Published in the United States by Anchor Books,
a division of Random House LLC, New York, and in Canada by
Random House of Canada Limited, Toronto,
Penguin Random House Companies.

Anchor Books and colophon are registered trademarks of Random House LLC.

Permissions appear at the end of the book.

The Library of Congress Cataloging-in-Publication Data has been applied for.

Anchor ISBN: 978-0-345-80325-2

www.anchorbooks.com

Printed in the United States of America
10 9 8 7 6 5 4 3 2

To Susan Williamson, with thanks
for friendship, stories, and Passovers.

The staff of Anchor Books—editorial, design, production, publicity—is devoted to publishing the highest-quality literature. Their intelligence, dedication, respect for writers, and professional skill make it an honor to work with them and a pleasure to participate in each *O. Henry Prize Stories* anthology. Editor Diana Secker Tesdell is a gentle, steady force for good. The series editor is grateful for Anchor's excellence.

Mimi Chubb and Kate Finlinson were devoted, invaluable, and brilliant editorial assistants for *The O. Henry Prize Stories 2013*. The series editor is grateful to them for their acuteness and hard work.

The Graduate School and Department of English of the University of Texas at Austin supports *The O. Henry Prize Stories* in many ways, especially with the editorial graduate fellowship. The series editor expresses her gratitude.

—LF

Publisher's Note

A BRIEF HISTORY OF THE
O. HENRY PRIZE STORIES

Many readers have come to love the short story through the simple characters, easy narrative voice and humor, and compelling plotting in the work of William Sydney Porter (1862–1910), best known as O. Henry. His surprise endings entertain readers, even those back for a second, third, or fourth look. Even now one can say " 'Gift of the Magi' " in a conversation about a love affair or marriage, and almost any literate person will know what is meant. It's hard to think of many other American writers whose work has been so incorporated into our national shorthand.

O. Henry was a newspaperman, skilled at hiding from his editors at deadline. A prolific writer, he wrote to make a living and to make sense of his life. He spent his childhood in Greensboro, North Carolina, his adolescence and young manhood in Texas, and his mature years in New York City. In between Texas and New York, he served out a prison sentence for bank fraud in Columbus, Ohio. Accounts of the origin of his pen name vary: one story dates from his days in Austin, where he was said to call the wandering family cat "Oh! Henry!"; another states that the name was inspired by the captain of the guard at the Ohio State Penitentiary, Orrin Henry.

Porter had devoted friends, and it's not hard to see why. He was charming and had an attractively gallant attitude. He drank too much and neglected his health, which caused his friends concern. He was often short of money; in a letter to a friend asking for a loan of fifteen dollars (his banker was out of town, he wrote), Porter added a postscript: "If it isn't convenient, I'll love you just the same." The banker was unavailable most of Porter's life. His sense of humor was always with him.

Reportedly, Porter's last words were from a popular song: "Turn up the light, for I don't want to go home in the dark."

Eight years after O. Henry's death, in April 1918, the Twilight Club (founded in 1883 and later known as the Society of Arts and Letters) held a dinner in his honor at the Hotel McAlpin in New York City. His friends remembered him so enthusiastically that a group of them met at the Biltmore Hotel in December of that year to establish some kind of memorial to him. They decided to award annual prizes in his name for short-story writers, and formed a Committee of Award to read the short stories published in a year and to pick the winners. In the words of Blanche Colton Williams (1879–1944), the first of the nine series editors, the memorial was intended to "strengthen the art of the short story and to stimulate younger authors."

Doubleday, Page & Company was chosen to publish the first volume, *O. Henry Memorial Award Prize Stories 1919*. In 1927, the society sold all rights to the annual collection to Doubleday, Doran & Company. Doubleday published *The O. Henry Prize Stories,* as it came to be known, in hardcover, and from 1984 to 1996 its subsidiary, Anchor Books, published it simultaneously in paperback. Since 1997 *The O. Henry Prize Stories* has been published as an original Anchor Books paperback.

HOW THE STORIES ARE CHOSEN

As of 2003, the series editor chooses the twenty O. Henry Prize Stories, and each year three writers distinguished for their fiction are asked to evaluate the entire collection and to write an appreciation of the story they most admire. These three writers receive the twenty prize stories in manuscript form with no identification of author or publication. They make their choices independent of each other and the series editor.

All stories originally written in the English language and published in an American or Canadian periodical are eligible for consideration. Individual stories may not be nominated; magazines must submit the year's issues in their entirety by July 1. Editors are invited to submit online fiction for consideration. Such submissions must be sent to the series editor in hard copy. (Please see pp. 445–446 for details.)

The goal of *The O. Henry Prize Stories* remains to strengthen the art of the short story.

To Mary McCarthy (1912–1989)

A middle-aged businessman with slightly porcine features and an attractive young woman meet in the club car, then spend an afternoon drinking highballs ("gold in the glasses") in his private compartment as the train carries them across the country. For propriety, they keep the door open. She forms many assumptions about him, socially, intellectually, emotionally; she prides herself on being perceptive and feels superior to him. When their bottle of whiskey is nearly empty, he interrupts her discourse on her many lovers and why none of them was quite right, and pronounces that she must still be in love with her ex-husband. The previously self-confident young woman changes: " 'Do you think so really?' she asked, leaning forward. 'Why?' Perhaps at last she had found him, the one she kept looking for, the one who could tell her what she was really like. For this she had gone to palmists and graphologists, hoping not for a dark man or a boat trip, but for some quick blaze of gypsy insight that would show her her own lineaments. If she once knew, she had no doubt that she could behave perfectly; it was merely a question of finding out."

For just such shifts and lightning understanding, we read Mary McCarthy now, more than one hundred years after her birth.

When "The Man in the Brooks Brothers Shirt" was published in 1941, it caused a sensation. Those were the days in which a short story could make a stir, and the stir in this case was about the wantonness of the heroine and the openness of her sexual behavior. Today, a reader's interest in the story is different.

Though it seems at first that the story is about sex on a cross-country train, the hardened twenty-first-century reader notices that while there's a lot of talk about sex and marriage, the secret, internal life of the protagonist is the real focus of the story. The young woman is not particularly likable. She is a snob who fancies herself a political radical; an independent thinker who nonetheless depends on the admiration and approval of men, both those she likes and those she dislikes; a woman who feels sexual desire and also repugnance, though what trumps her sexual feelings is her gratification at being desired. Sex for her is almost a business negotiation, one that can be analyzed and parsed endlessly.

The young woman, in her confusion, self-consciousness, and constant theorizing about herself, the man, her past, her feelings, and her unrelenting conscience, draws us into her complicated mind.

It is mind rather than sex that makes the story feel alive more than sixty years after its first publication. In the years since 1941, detailed and graphic descriptions and images of sex have become commonplace. What remains fresh and irresistible is a mind like Mary McCarthy's. By writing with laser power about the workings of thought and sensation, she is able to create a character as complicated as the story's protagonist.

It isn't a shock any longer that women feel sexual desire, but it is still fascinating to be put through a moral and intellectual wringer by Mary McCarthy's young woman as she locks in amorous combat with the man in the Brooks Brothers shirt.

Contents

Introduction

READING BLIND IS AN experience that we as readers most often have with a writer whose work is unknown to us. We feel exhilarated when we find a new writer; it's like meeting a new friend, sometimes like falling in love. The verb "envy" is the one most often used when we see someone embarking on a first reading of Virginia Woolf or Henry James.

Some of the stories in *The O. Henry Prize Stories* come from established writers, but they are given a chance to be read blind as well. Every year, a panel of three jurors reads a blind manuscript of the pieces selected as O. Henry Prize Stories; neither attribution nor provenance is given, so the jurors don't know which magazines the stories appeared in or who the authors are. All of the stories are in the same typeface and format. From these, each juror picks a favorite story and writes about it in the section "Reading *The O. Henry Prize Stories*."

This isn't to say that jurors don't on occasion detect a writer's identity. There can be clues in sentence structure, word choice, or subject matter. The biggest giveaway is what one might call the writer's presence, which includes all evidence of craft and meaning but goes beyond those elements. Each writer has a unique way of finding details in the material and natural world to create the story. The writer's presence—the way the writer sees—is as innate as the color of the writer's eyes.

Jim Shepard, a past O. Henry Prize winner and a 2013 juror, chose as his favorite story Andrea Barrett's "The Particles." He took note of the narrative's pacing and what he calls the writer's *restraint*. The word is a clue to a special quality of Barrett's work. Though she often writes about scientists and the past, she uses restraint to hold back an avalanche of extraneous or excessive detail and authorial observation—explanations the reader doesn't need. She restrains not only the superfluous but also the interesting when its presence would distract from her finely focused narrative. Implicit in her work is the fascination of what she leaves out (more science, more history), but we trust her to go on without it, pulled by the story exactly as she tells it. Her subject matter is often double—the human drama and the scientific. The reader can almost hear Barrett thinking.

In "Anecdotes," Ann Beattie traces the differences between friendship and acquaintanceship. Conversations between her characters, their overt sharing of anecdotes and the push and pull of their unspoken exchanges, are part of the pleasure of Beattie's writing. Little by little, the narrator of "Anecdotes" pulls away from the complications of what she thinks about a friend's mother, Lucia, and what the friend's mother thinks she should think, complications that extend to a choice between annoying involvement and happy disengagement. During this process, Beattie makes use of a minor character passing by in pink Uggs, and the criticism of the fuzzy boots by the cashmere-wearing Lucia. Beattie's combination of sharpness and humor might seem to add up to satire, but she doesn't make fun of her characters or reduce them to generalizations. Rather, she shows us that they're all worth a look, though some are worthier than others. Beattie's body of work is a testimonial against the unexamined life, and the title of her 1991 story collection *Secrets and Surprises* gives a clue to what awaits the reader in "Anecdotes."

Tash Aw's "Sail" is about a man who is isolated, estranged both from his country and his sense of who he is. Like the streamlined, arrowlike sailboat we see at the story's beginning, Yanzu moves lightly and, it seems, effortlessly. When we are introduced to him, he is considering buying the sailboat to help himself over a failed love affair. He does not, however, know how to sail, and his ignorance is parallel to his inability to occupy or direct his own life. Yanzu is different from other people, as different as the boat he contemplates buying is elegant and mysterious. At thirty-nine, he is a successful green businessman in Hong Kong, dresses in expensive "classic" clothing, and is married to a woman he doesn't like very much. At twenty, he studied chemistry, which the author calls the "intricate study of change," and left his native Beijing after minor participation in the Tiananmen Square protests. When Yanzu fled to Hong Kong, he wanted to become a writer who would reveal mainland China's faults and crimes. Yet "the more he wrote about Beijing, the more distant it seemed," until he gave up the idea of writing. Instead, through his ambitious, materialistic wife, he is introduced into a world of gain, and more or less accidentally makes money. He wishes to learn English, and at the advice of his wife, who treats him with less warmth than she would a designer handbag, he takes private lessons from a restless, rootless Englishwoman with whom he falls in love.

Tash Aw's story rings with the loneliness and absence of intimacy in Yanzu's life. As the tale unfolds, Yanzu gains the world in the form of property, status, and bespoke suits, but never finds his own meaning or identity. Aw's writing is elegant, guided by imagination, and skilled at showing how Yanzu appears to others in contrast to how he feels; the writer lets the reader understand how empty it feels inside Yanzu. Like the chemistry Yanzu once studied, "Sail" is an intricate study of change.

In contrast to the chilly vacancy of the marriage in "Sail," the marriage of Donald Antrim's Stephen and Alice in "He Knew" is a perfect synthesis. Antrim's skilled narration of their journey from Bergdorf Goodman to Madison Avenue and parts north reveals their marriage as a tight duet, perhaps a tango. The objects they covet, reject, and acquire are more than material; each has the shimmer of the spiritual, a communion made tangible. Stephen and Alice are tightly wound, both around each other and within their own screaming nervous systems. Drugged, alert, anxious, suffering, the two cling together during what at first looks like a shopping spree and eventually becomes a fantasy of fertility and stability. Antrim calibrates his story so perfectly that the walk up Madison Avenue past one luxury store after another resembles the Stations of the Cross. By the end of "He Knew," the reader feels as strung out as the characters, and wishes as much as Stephen does to believe in his desperate hopefulness.

Asako Serizawa's delicate and subtle story of suspicion and fear, "The Visitor," takes place in postwar Japan, during the brief visit of Murayama, an ex-soldier, to the narrator, a housewife. He claims to have been a friend of her missing, probably dead, son, also a soldier. Through small, telling details slowly parceled out in dialogue and exposition, we learn that civilians are near starvation, that returning soldiers are distrusted, and that the future is uncertain for all. Nationalism has been replaced by shame and deprivation.

There is a vase in the room where the mother entertains Murayama with food and tea from her scant supply. It is a "pale, ornamental vase [her] husband had sent from China during his tenure there. Like everything else, [she] did not expect the vase to stay long, its delicate color soon to be given up for a sack of grains and a few stalks of vegetables, but for the moment it cheered the room, its quiet shape attracting the eye, settling the soul. . . ." The absent husband is threatening, his wartime activities mysterious.

The narrator and the visitor exchange volleys of dialogue, and when the visitor finally leaves, she discovers a telling photograph he has left behind—which she mistakes for a scene of a mass execution before realizing it is an even more devastating image.

Interestingly, Serizawa mentions the idea of restraint in her commentary on "The Visitor" (see page 442), but in that case the restraint exists not as literary technique but as the human quality that keeps her characters at a distance from each other.

In Kelly Link's "The Summer People," juror Edith Pearlman's favorite, the mundane is transformed into the enchanted and back again. The story at first appears to be about year-round residents of a mountainous region who caretake for the rich summer visitors, and in particular about a clever and resourceful girl named Fran. Some of the summer people have more to them, though, than the usual breed of second-home owners: they have the power to transform, create, and heal. They also have the power to imprison, a device often seen in classic fairy tales. Fran tries throughout the story to slip the noose of enchantment, but, as in many fairy tales, learns that what seems like a triumph is not so desirable after all.

L. Annette Binder's "Lay My Head" makes use of a fairy tale as a story within a story. In a lament, elegiac and peaceful, the sickly Angela reviews the memories and emotions that bind her to life, including the tales of her childhood: "Strubelpeter with his wild hair and Hans im Glück who was happiest when all his gold was lost." Angela's mother still believes in remedies for the disease that's killing her daughter, but Angela believes only in her body's signals. As the story progresses, the reader is taken on a remarkable journey that lasts until Hans im Glück is free to go home happily, all his gold lost. Binder intersperses the decay of Angela's body with the progress of her spirit until, amazingly, the reader accepts Angela's death.

The subject of memory, or perhaps more accurately the condition of remembering, drives other stories in this year's collection:

"Leaving Maverley" by Alice Munro, "Your Duck Is My Duck" by Deborah Eisenberg, "The Mexican" by George McCormick, and "Pérou" by Lily Tuck.

Alice Munro's "Leaving Maverley" is steeped in memory, as announced by its opening: "In the old days when there was a movie theatre in every town. . . ." The story is not about nostalgia, which is a subspecies of memory. Rather, it shows the grace offered by memory and story in a life that otherwise might look like a cheat and a waste. The love story of Ray and Isabel is the umbrella plot protecting the story's deepest intention. Central as the events of their love and marriage are, it is the counterpoint to their long steadiness offered by the story of Leah that brings "Leaving Maverley" its depth and beauty. Unlike Ray and Isabel, Leah runs from one thing to another, coming in and out of their lives; she gives them something to talk about, and talking is one of the things they do best together. Ray is first seen as a night policeman in the small town of Maverley, working nights so he can spend his days with his invalid wife: "They had no children and could get talking anytime about anything. He brought her the news of the town, which often made her laugh, and she told him about the books she was reading." When they met, he was a young veteran, hoping to head to college. Isabel was from a rich family, married to another man. Each changed everything so that they could marry and be together. Then she fell ill, and their existence became a careful routine.

Leah is change itself, making surprising leaps among relationships and modes of living. When she reappears at a crucial moment in Ray and Isabel's life, Ray can't remember her name. When he does, it's "a relief out of all proportion, to remember her." Leah's name and what he knows about her is a fragment of his own story, something he can keep.

Deborah Eisenberg's "Your Duck Is My Duck," juror Lauren Groff's favorite, also begins with a look at the past: "Way back—oh, not all that long ago, actually, just a couple of years, but back before I'd gotten a glimpse of the gears and levers and pulleys that dredge the future up from the earth's core to its surface—I was going to a lot of parties." The subject, then, is time, perceptible and fantastic. The narrator, an artist who's stuck—unable to paint, working a boring job—is invited to leave all that behind and become the guest of Ray and Christa, a seemingly agreeable rich couple, at their beach place. The hope is that she'll be able to paint again. As in Alice Munro's "Leaving Maverley," we are treated to an umbrella story, that of the beach town's inhabitants, the household's servants, and the other (also compromised) guests of the couple. The ups and downs of Ray and Christa's relationship rule everything and everyone. Only one guest, a master puppeteer, has found a way to stay clear of these fluctuations; he goes on with his work in a state of detachment. Our narrator doesn't find peace and quiet or a way to return to her art during her stay, but by the end of the story, she is not only painting, she's selling. She has her own money in her pocket and the reader wants to congratulate her on her restored independence from the whimsical, slightly sinister rich. Time rolls along in Eisenberg's funny and involving story, whether we like it or not, for it's inexorable, and once it's gone, we can't retrieve it except in the glimpses that memory gives us. As the puppeteer says, "And the thing you mostly get to keep is leaving."

The question of using autobiography—another form of memory—in fiction is a touchy one. Where one writer might bristle at the idea that she takes her work from her life, another will admit cheerfully that this is the case. It is certainly true that, at a minimum, writers never escape fully from themselves, not even in their most fully imagined work: wherever you go, there you are.

In "Pérou," Lily Tuck makes a story out of what she cannot possibly remember about her own life. "Pérou" begins: "The year is 1940 and I lie fast asleep under a fur blanket in a Balmoral pram." No baby knows what the year is or the name of its carriage; this is not memory speaking. A similar complicated negotiation of fact and imagination continues in the naming of the street the baby rolls along, and the detailed description of what her nurse, Jeanne, is wearing. Jeanne, the narrator explains, "is nineteen years old and will devote five years of her life to looking after me—years she will spend in Peru."

And so the story continues, the story of Jeanne losing her family, country, language, everything she ever had. The story is told in a detached voice with occasional asides, letting us know that the narrator, the former baby, was as helpless as Jeanne to affect her fate. In part, this is the fault of the times, a period in European history of desperate displacement and flight. Reading, one is convinced of the helplessness the people in danger must have felt as they tried to save themselves and those they loved. The baby in the Balmoral pram is under threat, and uses the resource of memory to construct and pay tribute to someone who guarded her from danger and was herself abandoned. In "Pérou" memory is flexible and slippery, like trying to use a snake to measure a straight line.

The narrator of George McCormick's "The Mexican" tells us that when he was a boy he worked summers at a rail yard with his Uncle Alton and a fellow named Chicken, icing shipments of California oranges, fruit that would ripen as it crossed the continent. The first paragraph of the story is a song of place-names and colors, with evocations of the weather, the sky, and the imagination of a boy looking past Oklahoma, perhaps into his future.

The narrator lets us know that he has two ways of telling the story of an eventful night with Uncle Alton and Chicken: the accurate way he's telling it to us, and the other way, distorted and pressed into a different setting; frogs in one version, coyotes in the other. As an adult, the narrator trades his experience for the mythic West of tall tales, yet he makes us care for the prosaic, for everything and everyone he describes. "In the West," he tells us, "what we love most are lies." That night in Oklahoma the boy sees something unexpected and keeps it to himself, which is one kind of lying. Years later, when he tells the story to his sons, he changes everything—the oranges become Mexican steers who escape from the train car. "The Mexican" weighs two versions of a night against each other, and what seems likely to be the truer is rejected in favor of distortions that fulfill a cultural desire for another kind of story altogether.

Melinda Moustakis arranged "They Find the Drowned" in short sections that alternate in subject matter between the natural world and the human, with "the scientists" mediating between the two. As the story progresses, the two worlds touch: "The canopy has thinned by 70 percent and everything under it is changing—a beetle gnaws through the bark of a tree and the salmon count drops and then a fisherman drinks himself into a ditch." With poker-faced humor and tenderness, Moustakis brings alive the threatened world of her story. Titles count in a short story. Watch for the point at which "they find the drowned" appears in the text. It's a moment of heightened danger and simple reality at once.

It seems that danger has passed when Ayşe Papatya Bucak's "The History of Girls" opens. Until the end, the story is in first-person plural. There is coziness in the narrative voice, in tandem with horrors. The "ghosts of the girls who had already died" wait while the narrators do, and school rivalries and crushes, youthful dreams and ambitions, stories, poems, sheets and blankets, uniforms, gym skirts, head scarves, and stockings are revisited. The ephemera of the girls' communal life charm us, and we—the story's narrators and its readers alike—forget to ask, *What are we waiting for?* The answer comes in the singularity of the voice at the end when we realize that we've witnessed nothing less than a struggle between life and death.

Another kind of struggle is the subject of Jamie Quatro's intriguing "Sinkhole." The narrator, Benjamin Mills, is, he tells us, an amazing fifteen-year-old runner whose potential would have no end if it weren't for the sinkhole in the middle of his chest. Only he can feel it, and if he doesn't perform the Gesture, the sinkhole will "be the boss" of him. Because Ben's brother died of a heart defect, his own physical perfection seems suspect; only Ben knows the danger he's in from the sinkhole.

Ben is at summer camp, a place where a God impersonator is brought in to instruct the campers. He has a crush on his friend Wren, who, after surgeries for cancer, lacks her reproductive organs and her colon. Wren is lovely, damaged, and sexually curious. Ben has his sinkhole; she has a hole in her side for her colostomy bag. Wren is brave and determined, but Ben might be pulled into his sinkhole. How they come to terms with their afflictions and with their affection for each other is the essence of Quatro's story. It's easy to portray teenagers as morose and self-absorbed. It's hard to create characters like Wren and Ben who use their youthful energy and will to vault themselves, however clumsily, into adulthood.

In Samar Farah Fitzgerald's "Where Do You Go?" Henry and Vega, married two years, move to a suburban village and find themselves the only young people there. At first, they are self-sufficient, and the advantages of their new home balance the oddness of their situation. They are different from their elderly neighbors, whom they find amusing and a little repulsive. Little by little, they mix with them, and find within themselves and their relationship some frightening truths about love and companionship. Henry wonders, "If he hadn't found Vega when he did, ten years ago, if he came across her now for the first time, would she still manage to captivate him?" What they took for granted now seems fragile and at risk. Henry becomes the favorite of their female neighbors, and Vega has an adventure of sorts with cigarette-smoking Gordon, whose customary outfit is pajama bottoms and a suit jacket. They begin to understand what a difference age makes and how little. For the first time, they see that something is coming for them, as it comes for everyone.

Essie, the unreasonable, possessive mother in "Tiger" by

Nalini Jones, resembles the eponymous beast in her ferocious desire to make everyone in her household obey her every wish. Her daughter Marian, visiting Bombay from America, is married to Daniel, a prime target of Essie's contempt. Essie's granddaughters, Nicole and Tara, are delighted to find a mother cat and two kittens. Against Essie's commands, they play with the kittens and feed them, making them part of Essie's household. The children choose the name "Tiger" for the mother cat. There are other tigers in the story, including an imposing and entitled one who naps in the middle of a road while travelers wait hours for it to awaken and move out of their way. Essie moves a bit, too, after tribulation. Jones's portrait of a lonely, stubborn woman is touching not for Essie's virtues but for her all-too-understandable flaws.

"White Carnations" by Polly Rosenwaike is another disquisition on motherhood, particularly on the transition from being a daughter to being a mother. A group of motherless women meet annually to celebrate Mother's Day. The narrator's meditation on her own mother's life and way of mothering is woven throughout the story. When the discussion turns to adoption, she wonders, "Why such attachment to your own genetic lineage? I didn't mean to be accusatory or self-righteous. My interest in this topic was philosophical." *Is that true?* the reader wonders. *False?* The story's conversational tone, the women at the Mother's Day celebration, the narrator's slowly revealed dilemma—all are factors in the enjoyment of the story and its ending, which surprises its characters and uncovers what the reader might have known all along.

Derek Palacio's "Sugarcane" is set in post-revolutionary Cuba, not the Cuba of political rhetoric but of the daily rules and orders that control the life of every citizen. Armando is a rural doctor allowed to have a Jeep to travel to visit his far-flung patients. To sweeten his life, he agrees to take under his wing a sugar plantation manager's son, Eduardo, who is neither bright nor talented but wishes to become a doctor. In exchange for consenting to teach Eduardo, help him through entrance exams, and write him a letter of recommendation, Armando receives pounds of sugar at a time when Cubans are entitled to only one cup every Saturday. With the bounty of sweetness comes an affair with the sensual Mercedes, and some hard choices for Armando. The story is saturated with sugar and bureaucracy, limits and confinement, and the possibility of love. Underlying the sweetness and bitterness of life in Cuba is the nagging question of leaving or staying.

Joan Silber's "Two Opinions" begins with a family visit to federal prison, where the narrator's father is being held for refusing to register for the draft during World War II. The narrator, Louise, and her sister, Barbara, are dressed up and wear their Mary Janes, and on the way home their mother feeds them treats like "homemade brownies and date-nut squares," of which the narrator says, "We were very excited, the whole trip seemed to have been so we could have this food."

Thus begins Louise's evenhanded account of her life. Hidden within all the interesting details of her gains and losses is her continual contrast of the ideal and the quotidian. She is accused by her family of having no principles, but this isn't really so. Her principles are less easily articulated than the political and social goods her parents believe in; she wishes to lead an ordinary life, and she does, or tries to. She marries her high-school sweetheart, a teacher who has so few scruples that he bribes his students "to rat on each other." When he's fired, their lives take a different turn. Throughout, the narrator stands up for the goodness of the ordinary. Her principles are all her own.

In many of Joan Silber's short stories, her narrators, as in "Two Opinions," bear witness to their lives, speaking so openly, sharing themselves so willingly, that the reader can't help hoping for mercy for them.

Kishen, the main character in Ruth Prawer Jhabvala's "Aphrodisiac," is a Cambridge-educated Indian who wishes to write "the sort of novel that should be written about India." Several of Jhabvala's novels were set in India, though whether or not Kishen would consider them novels that *should* be written abut India is doubtful. Jhabvala, who died in April 2013, was not a writer who engaged in grandiose declarations about India or anything else.

Jhabvala's vision of her characters is so dry-eyed and clear-minded that Kishen would surely wish to duck her examination. Jhabvala excelled at creating frustrating characters who themselves are frustrated. At certain points in all her stories, the reader feels like telling a character or two to shape up, even as the reader is aware that the character's paradoxical problems require far more than willpower to be solved. Jhabvala was expert at portraying a certain kind of unwilling but fierce entanglement, as in "Aphrodisiac." By the time Kishen begins to understand how far things have gone wrong, he is beyond redemption. The reader can upbraid Kishen or feel sorry for him, or feel both emotions at once, knowing that he is hoisted with his own petard, as are we all. Ruth Prawer Jhabvala's vision, wisdom, and humor will be missed.

—*Laura Furman*
West Lake Hills, Texas

The O. Henry Prize Stories 2013

Deborah Eisenberg
Your Duck Is My Duck

W AY BACK—OH, NOT ALL that long ago, actually, just a
couple of years, but back before I'd gotten a glimpse of the
gears and levers and pulleys that dredge the future up from the
earth's core to its surface—I was going to a lot of parties.

And at one of these parties there was a couple, Ray and Christa,
who hung out with various people I sort of knew, or, anyhow,
whose names I knew. We'd never had much of a conversation,
just hey there, kind of thing, but I'd seen them at parties over the
years and at that particular party they seemed to forget that we
weren't actually friends ourselves.

Ray and Christa had a lot of money, a serious quantity, and
they were also both very good-looking, so they could live the way
they felt like living. Sometimes they split up, and one of them,
usually Ray, was with someone else for a while, always a splashy,
public business that made their entourage scatter like flummoxed
chickens, but inevitably they got back together, and afterwards,
you couldn't detect a scar.

Ray had a chummy arm around me and Christa was swaying
to the music, which was almost drowned out by the din of voices
in the metallic room, and smiling absently in my direction. I was

a little taken aback that I was being, I guess, anointed, but it was up to them how well they knew you, and I could only assume that their cordiality meant either that something good had happened to me which was not yet perceptible to me but was already perceptible to them, or else that something good was about to happen to me.

So, we were talking, shouting, really, over the noise, and after a bit I realized that what they were saying meant that they now owned my painting *Blue Hill*.

They owned *Blue Hill*? I had given *Blue Hill* to Graham once, in a happy moment, and he must have sold it to them when he up and moved to Barcelona. *Blue Hill* is not a bad painting, in my opinion, it's one of my best, still, the expression that I could feel taking charge of my face came and went without making trouble for anyone, thanks to the fact that, obviously, there were a lot of people in the room for Ray and Christa to be looking at, other than me.

How are you these days, they asked, and at this faint suggestion that they'd been monitoring me, a great wave of childish gratitude and relief washed over me, dissolving my dignity and leaving me stranded in self-pity.

Why did I keep going to these stupid parties? Night after night, parties, parties—was I hoping to meet someone? No one met people in person any longer—you couldn't hear what they were saying. Except for the younger women, who had piercing, high voices and sounded like Donald Duck, from whom they had evidently learned to talk. When had *that* happened? An adaptation? You could certainly hear *them*.

It was getting on my nerves and making me feel old. I'm exhausted, I told Ray and Christa. I can't sleep. I can't take the winter. I'm sick of my day job at Howard's photo studio, but on the other hand, Howard's having some problems—last week there were three of us, and this week there are two, and I'm scared I'm going to be the next to go. And as I told them that I was

frightened, that I was sick of the winter and my job, I understood
how deeply, deeply sick of the winter and my job, how frightened,
I really was.

Yeah, that's terrible, they said. Well, why don't you come stay
with us? We're taking off for our beach place on Wednesday.
There's plenty of room, and you can paint. We love your work.
It's a great place to work, everyone says so, really serene. The light
is great, the vistas are great.

I'm having some trouble painting these days, I said, I'm not
really, I don't know.

Hey, everyone needs some downtime, they said; you'll be
inspired, everyone who visits is inspired. You won't have to deal
with anything. There's a cook. You can lie around in the sun and
recuperate. You can take donkey rides down into the town, or
there are bicycles or the driver. What languages do you speak?
Well, it doesn't matter. You won't need to speak any.

Naturally I assumed they'd forget all about their invitation,
so I was startled, the day after the party, to get an email from
Christa, asking when I could get away. One of their people would
deal with the flights. I could stay as long as I liked, she said, and
if I wanted to send heavy working materials on ahead, that would
be fine. Lots of their guests did that. It could get cool at night, so
I should bring something warm, and if I wanted to hike, I should
bring boots, because snakes, as I knew, could be an issue, though
insects were generally not. I would not need a visa these days, so
not to worry about that, and not to worry about Wi-Fi—that was
all set up.

I doubted that anybody else who visited them would not know
exactly how to prepare, and yet there was Christa, informing me
so tactfully of everything, like snakes and visas, that I'd need
to know about, by pretending that of course I'd already have
thought of those things. A week or so later, a messenger brought
a plane ticket up the five flights of stairs to my little apartment,
which was when it dawned on me that the good thing Ray and

Christa had perceived happening to me was that they now owned one of my paintings, which meant, obviously, that it most likely was, or would soon be, worth acquiring.

My job at Howard's studio expired, along with the studio itself, at the end of the following month, just in time to save Howard and me from my quitting right before I got on the plane. At least it was no problem to sublet my apartment, even at a little profit, to a guy who liked cats, because, as everyone was observing with wonder, the real estate collapse had not flattened rents one bit.

Howard looked around at all the stuff that represented his last thirty years. "Bon voyage," he said. He gave me a little hug.

The plane took off in frosty grime and floated down across water, from which the sun was rising in sheer pink and yellow flounces. It was a different time here—must that not mean that different things were happening? I'd brought my computer, but maybe I could actually just not turn it on, and the dreary growth of little obligations that overran my screen would just disappear; maybe the news, which—like a magic substance in a fairy tale—was producing perpetually increasing awfulness from rock-bottom bad, would just disappear.

I had exuded a sticky coating of dirt during the night on the plane, but in the airport, ceiling fans were gracefully turning, and the heat was dry and benign, like a treatment. As everyone exited with their luggage, I kept peering at the email from Christa I'd printed out, which kept saying: *Someone will be waiting to pick you up.* I had her cell number on my phone, I remembered, and scrabbled in my purse for it, but as I pressed and tapped different bits of it and stared at its inert face, I was struck by how complete the difference is between a phone that works and a phone that doesn't work.

For a long time, whenever I traveled anywhere, it had been with Graham, who would have thought to deal with the issue of international phone service, even though Christa hadn't mentioned it. And as I stood there, a lanky apparition ballooned into the void at my side, frowning, mulling the situation over. Graham! But the apparition tossed back its fair, silky hair, kissed me lightly, and dissipated, leaving me so much more alone than I'd been an instant before.

Wheeling my bulging, creaking suitcase here and there as potential disasters stacked up in my mind in great, unstable piles, I located an exchange bureau, and my few sober monochromatic bills were replaced by a thick, fortifying sheaf of festive ones that looked like they were itching to get loose and party. Onward! I thought, and swayed on my feet from fatigue.

I was deciding which exit to march myself to and then do what, when Christa strode up. "The driver and Ray got into some big snarl," she said, hustling me along. "And he took off. He's acting out all over the place."

"He's, like, crashing into stuff?" I said.

I wasn't managing my suitcase fast enough to keep up with her, and she grabbed it from me irritably. "He's buying something."

"A car?"

"What? Did you remember to hydrate on the plane? Some subsidiary. It always makes him crazy, but, hey, nerves are a *weakness, I'm* the one who's nervous. So this morning Mr. Sang Froid accuses the driver, who by the way is also one of the gardeners and a general handyman, but what difference does it make if everything falls apart, of scratching the Mercedes, which I happen to be one hundred percent certain is something he himself did the other night when he came home blind drunk at dawn and almost demolished the gate. So the driver stormed off, just before he was supposed to leave to pick you up, and then Ray stormed off, too, in a black cloud to God knows where. Plus, the place has been crawling with, just who you want to hang out with, accountants. Well, one of them's a lawyer, and I think there's an engineer, too. They look like triplets, or maybe it's quadruplets, hard to tell how many of them there are, you'll see. They're Ray's guys, his pets, a week ago they were golden, guaranteed to go for the throat, now all of a sudden they're a heap of sloths who just lounge around swilling his wine and hogging up his food, which big surprise, and he fucking well better be back for dinner, because *I'm* not entertaining those turnip heads. Don't worry, you'll be okay, though—Amos Voinovich is here, too, except he's pretty anti-social, which I didn't really get until he showed up, and it turns out he hates the beach. He says he's working, which is great of course—maybe he'll do something for us while he's here. And anyhow, he's better than nothing."

"Amos Voinovich, the puppeteer?"

"Well, I mean, yeah. You know him?"

I didn't know him, but I'd seen one of his shows, which was about two explorers and their teams. There were puppet penguins and puppet dolphins and puppet dogsleds and of course puppet explorers fighting their way through blizzards and under brilliant, starry skies to be the first to get to the South Pole. Voinovich himself had written the lyrics and the music, which was vaguely operatic, and each explorer sang of his own megalomaniac ambitions, and various dogs from each team sang about doubts, longings, loyalties, resentments, and so on, and the penguins, who knew very well that one explorer's team would prevail and flourish and that the other explorer's team would die, down to the last man, sang a choral commentary, philosophical in nature, that sounded like choirs of drugged angels. The eerie melodies were often submerged, woven through the howling winds.

Christa chucked my suitcase into the trunk of her car, and as we sped along upwards on winding roads in the brilliant sunshine, the deluxe night of Amos Voinovich's puppet show wrapped around me, and while Christa groused about Ray, I kept dozing off, which was something I had not been doing much of for a very long time, and her voice was a harsh silver ribbon glinting in the fleecy dark.

We came to an abrupt stop in front of a smallish house, covered with flowering vines. "This is where you and Amos are. I put you in the same place, because you're the only two here right now and it's easier for the staff. You'll be sharing a kitchen, but I mean nothing else, obviously."

"Accountants?" I asked, stumbling out of the car.

"They're staying in the main house with us, unfortunately. Ray insisted, although we could perfectly well have given them a bungalow. They've got their own wing, at least, across the courtyard. You'll see them at dinner, but except for that you won't have to deal with them. I gather they're all taking off tomorrow."

She brought me into the little house, which was divided in two, except, as she'd said, for a kitchen downstairs, which both Amos and I had a door opening onto and which appeared to be very well equipped, though meals and snacks and coffee and so on would always be available in the main house. She showed me light switches, and temperature control for my part of the house, and where extra blankets and towels were kept. Dinner was early, she said, at eight, and no one dressed, except once in a while, if someone happened to be around. Lunch was at one. And breakfast was improvisatory. The cook would be on hand from six, because sometimes Ray liked to swim early. Did I have any questions?

I gaped. "Guess not," I said. "Um, should I . . . ?"

"Yeah, come on over whenever you want," she said, and gave me a quick, squeamish hug. "So, welcome."

What was not dressing? I was incredibly tired, despite the little nap in the car, but not even slightly sleepy. I opted for jeans, which were mostly what I'd brought, and when the clock on the night table informed me that it was 7:45, I went over to what I assumed was the main house and wandered through empty rooms until I happened upon Christa, who was wearing a little vintage sundress, the color of excellent butter.

Dinner meant helping yourself from a selection of possibilities, including some things on platters over little flame arrangements, and then sitting down at a long, polished table that probably seated thirty. Amos the puppeteer did not in fact show, but the accountants or accountants plus lawyer plus engineer were there. They didn't wear jackets, but they all wore exhaustingly playful ties, which suggested, I suppose, that Ray's forthcoming acquisition was so sound that chest-thumping frivolity was in order. Ray had reappeared, and said hello to me, but barely, giving me a bitter little smile as though he and I were petty thugs who had just been flagged down by a state trooper, and that was the last notice of me he took that evening.

I watched, through the glass wall, as evening slowly began to rise in the bowl of the valley below and soft lights glimmered on. Up over the mountains, though, it was still day. A dramatic terrain. The soft, mauve twilight currents were rising around the table, so you didn't really have to converse, or you could sort of pretend that you were conversing with someone else. Somewhere in that gently swirling dusk the accountants were talking among themselves—telling jokes, it seemed. Their bursts of raucous laughter sounded like reams of paper being shredded, and after each burst of laughter they would instantly sober up and swivel deferentially around to Ray.

Terrain—was that what I meant? "What language are they speaking?" I whispered to Christa, who was sitting in a darkening cloud of her own.

"You really better drink some water," she said. "Don't worry, it's all bottled. There are cases over at your place, by the way, I forgot to show you, in one of the cupboards, but tap is okay for your teeth."

It was English, I realized, but specialized. One of them was finishing up a joke that seemed to concern a pilgrim, a turkey, a squaw, and something called credit swap rates.

They all laughed raucously again. Ray was drumming his fingers on the table, making a sound of distant thunder. The accountants etc. swiveled around to him again with sweet boys' faces, and he stood up abruptly.

"Gentlemen," he said, with a tiny bow. "I have a great deal to gain from this transaction, assuming it all proceeds as anticipated. But if at zero hour, by some mishap, it should fall through, let me remind you that, owing to the billable hours clause you were so kind as to append to our contract, only you will be the losers. I salute your efforts. I have the highest hopes, for your sake as well as mine, that your irrepressible confidence in them is justified. But perhaps a moment of sobriety is in order at this point, a moment of reflection about the tenuous nature of careers. Or, to put it another way, don't think for a moment that if the boat is scuttled I'll throw you my rope. I'm sure you all recall the Zen riddle about the great Zen master, his disciple, and the duck trapped in the bottle?"

He drained his large glass of wine, glug glug glug. "Everyone recall the Master's lesson? *It's not my duck, it's not my bottle, it's not my problem*?" He slammed his empty glass down on the table, and wheeled out.

"What did I tell you?" Christa said.

What *did* she tell me? I had no idea. Presumably I'd been dozing at the time, soaring aloft on polar winds as the two explorers savagely pursued their pointless goal under the remote, ironically twinkling stars.

"Plus," she said. "I think he's seeing someone here."

"Oh, wow," I said, and I thought of the bite that every morning would be taking out of her beauty and glamour and how rapidly an individual's beauty and glamour could be rendered irrelevant by standards that had been embryonic only months before, or supplanted by some girl who was just about to walk through the door. "Oh, wow," I said again.

"You can say *that* again," she said. The accountants etc. had disappeared from the table, I realized. All that was left in their place were crumbs. "Yeah, you can sure say that again . . ."

"Well, so, goodnight, I guess," I said, as she wandered off. "Guess I'll just be going back over to the, to the . . ."

Upstairs in my bedroom, I began to unpack, but there was the issue of putting things wherever, so I decided I would leave all that until morning. I set up my laptop after all, though, as tossing out my old life seemed both less plausible and maybe less desirable than it had some hours earlier.

I fished my pj's out of my suitcase and opened the shuttered windows for the breeze. I was listing, as though I were drunk, which I supposed I was, from all the wine it had seemed appropriate to toss down at dinner, but mainly I was exhausted, though still wide awake, as I was so often—wide awake and thinking about things I couldn't do anything about. Couldn't do anything about. Couldn't do anything about. Also, an unfamiliar, somewhat rhythmic tapping suggested that there might be a beast, some brash snake, for example, in the vines just outside my window, trying to get me to open the screen and let it in.

To account for my snoozing in the car, I had mentioned to Christa my exasperating resistance to sleep, and just before we sat down at the table she gave me a few pills, wrapped in a Kleenex. "What are they?" I'd asked. "They're Ray's," she said. "He won't notice."

A few months back, I'd gone to a doctor about sleeping problems, and he'd asked me if I wanted pills.

"I'm afraid they'll blunt my affect," I said. He looked a little disgusted, as if to remind me that he had a downtown practice and I was not the first self-obsessed hysteric he'd dealt with that day. "Then your best bet is to figure out why you're not sleeping," he said.

"What's to figure out?" I said. "I'm hurtling through time, strapped to an explosive device, my life. Plus, it's beginning to look like a photo finish—me first, or the world. It's not so hard to figure out why I'm not sleeping. What I can't figure out is why everybody else is sleeping."

"Everybody else is sleeping because everybody else is taking pills," he said. So I got a prescription from him, and I took the pills for about five nights running and flushed the rest down the toilet. They got me straight to sleep all right, before I'd even had a chance to boot up the worries, and I would sleep for hours and hours, but then I would wake completely exhausted, having spent my night fighting my way through dark tunnels that stank of a charnel house, thwarted everywhere by slimy, pulsing lumps, my own organs, maybe, and in the morning, when I'd get to work painting, I seemed to be sloppier, or less demanding than I'd formerly been. Maybe my painting wasn't any worse than it had been, but I sure didn't mind enough that it wasn't better.

So then, when I stopped taking the pills and it mattered again that my painting wasn't better, I had to wonder *why* it mattered.

I had to face it—my affect was blunted, pills or no pills, unless weariness counted as affect. So, I decided that I'd make myself stop painting for a while, or maybe forever—that I'd stop unless something forced itself on me that I'd dishonor if I didn't paint better than I was able to. And so I did not send materials on ahead to Ray and Christa's, because the trip seemed like an ideal opportunity to clear my mind of whatever impediments to that, and even if I was left with nothing in place of the impediments, at least the sun would be shining.

I heaved my suitcase onto a luggage rack—things had been thought of—to get it out of the way of bugs, even though if there were bugs, I'd probably brought them along in my suitcase, and listed on my feet again. I needed to hydrate, probably, I thought, so I went downstairs and opened the door to the kitchen to search for water.

A bony little person wearing a red and black checked shirt and skinny red and black plaid pants was sitting at the table, regarding me with huge black eyes that looked as though they were rimmed with kohl. He had a lovely, large, downward-curving nose, and a face so waxen and intense in its penumbra of black curls that it left an afterimage.

"Am I disturbing you?" he said.

"Not yet," I said. "I mean, we've hardly met."

"The noise?" he said.

Spread out in front of him on the table were scraps of fabric and colored paper and little figures made out of clay and wood and various other materials, a pot of glue, and some tools, including a little hammer—oh.

"Hey, I loved *Terra Nova Dreaming*," I said. "I really did."

"Good," he said. "Because I could use your opinion on this new one. I want to try running it here, but it's gotten pretty out of control—there are a lot of characters, including some bats that have to turn into drone aircraft and back again, which is a pretty tricky maneuver. There are a couple of kids from the village who can help me backstage, and Fred can deal with the lights, but I'd appreciate a good supplementary eye out front."

"Fred?" I said.

"A guy who drives and gardens here and stuff. I don't know what his name really is. That's what Ray and Christa call him. He's good at doing things, but he's a bit erratic, I think. I don't want to take too much of your time, though. Christa told me you were coming, and I figured you wanted to get your own stuff done, or why else would you be here."

"Well, I mean, to relax?"

"Yeah? You must have a really unusual relaxation technique going."

I furrowed. "Why do you . . . ?"

"Hey, even some of the world's champ relaxers didn't show this season—haven't you noticed? The whole crowd has bailed—all the other freeloaders and the usual apparatchiks . . . I'm here because I got evicted from my apartment when the arts program at the school where I was teaching got cut, and what with putting the new show together and not exactly having an income, luxury handouts were definitely attractive, whatever the hidden costs. I figured you were coming for some similar reason. Anyhow, the onus is on us, obviously."

"The onus . . . ?"

"The onus? To entertain, to distract, to diffuse, to buffer? On us, as in on you and me? Which is why I hardly ever put in an appearance at the main house, and, as I established the policy immediately, it's been interpreted as a sign of genius, I hear from Fred, if I understand him correctly. Anyhow, I suggest that you adopt my example. ASAP, in fact, as things are clearly just about to get worse."

"Um . . . I'm kind of way behind you," I said.

"Hm." He looked at me with a blend of interest and distant pity, like an entomologist considering something in a jar.

"Two things," he said, and he started in, quietly but implacably, like a fortune teller laying out the pitiless cards.

"That can't be true," I said, when he had trailed off, gazing sadly out the window behind me. "Is that all true?"

"Have a look," he said. "See for yourself."

So I went to the window, and sure enough, off in the distance were bobbing lanterns, and I could see, as my eyes adjusted, the small line of people straggling down a dirt road toward the water, hauling little carts piled with bundles of stuff.

"They wait all night for the boats, sometimes longer. First come, first serve, I gather. Even a few weeks ago, you didn't see this too often, but now there are some almost every night."

Apparently most of the people in the area had lived for centuries by working little farms. But a few years earlier there had been relentless rain, and the flooding had washed out the crops, and then there was a second year of that. The third year was a drought, and so was the next one, so none of the new planting could establish roots, and it all blew away. People were exhausting their stores of food, but then Ray bought up lots of the farms, which, under the circumstances, he got at a very good price. And instead of planting grain or vegetables, he planted eucalyptus, which roots really fast, as a cash crop and to keep the bluffs from collapsing. So everyone was happy for a while. But in the summer there had been a few lightning storms, and the high oil content of the eucalyptus was graphically demonstrated when they burst into flame, burning down homes as well as whatever crops were still being grown by anyone who hadn't sold their land to Ray, and food prices were skyrocketing. So naturally local people who could leave were leaving, and a lot of the foreigners, like Ray and Christa, who had places in the area were pulling up stakes, too. "So, that's thing one," Amos said.

"Thing . . . one?" I said.

"And thing two is that Zaffran has rented a place about five miles further up the coast."

"Zaffran? You mean Zaffran the model, Zaffran?"

"Yup."

"But what does that, why should that be, oh."

"Yeah, it started back in the city, it seems. Or that's what Christa seems to think. Zaffran's Roshi is near here, and she comes every few months to study with him. She met him when she was here about a year ago, doing that preposterous spread for *Vogue*—all those idylls of her and the donkeys and the beaming peasants with the Photoshopped dental work. That's how that whole donkey ride business started, in fact, with the cute bells and fringe and so on—it was the stylist's idea. And anyhow, that's when she took up Zen. There weren't really any tourists here before the *Vogue* thing, but now there are plenty, so everyone in the village adores Zaffran because the tourist income is about all anybody here has to live on. And a couple of months ago Ray ran into her at some party at home, and she said she needed his advice about buying a place in the area, and, well, so that's the story."

"Oh, God."

"Yeah," he said. "Anyhow, the cook is great, Marya, and she's a real sweetheart. She'll give you food to bring over here and heat up if you don't want to eat at the house."

"Oh, God. Poor Christa. I just can't do that to her."

"Suit yourself," Amos said. "But remember that she'd do it to you."

His point reverberated through my head like a slammed door. I should go upstairs, I thought, and leave him alone to work, but it was hard to move, so just to stall, I asked him what his new show was about.

"Same old, same old," he said. "Never loses its sparkle, unfortunately."

And as Amos began to present the familiar elements and entwine them in a simple moral fable, I began once again to feel that I was falling into a dream. There was the castle, the greedy king, the trophy queen. There were the ravenous alligators, watchfully circling the moat. Soldiers in armor poised at the parapet walls with vats of boiling oil at the ready, and behind them, inside the towers, the king's generals programmed drone aircraft, whose shadows blighted the countryside.

Who was the enemy? Serfs, of course, potentially, who mined underground caves with the help of pit donkeys, and brought back huge sacks of gold and jewels to swell the royal coffers. Because what if the serfs and donkeys became inflamed with rage? They were many.

"But what the king and queen don't understand," Amos said, "is that the serfs and donkeys are already inflamed with rage, and the bats, who fly between the castle turrets and the mines, are couriers. They're on the side of the serfs, because they love freedom and flying at night and justice, which is blind, too. And the donkeys, once roused, turn out to be indefatigable strategists."

"Huh," I said. "Interesting."

"Yeah? I'm glad. It sure didn't require much thought. But it's got possibilities, I guess."

"What are you going to call it?" I asked.

"What will I call it, what will I call it . . ." His attention seemed to be mainly on one of the little figures, onto which he was gluing something that looked, I noticed, like an orange prison jumpsuit. "Hm. I think I'll call it *The Hand That Feeds You*."

"I'm not sure that's such a—"

"Yes, it is," he said. "It's a great title. Hey, relax, I'll find something more appropriate to call it for this audience."

"So how does it end?" I asked.

"I'm not exactly sure yet, but this is what I'm trying out: there's a huge popular uprising, and for about three minutes, there'll be a rhapsodic ode, during which the serfs, the donkeys, the bats, and the audience rejoice. The end! everyone thinks. But no, because there's a second act, and it turns out that the greedy king and queen are only a puppet government, keeping a client state in order for an unseen, unnamed greater power."

"You mean, like . . . God?"

"I mean, like, corporate executives. And now that the king and queen have been toppled, a state of emergency has been declared and the laws of the land, such as they were, have been indefinitely suspended, and the corporate executives empower the army to raze the countryside and imprison the bats and the king and queen—everyone, in fact, except the strongest serfs and donkeys, who will continue to toil in the mines, but under worse conditions than before."

"Wow," I said. "That's very . . . that's pretty depressing."

"Well, yeah, sure. But I mean, these are the facts."

"You know, I'm so tired," I said. "Who knows what time it is at home. I think I better go upstairs. Do you have any idea where they keep the water?"

"Here you go," he said, opening a cupboard that held cases and cases of fancy bottled water. "So, good luck with that relaxing thing."

Back up in my room, it seemed to me that I could hear a low, steady rumbling, rising up from the village—just regular night sounds, of course. Just . . . the night sounds of anywhere . . .

I studied the small, white pills Christa had given me. They were not very alarming, swaddled there in their tissue. They hardly seemed to count. Not that anything else did, either . . .

I woke up not exactly refreshed, more sort of blank, really, as if the night had been not just dreamless, but expunged. In fact, where was I? I padded across the unfamiliar floor to the unfamiliar window, and the implausible reality reasserted itself. From here, I was looking out at cliffs and the sea, all sluiced in delicate pinks and yellows and greens and blues, as if the sun were imparting to the sleeping rock and water dreams of their youth, dreams of the rock's birth in the earth's molten core, the water's ecstatic purity before it was sullied by life—as if the play of soft colors were the sun's lullaby to the cliffs and the sea, of endurance and transformation.

There was no trace of the people I'd seen the night before from the kitchen window. Could the whole conversation with Amos have been an illusion? There was not a ripple on the glassy water.

A faint jingling was coming my way. I craned out and could just make out one of the local villagers, I presumed, or farmers—a dark-skinned man, wearing loose white clothing and a colorful broad-brimmed hat—leading a procession of little gray donkeys festooned with bells and fringed harnesses and rosettes, picking their way up a steep track, each carrying a big, sacklike tourist.

I wandered over to my laptop, which apparently I'd left on, and called up my email—the Wi-Fi worked, just as Christa had promised—hoping for something to indicate that the world still in fact existed so that someday I might return to it. And—good heavens—there was something from Graham!

All the fragrance from the vines outside blossomed in my room, as though there had just been a quenching rain. Happiness slammed through my body. I, in my desolation—despite the distance, despite our estrangement—had evidently succeeded in calling forth the true Graham, not just the apparition who had come to me in the airport. The lavish air enfolded me, and I breathed it in, expanding as though I'd been constricted in cold shackles for a long, long time. I restrained myself for one more voluptuous second, then opened his email.

Prisoner?—it began—The world is large. You're only a prisoner of your own fears. If you don't like it in the prison of your fears, go somewhere else. Or stay there if you need to. But don't blame me. You obviously expect me to be your solution, as if I were an arcane number of some sort by which you were neatly divisible. Why do you think any-body could be that for you? Why do you think anybody could be that for anybody? I'm not someone who falls short of me—I'm me. I'm not a magic number, I'm just some biped. Look, maybe my soul really is dust, but I mean pris-oner? Slippers? Granary? Of course, I really don't get what you're talking—

What? "Prisoner?" "Slippers?" "Granary?" Was Graham crack-ing up over there in Barcelona? And yet . . . Had some fleeting thoughts of mine actually reached him, bent, like little bent darts from Cupid? Or what was happening? I'd begun to tingle, as though I were thinning out, strangely; something strange was happening—Oh! No, no, no, no, no, no, *no*—Graham's note was a response . . . a response to . . . to an email from me—apparently sent at 3 a.m.:

When you sold me to them—I'd written—did you envi-sion the consequences for me, the wandering in the tun-nels, the sunless life underground, lit only by baskets of cold, glittering gems? What did you hope to gain by divest-ing me? A subsidiary? Gone are my days of sitting at the hearth, embroidering slippers for the little bats—as inno-cent as the king and queen are vicious—singing all the whilst I adorned the panels of the granary. Your support for their corrupt regime has cost you more than it has cost me! Yes I am a prisoner now, but your soul has turned to dust, these are the facts. The word "l***," is that what I mean? I "l***" you? I am in a different country and speak a different language, where there is no word for "l***." Oh Graham, Graham, am I going to die here?

And then I finished reading his note:

—about. (As usual, right? I know, I know.) Anyhow, I'm okay, in case you have the slightest interest in the actual me. Barcelona hasn't really worked out, though, so it's time to move on, I guess. Europe is really expensive, and it's hard to get work if you're not a member of the EU. But Africa is mostly in turmoil, and so is Latin America. Australia? What would be the point? China's impossible, and Japan is hurting these days, obviously. Maybe I'll come back to the States just to regroup for a bit, though God knows it's finished there, isn't it—really, truly finished. Well, I hope you're okay. You really, really don't sound okay. Maybe you should see somebody and get some pills or something. Oh, by the way, I had to sell *Blue Hill*. I wish I didn't, but I couldn't bring it with me when I moved, and I couldn't afford to put stuff in storage, and I figured that you might get some benefit out of the sale because the buyers were crazy about it and they own a lot of stuff, and maybe the guy will commission you to do a mural for one of his banks, or something. I'll let you know if I'm coming back. Maybe we could get together for a drink. xo Graham

"*Whilst?*" I thought—"singing all the *whilst?*" No wonder I couldn't sleep—who would allow themselves to go to sleep, with all the stupid, rotting brain trash that would be waiting for you when you got there! How mortifying, how mortifying—and furthermore, Graham was right, if, in fact, I'd ever l***d him, it was the Graham—his very email made it all too clear—of my own devising. I reread what he had written, and then I read it again, and when I had recovered sufficiently I steamed over to the main house, where I found Christa and Ray at lunch, apparently not looking at each other or speaking. "What the fuck are those pills!" I said. "I wrote someone an email in my sleep!"

Now Ray looked at Christa. "Did you give her one of my Serenitols? You gave her one of my Serenitols, didn't you!"

"So what?" she said. "I told you to throw that shit out."

I was just standing there agape. "You gave me some pills that make you *email* in your *sleep?*"

" 'Some!' " Ray yelled. "You gave her *some?*"

"I'm sorry," Christa said to me, "but you said you were desperate. And they don't do anything to most people."

"They do something to me," Ray yelled. "They're the only things that get me to sleep!"

"They fucking decerebrate you!" Christa turned to me. "Ray *drives* in his sleep."

"I do not drive in my sleep!"

"Oh, you're *awake* when you jump in your car at two a.m. and go tearing up the coast to see that loony anorexic bitch?"

"She is *not* anorexic—that's just the way she looks! How many of those things do I have left now?"

"In one second you're not going to have any," Christa yelled, tearing out of the room after him, "because I'm going to flush them down—"

And then, happily, both of them were out of sight and earshot. So I helped myself to lunch, and it was all delicious. That night there was the first in a long series of freakish storms, and the sky erupted over and over into webs of lightning that crackled across the water and mountains and valley. Ray didn't show up for dinner, and he didn't show up the next day, either. In fact, he didn't return for nearly a month, during which time Christa alternated between shutting herself up in the bedroom, pounding on my door to talk incoherently for hours, and scaring up whatever expats and aimless travellers she could, for wild parties that lasted days. I was pretty worried about her, especially when I realized she was taking not only Crestilin, but Levelal and Hedonalex, too.

When I could, I would hide myself away from the noise and

confusion of the parties, and ask Marya for meals to bring to the little house for myself. And sometimes Amos and I would stand together at the kitchen window to watch the storms, and the fires springing up on distant slopes. And I would also sneak peeks at Amos, whose face reflected the flames as an entrancing opalescence, as if the light were coming from his lunar skin.

Ray was still gone, and one day Christa came to my room wearing baggy pajamas and carrying a huge armload of beautiful, beautiful dresses. "Here," she said. "These are for you. I don't want them anymore." In her eyes, tears were welling and subsiding and welling. I took the clothes from her, and we stood and looked at each other, and then she turned away and was gone. Naturally, during that time, I thought about Graham quite a bit, and I longed not for him, but for the apparition he fell so far short of, which I called up over and over, and gradually wore away until there was nothing left of it, though the loss wasn't exactly a nullity—I could feel an uncomfortable splotch marking its spot, like a darned patch on a sock.

I watched the ravenous flames devouring Ray's eucalyptus, where there had once been small farms and living crops, and I was sorry that I hadn't sent myself my paints and brushes. So Fred drove me to the nearest large town, where I spent most of the frisky money that had made me feel so powerful to acquire some passable materials.

We passed some donkeys on the road, sweet little gray things with eyes as black as Amos's. "Donkeys!" Fred said affectionately.

Fred spoke only a bit of English, so I'm not sure exactly what he was telling me—I think it was that he had a wife and lots of children, and that his wife was a baker, who made the delicious pastries that Marya served every day, but that the price of flour was now so high that the remaining local people could barely afford to buy her bread.

Fred himself was an electrician, I think he said, but these days there wasn't much paying work, so he had started to do any sort of thing he could for Christa and Ray, to make ends meet. I'm not sure, but I think he said that he was helping build a generator, too, for the little hospital in the area, and that there were sometimes electrical emergencies, so he had to drop whatever he was doing for Ray or Christa and go attend to the problem.

Anyhow, he was good at doing a lot of things, and he was kind enough to help me stretch some canvases. Accident had selected me to observe, in whatever way I could, the demonic, vengeful, helpless, ardent fires as they consumed the trees that had replaced the crops—to observe the moment when, at the heart of the conflagration, the trees that sustained it became phantoms, the fire's memory.

In those days, I was neither awake nor asleep. The fires, the sea, the parties, Christa, Marya, Amos, and Fred wove through the troubled light, the dusk, the smoky, phosphorescent nights. The water had become rough and gray, and down by the shore a little group of shacks had sprung up, where people waited for a boat to appear on the horizon. Sometimes I thought of my former employer, Howard, just standing there, as I left, not looking at me.

I was getting fed; at home, so was my cat. I arranged to stay another month. Ray returned, and the wild parties came to an abrupt end, though now and again a fancy car would still roar up, and some flashy, drunken teenagers would tumble out at the door and have to be shooed away. I learned, online, that Zaffran had taken up with a young actor. The first few days Ray was back, he was irritable and silent, but soon he became cheery and expansive, as though he had achieved something of note, and Christa began to make plans to redecorate. "Would you like the dresses back?" I asked. "I don't really have any place to wear them."

"The dresses?" she said. She smiled vaguely, and patted me, as though I had barked.

Three weeks of drenching rains kept us all indoors, and by the next week, when the rain began to let up, I had completed almost what I could, and Amos was ready to run his show, which he was provisionally calling *State of Emergency*.

The dank fires were still smoldering, and several donkeys had slid into a ravine, where they died, heaps of blood and shattered bone, though no tourists had been hurt. With the help of Fred and some kids from the village, Amos had constructed a little theatre inside the main house, and we all settled in to watch— Christa and Ray and me, of course, and Marya, and a few Europeans and Saudis, who still had vacation places in the area, and a visitor from Jaipur, who designed software for a big U.S. corporation, and his elegant wife. I wore one of Christa's lovely dresses for the occasion, the only one that didn't make me look seriously delusional.

The curtain rose, over a vibrant and ominous bass line. You could hear the plashing of the alligators in the moat and the lethal tapping of the computer keys in the towers. A queasy buzzing of the synthetic string section slowly became audible as the murky dawn disclosed drone aircraft circling the skies around the castle. Fred had done an amazing job with the lights, and the set, with its beautiful painted backdrops, was so vivid and alluring that sitting there in front of it you felt as though you had been miniaturized and were living in the splendid castle, pacing its red stone floors among the silk hangings. In the caves, where the serfs and donkeys toiled, at a throb of the woodwinds, pinpoints of brilliant yellow eyes flicked open, revealing hundreds of upside-down bats.

Amos had made a makeshift recording in his own strange, quavering, slightly nasal voice, of all the vocal tracks laid over an electronic reduction of the score—the forceful recitatives, and the complex, intertwining vocal lines. As the conflict built toward a climax, the powerful despots—the king and queen, the generals, and the alligators in the moat—sang of rage and growing fears. The twilight deepened, and the hills beyond the castle grew pink. Small black blobs massing on them became columns of donkeys and serfs, advancing. The sound of piccolos flared, and Marya grabbed my wrist as a great funnel of dots swirled from the turrets and bats filled the sky, and Amos's quavering voice, in a gorgeous and complicated sextet, not only mourned the downfall of the brutal regime but also celebrated the astonishing triumph of the innocents.

The curtain dropped, and there was a brief silence until Marya and I began to clap. The others joined in tepidly. "Nicely done, nicely done," the man from Jaipur said.

"We love to have artists working here," Christa said to his elegant wife. "It's an atmosphere that promotes experimentation. Sometimes things succeed and sometimes they fail. That's just how it works."

"That was only the first act," Amos said. "This is intermission."

"Ah," Ray said, grimly. "Well, let's all have a stretch and a drink, then, before we sit down again."

"I'm afraid we won't be able to stay for the second act," one of the Saudis said. "An early flight. Thank you. It was a most enjoyable evening, most unexpected."

So the rest of us had a stretch and a drink and sat down for the short second act.

The curtain rose over a blasted landscape. The bodies of the king and the queen swung stiffly from barren trees. With a moaning and creaking of machinery, the ruins of the castle rose unsteadily up from the earth. Heaps of smoking corpses clogged the moat.

Three generals, formerly in the service of the hanged royal couple and now in the service of the absent executives, appeared at the front of the stage. One sang of the dangers to prosperity and social health that the conquered rebels had represented. A second joined in, with a lyrical memory of his beloved father, also a general, who had died in the line of duty. And the third sang of a hauntingly beautiful serf rebel, whom he had been obliged to kill.

There was more mechanical moaning and creaking, and up from the earth in front of the castle rose a line of skeletons—serfs, bats, and donkeys—linked by heavy chains. The generals, now in the highest turret, swigged from a bottle of champagne, and as the grand finale, the skeletons, heads bowed, sang a dirge in praise of martial order.

The curtain came down again, heavily. There were another few moments of confused silence, and then Marya and I began to clap loudly, and the others joined in a bit, after which Marya disappeared quietly into the kitchen, to put out the scrumptious dinner she had prepared, and Ray stood up. "Well," he said. "So."

I rarely go to parties any longer, but I did go to one the other evening, and there were Ray and Christa, looking wonderful. The milling crowd jostled us together for a moment, and they each gave me a quick kiss on the cheek and moved on, not seeming to remember me, exactly.

In the morning, I called Amos, with whom I have coffee now and again, and we arranged to meet up that afternoon. He had just gotten back from touring *The Hand That Feeds You* in Sheffield, Delft, and Leipzig, where it had a modest success, apparently. "Gosh, I'd love to see that show again," I said. "Yeah," he said, "it's changed. I've worked out some of the kinks, and of course I got together some people who can actually sing to record the music, but I can't get it put on here. Too expensive. And my former producer says the stuff about serfs is cliché."

He was thinner than ever, drawn, actually, and I noticed for the first time that his wonderful, pallid luster had dimmed. "Amos, hey, I really cleaned up with my last show," I said. "Let me take you to a decent dinner."

"Sure," he said, in such a concertedly neutral tone that I realized I'd upset him.

"Wow, Christa and Ray," I said, retreating to more comfortable ground. "I think about them sometimes, don't you? It's odd—no matter how you feel about a place, it's as though you exchange something with it. It keeps a little bit of you, and you keep a little bit of it."

"I know," he said. "And the thing you mostly get to keep is leaving."

A while after we'd both returned home, or so Amos had heard, the last of Ray's eucalyptus trees had been torn out to prevent further fires, and then the bluffs collapsed, sweeping away the remaining huts of the village in mudslides, and Ray and Christa had shut up the place and left, shortly before it was torched. So we wouldn't be seeing it again, obviously, and nobody else would, either.

And in fact it was hard to believe, as we sat there in the rather grubby coffee shop about halfway between our apartments, that the place had ever actually existed, and that Amos had first done his show there that evening when the rains finally stopped and the sky cleared and the stars came out and the moon made a path on the sea that looked as though it led straight to heaven.

No one had mentioned the show at dinner, but there was plenty to talk about that night anyway—a new drug against hair loss that was being developed in Germany, an animated film about space aliens that was grossing an immense profit despite its unprecedented cost, and a bestselling memoir detailing a teenager's abusive upbringing that turned out to have been written by a prankster. And after we'd all had a lot of very good wine and Marya brought out an incredible fruit tart, the man from Jaipur stood to raise his glass and said, "Let us be thankful—let us be thankful for our generous hosts, for art, for this beautiful evening, and for the mild, sunny days ahead!"

Derek Palacio

Sugarcane

Aʀᴍᴀɴᴅᴏ sʜᴏᴜʟᴅ ɴᴇᴠᴇʀ ʜᴀᴠᴇ taken on the boy, but the food lines were long, and despite being the town doctor, he was not privileged beyond the standard cup of sugar every Saturday. He had a jeep, no roof, paid for by the barracks, but he was allowed no passengers (other than the boy) and he could not drive the vehicle except on house calls to the base, which he made daily. He'd thought about taping boards where the windows should be and driving south to the city beaches on weekends, but he'd also thought about setting fire to his house, hiking to Guardalavaca, slipping into the ocean at midnight and trying for Duncan Town. The bad joke was most of the sugar left the island, and even if Armando could drive the jeep to another food station, he'd still have to produce a clean rations book, which his was not. People eyed him jealously when the truck sputtered by on uneven roads, but his luxury meant only that he could work longer hours and see patients farther away. So when a pound of raw sugar appeared five months ago in his mailbox with a note requesting an internship for the plantation manager's son, Armando wrote back "yes" and "of course" while shoveling four teaspoons of amber crystal into his evening coffee.

But the boy, Eduardo, was thick in the hands, and recently he'd proven himself thick in the ears. Entrance exams were now sixteen days away, and the week before he confessed to not having read the books Armando had given him back in April. He said they were all lists and diagrams, and he was learning more by watching.

"You have to make the marks first," Armando told him.

"I will study between now and then," Eduardo replied, "and you will write a letter."

José Martí could not write a letter that would justify Eduardo's place in school. Not only did he shirk the books, but he was also rotten with patients, especially late in the long evenings when the two of them left the barracks and returned to the high town to see pregnant housewives, coughing toddlers, and fevered state laborers. Armando was trained as a surgeon, but the government made no distinction between physicians and specialists, and he saw anyone who ailed. Someone always had a fever. He'd tried telling Eduardo that many sicknesses could be frailties of the mind. He'd explained the little white capsules with a false name, Diocyclin, which he gave out to the ambiguously ill. He even broke one in front of the boy to show him how it was just water inside. He was trying to teach Eduardo that his job was to cure people, not just symptoms. But then Eduardo began to think that most patients were faking and made a game of proving their symptoms exaggerated. Just three days ago the boy had asked a lieutenant at the barracks to describe his pains *more specifically* and *with greater detail*.

"I see," Eduardo had said during the consult. He'd stood in front of a soldier sitting on a stool and complaining of a sore throat. Armando had promised an easy interview to Eduardo that week.

"But can you describe what it *feels like?*"

Armando had raised an eyebrow at that and almost put an end to the charade, but the boy backed down when he heard the doctor stir. " 'Hot and tender' are just a little vague," Eduardo said. "If you can be more precise, I can better help you." He shrugged and added, "I am still learning."

The lieutenant coughed and said it felt like hot sand had been poured down his throat, and he couldn't swallow for his life. Eduardo nodded in satisfaction, but then forgot to take the man's temperature and Armando had to relieve him.

In the jeep he'd scolded Eduardo, yelling over the spitting engine to never second-guess a patient. If the symptoms were not there, he would find out during the examination. You cannot help them if they do not trust you, he said. Eduardo had been quiet for the remainder of the day and followed Armando's orders with a mechanical agency. A young girl said he pinched her too hard when taking her pulse, but that was all, and the next morning he was fine again.

A country boy, Armando often thought, and too accustomed to mules and sows. Eduardo prodded people like a horseman pokes a steer. Armando knew this from the beginning. He had been invited to the manager's house after he wrote back "yes" and met the man and his son in the stables. The plantation was in the valley below Patalón and drew its water from two streams that started in the hills. The stables were large and could have entertained more animals, maybe once had, and the father, the manager, had stood just inside the barn, wearing a hat with a wide brim. He was short and his handshake was weak, but his black eyes cut into your chest.

"Eduardo is smart," the manager had said. "He holds onto things like a barnacle to stone."

Armando stood by the father then and watched Eduardo saddle a mule. He was quick with the cinch and knew to poke the ribs before tightening. They took Armando into the sugarcane but did not ride themselves. The father walked beside him, and Eduardo led the mule between the rows. Armando felt like an idiot, but said nothing. The father's plantation was no small part of the country's export, and the man sported a machete in a chipped leather holster attached at his hip.

"He was a fine student, but he had obligations here, so his scores were not as they should have been."

"He doesn't want to follow in your footsteps?" Armando asked.

"My older son is at business school and will return in the spring. This is his."

Armando looked at Eduardo, but the boy didn't flinch at his father's words. He walked with his head up, never watching the ground, and he led the mule flawlessly over rocks and across small ditches.

"So a surgeon?" Armando continued, still watching Eduardo.

"He is good with his hands," the manager replied. As if on cue, a rat in a nearby row scurried past. The mule bucked and whinnied. Eduardo turned quickly and grabbed for the bit, slipping his hand between the cheek and the curb chain. He pulled down hard until the teeth snapped shut. Armando did not have the chance to even consider falling off.

They returned to the stable and the father stated that Eduardo would begin the next morning. He would ride over to the doctor's house by horse so as not to upset Armando's routine and would wait outside. He would follow Armando every day thereafter, and in half a year he would help with his last harvest, see his last cane fire, and go off to university.

The men shook hands once more, and when Armando made it home an hour later, he found another three pounds of sugar on his doorstep. Lifting his bounty off the ground, Armando believed, however foolishly, that diligent study and his own patience might somehow prepare Eduardo for the primary exams, maybe even for the college of dentistry.

But that had been April. It was September now, and Armando awoke in bed next to a woman he'd cooked plantains for the previous night. The sheet was pulled down to their waists, and the woman's breasts were exposed. Armando looked at the clock and saw that it was early still, so he touched the woman in the ribs. When she sighed, he bent over her chest and kissed her right nipple. He put a hand at her navel and with his long middle finger tickled the hairs growing up from her crotch. She opened her eyes and smiled. She kept them open the whole time, and she bit his ear when they were finished.

Everyone here is hungry, Armando thought.

Her name was Mercedes, and she had a sweet tooth, the same kind as Armando, weak and malleable. She was the fourth woman in a month he'd invited over for dinner and the third to have slept with him after dessert. She was the first he'd made advances upon the morning after, and he had not minded her sour, waking breath. Her sugary gums were gone from the night before, but Armando found her dry lips just as pleasant, their taste a mixture of sweat and stale fruit, and he wished he had the strength and time to touch her again. He wondered what other desserts he could make.

Armando left her in bed for a cup of coffee that was gritty from too much sugar. Alone in the kitchen, he contemplated the economy of sugar, which, since that first sack in April, had become the economy of women and the economy of sex. Eduardo's father plants a crop and waits for rain. A few months pass and the state laborers arrive. They burn the fields and harvest the stalks. The cane is bundled and shipped west to the processing plant. The sugar is refined and then it is bleached. It is sent to the Soviets or someone else, anywhere but north, and only the worst of it stays, given out in cups once a week to the farmhands, to the doctors, to the army, to everyone. Long live the state. I retrieve my cup every Saturday morning, along with rice and beans, perhaps some fish, a little salt, just enough for one good meal. I come back to my house and there is another sack of sugar for me, milled privately by the plantation manager. It is mine because I teach his son. We exchange food for thought. I take my sugar and grow fat on it. Every cup of coffee is a meal. When I realize there is too much and that I am losing my taste for it, I invite a woman over. She comes not because I am a handsome man, but because I am a doctor. I cook her dinner, and then dessert, which is when she decides to stay, because no one has enough sugar for candied plantains, or they have been saving up for a month. The woman is delighted, and we exchange food for sex. When I taste my sugar on her lips, it mixes with her spit and makes a syrup. My tooth aches once more, and I spend another week with Eduardo, waiting happily on another bag of crudely milled crystal. The system plays again.

Mercedes walked into the kitchen wearing the light blue dress from the night before. The hem fluttered across her knees, and Armando remembered her walking into his room the same way, weightless and airy.

"Where is your student?" she asked. Armando had told her about Eduardo over their salted fish and pinto beans.

"It's too early still."

"What will you teach him today?"

"Bones." It would be a start.

Armando thought back to his own primaries twenty-one years ago. He tried to recall what they asked of him and how specific they were. He remembered naming the bones, identifying the muscles, marking tendons. Plenty of Latin.

Mercedes poured herself a cup from the metal percolator and sat across from Armando at the table. Her hair was up, as it was at the tailor's shop where Armando had found her. She was a seamstress, and she sipped the black water without adding any sugar.

"You like it plain?" Armando asked.

"I've gotten used to it this way."

"I have plenty."

She waved him off and then touched her cheek, which was red. "Perhaps you should shave this morning."

Armando blushed and felt his chin. The stubble was coarse

and he could only imagine how gray. Thirty-nine was not so old, but he was an ancient bachelor. Mercedes could not have been more than thirty-six, and she had been the youngest so far. The others were forty-five, forty-seven, even fifty. Armando had been lucky, because there were not so many of them left, the women his age. Not enough, at least, for all the men who remained to marry, so he wondered how Mercedes was in Cuba.

"Your family stayed?" he asked.

"We had no money, and my uncle was a police officer. We thought he would join the army."

"He did not?"

"They wanted only new men, no Batistianos. My uncle now runs our shop. We are from Camagüey but move between Cienfuegos and Guayabal. We follow the harvesters. Their denim always needs mending."

"Gypsies," Armando teased. "How do you like these hills?"

"They're pretty at dusk."

"The rest of the time?"

"Like any other hills," she told him.

"You would leave?"

"Patalón?"

"The island."

She answered quickly, "Yes."

"Why?"

"Because the days here are all the same," she said. "They believe monotony is stability."

"You travel across the country."

"Going nowhere."

She looked down and sipped her black coffee. Armando nodded. Mercedes was not sad when she spoke, and there was a blank detachment in her voice. She was unlike the older women whose faces darkened when he asked them why they hadn't left with relatives. It was as if she had not yet judged her circumstance fixed or fleeting, so why feel anything? Or perhaps she still believed she was going and that the journey was just long, circuitous, and one had to travel the island before finding a way out.

"And you?" Mercedes asked.

"I've thought about it."

"Everyone thinks about it."

"Not everyone."

"You have enough money?"

"Some," he answered, "but they would never let me go." He showed his hands. "I am a good doctor here."

"You could be that somewhere else," she chided. But then, politely, "You are also a good cook."

"Then we can eat again?" he asked.

"Will you make plantains?"

"If you like. If I can find some." Armando had not tried to please a woman in a long time, and he hadn't asked any of the other women to return. He felt his brow twitch. You attract flies with honey, but once they found it, would they stay?

"To be honest, I like them for the sugar."

"It's precious now."

"I don't remember anyone, even my mother when I was a child, using it with such carelessness. It was criminal how you burned it in the pan."

"I have plenty," Armando said.

"Where do you get it from?" she finally asked. She added, "I won't tell."

"You can't tell. You've eaten some. You are my accomplice."

"So you steal it? From who? Your patients? How cruel!"

She feigned disgust and Armando laughed. "Eduardo's father. He is the plantation manager."

"A retired *escopetero* then, fed by *Ortodoxo* cane farmers."

"I was not a rebel."

"But you are now," she joked.

"Not quite," he answered. She pressed her lips together and Armando wished he had played along.

"But then you must be a wonderful teacher," Mercedes offered.

"The father hopes so."

"But you said the boy is not smart."

"No. He will probably fail."

"Then what becomes of your sugar?"

"I have enough for one cup of coffee a day for three months."

"You would ration it like that?"

Armando thought for a moment and said, "No. I would eat it all in a night and then tell stories of it for the rest of my life." He had grown bold in the last month.

She leaned across the table and kissed him.

"I will come," she said.

"For another meal?"

"For another dessert."

In the jeep Armando tried to quiz Eduardo on the bones of the body. "The humerus," he said.

"My arm."

"Which part?"

The boy tapped near his elbow.

"You will have to be specific," Armando shouted over the engine.

"The muscles are easier."

"Peroneus brevis?" Armando asked.

"My leg," Eduardo replied.

Just outside the base, which was higher up in the hills, Armando stopped the car to put on his barracks coat. The ranking colonel had given it to him to wear when working at the infirmary, and it served as his army attire. He would see the colonel that morning. Armando had received a phone call at his office in town that the man was feeling ill and to come as soon as possible. Armando canceled two early appointments and prayed for a pregnant patient's contractions not to get any closer. He'd told Eduardo to hurry and grab the travel kit.

"You look like a recruit in your green jacket," Eduardo said.

"I am just following the rules."

"You also walk taller when we visit the barracks."

Armando looked at the boy before turning the ignition. He was slightly taller than his father, but had the same broad shoulders and the same coal-dark eyes. Eduardo had been born after 1959 and had no recollection of anything but his father's sugarcane and the edges of this town. He was the first generation after the lost generation, the men and women who'd mostly left with their families before the coup.

Armando had himself been in medical school, was almost done, and if he'd gone to Spain with his uncle, what would he have become? Maybe a paltry line cook like his uncle (who'd had his own restaurant in Colón), but more likely some laborer. A farmhand. The boy was a farmhand. He would have become Eduardo. And by the time he was a doctor, it was too late. But still he found himself thinking, I'd rather be a doctor in Cuba than a vagrant in Spain. Eduardo blinked his black eyes and Armando thought, he will never leave. He will never think to leave.

"When you work with the army," Armando said, "you will need to be as determined as they are." Lies.

Armando spun the tires out and raced toward the gate.

The colonel was a large-nosed man who chewed on the end of an unlit cigar. He sat on an exam table with his shirt off and spoke to the ceiling. Armando walked up next to him, but Eduardo stood back near a table upon which he placed the travel kit.

"It's my carrot, Doctor. I can taste the leaf inside, and it keeps me going. Always more to be done for the state."

"Noble work," Armando answered.

"Yes," the colonel said heavily, and he bit down on the cigar as if to reassure himself.

His face sagged at the cheeks, and Armando thought, all the soldiers look the same. It must be tiresome to talk like that all day.

"I hope I did not inconvenience you by asking you here so soon."

"Of course not."

"Good. I told the lieutenant to fix the window screen in my quarters yesterday, but he neglected to do so. When I woke this morning, my arm was covered in mosquitoes, and now I feel like the plague. Malaria, I suspect."

"A reasonable conclusion, sir." Armando leaned over the prostrate colonel. "May I take your temperature first?"

The man grunted.

Eduardo brought out a thermometer and carried it to the examination table. Armando took it from the boy and placed it inside the colonel's mouth. He checked the man's forehead. The skin was dry and cool. He felt the man's throat, pushing his thumbs into the brown skin. But the colonel was thick in the neck, and Armando had to search for the glands.

"Excuse the pressure, sir." There was no swelling, and Armando took his hands away.

"How did you sleep last night?" he asked.

"Fine," the colonel mumbled. "Better than I should have, considering the bugs."

"No tossing or turning? No trembling?"

The colonel shook his head.

Armando examined the eyes. The colonel looked left, right, down, and up. The sclera were clean and white.

"Blink, please."

The pupils expanded and retracted nicely. With his chin so close to the colonel's mouth, Armando could smell his breath. Salt and fish. He stood back up and took the thermometer out from under the colonel's tongue. His temperature was normal.

"The pain is more abdominal, Doctor."

Armando quickly prodded the man's girth. His hands slid from the sternum down to the navel. He pushed down on the bowels, and when the colonel let out a small sigh, Armando stopped.

"It might be malaria, sir, but it is impossible to tell just now. You are right to worry about the mosquitoes. I will leave some medicine, just a few pills, and should you take them tonight and tomorrow, you will be fine. As I said, it might or might not be malaria. Too soon to tell. But the pills—two today, four tomorrow, two the next morning—and some rest will ensure that if it is indeed malaria, we will take it out before it gets underway."

"Fine, Doctor."

Armando walked over to his travel kit and spoke to Eduardo. "Fix a bottle for the colonel. Eight capsules of Diocyclin." Eduardo stared a moment but then did as he was told.

"We will check with you tomorrow morning and then again the day after," Armando told the colonel.

On the road Armando drove as fast as he could up the hill toward town. He checked his watch and determined that his pregnant patient would be fully dilated in about an hour. Eduardo had been quiet since leaving the barracks.

"Does the colonel have malaria?" he asked.

Armando could not hear him. "What?"

"Is the colonel really sick?"

"No," Armando shouted, then, "sort of. He has a loose stool. Two months ago he complained the same way after attending a fishing competition and eating grouper. He cannot stomach fish oil. He had something on his breath, probably sardines. He was not really sick. Just suffering from bad digestion."

"Then why did you pretend?"

"The man would not believe me if I told him his pain was just indigestion."

"But you are the doctor."

Armando could see then what Eduardo thought of medicine. It was like the boy and his mule. One held the secret knowledge. One was stupid. One led and one followed. Eduardo would be the master and his patients would listen, mindful of the curb chain.

"My job is to make people feel better."

"Even if it is a lie?" Eduardo asked.

"It is not a lie."

"Then what is it?"

Armando thought of his maxim: better to be a doctor in Cuba . . . No, a doctor helps people however he can. "Never mind. You can't understand."

"Understand what?"

"Forget it."

"Tell me," Eduardo demanded.

"Enough!" Armando shouted. He put his hand up, and the boy sank into his seat. "You can't understand," he said, and the jeep lumbered back down the hill toward Patalón.

Armando's pregnant patient had already miscarried twice before, and it was a small miracle she'd come to full term. He ordered Eduardo to arrange the back room as quickly as possible, and when the boy lagged, Armando did not hesitate to raise his voice.

The woman was twenty-seven, and her husband worked at the post office in town. He used to deliver the mail, but now he sorted envelopes. The woman was a schoolteacher, and she would have two weeks after their child was born before returning to work. Armando told the woman she would need more time. She'd shrugged at him.

When Eduardo called that the room was ready, Armando and the woman's midwife, an aunt perhaps, lifted her onto the bed and the clean sheets Eduardo had drawn. The boy watched from a corner of the room as Armando undid the woman's gown and positioned her on the mattress, pushing her legs up into the stirrups and propping her head against an old pillow.

"Lots of towels, Eduardo, and two basins of clean, warm water. Then go to the rations house and ask for ice."

Armando prepped a side table with forceps, retractors, clamps, and a scalpel. Before pulling it up to the bed, he draped a towel across the top and hid the knife. He did not want to frighten the woman. Since the morning, her contractions had peaked, coming in quick waves. The midwife squeezed the woman's hand and pressed down on her forehead. The woman's breaths were short, but when Armando tested her pulse, it held. The child's head was turned by the time Eduardo returned.

Armando had not asked the boy if he'd wanted to see this. He had never asked him what he did or did not want to see, and Eduardo had never shied away from a procedure or sick patient. You could see as much on the plantation: farm accidents were not uncommon, and machetes cut fingers off every season. Sows were slaughtered, mares gave birth to foals, and this arrangement had been the father's idea anyway.

But the boy moved off to the side of the bed, and he did not stop to look. In his hands the bag of ice shook. Armando thought, the boy has not had sex yet. He is a nervous virgin.

"Good," Armando said to him. "Put the bag in the sink and bring a cup of ice to our patient."

Eduardo dumped the wet bag in the steel sink by the cupboard and then planted himself next to the bed. He held the cup in front of the woman, but when he realized she would not reach for it, he hesitantly poured some cubes into her open mouth. Eduardo spilled some water from the cup and the expectant mother tried smiling at him, but he just looked to the floor.

It was another hour before the woman was fully dilated, which was when Armando saw a deepening shade of purple spread across the infant's breaching crown. It could not breathe. Armando looked at the woman and saw the exhaustion on her face. He could not push the fetus back in and cut it out now. She would die. He needed the baby to come quickly, and when the head was mostly through, he could slip his long, middle finger into the woman's vagina and pry the umbilical cord from around the child's neck.

"You have to push," Armando said softly. "Hard, three times."

The woman seemed unable to take in air.

"It will be the greatest pain, but also the quickest," he lied.

"Three hard pushes, and you will hear a cry because your baby will be out." Armando squeezed the woman's ankle.

"Listen to the doctor," the midwife pleaded. "It's close to done."

"No," she said.

Armando reached for the side table and slid his hand under the white towel.

"Hold her tight," he said to Eduardo and the midwife. The boy hesitated and Armando said, "Take her shoulder and press down on it."

Eduardo dropped the empty cup he held, and as soon as his hands were on the woman's arm, Armando pulled the scalpel from the side table and made a hasty incision along the woman's perineum. She screamed, and the midwife leaned down on her. Eduardo had only her forearm in his grasp and this she tried to free. "Stop!" she yelled, and the boy bit his lip, then sobbed, "I'm sorry! I'm sorry!"

The head still did not move, and after a failed effort with the forceps, Armando slipped around Eduardo and chastised his patient.

"There's no time," he said, fearful for the child, but mostly scared for this mother and the father who was at work. They would not try again.

"Push," he commanded her. "Push now!"

The woman closed her eyes and pressed her lips together. She pushed once, but then started crying and tried again to wrench her hand from Eduardo's grip.

"Twice more!" he shouted. "Twice more!"

The midwife grabbed the woman's left leg and pulled it wide. "Push!" she said.

The woman tensed again, and Armando looked down to her crotch. The head was beginning to crown. The purple was turning blue.

"Just once more for your baby," Armando said into the woman's ear. "One more—"

But then Eduardo grabbed Armando's arm and shouted,

"Blood!" The mattress below the woman was a dark, wet red, and the boy tugged incessantly on Armando's sleeve. "There is so much blood!" He shook the boy off him but looked closer. The head was still not there, and Armando leaned into the woman then, put his lips as close as he could to her ears. He smelled her sweat, heard her shallow breaths, and it reminded him of the night just gone by with Mercedes, the damp heat and the one thin sheet. He recalled her wide hips, which moved effortlessly up and down, and he thought he could love her just as easily. Then he imagined the pregnant woman Mercedes and the baby theirs, and it gave him the courage to be cruel.

He said, "We cannot let the child die," and gripping the tendon between her shoulder and her neck, Armando pinched the woman as hard as he could until she tensed. She wailed terribly, but her muscles, all the muscles in her body, contracted.

"You're killing her!" It was Eduardo's voice over the mother's screams, though it was different, scared and human, and Armando felt a set of hands grabbing for him. But the mother was pushing and Armando was a good doctor; he was performing his duties and saving two lives, so he shoved the boy much harder than he'd needed to.

When the head came, Armando was quick, and he cut the cord as well as freeing it from the neck. The baby's lips were blue, but there was some red in its nose and cheeks. With a small suction-bulb syringe he cleared the nose and throat, and Armando only had to slap the tiny creature twice before it coughed and began to cry. Only when the midwife took the baby to clean and wrap it did Armando turn around and see Eduardo sitting on the floor, slumped against the wall. He offered the boy his bloody hand, but Eduardo scrambled to his feet and stormed out of the room. The newborn was a girl.

"I'm sorry," Armando said.

Eduardo sat at the desk in the small room with a metal cabinet that Armando used for filing and paperwork. He sat straight up with his hands in his lap, and he did not look Armando in the eye when he spoke.

He said, "You are a coward."

"I should not have pushed you so hard, but the baby—"

"You are a coward for screaming at that poor woman."

"The mother?" Armando asked.

"And for lying to the colonel. You are afraid of the colonel, but not the woman. You treated her like an animal. Like a dog and its litter. You were not afraid to bully her. Or me."

"You don't understand," Armando began. "She would have died."

"Do you mean I don't understand or I can't understand?"

"The child was choking," he said. "She needed to push, not to be coddled. The infant would be a corpse if the mother had stopped."

Eduardo stood up and pushed out his chest.

"I am not afraid of you," he whispered, and Armando slapped the boy.

He had nothing prepared, nothing cooking, by the time Mercedes arrived. She wore another dress, yellow, and Armando told her about Eduardo in his office.

"No more desserts," he said sheepishly.

"A brief joy," she replied. "Most are."

It terrified him that she maybe spoke of more than sugar.

"I suppose," he said.

"When are his exams? Next week?"

"Two weeks. Or maybe ten days. When is the burning? It's after the harvest."

Armando had a third of a bottle of rum, which he'd saved for a long time, and he drank very slowly from a short glass.

"You would have had two more pounds in your cupboard."

"Yes."

"The boy won't pass?" she asked.

"Not a chance." He paused. "I'm sorry."

"For what?"

He waved at the stove. "For teasing you."

Mercedes shrugged. "Brief," she repeated, "but the sweeter for it." She went to the cabinet and retrieved a wine glass. She filled it more than halfway with Armando's rum. Going to the window, she snatched the open sack of sugar he'd left by the sink and brought it to the table. With a spoon she heaped little hills of brown crystal into the liquor until the rum nearly met the rim. She carefully stirred it and then gingerly pulled a soaked mound of sugar out of the glass. It dripped onto the kitchen table, and Mercedes held it up to Armando's mouth.

"To drink away the troubles?" he asked.

"To forget you ever had them," she said.

"And what happens when I wake tomorrow morning?"

"Your head will hurt to the point of cursing sugar. You won't want it then."

"Sounds terrible."

"The doctor's medicine," she told him. "Or my gypsy potion, if you prefer."

He smiled at last. "Who knows then where I will wake up?"

"If you are lucky, somewhere far away."

It reminded Armando of a dessert his uncle used to serve in his restaurant: brown rum syrup over ice cream with fried mangoes and raisins. The hot topping would melt the ice cream, and something like rum-milk would collect at the bottom. Armando would take the bowl with both hands and drink the cream and liquor and lick his lips. They would be sticky with the sugar, but his throat would ache from the rum.

"Thank you," he said, but he put his hand up when she offered him another.

"You promised," Mercedes said, "to make a story of this. The awful sugar that you ate until you nearly burst."

"You won't miss it?"

"I'll remember Patalón for the sugar. Something different once. Something I had not expected."

"After the harvest, you mean. When you are gone."

She said nothing and instead ate the spoonful he rejected, but then dipped another for him.

"Eat and say farewell. Good-bye, sugar."

He accepted this reluctantly, and they traded mouthfuls until the glass was nearly empty and Mercedes finished the rum as a thirsty priest finished the wine at Mass.

Mercedes stood in front of her chair and undid her dress. She wore a slip but no bra, and the slip she removed as well. Her hair was up still from her day at work, out of the way and nothing dragging behind, and she left it there but removed her earrings, tiny wooden beads painted gold. She took a step toward Armando and leaned back some, and her breasts stretched above her ribs. Her left hand found her mouth and then found the open sack on the table. The sugarcoated fingers paused at both her nipples, and Mercedes put a hand behind Armando's head. She pulled him to her chest, and he opened his mouth and licked her.

When Armando tried to remove his pants, she seized his hands and said, "Wait." She lifted herself onto the table and spread her legs. With the sticky spoon she dug more sugar from out of the bag, but instead of offering him the mouthful, she poured it over her crotch.

"Kiss me," she said.

Armando rarely drove the jeep at night, so after leaving Mercedes alone in the house, he struggled in the driver's seat to find the switch for the headlamps. There was no moon, just some scattered stars, and a haze drifting overhead. Armando smelled the faintest bit of smoke, but then his hand found the knob and the lights were on. He drove half-mad and fuming, and he wondered if he had a fever from all the sugar. In his head there was still hope. It was supply and demand, sugar and a woman, and he thought he could possibly keep them both. At the very least he believed one might stay the other, a good doctor and some sweets perhaps just enough to convince a woman to linger.

Topping the last ridge above the plantation, the jeep came off the ground perhaps a centimeter, and when Armando saw down the slopes and into the valley, he realized there was smoke in the air. The harvest was sooner than he'd thought, and the laborers were burning the fields to chase out the vermin and lighten the load. The flames would turn to dust the silk leaves and stalk tops, and the remaining bundles, charred and sooty but otherwise fine, would be easier to collect and carry.

At the western gate a farmhand told Armando which dirt road to follow and for how long. He said to be careful of gouges in the track. He did not want Armando to flip the vehicle and land in a fire. The winds were high that night, and fields were burning that shouldn't have been. Armando drove carefully until the gate was out of sight and then tested the jeep's suspension against the rutted path.

He saw Eduardo before he saw the plantation manager. The boy stood in a wide open road, a bigger dirt path than the one Armando came in on, holding the reins of two horses at a distance from a small group of men. To Armando's left were two other jeeps, and he parked his truck alongside them. When Eduardo saw him, the boy's face dropped. But Armando walked toward the group of men, which was breaking up, instead of acknowledging his pupil. Eduardo's father was there, and he pointed to a field not on fire, and the other men, all uniformed, fanned out into the sugarcane. When he turned and saw Armando, he looked angry.

"Doctor," he said.

"Señor Valdes," Armando gasped. He had some smoke or dust in his lungs.

"We are busy, sir," the manager told him. "The auditors have come early," by which he meant they had arrived unannounced.

"Yes, of course. Just a small matter." Armando looked beyond the father's shoulder at the son, and he was certain the boy was too far away to hear.

"This afternoon, at my office, Eduardo and I—"

"It's fine," the manager said, and he turned away and started walking toward the stalks. Armando followed. "Fine, sir?"

"Eduardo told me how you struck him. He also told me about the colonel and the pregnant peasant."

Armando almost laughed at the manager's archaic term. *All Comrades Are King in Cuba.* "I lost my temper."

"You did no such thing. You taught the boy a lesson, one he should already know. The agents," the manager said, waving at the field, "are no different from your colonel. They are representatives of the state. The boy knows how I treat these men, what I give them to keep my numbers high. He called you a coward when he shouldn't have, and you are certainly not. But you're also not a fool, which is why you humor the brass."

Armando watched the man's black eyes. They were sincere. It amazed him that he'd taught Eduardo anything. He was a better instructor than he knew.

The wind blew fiercely then, and the stalks bent to the east. Armando could hear the weaker ones snapping. A rush of heat flooded the dirt road, and his eyes watered.

"Why are they here?" he asked.

"To check the interior before we burn. They want to know that I'm not cutting from the middle for private sales."

They both looked to the distant fields and saw flames drawing wind.

"Will they find anything?" Armando asked.

"Only sugar. Work as hard as you can and take only what you need. Are we not communists?"

"We are."

"A man doesn't need much. Enough for family and maybe some small gifts."

"No shame in that."

"I'm glad you agree," the manager finished.

In the moment that followed, the distant flames were suddenly much nearer, and the wind gathered into blows.

"It's getting too close," the manager said, and his eyes narrowed.

The fire, which had loomed on the horizon, was then riding gusts across the dirt paths, and in an instant the flames spread over the dark field in front of them. It sparked the cane the auditors surveyed. Both Armando and the manager approached the wall of green stalks and listened. Some voices rose, and then a scream. A call for help. Armando did not wait for Eduardo's father, but bent his shoulder and rushed forward.

He found smoke first and a body second. A man curled on the ground, and a suffocating heat throbbing nearby. The crippled man coughed violently, and there was blood seeping down his leg and into his boot. He'd tripped and gashed himself on a spiked ratoon. But the man seemed unaware of his leg and with clenched fists covered his eyes. Armando tried to pull the hands away from the sockets, but even when the man stood he would not uncover his eyes. The smoke has clouded them, Armando thought, and he gripped the auditor and dragged him out to the road.

There he laid the man on the ground and tore the fabric from the man's pant leg. The cut was deep and gushing, but he could not see the bone, and the man groaned only slightly when Armando prodded the flesh around the wound. When he looked up, Eduardo was there with a canteen, and he took it from the boy's outstretched hands. He rinsed the leg and with the torn fabric wrapped the shin. The remaining water he poured over the hands and face of the auditor until at last the man removed his palms from his eyes. The man, dazed, looked between Eduardo and Armando.

He tried to speak but coughed, then tried again. "Thank you," he sputtered.

"It was the boy. He found you and pulled you out."

Eduardo said nothing. He was motionless, and when Armando caught his eyes, his black eyes, the gifts of his father, he said, "He came rushing out of the sugarcane with you on his back. It was remarkable."

The auditor looked up and coughed again. He smiled slightly and then reached for Eduardo's arm, which hung limply at his side, and gripped the boy around the wrist.

"Amazing. Your father is a hard man, and I suppose you are the same. Amazing."

"You've cut your leg," Armando said, "but it is not deep. I think you will be fine."

"He is the town doctor," Eduardo said, finally speaking.

The auditor said, "How lucky am I."

Armando fiddled with the bandage on the leg, and in the quiet moment they heard the sound of men hacking through the sugarcane. Eduardo's father and the other auditors suddenly emerged from the stalks, and it seemed no one else was injured. They all wheezed, but they all stood, and there were smiles on their faces, the joy of being alive. Eduardo ran to his father, and Armando thought to himself, if the man had not just come through the stalks, the boy would no doubt have gone in after him, his own father. He would have forgotten himself and gone for his father. Armando then remembered the pregnant woman and Eduardo's brief cry. He was capable of acting for others, wasn't he? And if he could do that, then surely he could be a doctor, maybe even a surgeon. Couldn't he?

"The boy wants to go to medical school," Armando told the auditor. "I've been working with him these past two months. He is very dedicated, although his scores are not so high. But tests do not consider dedication or ambition."

"He seems capable of anything," the man offered.

"Something like this could speak to his will, could help his cause."

"No doubt."

"And maybe a letter from the patient himself, vouching for the boy's abilities? They would trust a man like yourself."

The man nodded. He asked, "Is he as good a pupil as he is a fireman?"

"He is a fine student, very diligent, and he will make a fine doctor."

The light outside was gray when Armando returned to the bedroom and Mercedes. He did not notice that she had dressed. He went straight to where she sat on the bed and said, "We can have sugar for breakfast."

"What?" she asked.

"We can have sugar for lunch and dinner. The boy will be a doctor," Armando said, "and we will have all the sugar we can possibly eat."

"Today?"

"Always."

Mercedes leaned away from him, and her eyes were large. She smelled like rum and when Armando touched her elbow, it was sticky. "We can make sweet breakfast pies and plantain. Sugared apples. Coffee with sugar. Or cream with sugar."

He stroked her arm and then pushed the hair out of her face. Her eyes were as white as polished clam shells.

"Sweetened pork and beans. Cocoa mixed with sugar, melted on pineapple. Sugared bacon and sweet tea. Candied pears. Soft cake bread. Something different every meal."

"Every day?" she asked.

"Yes, love. Every day we can have sugar. From now until eternity."

"And every day will be sweet?" she asked.

"Yes," Armando said, "some sweet thing always." He looked and saw in her eyes the years of sugar ahead of them, the weight of all that sugarcane, the fire in the fields, the rotating crops, the sharp ratoons, the sea of stalks, and the inevitable monotony of sweetness. And then Armando knew she could never stay, that she could not think of staying.

Kelly Link

The Summer People

Fran's daddy woke her up wielding a mister. "Fran," he said, spritzing her like a wilted houseplant. "Fran, honey. Wake up for just a minute."

Fran had the flu, except it was more like the flu had Fran. In consequence of this, she'd lain out of school for three days in a row. The previous night, she'd taken four NyQuil caplets and fallen asleep on the couch, waiting for her daddy to come home, while a man on the TV threw knives. Her head felt stuffed with boiled wool and snot. Her face was now wet with watered-down plant food. "Hold up," she croaked. "I'm awake!" She began to cough, so hard she had to hold her sides. She sat up.

Her daddy was a dark shape in a room full of dark shapes. The bulk of him augured trouble. The sun wasn't up the mountain yet, but there was a light in the kitchen. There was a suitcase, too, beside the door, and on the table a plate with a mess of eggs. Fran was starving.

Her daddy went on. "I'll be gone some time. A week or three. Not more. You'll take care of the summer people while I'm gone. The Roberts come up next weekend. You'll need to get their groceries tomorrow or next day. Make sure you check the expiration date on the milk when you buy it, and put fresh sheets on all the beds. I've left the house schedule on the counter, and there should be enough gas in the car to make the rounds."

"Wait," Fran said. Every word hurt. "Where are you going?" He sat down on the couch beside her, then pulled something out from under him. He held it out on his palm; one of Fran's old toys, the monkey egg. "Now you know I don't like these. I wish you'd put 'em away."

"There's lots of stuff I don't like," Fran said. "Where you going?"

"Prayer meeting in Miami. Found out about it on the Internet," her daddy said. He shifted on the couch, put a hand against her forehead, so cool and soothing it made her eyes leak. "You don't feel near so hot right now."

"I know you need to stay here and look after me," Fran said. "You're my daddy."

"Now, how can I look after you if I'm not right?" he said. "You don't know the things I've done."

Fran didn't know, but she could guess. "You went out last night," she said. "You were drinking."

Her daddy spread out his hands. "I'm not talking about last night," he said. "I'm talking about a lifetime."

"That is—" Fran said, and then began to cough again. She coughed so long and so hard she saw bright stars. Despite the hurt in her ribs, and despite the truth that every time she managed to suck in a good pocket of air, she coughed it all right back out again, the NyQuil made it all seem so peaceful, her daddy might as well have been saying a poem. Her eyelids were closing. Later, when she woke up, maybe he would make her breakfast.

"Any come around, you tell 'em I'm gone on ahead. Any man tells you he knows the hour or the day, Fran, that man's a liar or a fool. All a man can do is be ready."

He patted her on the shoulder, tucked the counterpane up around her ears. When she woke again, it was late afternoon, and her daddy was long gone. Her temperature was 102.3. All across her cheeks, the plant mister had left a red raised rash.

On Friday, Fran went to school, because she wasn't sure what else to do. Breakfast was a spoon of peanut butter and dry cereal. She couldn't remember the last time she'd eaten. Her cough scared off the crows when she went down to the county road to catch the school bus.

She dozed through three classes, including calculus, before having such a fit of coughing the teacher sent her off to see the nurse. The nurse, she knew, was liable to call her daddy and send her home. This might have presented a problem, but on the way to the nurse's station, Fran came upon Ophelia Merck at her locker.

Ophelia Merck had her own car, a Lexus. She and her family had been summer people, except now they lived in their house up at Horse Cove on the lake all year round. Years ago, Fran and Ophelia had spent a summer of afternoons playing with Ophelia's Barbies while Fran's father smoked out a wasps' nest, repainted cedar siding, tore down an old fence. They hadn't really spoken since then, though once or twice after that summer, Fran's father brought home paper bags full of Ophelia's hand-me-downs, some of them still with the price tags.

Fran eventually went through a growth spurt, which put a stop to that; Ophelia was still tiny, even now. And far as Fran could figure, Ophelia hadn't changed much in most other ways: pretty, shy, spoiled, and easy to boss around. The rumor was her family'd moved full-time to Robbinsville from Lynchburg after a teacher caught Ophelia kissing another girl in the bathroom at a school dance. It was either that or Mr. Merck being up for malpractice, which was the other story, take your pick.

"Ophelia Merck," Fran said. "I need you to tell Nurse Tannent you're gone to give me a ride home right now."

Ophelia opened her mouth and closed it. She nodded.

Fran's temperature was back up again, at 102. Tannent even wrote Ophelia a note to go off campus.

"I don't know where you live," Ophelia said. They were in the parking lot, Ophelia searching for her keys.

"Take the county road," Fran said. "129." Ophelia nodded. "It's up a ways on Wild Ridge, past the hunting camps." She lay back against the headrest and closed her eyes. "Oh, hell. I forgot. Can you take me by the convenience first? I have to get the Roberts' house put right."

"I guess I can do that," Ophelia said.

At the convenience, she picked up milk, eggs, whole wheat sandwich bread, and cold cuts for the Roberts, Tylenol and more NyQuil for herself, as well as a can of frozen orange juice, microwave burritos, and Pop-Tarts. "On the tab," she told Andy.

"I hear your pappy got himself into trouble the other night," Andy said.

"That so," Fran said. "He went down to Florida yesterday morning. He said he needs to get right with God."

"God ain't who your pappy needs to get on his good side," Andy said.

Fran coughed and bent over. Then she straightened right back up. "What's he done?" she said.

"Nothing that can't be fixed with the application of some greaze and good manners," Andy said. "You tell him we'll get it all settled when he come back."

Half the time her daddy got to drinking, Andy and Andy's cousin Ryan were involved, never mind it was a dry county. Andy kept the liquor out back in his van for everwho wanted it and knew to ask. The good stuff came from over the county line, in Andrews. The best stuff, though, was the liquor Fran's daddy brought Andy every once in a while. Everyone said that Fran's daddy's brew was too good to be strictly natural. Which was true. When he wasn't getting right with God, Fran's daddy got up to all kinds of trouble. Fran's best guess was that, in this particular situation, he'd promised to supply something that God was not now going to let him deliver. "I'll tell him you said so."

Ophelia was looking over the list of ingredients on a candy wrapper, but Fran could tell she was interested. When they got back into the car Fran said, "Just because you're doing me a favor doesn't mean you need to know my business."

"Okay," Ophelia said.

"Okay," Fran said. "Good. Now maybe you can take me by the Roberts' place. It's over on—"

"I know where the Roberts' house is," Ophelia said. "My mom played bridge over there all last summer."

The Roberts hid their spare key under a fake rock just like everybody else. Ophelia stood at the door like she was waiting to be invited in. "Well, come on," Fran said.

There wasn't much to be said about the Roberts' house. There was an abundance of plaid, and everywhere Toby mugs and statuettes of dogs pointing, setting, or trotting along with birds in their gentle mouths.

Fran made up the smaller bedrooms and did a quick vacuum downstairs while Ophelia made up the master bedroom and caught the spider that had made a home in the wastebasket. She carried it outside. Fran didn't quite have the breath to make fun of her for this. They went from room to room, making sure that there were working bulbs in the light fixtures and that the cable wasn't out. Ophelia sang under her breath while they worked. They were both in choir, and Fran found herself evaluating Ophelia's voice. A soprano, warm and light at the same time, where Fran was an alto and somewhat froggy, even when she didn't have the flu.

"Stop it," she said out loud, and Ophelia turned and looked at her. "Not you," Fran said. She ran the tap water in the kitchen sink until it was clear. She coughed for a long time and spat into the drain. It was almost four o'clock. "We're done here."

"How do you feel?" Ophelia said.

"Like I've been kicked all over," Fran said.

"I'll take you home," Ophelia said. "Is anyone there, in case you start feeling worse?"

Fran didn't bother answering, but somewhere between the school lockers and the Roberts' master bedroom, Ophelia seemed to have decided that the ice was broken. She talked about a TV show, about the party neither of them would go to on Saturday night. Fran began to suspect that Ophelia had had friends once, down in Lynchburg. She complained about the calculus homework and talked about a sweater she was knitting. She mentioned a girl rock band that she thought Fran might like, even offered to burn her a CD. Several times, she exclaimed as they drove up the county road.

"I never get used to it, to living up here year-round," Ophelia said. "I mean, we haven't even been here a whole year, but . . . It's just so beautiful. It's like another world, you know?"

"Not really," Fran said. "Never been anywhere else."

"Oh," Ophelia said, not quite deflated by this comeback. "Well, take it from me. It's freaking gorgeous here. Everything is so pretty it almost hurts. I love the morning, the way everything is all misty. And the trees! And every time the road snakes around a corner, there's another waterfall. Or a little pasture, and it's all full of flowers. All the *hollers*." Fran could hear the invisible brackets around the word. "It's like you don't know what you'll see, what's there, until suddenly you're in them. Are you applying to college anywhere next year? I was thinking about vet school. I don't think I can take another English class. Large animals. No little dogs or guinea pigs. Maybe I'll go out to California."

Fran said, "We're not the kind of people who go to college."

"Oh," Ophelia said. "You're a lot smarter than me, you know? So I just thought . . ."

"Turn here," Fran said. "Careful. It's not paved."

They went up the dirt road, through the laurel beds, and into the little meadow with the nameless creek. Fran could feel Ophelia suck in a breath, probably trying her hardest not to say something about how beautiful it was. And it was beautiful, Fran knew. You could hardly see the house itself, hidden like a bride behind her veil of climbing vines: virgin's bower and Japanese honeysuckle, masses of William Baffin and Cherokee roses overgrowing the porch and running up over the sagging roof. Bumblebees, their legs armored in gold, threaded through the meadow grass, almost too weighed down with pollen to fly.

"It's old," Fran said. "Needs a new roof. My great-grandaddy ordered it out of the Sears catalog. Men brought it up the side of the mountain in pieces, and all the Cherokee who hadn't gone away yet came and watched." She was amazed at herself: next thing she would be asking Ophelia to come for a sleepover.

She opened the car door and heaved herself out, plucked up the poke of groceries. Before she could turn and thank Ophelia for the ride, Ophelia was out of the car, as well. "I thought," Ophelia said uncertainly. "Well, I thought maybe I could use your bathroom?"

"It's an outhouse," Fran said, deadpan. Then she relented: "Come on in, then. It's a regular bathroom. Just not very clean."

Ophelia didn't say anything when they came into the kitchen. Fran watched her take it in: the heaped dishes in the sink, the pillow and raggedy quilt on the sagging couch. The piles of dirty laundry beside the efficiency washer in the kitchen. The places where hairy tendrils of vine had found a way inside around the windows. "I guess you might be thinking it's funny," she said. "My dad and I make money doing other people's houses, but we don't take no real care of our own."

"I was thinking that somebody ought to be taking care of you," Ophelia said. "At least while you're sick."

Fran gave a little shrug. "I do fine on my own," she said. "The washroom's down the hall."

She took two NyQuil while Ophelia was gone and washed them down with the last swallow or two of ginger ale out of the refrigerator. Flat, but still cool. Then she lay down on the couch and pulled the counterpane up around her face. She huddled into the lumpy cushions. Her legs ached, her face felt hot as fire. Her feet were ice cold.

A minute later Ophelia sat down on the couch beside her.

"Ophelia?" Fran said. "I'm grateful for the ride home and for the help at the Roberts', but I don't go for the girls. So don't lez out."

Ophelia said, "I brought you a glass of water. You need to stay hydrated."

"Mmm," Fran said.

"You know, your dad told me once that I was going to hell," Ophelia said. "He was over at our house doing something. Fixing a burst pipe, maybe? I don't know how he knew. I was eleven. I don't think I knew, not yet, anyway. He didn't bring you over to play after he said that, even though I never told my mom."

"My daddy thinks everyone is going to hell," Fran said into the counterpane. "I don't care where I go, as long as it isn't here, and he isn't there."

Ophelia didn't say anything for a minute or two, and she didn't get up to leave, either, so finally Fran poked her head out. Ophelia had a toy in her hand, the monkey egg. She turned it over, and then over again. She looked a question at Fran.

"Give here," Fran said. "I'll work it." She wound the filigreed dial and set the egg on the floor. The toy vibrated ferociously. Two pincerlike legs and a scorpion tail made of figured brass shot out of the bottom hemisphere, and the egg wobbled on the legs in one direction and then another, the articulated tail curling and lashing. Portholes on either side of the top hemisphere opened and two arms wriggled out and reached up, rapping at the dome of the egg until that, too, cracked open with a click. A monkey's head, wearing the egg dome like a hat, popped out. Its mouth opened and closed in chattering ecstasy, red garnet eyes rolling, arms describing wider and wider circles in the air until the clockwork ran down and all of its extremities whipped back into the egg again.

"What in the world?" Ophelia said. She picked up the egg, tracing the joins with a finger.

"It's just something that's been in our family," Fran said. She stuck her arm out of the quilt, grabbed a tissue, and blew her nose for maybe the thousandth time. "We didn't steal it from no one, if that's what you're thinking."

"No," Ophelia said, and then frowned. "It's just—I've never seen anything like it. It's like a Fabergé egg. It ought to be in a museum."

There were lots of other toys. The laughing cat and the waltzing elephants; the swan you wound up, who chased the dog. Other toys that Fran hadn't played with in years. The mermaid who combed garnets out of her own hair. Bawbees for babies, her mother had called them.

"I remember now," Ophelia said. "When you came and played at my house. You brought a minnow made out of silver. It was smaller than my little finger. We put it in the bathtub, and it swam around and around. You had a little fishing rod, too, and a golden worm that wriggled on the hook. You let me catch the fish, and when I did, it talked. It said it would give me a wish if I let it go."

"You wished for two pieces of chocolate cake," Fran said.

"And then my mother made a chocolate cake, didn't she?" Ophelia said. "So the wish came true. But I could only eat one piece. Maybe I knew she was going to make a cake? Except why would I wish for something that I already knew I was going to get?"

Fran said nothing. She watched Ophelia through slit eyes.

"Do you still have the fish?" Ophelia asked.

Fran said, "Somewhere. The clockwork ran down. It didn't give wishes no more. I reckon I didn't mind. It only ever granted little wishes."

"Ha, ha," Ophelia said. She stood up. "Tomorrow's Saturday. I'll come by in the morning to make sure you're okay."

"You don't have to," Fran said.

"No," Ophelia said. "I don't have to. But I will."

When you do for other people (Fran's daddy said once upon a time when he was drunk, before he got religion) things that they could do for themselves, but they pay you to do it instead, you both will get used to it. Sometimes they don't even pay you, and that's charity. At first, charity isn't comfortable, but it gets so it is. After some while, maybe you start to feel wrong when you ain't doing for them, just one more thing, and always one more thing after that. Maybe you start to feel as you're valuable. Because they need you. And the more they need you, the more you need them. Things go out of balance. You need to remember that, Franny. Sometimes you're on one side of that equation, and sometimes you're on the other. You need to know where you are and what you owe. Unless you can balance that out, here is where y'all stay.

Fran, dosed on NyQuil, feverish and alone in her great-grandfather's catalog house, hidden behind walls of roses, dreamed—as she did every night—of escape. She woke every few hours, wishing someone would bring her another glass of water. She sweated through her clothes, and then froze, and then boiled again. Her throat was full of knives.

She was still on the couch when Ophelia came back, banging through the screen door. "Good morning!" Ophelia said. "Or maybe I should say good afternoon! It's noon, anyhow. I brought oranges to make fresh orange juice, and I didn't know if you liked sausage or bacon, so I got you two different kinds of biscuit."

Fran struggled to sit up.

"Fran," Ophelia said. She came and stood in front of the sofa, still holding the two cat-head biscuits. "You look terrible." She put her hand on Fran's forehead. "You're burning up! I knew I oughtn't've left you here all by yourself! What should I do? Should I take you down to the emergency?"

"No doctor," Fran managed to say. "They'll want to know where my daddy is. Water?"

Ophelia scampered back to the kitchen. "How many days have you had the flu? You need antibiotics. Or something. Fran?"

"Here," Fran said. She lifted a bill off a stack of mail on the floor, pulled out the return envelope. She plucked out three strands of her hair. She put them in the envelope and licked it shut. "Take this up the road where it crosses the drain," she said. "All the way up." She coughed a rattling, deathly cough. "When you get to the big house, go around to the back and knock on the door. Tell them I sent you. You won't see them, but they'll know you came from me. After you knock, you can just go in. Go upstairs directly, you mind, and put this envelope under the door. Third door down the hall. You'll know which. After that, you oughter wait out on the porch. Bring back whatever they give you."

Ophelia gave her a look that said Fran was delirious. "Just go," Fran said. "If there ain't a house, or if there is a house and it ain't the house I'm telling you about, then come back, and I'll go to the emergency with you. Or if you find the house, and you're afeared and you can't do what I asked, come back, and I'll go with you. But if you do what I tell you, it will be like the minnow."

"Like the minnow?" Ophelia said. "I don't understand."

"You will. Be bold," Fran said, and did her best to look cheerful. "Like the girls in those ballads. Will you bring me another glass of water afore you go?"

Ophelia went.

Fran lay on the couch, thinking about what Ophelia would see. From time to time, she raised a pair of curious-looking spyglasses—something much more useful than any bawbee—to her eyes. Through them she saw first the dirt track, which only seemed to dead-end. Were you to look again, you found your road crossing over the shallow crick once, twice, the one climbing the mountain, the drain running away and down. The meadow disappeared again into beds of laurel, then low trees hung with climbing roses, so that you ascended in drifts of pink and white. A stone wall, tumbled and ruined, and then the big house. The house, dry-stack stone, stained with age like the tumbledown wall, two stories. A slate roof, a long covered porch, carved wooden shutters making all the eyes of the windows blind. Two apple trees, crabbed and old, one green and bearing fruit and the other bare and silver black. Ophelia found the mossy path between them that wound around to the back door with two words carved over the stone lintel: Be bold.

And this is what Fran saw Ophelia do: having knocked on the door, Ophelia hesitated for only a moment, and then she opened it. She called out, "Hello? Fran sent me. She's ill. Hello?" No one answered.

So Ophelia took a breath and stepped over the threshold and into a dark, crowded hallway with a room on either side and a staircase in front of her. On the flagstone in front of her were carved the words: Be bold, be bold. Despite the invitation, Ophelia did not seem tempted to investigate either room, which Fran thought wise of her. The first test was a success. You might expect that through one door would be a living room, and you might expect that through the other door would be a kitchen, but you would be wrong. One was the Queen's Room. The other was what Fran thought of as the War Room.

Fusty stacks of old magazines and catalogs and newspapers, old encyclopedias and gothic novels leaned against the walls of the hall, making such a narrow alley that even lickle, tiny Ophelia turned sideways to make her way. Dolls' legs and old silverware sets and tennis trophies and mason jars and empty match boxes and false teeth and stranger things still poked out of paper bags and plastic carriers. You might expect that through the doors on either side of the hall there would be more crumbling piles and more odd jumbles, and you would be right. But there were other things, too. At the foot of the stairs was another piece of advice for guests like Ophelia, carved right into the first riser: Be bold, be bold, but not too bold.

The owners of the house had been at another one of their frolics, Fran saw. Someone had woven tinsel and ivy and peacock feathers through the banisters. Someone had thumbtacked cut silhouettes and Polaroids and tintypes and magazine pictures on the wall alongside the stairs, layers upon layers upon layers; hundreds and hundreds of eyes watching each time Ophelia set her foot down carefully on the next stair.

Perhaps Ophelia didn't trust the stairs not to be rotted through. But the stairs were safe. Someone had always taken very good care of this house.

At the top of the stairs, the carpet underfoot was soft, almost spongy. Moss, Fran decided. They've redecorated again. That's going to be the devil to clean up. Here and there were white and red mushrooms in pretty rings upon the moss. More bawbees, too, waiting for someone to come along and play with them. A dinosaur, only needing to be wound up, a plastic dime-store cowboy sitting on its shining shoulders. Up near the ceiling, two armored dirigibles, tethered to a light fixture by scarlet ribbons. The cannons on these zeppelins were in working order. They'd chased Fran down the hall more than once. Back home, she'd had to tweeze the tiny lead pellets out of her shin. Today, though, all were on their best behavior.

Ophelia passed one door, two doors, stopped at the third door. Above it, the final warning: BE BOLD, BE BOLD, BUT NOT TOO BOLD, LEST THAT THY HEART'S BLOOD RUN COLD. Ophelia put her hand on the doorknob, but didn't try it. Not afeared, but no fool neither, Fran thought. They'll be pleased. Or will they?

Ophelia knelt down to slide Fran's envelope under the door. Something else happened, too: something slipped out of Ophelia's pocket and landed on the carpet of moss.

Back down the hall, Ophelia stopped in front of the first door. She seemed to hear someone or something. Music, perhaps? A voice calling her name? An invitation? Fran's poor, sore heart was filled with delight. They liked her! Well, of course they did. Who wouldn't like Ophelia?

She made her way down the stairs, through the towers of clutter and junk. Back onto the porch, where she sat on the porch swing, but didn't swing. She seemed to be keeping one eye on the house and the other on the little rock garden out back, which ran up against the mountain right quick. There was even a waterfall, and Fran hoped Ophelia appreciated it. There'd never been no such thing before. This one was all for her, all for Ophelia, who opined that waterfalls are freaking beautiful.

Up on the porch, Ophelia's head jerked around, as if she were afraid someone might be sneaking up the back. But there were only carpenter bees, bringing back their satchels of gold, and a woodpecker, drilling for grubs. There was a groundpig in the rumpled grass, and the more Ophelia set and stared, the more she and Fran both saw. A pair of fox kits napping under the laurel. A doe and a faun peeling bark runners off young trunks. Even a brown bear, still tufty with last winter's fur, nosing along the high ridge above the house. Fran knew what Ophelia must be feeling. As if she were an interloper in some Eden. While Ophelia sat on the porch of that dangerous house, Fran curled inward on her couch, waves of heat pouring out of her. Her whole body shook so violently her teeth rattled. Her spyglasses fell to the floor. Maybe I am dying, Fran thought, and that is why Ophelia came here.

Fran, feverish, went in and out of sleep, always listening for the sound of Ophelia coming back down. Perhaps she'd made a mistake, and they wouldn't send something to help. Perhaps they wouldn't send Ophelia back at all. Ophelia, with her pretty singing voice, that shyness, that innate kindness. Her long, straight hair, silvery blond. They liked things that were shiny. They were like magpies that way. In other ways, too.

But here was Ophelia, after all, her eyes enormous, her face lit up like Christmas. "Fran," she said. "Fran, wake up. I went there. I was bold! Who lives there, Fran?"

"The summer people," Fran said. "Did they give you anything for me?"

Ophelia set an object upon the counterpane. Like everything the summer people made, it was right pretty. A lipstick-sized vial of pearly glass, an enameled green snake clasped around it, its tail the stopper. Fran tugged at the tail, and the serpent uncoiled. A pole ran out the mouth of the bottle, and a silk rag unfurled. Embroidered upon it were the words DRINK ME.

Ophelia watched this, her eyes glazed with too many marvels. "I sat and waited, and there were two fox kits! They came right up to the porch, and then went to the door and scratched at it until it opened. They trotted right inside and came out again. One came over to me then, with something in its jaw. It laid down that bottle right at my feet, and then they ran down the steps and into the woods. Fran, it was like a fairy tale."

"Yes," Fran said. She put her lips to the mouth of the vial and drank down what was in it. It tasted sour and hot, like bottled smoke. She coughed, then wiped her mouth and licked the back of her hand.

"I mean, people say something is like a fairy tale all the time," Ophelia said. "And what they mean is somebody falls in love and gets married. But that house, those animals, it really is a fairy tale. Who are they? The summer people?"

"That's what my daddy calls them," Fran said. "Except, when he gets religious, he calls them devils come up to steal his soul. It's because they supply him with drink. But he weren't never the one who had to mind after them. That was my mother. And now she's gone, and it's only ever me."

"You take care of them?" Ophelia said. "You mean, like the Roberts?"

A feeling of tremendous well-being was washing over Fran. Her feet were warm for the first time in what seemed like days, and her throat felt coated in honey and balm. Even her nose felt less raw and red. "Ophelia?" she said.

"Yes, Fran?"

"I think I'm going to be much better," Fran said. "Which is something you done for me. You were brave and a true friend, and I'll have to think how I can pay you back."

"I wasn't—" Ophelia protested. "I mean, I'm glad I did. I'm glad you asked me. I promise I won't tell anyone."

If you did you'd be sorry, Fran thought but didn't say. "Ophelia? I need to sleep. And then, if you want, we can talk. You can even stay here while I sleep. If you want. I don't care if you're a lesbian. There are Pop-Tarts on the kitchen counter. And those two biscuits you brung. I like sausage. You can have the one with bacon."

She fell asleep before Ophelia could say anything else.

The first thing she did when she woke up was take a bath. In the mirror, she took a quick inventory. Her hair was lank and greasy, all witch knots and tangles. There were circles under her eyes, and her tongue, when she stuck it out, was yellow. When she was clean and dressed again, her jeans were loose and she could feel her hip bones protruding. "I could eat a whole mess of food," she told Ophelia. "But a cat-head and a box of Pop-Tarts will do for a start."

There was fresh orange juice, and Ophelia had poured it into a stoneware jug. Fran decided not to tell her that her daddy used it as a sometime spittoon. "Can I ask you some more about them?" Ophelia said. "You know, the summer people?"

"I don't reckon I can answer every question," Fran said. "But go on."

"When I first got there," Ophelia said, "when I went inside, at first I decided that it must be a shut-in. One of those, you know, hoarders. I've watched that show, and sometimes they even keep their own poop. And dead cats. It's just horrible.

"Then it just kept on getting stranger. But I wasn't ever scared.

It felt like there was somebody there, but they were happy to see me."

"They don't get much in the way of company," Fran said.

"Yeah, well, why do they collect all that stuff? Where does it come from?"

"Some of it's from catalogs. I have to go down to the post office and collect it for them. Sometimes they go away and bring things back. Sometimes they tell me they want something and I have to go get it for them. Mostly it's stuff from the Salvation Army. Once I had to buy a hunnert pounds of copper piping."

"Why?" Ophelia said. "I mean, what do they do with it?"

"They make things," Fran said. "That's what my momma called them, makers. I don't know what they do with all of it. They give away things. Like the toys. They like children. When you do things for them, they're beholden to you."

"Have you seen them?" Ophelia said.

"Now and then," Fran said. "Not very often. Not since I was much younger. They're shy."

Ophelia was practically bouncing on her chair. "You get to look after them? That's the best thing ever! Have they always been here? Is that why you aren't going to go to college?"

Fran hesitated. "I don't know where they come from. They aren't always there. Sometimes they're . . . somewhere else. My momma said she felt sorry for them. She thought maybe they couldn't go home, that they'd been sent away, like the Cherokee, I guess. They live a lot longer, maybe forever, I don't know. I don't think time works the same way where they come from. Sometimes they're gone for years. But they always come back. They're summer people. That's just the way it is with summer people."

"And you're not," Ophelia said. "And now I'm not, either."

"*You* can go away again whenever you want," Fran said, not caring how she sounded. "I can't. It's part of the bargain. Whoever takes care of them has to stay here. You can't leave. They don't let you."

"You mean, you can't leave, ever?"

"No," Fran said. "Not ever. My mother was stuck here until she had me. And then when I was old enough, she told me I had to take over. She took off right after that."

"Where did she go?"

"I'm not the one to answer that," Fran said. "They gave my momma a tent that folds up no bigger than a kerchief, that sets up the size of a two-man tent, but on the inside, it's teetotally different, a cottage with two brass beds and a chifforobe to hang your things in, and a table, and windows with glass in them. When you look out one of the windows, you see wherever you are, and when you look out the other window, you see those two apple trees, the ones in front of the house with the moss path between them?"

Ophelia nodded.

"Well, my momma used to bring out that tent for me and her when my daddy had been drinking. Then my momma passed the summer people on to me, and one morning after we spent the night in the tent, I woke up and saw her climb out that window. The one that shouldn't ought to be there. She disappeared down that path. Maybe I should have followed on after her, but I stayed put."

"Where did she go?" Ophelia said.

"Well, she ain't here," Fran said. "That's what I know. So I have to stay here in her place. I don't expect she'll be back, neither."

"Well, that sucks," Ophelia said.

"I wish I could get away for just a little while," Fran said. "Maybe go out to San Francisco and see the Golden Gate Bridge. Dip my toes in the Pacific. I'd like to buy me a guitar and play some of those old ballads on the streets. Just stay a little while, then come back and take up my burden again."

"I'd sure like to go out to California," Ophelia said.

They sat in silence for a minute.

"I wish I could help out," Ophelia said. "You know, with that house and the summer people. You shouldn't have to do everything, not all of the time."

"I already owe you," Fran said, "for helping with the Roberts' house. For looking in on me when I was ill. For what you did when you went up to fetch me help."

"I know what it's like when you're all alone," Ophelia said. "When you can't talk about stuff. And I mean it, Fran. I'll do whatever I can to help."

"I can tell you mean it," Fran said. "I just don't think you know what it is you're saying. I ought to explain at least one thing. If you want, you can go up there again one more time. You did me a favor, and I don't know how else to pay you back. There's a bedroom up in that house, and if you sleep in it, you see your heart's desire. I could take you back tonight and show you that room. Besides, I think you lost something up there."

"I did?" Ophelia said. "What was it?" She reached down in her pockets. "Oh, hell. My iPod. How did you know?"

Fran shrugged. "Not like anybody up there is going to steal it. Expect they'd be happy to have you back up again. If they didn't like you, you'd know it already."

Fran was straightening up her and her daddy's mess when the summer people let her know that they needed a few things. "Can't I just have a minute to myself?" she grumbled.

They told her that she'd had a good four days. "And I surely do appreciate it," she said, "considering I was laid so low." But she put the skillet down in the sink to soak and wrote down what they wanted.

She tidied away all of the toys, not quite sure what had come over her to take them out.

When Ophelia came back at five, she had her hair in a ponytail and a flashlight and a thermos in her pocket, like she thought she was Nancy Drew.

"It gets dark up here so early," Ophelia said. "I feel like it's Halloween or something. Like you're taking me to the haunted house."

"They ain't haints," Fran said. "Nor demons or any such thing. They don't do no harm unless you get on the wrong side of them. They'll play a prank on you then, and count it good fun."

"Like what?" Ophelia said.

"Once I did the warshing up and broke a teacup," Fran said. "They'll sneak up and pinch you." She still had marks on her arms, though she hadn't broken a plate in years. "Lately, they've been doing what all the people up here like to do, that reenacting. They set up their battlefield in the big room downstairs. It's not the War Between the States. It's one of theirs, I guess. They built themselves airships and submersibles and mechanical dragons and knights and all manner of wee toys to fight with. Sometimes, when they get bored, they get me up to be their audience, only they ain't always careful where they go pointing their cannons."

She looked at Ophelia and saw she'd said too much. "Well, they're used to me. They know I don't have no choice but to put up with their ways."

That afternoon, she'd had to drive over to Chattanooga to visit a particular thrift store. They'd sent her for a used DVD player and all the bathing suits she could buy up. Between that and paying for gas, she'd gone through seventy dollars. And the service light had been on the whole way. At least it hadn't been a school day. Hard to explain you were cutting out because voices in your head were telling you they needed a saddle.

She'd gone on ahead and brought it all up to the house after. No need to bother Ophelia with any of it. The iPod had been a-laying right in front of the door.

"Here," she said. "I went ahead and brought this back down."

"My iPod!" Ophelia said. She turned it over. "They did this?"

The iPod was heavier now. It had a little walnut case instead of pink silicone, and there was a figure inlaid in ebony and gilt.

"A dragonfly," Ophelia said.

"A snake doctor," Fran said. "That's what my daddy calls them."

"They did this for me?"

"They'd embellish a Bedazzled jean jacket if you left it there," Fran said. "No lie. They can't stand to leave a thing alone."

"Cool," Ophelia said. "Although my mom is never going to believe me when I say I bought it at the mall."

"Just don't take up anything metal," Fran said. "No earrings, not even your car keys. Or you'll wake up and they'll have smelted them down and turned them into doll armor or who knows what all."

They took off their shoes when they got to where the road crossed the drain. The water was cold with the last of the snow-melt. Ophelia said, "I feel like I ought to have brought a hostess gift."

"You could pick them a bunch of wildflowers," Fran said. "But they'd be just as happy with a bit of kyarn."

"Yarn?" Fran said.

"Roadkill," Fran said. "But yarn's okay too."

Ophelia thumbed the wheel of her iPod. "There's songs on here that weren't here before."

"They like music, too," Fran said. "They like it when I sing."

"What you were saying about going out to San Francisco to busk," Ophelia said. "I can't imagine doing that."

"Well," Fran said. "I won't ever do it, but I think I can imagine it okay."

When they got up to the house, there were deer grazing on the green lawn. The living tree and the dead were all touched with the last of the sunlight. Chinese lanterns hung in rows from the rafters of the porch.

"You always have to come at the house from between the trees," Fran said. "Right on the path. Otherwise, you don't get nowhere near it. And I don't ever use but the back door."

She knocked at the back door. BE BOLD, BE BOLD. "It's me again," she said. "And my friend Ophelia. The one who left the iPod."

She saw Ophelia open her mouth and went on, hastily, "Don't say it, Ophelia. They don't like it when you thank them. They're allergic to that word. Come on in. *Mi casa es su casa*. I'll give you the grand tour."

They stepped over the threshold, Fran first.

"There's the pump room out back, where I do the wash," she said. "There's a big ole stone oven for baking in, and a pig pit, although why I don't know. They don't eat meat. But you prob'ly don't care about that."

"What's in this room?" Ophelia said.

"Hunh," Fran said. "Well, first, it's a lot of junk. They just like to accumulate junk. Way back in there, though, is what I think is a queen."

"A queen?"

"Well, that's what I call her. You know how, in a beehive, way down in the combs, you have the queen, and all the worker bees attend on her?

"Far as I can tell, that's what's in there. She's real big and not real pretty, and they are always running in and out of there with food for her. I don't think she's teetotally growed up yet. For a while now, I've been thinking on what my momma said, about how maybe these summer people got sent off. Bees do that too, right? Go off and make a new hive when there are too many queens?"

"Honestly?" Ophelia said. "It sounds kind of creepy."

"The queen's where my daddy gets his liquor, and she don't bother him none. They have some kind of still set up in there, and every once in a while when he ain't feeling too religious, he goes in and skims off a little bitty bit. It's awful sweet stuff."

"Are they, uh, are they listening to us right now?"

In response came a series of clicks from the War Room.

Ophelia jumped. "What's that?" she said.

"Remember I told you 'bout the reenactor stuff?" Fran said. "Don't get freaked out. It's pretty cool."

She gave Ophelia a little push into the War Room.

Of all the rooms in the house, this one was Fran's favorite, even if they dive-bombed her sometimes with the airships, or fired off the cannons without much thought for where she was standing. The walls were beaten tin and copper, scrap metal held down with two-penny nails. Molded forms lay on the floor representing scaled-down mountains, forests, and plains where miniature armies fought desperate battles. There was a kiddie pool over by the big picture window with a machine in it that made waves. There were little ships and submersibles, and occasionally one of the ships sank, and bodies would go floating over to the edges. There was a sea serpent made of tubing and metal rings that swam endlessly in a circle. There was a sluggish river, too, closer to the door, that ran red and stank and stained the banks. The summer people were always setting up miniature bridges over it, then blowing the bridges up.

Overhead were the fantastic shapes of the dirigibles, and the dragons that were hung on string and swam perpetually through the air above your head. There was a misty globe, too, suspended in some way that Fran could not figure, and lit by some unknown source. It stayed up near the painted ceiling for days at a time, and then sunk down behind the plastic sea according to some schedule of the summer people's.

"It's amazing," Ophelia said. "Once I went to the house of some friend of my father's. An anesthesiologist? He had a train set down in his basement and it was crazy complicated. He would die if he saw this."

"Over there is a queen, I think," Fran said. "All surrounded by her knights. And here's another one, much smaller. I wonder who won, in the end."

"Maybe it's not been fought yet," Ophelia said. "Or maybe it's being fought right now."

"Could be," Fran said. "I wish there was a book told you everything that went on. Come on. I'll show you the room you can sleep in."

They went up the stairs. BE BOLD, BE BOLD, BUT NOT TOO BOLD. The moss carpet on the second floor was already looking a little worse for wear. "Last week I spent a whole day scrubbing these boards on my hands and knees. So, of course, they need to go next thing and pile up a bunch of dirt and stuff. They won't be the ones who have to pitch in and clean it up."

"I could help," Ophelia said. "If you want."

"I wasn't asking for help. But if you offer, I'll accept. The first door is the washroom," Fran said. "Nothing queer about the toilet. I don't know about the bathtub, though. Never felt the need to sit in it."

She opened the second door.

"Here's where you sleep."

It was a gorgeous room, all done up in shades of orange and rust and gold and pink and tangerine. The walls were finished in leafy shapes and vines cut from all kinds of dresses and T-shirts and what have you. Fran's momma had spent the better part of a year going through stores, choosing clothes for their patterns and textures and colors. Gold-leaf snakes and fishes swam through the leaf shapes. When the sun came up in the morning, Fran remembered, it was almost blinding.

There was a crazy quilt on the bed, pink and gold. The bed itself was shaped like a swan. There was a willow chest at the foot of the bed to lay out your clothes on. The mattress was stuffed with the down of crow feathers. Fran had helped her mother shoot the crows and pluck their feathers. She thought they'd killed about a hundred.

"I'd say wow," Ophelia said, "but I keep saying that. Wow, wow, wow. This is a crazy room."

"I always thought it was like being stuck inside a bottle of orange Nehi," Fran said. "But in a good way."

"Oh yeah," Ophelia said. "I can see that."

There was a stack of books on the table beside the bed. Like everything else in the room, all the books had been picked out for the colors on their jackets. Fran's momma had told her that once the room had been another set of colors. Greens and blues, maybe? Willow and peacock and midnight colors? And who had brought the bits up for the room that time? Fran's great-grandfather or someone even farther along the family tree? Who had first begun to take care of the summer people? Her mother had doled out stories sparingly, and so Fran only had a piecemeal sort of history.

Hard to figure out what it would please Ophelia to hear any-way, and what would trouble her. All of it seemed pleasing and troubling to Fran in equal measure after so many years.

"The door you slipped my envelope under," she said, finally. "You oughtn't ever go in there."

Ophelia yawned. "Like Bluebeard," she said.

Fran said, "It's how they come and go. Even they don't open that door very often, I guess." She'd peeped through the keyhole once and seen a bloody river. She'd bet if you passed through that door, you weren't likely to return.

"Can I ask you another stupid question?" Ophelia said. "Where are they right now?"

"They're here," Fran said. "Or out in the woods chasing night-jars. I told you I don't see them much."

"So how do they tell you what they need you to do?"

"They get in my head," Fran said. "I guess it's kind of like being schizophrenic. Or like having a really bad itch or some-thing that goes away when I do what they want me to."

"Not fun," Ophelia said. "Maybe I don't like your summer people as much as I thought I did."

Fran said, "It's not always awful. I guess what it is, is compli-cated."

"I guess I won't complain the next time my mom tells me I have to help her polish the silver, or do useless crap like that. Should we eat our sandwiches now, or should we save them for when we wake up in the middle of the night?" Ophelia asked. "I have this idea that seeing your heart's desire probably makes you hungry."

"I can't stay," Fran said, surprised. She saw Ophelia's expression and said, "Well, hell. I thought you understood. This is just for you."

Ophelia continued to look at her dubiously. "Is it because there's just the one bed? I could sleep on the floor. You know, if you're worried I might be planning to lez out on you."

"It isn't that," Fran said. "They only let a body sleep here once. Once and no more."

"You're really going to leave me up here alone?" Ophelia said.

"Yes," Fran said. "Unless you decide you want to come back down with me. I guess I'd understand if you did."

"Could I come back again?" Ophelia said.

"No."

Ophelia sat down on the golden quilt and smoothed it with her fingers. She chewed her lip, not meeting Fran's eye.

"Okay. I'll do it." She laughed. "How could I not do it? Right?"

"If you're sure," Fran said.

"I'm not sure, but I couldn't stand it if you sent me away now," Ophelia said. "When you slept here, were you afraid?"

"A little," Fran said. "But the bed was comfortable, and I kept the light on. I read for a while, and then I fell asleep."

"Did you see your heart's desire?" Ophelia said.

"I guess I did," Fran offered, and then said no more.

"Okay, then," Ophelia said. "I guess you should go. You should go, right?"

"I'll come back in the morning," Fran said. "I'll be here afore you even wake."

"Thanks," Ophelia said.

But Fran didn't go. She said, "Did you mean it when you said you wanted to help?"

"Look after the house?" Ophelia said. "Yeah, absolutely. You really ought to go out to San Francisco someday. You shouldn't have to stay here your whole life without ever having a vacation or anything. I mean, you're not a slave, right?"

"I don't know what I am," Fran said. "I guess one day I'll have to figure that out."

Ophelia said, "Anyway, we can talk about it tomorrow. Over breakfast. You can tell me about the suckiest parts of the job and I'll tell you what my heart's desire turns out to be."

"Oh," Fran said. "I almost forgot. When you wake up tomorrow, don't be surprised if they've left you a gift. The summer people. It'll be something that they think you need or want. But you don't have to accept it. You don't have to worry about being rude that way."

"Okay," Ophelia said. "I will consider whether I really need or want my present. I won't let false glamour deceive me."

"Good," Fran said. Then she bent over Ophelia where she was sitting on the bed and kissed her on the forehead. "Sleep well, Ophelia. Good dreams."

Fran left the house without any interference from the summer people. She couldn't tell if she'd expected to find any. As she came down the stairs, she said rather more fiercely than she'd meant to: "Be nice to her. Don't play no tricks." She looked in on the queen, who was molting again.

She went out the front door instead of the back, which was something that she'd always wanted to do. Nothing bad happened, and she walked down the hall feeling strangely put out. She went over everything in her head, wondering what still needed doing that she hadn't done. Nothing, she decided. Everything was taken care of.

Except, of course, it wasn't. The first thing was the guitar, leaned up against the door of her house. It was a beautiful instrument. The strings, she thought, were pure silver. When she struck them, the tone was pure and sweet and reminded her uncomfortably of Ophelia's singing voice. The keys were made of gold and shaped like owl heads, and there was mother-of-pearl inlay across the boards like a spray of roses. It was the gaudiest gewgaw they'd yet made her a gift of.

"Well, all right," she said. "I guess you didn't mind what I told her." She laughed out loud with relief.

"Why, everwho did you tell what?" someone said.

She picked up the guitar and held it like a weapon in front of her. "Daddy?"

"Put that down," the voice said. A man stepped forward out of the shadow of the rosebushes. "I'm not your damn daddy. Although, come to think of it, I would like to know where he is."

"Ryan Shoemaker," Fran said. She put the guitar down on the ground. Another man stepped forward. "And Kyle Rainey."

"Howdy, Fran," said Kyle. He spat. "We were lookin' for your pappy, like Ryan says."

"If he calls I'll let him know you were up here looking for him," Fran said. "Is that all you wanted to ask me?"

Ryan lit up a cigarette, looked at her over the flame. "It was your daddy we wanted to ask, but I guess you could help us out instead."

"It don't seem likely somehow," Fran said. "But go on."

"Your daddy was meaning to drop off some of the sweet stuff the other night," Kyle said. "Only, he started thinking about it on the drive down, and that's never been a good idea where your daddy is concerned. He decided Jesus wanted him to pour out every last drop, and that's what he did all the way down the mountain. If he weren't a lucky man, some spark might have cotched while he were pouring, but I guess Jesus doesn't want to meet him face to face just yet."

"And if that weren't bad enough," Ryan said, "when he got to the convenience, he decided that Jesus wanted him to get into the van and smash up all Andy's liquor, too. By the time we realized what was going on, there weren't much left besides two bottles of Kahlua and a six-pack of wine coolers."

"One of them smashed, too," Kyle said. "And then he took off afore we could have a word with him."

"Well, I'm sorry for your troubles, but I don't see what it has to do with me," Fran said.

"What it has to do is that we've come up with an easy payment plan. We talked about it, and the way it seems to us is that your pappy could provide us with entrée to some of the finest homes in the area."

"Like I said," Fran said. "I'll pass on the message. You're hoping my daddy will make his restitution by becoming your accessory in breaking and entering. I'll let him know if he calls."

"Or he could pay poor Andy back in kind," Ryan said. "With some of that good stuff."

"He'll have to run that by Jesus," Fran said. "Frankly, I think it's a better bet than the other, but you might have to wait until he and Jesus have had enough of each other."

"The thing is," Ryan said, "I'm not a patient man. And what has occurred to me is that your pappy may be out of our reach at present moment, but here you are. And I'm guessing that you can get us into a house or two. Preferably ones with quality flat screens and high-thread-count sheets. I promised Mandy I was going to help her redecorate."

"Or else you could point us in the direction of your daddy's private stash," Kyle said.

"And if I don't choose to do neither?" Fran asked, crossing her arms.

"I truly hope that you know what it is you're doing," Kyle said. "Ryan has not been in a good mood these last few days. He bit a sheriff's deputy on the arm last night in a bar. Which is why we weren't up here sooner."

"He was pigheaded, just like you," Ryan said. "No pun intended. But I bet you'd taste better."

Fran stepped back. "Fine. There's an old house farther up the road that nobody except me and my daddy knows about. It's ruint. Nobody lives there, and so my daddy put his still up in it. He's got all sorts of articles stashed up there. I'll take you up. But you can't tell him what I done."

"Course not, darlin'," Kyle said. "We don't aim to cause a rift in the family. Just to get what we have coming."

And so Fran found herself climbing right back up that same road. She got her feet wet in the drain but kept as far ahead of Kyle and Ryan as she dared. She didn't know if she felt safe with them at her back.

When they got up to the house, Kyle whistled. "Fancy sort of ruin."

"Wait'll you see what's inside," Fran said. She led them around to the back, then held the door open. "Sorry about the lights. The power goes off more than it stays on. My daddy usually brings up a torch. Want me to go get one?"

"We've got matches," Ryan said. "You stay right there."

"The still is in the room over on the right. Mind how you go. He's got it set up in a kind of maze, with the newspapers and all."

"Dark as the inside of a mine at midnight," Kyle said. He felt his way down the hall. "I think I'm at the door. Sure enough, smells like what I'm lookin' for. Guess I'll just follow my nose. No booby traps or nothing like that?"

"No sir," Fran said. "He'd have blowed himself up a long time before now if he tried that."

"I might as well take in the sights," Ryan said, the lit end of his cigarette flaring. "Now that I'm getting my night vision."

"Yes sir," Fran said.

"And might there be a pisser in this heap?"

"Third door on the left, once you go up," Fran said. "The door sticks some."

She waited until he was at the top of the stairs before she slipped out the back door again. She could hear Kyle fumbling toward the center of the Queen's Room. She wondered what the queen would make of Kyle. She wasn't worried about Ophelia at all. Ophelia was an invited guest. And anyhow, the summer people didn't let anything happen to the ones who looked after them.

One of the summer people was sitting on the porch swing when she came out. He was whittling a stick with a sharp knife.

"Evening," Fran said and bobbed her head.

The summer personage didn't even look up at her. He was one of the ones so pretty it almost hurt to peep at him, but you couldn't not stare, neither. That was one of the ways they cotched you, Fran figured. Just like wild animals when you shone a light at them. She finally tore her gaze away and ran down the stairs like the devil was after her. When she stopped to look back, he was still setting there, smiling and whittling that poor stick down.

She sold the guitar when she got to New York City. What was left of her daddy's two hundred dollars had bought her a Greyhound ticket and a couple of burgers at the bus station. The guitar got her six hundred more, and she used that to buy a ticket to Paris, where she met a Lebanese boy who was squatting in an old factory. One day she came back from her under-the-table job at a hotel and found him looking through her backpack. He had the monkey egg in his hand. He wound it up and put it down on the dirty floor to dance. They both watched until it ran down. *"Très jolie,"* he said.

It was a few days after Christmas, and there was snow melting in her hair. They didn't have heat in the squat, or even running water. She'd had a bad cough for a few days. She sat down next to her boy, and when he started to wind up the monkey egg again, she put her hand out to make him stop.

She didn't remember packing it. And of course, maybe she hadn't. For all she knew, they had winter places as well as summer places. Just because she'd never been able to travel didn't mean they didn't get around.

A few days later, the Lebanese boy disappeared off, probably looking for someplace warmer. The monkey egg went with him.

After that, all she had to remind herself of home was the tent that she kept folded up like a dirty handkerchief in her wallet.

It's been two years, and every now and again, while Fran is cleaning rooms in the pension, she closes the door and sets up the tent and gets inside. She looks out the window at the two apple trees. She tells herself that one day soon she will go home again.

Alice Munro
Leaving Maverley

In the old days when there was a movie theatre in every town there was one in this town, too, in Maverley, and it was called the Capital, as such theatres often were. Morgan Holly was the owner and the projectionist. He didn't like dealing with the public—he preferred to sit in his upstairs cubbyhole managing the story on the screen—so naturally he was annoyed when the girl who took the tickets told him that she was going to have to quit, because she was having a baby. He might have expected this—she had been married for half a year, and in those days you were supposed to get out of the public eye before you began to show—but he so disliked change and the idea of people having private lives that he was taken by surprise.

Fortunately, she came up with somebody who might replace her. A girl who lived on her street had mentioned that she would like to have an evening job. She was not able to work in the daytime, because she had to help her mother look after the younger children. She was smart enough to manage, though shy.

Morgan said that that was fine—he didn't hire a ticket-taker to gab with the customers.

So the girl came. Her name was Leah, and Morgan's first and

last question for her was to ask what kind of name that was. She said that it was out of the Bible. He noticed then that she did not have any makeup on and that her hair was slicked unbecomingly tight to her head and held there with bobby pins. He had a moment's worry about whether she was really sixteen and could legally hold a job, but close up he saw that it was likely the truth. He told her that she would need to work one show, starting at eight o'clock, on week nights and two shows, starting at seven, on Saturday nights. After closing, she would be responsible for counting the take and locking it away.

There was only one problem. She said that she would be able to walk herself home on week nights but it would not be allowed on Saturday nights and her father could not come for her then, because he himself had a night job at the mill.

Morgan said that he did not know what there was to be scared of in a place like this, and was about to tell her to get lost, when he remembered the night policeman who often broke his rounds to watch a little of the movie. Perhaps he could be charged with getting Leah home.

She said that she would ask her father.

Her father agreed, but he had to be satisfied on other accounts. Leah was not to look at the screen or listen to any of the dialogue. The religion that the family belonged to did not allow it. Morgan said that he did not hire his ticket-takers to give them a free peek at the show. As for the dialogue, he lied and said that the theatre was soundproofed.

Ray Elliot, the night policeman, had taken the job so that he would be able to help his wife manage for at least some part of the daytime. He could get by with about five hours' sleep in the morning and then a nap in the late afternoon. Often, the nap did not materialize, because of some chore that had to be done or just because he and his wife—her name was Isabel—got to talking. They had no children and could get talking anytime about anything. He brought her the news of the town, which often made her laugh, and she told him about the books she was reading.

Ray had joined up for the war as soon as he was eighteen. He chose the Air Force, which promised, as was said, the most adventure and the quickest death. He had been a mid-upper gunner—a position that Isabel could never get straight in her head—and he had survived. Close to the end of the war, he'd been transferred to a new crew, and within a couple of weeks his old crew, the men he'd flown with so many times, were shot down and lost. He came home with a vague idea that he had to do something meaningful with the life that had so inexplicably been left to him, but he didn't know what.

First, he had to finish high school. In the town where he had grown up, a special school had been set up for veterans who were doing just that and hoping to go on to college, courtesy of the grateful citizens. The teacher of English Language and Literature was Isabel. She was thirty years old and married. Her husband, too, was a veteran, who considerably outranked the students in her English class. She was planning to put in this one year of teaching out of general patriotism, and then she was going to retire and start a family. She discussed this openly with her students, who said, just out of her earshot, that some guys got all the luck.

Ray disliked hearing that kind of talk, and the reason was that he had fallen in love with her. And she with him, which seemed infinitely more surprising. It was preposterous to everybody except themselves. There was a divorce—a scandal to her well-connected family and a shock to her husband, who had wanted to marry her since they were children. Ray had an easier time of it than she did, because he had little family to speak of, and those he did have announced that they supposed they wouldn't be good enough for him now that he was marrying so high up, and they would just stay out of his way in the future. If they expected any denial or reassurance in response to this, they did not get it.

Okay with him was what he more or less said. Time to make a fresh start. Isabel said that she could go on teaching until Ray had finished college and got established in whatever it was that he wanted to do.

But the plan had to change. She was not well. At first, they thought it was nerves. The upheaval. The foolish fuss.

Then the pains came. Pain whenever she took a deep breath. Pain under the breastbone and in her left shoulder. She ignored it. She joked about God punishing her for her amorous adventure and said that he, God, was wasting his time when she didn't even believe in him.

She had something called pericarditis. It was serious and she had ignored it to her peril. It was something she would not be cured of but could manage, with difficulty. She could never teach again. Any infection would be dangerous, and where is infection more rampant than in a schoolroom? It was Ray now who had to support her, and he took a job as a policeman in this small town called Maverley, just over the Grey-Bruce border. He didn't mind the work and she didn't mind, after a while, her semi-seclusion.

There was one thing they didn't talk about. Each of them wondered whether the other minded not being able to have children. It occurred to Ray that that disappointment might have something to do with Isabel's wanting to hear all about the girl he had to walk home on Saturday nights.

"That is deplorable," she said when she heard about the ban on movies, and she was even more upset when he told her that the girl had been kept out of high school to help at home.

"And you say she's intelligent."

Ray did not remember having said that. He had said that she was weirdly shy, so that during their walks he had to rack his brains for a subject of conversation. Some questions he thought of wouldn't do. Such as, What is your favorite subject at school? That would have had to go into the past tense and it would not matter now whether she'd liked anything. Or, What did she want to do when she was grown up? She was grown up now, for all intents and purposes, and she had her work cut out for her, whether she wanted it or not. Also the question of whether she liked this town, and did she miss wherever it was that she used to live—pointless. And they had already gone through, without elaboration, the names and ages of the younger children in her family. When he inquired after a dog or a cat, she reported that she didn't have any.

She did come up with a question for him eventually. She asked what it was that people had been laughing about in the movie that night.

He didn't think he should remind her that she wasn't supposed to have heard anything. But he could not remember what might have been funny. So he said that it must have been some stupid thing—you could never tell what would make the audience laugh. He said that he didn't get too involved in the movies, seeing them as he did, in bits and pieces. He seldom followed the plots.

"Plots," she said.

He had to tell her what that meant—that there were stories being told. And from that time on there was no problem making conversation. Nor did he need to warn her that it might not be wise to repeat any of it at home. She understood. He was called upon not to tell any specific story—which he could hardly have done anyway—but to explain that the stories were often about crooks and innocent people and that the crooks generally managed well enough at first by committing their crimes and hoodwinking people singing in night clubs (which were like dance halls) or sometimes, God knows why, singing on mountaintops or in some other unlikely outdoor scenery, holding up the action. Sometimes the movies were in color. With magnificent costumes if the story was set in the past. Dressed-up actors making a big show of killing one another. Glycerin tears running down ladies' cheeks. Jungle animals brought in from zoos, probably, and teased to act ferocious. People getting up from being murdered in various ways the moment the camera was off them. Alive and well, though you had just seen them shot or on the executioner's block with their heads rolling in a basket.

"You should take it easy," Isabel said. "You could give her nightmares."

Ray said he'd be surprised. And certainly the girl had an air of figuring things out, rather than being alarmed or confused. For instance, she never asked what the executioner's block was or seemed surprised at the thought of heads on it. There was something in her, he told Isabel, something that made her want to absorb whatever you said to her, instead of just being thrilled or mystified by it. Some way in which he thought she had already shut herself off from her family. Not to be contemptuous of them, or unkind. She was just rock-bottom thoughtful.

But then he said what made him sorrier than he knew why.

"She hasn't got much to look forward to, one way or the other."

"Well, we could snatch her away," Isabel said.

Then he warned her. Be serious.

"Don't even think about it."

Shortly before Christmas (though the cold had not really set in yet), Morgan came to the police station around midnight one night in the middle of the week to say that Leah was missing.

She had sold the tickets as usual and closed the window and put the money where it was supposed to go and set off for home, so far as he knew. He himself had shut things up when the show was done, but when he got outside this woman he didn't know had appeared, asking what had become of Leah. This was the mother—Leah's mother. The father was still at his job at the mill, and Morgan had suggested that the girl might have taken it into her head to go and see him at work. The mother didn't seem to know what he was talking about, so he said that they could go to the mill and see if the girl was there, and she—the mother—cried and begged him not to do any such thing. So Morgan gave her a ride home, thinking that the girl might have turned up by now, but no luck, and then he thought he had better go and inform Ray.

He didn't relish the thought of having to break the news to the father.

Ray said that they should go to the mill at once—there was a slim chance she might be there. But of course when they located the father he hadn't seen anything of her, and he got into a rage about his wife's going out like that when she did not have permission to leave the house.

Ray asked about friends and was not surprised to learn that Leah didn't have any. Then he let Morgan go home and went himself to the house, where the mother was very much in the distracted state that Morgan had described. The children were still up, or some of them were, and they, too, proved to be speechless. They trembled either from fright and their misgivings about the stranger in the house or from the cold, which Ray noticed was definitely on the rise, even indoors. Maybe the father had rules about the heat as well.

Leah had been wearing her winter coat—he got that much out of them. He knew the baggy brown checked garment and thought that it would keep her warm for a while, at least. Between the time that Morgan had first shown up and now, snow had begun to fall fairly heavily.

When his shift was over, Ray went home and told Isabel what had happened. Then he went out again and she didn't try to stop him.

An hour later, he was back with no results, and the news that the roads were likely to be closed for the first big snowstorm of the winter.

By morning, that was in fact the case; the town was boxed in for the first time that year and the main street was the only one that the snowplows tried to keep open. Nearly all the stores were closed, and in the part of town where Leah's family lived the power had gone out and there was nothing that could be done about it, with the wind arching and bowing the trees until it looked as if they were trying to sweep the ground.

The day-shift policeman had an idea that had not occurred to Ray. He was a member of the United Church and he was aware—or his wife was aware—that Leah did ironing every week for the minister's wife. He and Ray went to the parsonage to see if anybody there knew anything that could account for the girl's disappearance, but there was no information to be had, and after that brief stirring of hope the trail seemed even more hopeless than before.

Ray was a little surprised that the girl had taken on another job and not mentioned it. Even though, compared with the theatre, it hardly seemed like much of a foray into the world.

He tried to sleep in the afternoon and did manage an hour or so. Isabel attempted to get a conversation going at supper but nothing lasted. Ray's talk kept circling back to the visit to the minister, and how the wife had been helpful and concerned, as much as she could be, but how he—the minister—had not exactly behaved as you might think a minister should. He had answered the door impatiently, as if he had been interrupted while writing his sermon or something. He'd called to his wife and when she came she'd had to remind him who the girl was. Remember the girl who comes to help out with the ironing? Leah? Then he'd said that he hoped there would be some news soon, while trying to inch the door shut against the wind.

"Well, what else could he have done?" Isabel said. "Prayed?"

Ray thought that it wouldn't have hurt.

"It would just have embarrassed everybody and exposed the futility," Isabel said. Then she added that he was probably a very up-to-date minister who went in more for the symbolic.

Some sort of search had to be carried out, never mind the weather. Back sheds and an old horse barn unused for years had to be pried open and ransacked in case she had taken shelter there. Nothing came to light. The local radio station was alerted and broadcast a description.

If Leah had been hitchhiking, Ray thought, she might have been picked up before the storm got started, which could be good or bad.

The broadcast said that she was a little under average height— Ray would have said a little over—and that she had straight medium-brown hair. He would have said very dark brown, close to black.

Her father did not take part in the search; nor did any of her brothers. Of course, the boys were younger than she was and would never have got out of the house without the father's consent anyway. When Ray went around to the house on foot and made it through to the door, it was hardly opened, and the father didn't waste any time telling him that the girl was most likely a runaway. Her punishment was out of his hands and in God's now. There was no invitation to Ray to come in and thaw himself out. Perhaps there was still no heat in the house.

The storm did die down, around the middle of the next day. The snowplows got out and cleared the town streets. The county plows took over the highway. The drivers were told to keep their eyes open for a body frozen in the drifts.

The day after that, the mail truck came through and there was a letter. It was addressed not to anyone in Leah's family but to the minister and his wife. It was from Leah, to report that she had got married. The bridegroom was the minister's son, who was a saxophone player in a jazz band. He had added the words "Surprise Surprise" at the bottom of the page. Or so it was reported, though Isabel asked how anybody could know that, unless they were in the habit of steaming envelopes open at the post office.

The sax player hadn't lived in this town when he was a child. His father had been posted elsewhere then. And he had visited very rarely. Most people could not even have told you what he looked like. He never attended church. He had brought a woman home a couple of years ago. Very made-up and dressy. It was said that she was his wife, but apparently she hadn't been.

How often had the girl been in the minister's house, doing the ironing, when the sax player was there? Some people had worked it out. It would have been one time only. This was what Ray heard at the police station, where gossip could flourish as well as it did among women.

Isabel thought it was a great story. And not the elopers' fault. They had not ordered the snowstorm, after all.

It turned out that she herself had some slight knowledge of the sax player. She had run into him at the post office once, when he happened to be home and she was having one of her spells of being well enough to go out. She had sent away for a record but it hadn't come. He had asked her what it was and she had told him. Something she could not remember now. He'd told her then about his own involvement with a different kind of music. Something had already made her sure that he wasn't a local. The way he leaned into her and the way he smelled strongly of Juicy Fruit gum. He didn't mention the parsonage, but somebody else told her of the connection, after he had wished her goodbye and good luck.

Just a little bit flirtatious, or sure of his welcome. Some nonsense about letting him come and listen to the record if it ever arrived. She hoped she was meant to take that as a joke.

She teased Ray, wondering if it was on account of his descriptions of the wide world via the movies that the girl had got the idea.

Ray did not reveal and could hardly believe the desolation he had felt during the time when the girl was missing. He was, of course, greatly relieved when he found out what had happened.

Still, she was gone. In a not entirely unusual or unhopeful way, she was gone. Absurdly, he felt offended. As if she could have shown some inkling, at least, that there was another part of her life.

Her parents and all the other children were soon gone as well, and it seemed that nobody knew where.

The minister and his wife did not leave town when he retired.

They were able to keep the same house and it was often still referred to as the parsonage, although it was not really that anymore. The new minister's young wife had taken issue with some features of the place, and the church authorities, rather than fix it up, had decided to build a new house so that she could not complain anymore. The old parsonage was then sold cheaply to the old minister. It had room for the musician son and his wife when they came to visit with their children.

There were two, their names appearing in the newspaper when they were born. A boy and then a girl. They came occasionally to visit, usually with Leah only; the father was busy with his dances or whatever. Neither Ray nor Isabel had run into them at those times.

Isabel was better; she was almost normal. She cooked so well that they both put on weight and she had to stop, or at least do the fancier things less often. She got together with some other women in the town to read and discuss Great Books. A few had not understood what this would really be like and dropped out, but aside from them it was a startling success. Isabel laughed about the fuss there would be in Heaven as they tackled poor old Dante.

Then there was some fainting or near-fainting, but she would not go to the doctor till Ray got angry with her and she claimed it was his temper that had made her sick. She apologized and they made up, but her heart took such a plunge that they had to hire a woman who was called a practical nurse to stay with her when Ray could not be there. Fortunately, there was some money— hers from an inheritance and his from a slight raise, which materialized even though, by choice, he kept on with the night shift.

One summer morning, on his way home, he checked at the

post office to see if the mail was ready. Sometimes they had got it sorted by this time; sometimes they hadn't. This morning they hadn't.

And now on the sidewalk, coming toward him in the bright early light of the day, was Leah. She was pushing a stroller, with a little girl about two years old inside it, kicking her legs against the metal footrest. Another child was taking things more soberly, holding on to his mother's skirt. Or to what was really a long orangey pair of trousers. She was wearing with them a loose white top, something like an undervest. Her hair had more shine than it used to have, and her smile, which he had never actually seen before, seemed positively to shower him with delight.

She could almost have been one of Isabel's new friends, who were mostly either younger or recently arrived in this town, though there were a few older, once more cautious residents, who had been swept up in this bright new era, their former viewpoints dismissed and their language altered, straining to be crisp and crude.

He had been feeling disappointed not to find any new magazines at the post office. Not that it mattered so much to Isabel now. She used to live for her magazines, which were all serious and thought-provoking but with witty cartoons that she laughed at. Even the ads for furs and jewels had made her laugh, and he hoped, still, that they would revive her. Now, at least, he'd have something to tell her about. Leah.

Leah greeted him with a new voice and pretended to be amazed that he had recognized her, since she had grown—as she put it—into practically an old lady. She introduced the little girl, who would not look up and kept a rhythm going on the metal footrest, and the boy, who looked into the distance and muttered. She teased the boy because he would not let go of her clothes.

"We're across the street now, honeybunch."

His name was David and the girl's was Shelley. Ray had not remembered those names from the paper. He had an idea that both were fashionable.

She said that they were staying with her in-laws.

Not visiting them. Staying with them. He didn't think of that till later and it might have meant nothing.

"We're just on our way to the post office."

He told her that he was coming from there, but they weren't through with the sorting yet.

"Oh, too bad. We thought there might be a letter from Daddy, didn't we, David?"

The little boy had hold of her clothing again.

"Wait till they get them sorted," she said. "Maybe there'll be one then."

There was a feeling that she didn't quite want to part with Ray yet, and Ray did not want it, either, but it was hard to think of anything else to say.

"I'm on my way to the drugstore," he said.

"Oh, are you?"

"I have to pick up a prescription for my wife."

"Oh, I hope she's not sick."

Then he felt as if he had committed a betrayal and said rather shortly, "No. Nothing much."

She was looking past Ray now, and saying hello in the same delighted voice with which she had greeted him, some moments ago.

Speaking now to the United Church minister, the new, or fairly new, one, whose wife had demanded the up-to-date house.

She asked the two men if they knew each other and they said yes, they did. Both spoke in a tone that indicated *not well,* and that maybe showed some satisfaction that it should be so. Ray noticed that the man was not wearing his dog collar.

"Hasn't had to haul me in for any infractions yet," the minister said, perhaps thinking that he should have been jollier. He shook Ray's hand.

"This is so lucky," Leah said. "I've been wanting to ask you some questions and now here you are."

"Here I am."

"I mean about Sunday school," Leah said. "I've been wondering. I've got these two little creatures growing up and I've been wondering how soon and what's the procedure and everything."

"Oh, yes," the minister said.

Ray could see that he was one of those who didn't particularly like doing their ministering in public. Didn't want the subject brought up, as it were, every time they took to the streets. But the minister hid his discomfort as well as he could and there must have been some compensation for him in talking to a girl who looked like Leah.

"We should discuss it," he said. "Make an appointment anytime."

Ray was saying that he had to be off.

"Good to run into you," he said to Leah, and gave a nod to the man of the cloth.

He went on, in possession of two new pieces of information. She was going to be here for some time, if she was trying to make arrangements for Sunday school. And she had not got out of her system all the religion that her upbringing had put into it.

He looked forward to running into her again, but that did not happen.

When he got home, he told Isabel about how the girl had changed, and she said, "It all sounds pretty commonplace, after all."

She seemed a little testy, perhaps because she had been waiting for him to get her coffee. Her helper was not due till nine o'clock and she was forbidden, after a scalding accident, to try to manage it herself.

It was downhill and several scares for them till Christmastime, and then Ray got a leave of absence. They took off for the city, where certain medical specialists were to be found. Isabel was admitted to the hospital immediately and Ray was able to get into one of the rooms provided for the use of relatives from out of town. Suddenly, he had no responsibilities except to visit Isabel for long hours each day and take note of how she was responding to various treatments. At first, he tried to distract her with lively talk of the past, or observations about the hospital and other patients he got glimpses of. He took walks almost every day, in spite of the weather, and he told her all about those as well. He brought a newspaper with him and read her the news. Finally, she said, "It's so good of you, darling, but I seem to be past it."

"Past what?" he countered, but she said, "Oh, please," and after that he found himself silently reading some book from the hospital library. She said, "Don't worry if I close my eyes. I know you're there."

She had been moved some time ago from Acute Care into a room that held four women who were more or less in the same condition as she was, though one occasionally roused herself to holler at Ray, "Give us a kiss."

Then one day he came in and found another woman in Isabel's bed. For a moment, he thought she had died and nobody had told him. But the voluble patient in the kitty-corner bed cried out, "Upstairs." With some notion of jollity or triumph.

And that was what had happened. Isabel had failed to wake up that morning and had been moved to another floor, where it seemed they stashed the people who had no chance of improving—even less chance than those in the previous room—but were refusing to die.

"You might as well go home," they told him. They said that they would get in touch if there was any change.

That made sense. For one thing, he had used up all his time in the relatives' housing. And he had more than used up his time away from the police force in Maverley. All signs said that the right thing to do was to go back there.

Instead, he stayed in the city. He got a job with the hospital maintenance crew, cleaning and clearing and mopping. He found a furnished apartment, with just essentials in it, not far away.

He went home, but only briefly. As soon as he got there, he started making arrangements to sell the house and whatever was in it. He put the real-estate people in charge of that and got out of their way as quickly as he could; he did not want to explain anything to anybody. He did not care about anything that had happened in that place. All those years in the town, all he knew about it, seemed to just slip away from him.

He did hear something while he was there, a kind of scandal involving the United Church minister, who was trying to get his wife to divorce him, on the ground of adultery. Committing adultery with a parishioner was bad enough, but it seemed that the minister, instead of keeping it as quiet as possible and slinking off to get rehabilitated or to serve in some forsaken parish in the hinterlands, had chosen to face the music from the pulpit. He had more than confessed. Everything had been a sham, he said. His mouthing of the Gospels and the commandments he didn't fully believe in, and most of all his preachings about love and sex, his conventional, timid, and evasive recommendations: a sham. He was now a man set free, free to tell them what a relief it was to celebrate the life of the body along with the life of the spirit. The woman who had done this for him, it seemed, was Leah. Her husband, the musician, Ray was told, had come back to get her sometime before, but she hadn't wanted to go with him. He'd blamed it on the minister, but he was a drunk—the husband was—so nobody had known whether to believe him or not. His mother must have believed him, though, because she had kicked Leah out and hung on to the children.

As far as Ray was concerned, this was all revolting chatter. Adulteries and drunks and scandals—who was right and who was wrong? Who could care? That girl had grown up to preen and bargain like the rest of them. The waste of time, the waste of life, by people all scrambling for excitement and paying no attention to anything that mattered.

Of course, when he had been able to talk to Isabel, everything had been different. Not that Isabel would have been looking for answers—rather, that she would have made him feel as if there were more to the subject than he had taken account of. Then she'd have ended up laughing.

He got along well enough at work. They asked him if he wanted to join a bowling team and he thanked them but said he didn't have time. He had plenty of time, actually, but had to spend it with Isabel. Watching for any change, any explanation. Not letting anything slip away.

"Her name is Isabel," he used to remind the nurses if they said, "Now, my lady," or "Okay, missus, over we go."

Then he got used to hearing them speak to her that way. So there were changes, after all. If not in Isabel, he could find them in himself.

For quite a while, he had been going to see her once a day.

Then he made it every other day. Then twice a week.

Four years. He thought it must be close to a record. He asked those who cared for her if that was so and they said, "Well. Getting there." They had a habit of being vague about everything.

He had got over the persistent idea that she was thinking. He was no longer waiting for her to open her eyes. It was just that he could not go off and leave her there alone.

She had changed from a very thin woman not to a child but to an ungainly and ill-assorted collection of bones, with a birdlike crest, ready to die every minute with the erratic shaping of her breath.

There were some large rooms used for rehabilitation and exercise, connected to the hospital. Usually he saw them only when they were empty, all the equipment put away and the lights turned off. But one night as he was leaving he took a different route through the building for some reason and saw a light left on.

And when he went to investigate he saw that somebody was

still there. A woman. She was sitting astride one of the blown-up exercise balls, just resting there, or perhaps trying to remember where she was supposed to go next.

It was Leah. He didn't recognize her at first, but then he looked again and it was Leah. He wouldn't have gone in, maybe, if he'd seen who it was, but now he was halfway on his mission to turn off the light. She saw him.

She slid off her perch. She was wearing some sort of purposeful athletic outfit and had gained a fair amount of weight.

"I thought I might run into you sometime," she said. "How is Isabel?"

It was a bit of a surprise to hear her call Isabel by her first name, or to speak of her at all, as if she'd known her.

He told her briefly how Isabel was. No way to tell it now except briefly.

"Do you talk to her?" she said.

"Not so much anymore."

"Oh, you should. You shouldn't give up talking to them."

How did she come to think she knew so much about everything?

"You're not surprised to see me, are you? You must have heard?" she said.

He did not know how to answer this.

"Well," he said.

"It's been a while since I heard that you were here and all, so I guess I just thought you'd know about me being down here, too."

He said no.

"I do recreation," she told him. "I mean for the cancer patients. If they're up to it, like."

He said he guessed that was a good idea.

"It's great. I mean for me, too. I'm pretty much okay, but sometimes things get to me. I mean particularly at suppertime. That's when it can start to feel weird."

She saw that he didn't know what she was talking about and she was ready—maybe eager—to explain.

"I mean without the kids and all. You didn't know their father got them?"

"No," he said.

"Oh, well. It's because they thought his mother could look after them, really. He's in AA and all, but the judgment wouldn't have gone like that if it wasn't for her."

She snuffled and dashed away tears in an almost disregarding way.

"Don't be embarrassed—it isn't as bad as it looks. I just automatically cry. Crying isn't so bad for you, either, so long as you don't make a career of it."

The man in AA would be the sax player. But what about the minister and whatever had been going on there?

Just as if he had asked her aloud, she said, "Oh. Then. Carl. That stuff was such a big deal and everything? I should have had my head examined.

"Carl got married again," she said. "That made him feel better. I mean because he'd sort of got past whatever it was he had on me. It was really kind of funny. He went and married another minister. You know how they let women be ministers now? Well, she's one. So he's like the minister's wife. I think that's a howl."

Dry-eyed now, smiling. He knew that there was more coming, but he could not guess what it might be.

"You must have been here quite a while. You got a place of your own?"

"Yes."

"You cook your own supper and everything?"

He said that that was the case.

"I could do that for you once in a while. Would that be a good idea?"

Her eyes had brightened, holding his.

He said maybe, but to tell the truth there wasn't room in his place for more than one person to move around at a time.

Then he said that he hadn't looked in on Isabel for a couple of days, and he must go and do it now.

She nodded just slightly in agreement. She did not appear hurt or discouraged.

"See you around."

"See you."

They had been looking all over for him. Isabel was finally gone. They said "gone," as if she had got up and left. When someone had checked her about an hour ago, she had been the same as ever, and now she was gone.

He had often wondered what difference it would make.

But the emptiness in place of her was astounding.

He looked at the nurse in wonder. She thought he was asking her what he had to do next and she began to tell him. Filling him in. He understood her fine, but was still preoccupied.

He'd thought that it had happened long before with Isabel, but it hadn't. Not until now.

She had existed and now she did not. Not at all, as if not ever. And people hurried around, as if this could be overcome by making arrangements. He, too, obeyed the customs, signing where he was told to sign, arranging—as they said—for the remains.

What an excellent word—"remains." Like something left to dry out in sooty layers in a cupboard.

And before long he found himself outside, pretending that he had as ordinary and good a reason as anybody else to put one foot ahead of the other.

What he carried with him, all he carried with him, was a lack, something like a lack of air, of proper behavior in his lungs, a difficulty that he supposed would go on forever.

The girl he'd been talking to, whom he'd once known—she had spoken of her children. The loss of her children. Getting used to that. A problem at suppertime.

An expert at losing, she might be called—himself a novice by comparison. And now he could not remember her name. Had lost her name, though he'd known it well. Losing, lost. A joke on him, if you wanted one.

He was going up his own steps when it came to him.

Leah.

A relief out of all proportion, to remember her.

Polly Rosenwaike

White Carnations

WE DIDN'T HAVE MOTHERS anymore, nor were we mothers ourselves, so we got together on Mother's Day at a
down-and-out pub frequented by gay men and regular drunks.
There weren't any mothers there, as far as we could tell, and the
day gave us that kind of radar. We knew who was a mother and
who wasn't. It was the third anniversary of our early May outing,
and we all showed up on time, at two o'clock on this sun-struck
afternoon, as if we couldn't wait to get inside where it felt dark
and smoky, even though smoking had been banned in New York
City bars and restaurants for several years now.

The tradition started with Elaine and Lara, who worked
together at a museum. When Elaine came back to the office after
her mother died, Lara took her out for a fancy lunch and made
her weep at the hazelnut-encrusted salmon and the chocolate
turtle cake with caramel beurre salé. Sometime after that, Elaine
and Anne met at a fundraiser and discovered what they had in
common.

Then Lara and I met at a party. It was the first party I had
gone to since my mother's death. I wore a red strapless dress and
felt insanely cheerful and dangerously cavalier. I talked to women

about bikini waxing and bedbugs. I found a way to touch every man I met: hand, shoulder, hip. At the punch bowl Lara introduced herself.

"What do you do?" she asked. I told her that I did program administration for a ballet school, where I used to dance myself. Before I had time to reciprocate the question, she asked, "And what do your parents do?" The snobbery surprised me from this woman in jeans and a ponytail, but I was prepared for all questions that night, prepared to hold myself apart from whatever was asked of me.

"I don't know my father, and my mother is dead."

"Yes," Lara said.

I didn't go home with a man that night. I drank spiked punch with Lara, who, it turned out, was not the kind of snob who dealt in pedigree or career. Parental loss was her stock-in-trade.

So when Mother's Day came around, with its bouquets and dinner specials, Elaine invited Anne, and Lara invited me, and there were four of us. But I imagined that our numbers were secretly legion, that in windowless joints throughout the city, huddled groups of women gathered, not a mother among them. We weren't quite commemorating, and we weren't quite commiserating, though we weren't in denial either. We spent hours together in the hard wooden booth, and we ate and drank, talked and laughed, and it was a kind of fun fueled by each of our particular experiences of death.

For Elaine's mother it was Alzheimer's. At the end, as if to prove to Elaine that she'd always favored her younger sister, she could remember the name Janice, but not Elaine, though Elaine was the one who visited her mother more often, who had to explain over and over again why she couldn't go back to her sweet little house with the Victory Garden she had planted for when the soldiers came home. Anne's mother had died of cancer, the super fast kind, for which the relatives flew in right away to say goodbye. And Lara's mother killed herself many years ago. Lara was twelve, away at camp for the summer. One morning she dropped a letter to her mother in the camp mailbox. That afternoon, her uncle came to take her home. The letter arrived a few days later. Lara retrieved it from the mailbox, lit a match, and burned it. When the paper was consumed, she let the flame burn her skin.

When you think about it afterward, there is always something, in addition to the death, that marks the occasion. My mother was killed in a car accident three and a half years ago. Taxi drivers are known for their death-defying skills: you lurch and you cringe, but you get to where you're going sooner than the other guys on the road, except in my mother's case. And what else happened earlier that day? I sat in my office at the ballet school and watched the gingko leaves glide off the tree outside my window, the way gingko trees divest themselves, stunningly all at once.

At the pub, Lara and I sat on one side of the booth, Anne and Elaine on the other. I was the youngest at twenty-six, and Lara, thirty-three, was the second-youngest. We both favored eyeliner that made our eyes seem darker and not entirely trustworthy. We wore jeans that skinnied our already skinny legs. Elaine was fifty-two, with the skin of a woman who swore by an excellent facial cream, her hair a pretty, well-maintained white. Anne was a determined blonde at forty; her roots barely showed. She was good-looking in a hard way, with the polished directness of an anchorwoman. Lara's mother and my own had died before their time, by choice and by accident, and Elaine's and Anne's mothers had died in their seventies, a reasonable age to go. But we, their daughters, wanted to make ourselves attractive not just for partners or lovers or co-workers or each other. When we looked in the mirror, we wanted to place ourselves far away from our mothers' fate.

Soon my body would escape the tight control I had always imposed as a dancer. It had already begun, with inflated breasts and a slight slackening of my belly. I was three months pregnant, and though, five weeks earlier, I went to an abortion clinic, I had left the clinic still pregnant. I went through all of the preliminary steps: blood draw, ultrasound, counseling. The nurse asked if I was sure of my decision and I told her I was. Then I lay on the table, waiting for the doctor. I expected a woman, I suppose because I'd always had female doctors. I preferred it that way. When men tended to my body, I wanted it to be for pleasure. Women were the clinicians, women older than I was, who had chosen this depressing profession that seemed the opposite of dance. Doctors worked with the body immobilized, the body unhealthy and unbeautiful. I felt sorry for them in their white coats and sensible shoes.

The doctor came in. "Hi, Karyn," he said amiably, as if he knew me. He was tall, fiftyish, with grayish-brown hair, good-looking in a mild way. With the nurse's help, he began to prepare his instruments. Because I had never known my father, it was my habit to recognize him in a man of a certain age. His features, his voice, whatever task or gesture his hands were engaged in—I studied them all. I looked enough like my mother that lack of resemblance did not disqualify a man. I didn't expect my father to be like me; I expected him to be as strange and remote as he was to my life. And vis-à-vis the inevitable converging paths of lost parents and children, well-documented in fairy tales and movies, here he was: my seventh-grade biology teacher, a proctor at the SATs, the college dance department advisor, a docent at the Met, the super of my apartment building, the doctor who was about to perform my abortion.

He sat down by my stirruped feet, his gloved hands outstretched. "First I'm going to feel your cervix. It shouldn't hurt. You'll just feel some pressure." I dug my nails into my palms. No, it didn't hurt. I had heard that the cervix softened during pregnancy, and I wondered what that softness felt like to a practiced hand. The doctor disengaged himself. I watched his mild handsome competence and I wanted to stop it.

"I'm sorry." I scooted up the table to an upright position. "I have to go." I was blazing with embarrassment and freedom.

The nurse looked at the doctor, and I wondered how common

last-minute defections were, and if they scored it as a point for the anti-abortion gang.

"Are you sure?" the doctor asked.

"Yes," I lied. I was sure I wouldn't see him again, though perhaps I would make an appointment somewhere else, ask for a female doctor, keep my eyes shut.

"Okay," he said, with a slight edge to his voice, the edge I imagined a father would have, thinking, but not saying to his squirming child, and why didn't you go to the bathroom earlier, when I asked if you needed to? "Okay. We'll let you get dressed."

I let time pass. I did not exactly say to myself, I will keep this baby. I was waiting to see what would happen. In the early mornings I ran in the park, around the murky reservoir, fighting off exhaustion. At work I watched girls in leotards and tights, girls with sweet, silky skin practicing before class. I met friends for dinner and told them I was taking antibiotics and couldn't drink. Sometimes I thought of the doctor, who had known my secret and didn't care, and sometimes I lingered over another man of fifty or so who could, if a great accident of time and place allowed, be the one who had brought me into being, unbeknownst to him. I had always seen my father everywhere, but my mother I had not seen since a few weeks before her death.

The pub menus were stained and familiar, with their selection of unwholesome food. Bacon-cheese melt, fish and chips, clam chowder. The closest you could get to healthy was Caesar salad. Today we all agreed to enjoy things that tasted great and bad at the same time, that left us feeling bloated and satisfied.

"My neighbor gave me a white carnation this morning," Anne said. "A nice gesture, but you know."

"Ugh," Elaine said.

"Why aren't you wearing it in your buttonhole?" Lara mocked.

"I don't get it," I said.

"Carnations—the Mother's Day flower," Lara said. "Red for the living. White for the purity of a dead mother's love."

"How did Mother's Day get started, anyway?"

"A woman named Anna Jarvis," Anne said. "She wanted to create this memorial to her mother, and it caught on and was declared a national holiday in 1914. But she got disgusted with it. The commercialism, Hallmark, and chocolates—you know the whole bit. She ended up spending her family inheritance campaigning against Mother's Day and died in poverty. She never married, never had children."

Anne had been trying to get pregnant for years. She filled us in on her methods: basal thermometers, Clomid, IVI, and IVF. She wanted a baby so badly, and yet the more desperate energy she poured into the baby-making project, the less sympathetic I had felt. Now I sat across from her, my womb occupied by an inhabitant I hadn't meant to encourage. Looking at Anne's carefully concealed frown lines, I felt guilty. She was an earnest social worker with an architect husband and a nice house in Tarrytown. Why shouldn't they do everything to try to have a child? But it bothered me to think of them having sex on designated days in the missionary position to allow the sperm the shortest trip to the egg—or worse, making regular visits to the fertility clinic, where sex was a matter of extracting and inserting the necessary material.

The waiter arrived with our drinks. A gin and tonic, a whiskey sour, a Molson, and a root beer. I was prepared with my antibiotics excuse, but no one commented. Elaine began talking about her mother.

"Did I tell you she didn't even recognize herself in the mirror? But when she looked at an old photo of herself as a young woman—*oh yeah, that's me.* Smooth skin and hair, and smiling on a bicycle seat. I could never figure out if she knew it was from the past, or if she actually thought that was what she looked like."

"When she saw herself in the mirror, who did she think it was?" Lara asked.

"Just some old lady, I think. Another lady who happened to be in the room, like a roommate. But the one good thing about it all, for me, was that as soon as she started losing her memory, she didn't care who Nancy was anymore. It seemed plausible to her that Nancy was just a friend I'd invited over. Then eventually, of course, she didn't recognize either of us. So maybe we should give all the homophobes just a little bit of Alzheimer's."

Elaine and Nancy had been together for years, as had Anne and Robert. It was incumbent upon Lara and me to provide the dating stories. When she wasn't at parties, bobbing for orphans, Lara was online. She liked the way you could scrutinize a guy, pore over photos and read into chats, before actually meeting him. My boyfriends, flings, and one-night stands were usually men I met by dancing with them, feeling first the tension in their arms, the concentration or abandon of their faces near mine. Since I'd stopped dancing ballet in college, I went to clubs with bump and grind music. More and more, I went alone. Sometimes I brought men home, and who was around to tell me that I shouldn't?

In January I'd met Philippe that way. He wasn't a great dancer, but he was determined, keeping up with me for three hours, his clammy fingers stuck in mine. He was French, from Nice or Nantes, I forgot which. A gawkily handsome man, he would probably seem a boy until he was forty and then he'd retreat into bony limbs and wrinkles.

"Do you live here?" he asked, when it was clear that we were dancing with each other and wanted to keep on doing it.

"You might say that," I said. "I come here often."

"But in New York, do you live?" I liked his accent. I liked that it made him seem both sophisticated and unsure.

"Yes," I said. "For my whole life."

"Great. Do you love it?"

"I try to love it," I said, but I think the qualification was lost on him.

Philippe was visiting the East Coast, with a backpack and an English pocket dictionary. He'd gone to D.C. and Philadelphia. After New York, he was on to Boston and Vermont.

"Vermont in January. You know it'll be really cold."

"Yes, all the snow. Like a fairy tale. I want to see it." He pulled me closer, and I thought of the romance: New York for the first time. And I would be the girl he had met there, who used to be a dancer, and who danced him into her bed.

Since my mother had died and left me some money, I could afford to have my own place. It was on the border of the Upper West Side and Harlem, in a building with a Christmas tree in the lobby six months out of the year. In the elevator there was a black and white framed picture of somebody's son from long ago, with pomaded hair and pink cheeks painted on. My apartment was white and empty, bare walls, no rugs on the hardwoods, though I'd been told when I moved in that New York City law required carpeting on 80 percent of the floors. When he came up occasionally to fix my toilet, the landlord glanced around but didn't comment. I kept the place clean and the neighbors didn't complain. In the elevator we smiled at each other and then studied the door. A storage unit in Westchester held most of the things I'd saved from my mother's apartment. An old oak stereo and boxes of records, dreamy folksongs I used to twirl to as a little girl. A series of antique lamps we'd hauled onto the subway. An armchair she settled into in the evenings. I sometimes found her there in the morning, with a mystery novel nearing the end of its mystery, her thigh a prominent bookmark. Sometimes I thought about renting a truck and furnishing my apartment with those things that were gathering dust out in Westchester. But I left them there. My mother and I had lived in a small East Village apartment that could barely hold the two of us. I had always loved the gleaming bareness of the dance studio, free of the oppressiveness of stuff. No stuff could survive on the dance floor. It would be pliéd and pas de deuxed and jetéd aside.

My bed was high and firm and piled with white blankets. Philippe pulled me on top of him. "You are all so pretty," he said.

This moment when sex began with an almost stranger was

always something of a puzzlement. Why do this, of all things, with a man whose name was still new on my tongue? But by then it was too late. Our limbs were artfully arranged, our chests pressed together, our mouths hovering near each other with embattled breath. I liked it. I wanted it. If on some level I also disapproved, so be it. I had trained for years to keep my body in alignment, to follow strict orders, to perform on command. Let my mind stumble and stagger about. Let it simper and second-guess. My body would carry on with its amorous work.

Still, I wasn't such a fool that I didn't use condoms. The top drawer of my nightstand was reserved for only an eye pillow and a box of Trojans. But Philippe couldn't seem to manage with one on. We spent an hour trying. Finally, I threw it aside.

"Is it okay?" he asked. For three years, whenever someone asked if I was okay, I thought of my mother. She was thrown out of a car window on her way to the airport. She died on the shoulder of the Cross Bronx Expressway at forty-five years old. How could things be okay?

I kissed Philippe's tender neck. "Yes," I whispered. I trusted his polite and eager foreignness, and sex was always a diversionary gamble anyway. I just didn't really care.

At the pub, we had consumed seven alcoholic drinks, two root beers, and an assortment of things sauce-smothered and fried.

"Okay, last one," Anne said, plucking an onion ring from Lara's plate. "We have to go out with Robert's parents tonight."

"Can't you get out of it? Tell them you need to see a sick friend. After a few more beers, I'll throw up for you," Elaine said.

"You know what my mother-in-law would say? *She wants to see you, this sick friend? You're a doctor now? What happened to the social work?* The way she says social work, it's like I'm planning parties. Her faith in doctors is insane. According to her I just haven't gone to the doctor enough—that's why I can't have kids. You find a good doctor, and you go to him, and you keep on going to him until he fixes you. Unless you have cancer, and then there's no hope."

Anne ate another onion ring. "But I have some good news for a change. We put an application in with an adoption agency in China. They approved it last week."

We all agreed this was great and clinked our glasses with Anne's.

"Do you know how long it might take?" Lara asked.

"It could be a month. It could be six months. We have to be ready to buy a ticket to China. They tell you when to come, and then they send you on a tour with these other prospective parents. It's this weird vacation where you get a baby prize at the end."

I let Lara and Elaine continue to ask the questions. Last Mother's Day, Anne and I had clashed over adoption. She was going through what seemed to be an unsuccessful round of IVF, and I wanted to know whether she was considering adopting. Yes, of course, she said coldly. But they really wanted their own baby. I pressed her on it. Why such attachment to your own genetic lineage? I didn't mean to be accusatory or self-righteous. My interest in this topic was philosophical. Wasn't motherhood essentially a matter of care? Was origin so important? True, I had fantasized all my life about finding my father. But wasn't that because I didn't have any father at all?

"Okay, Karyn," Anne had said. "You make a good case. But do me a favor? Let me have my fantasy. Let me have it until I'm out of patience and stamina and spirit, which will happen soon, and then maybe I'll come around to your point of view." I was chastened by her tone. I felt like I'd been put in my place by a teacher or a mother, though not by my mother, who wouldn't be so direct. But then, I hadn't pushed her the way I pushed Anne. I had never asked her what she thought motherhood was. I had never asked her for my father's name. In the following year, Anne and I saw each other at a few different social occasions. We weren't friends exactly. There was formality and tension, a kind of tightly controlled uncertainty between us, the kind that makes you think either you'll never connect with this person, or you will eventually, in a deep and intractable way.

"They're all girls, of course," Anne said about the Chinese babies. "I've always wanted a girl. I remember thinking at nine or so, in an extreme boy-hating stage, maybe I'll adopt a baby when I get older so I won't get stuck with a stupid boy. I was always planning ahead."

"Girls are the best," Elaine said.

"Girls are smarter," Lara said.

It was hard to tell how happy Anne was about the prospect of adoption. But then, we weren't a happy bunch. We descended into this below-street-level pub on Mother's Day, holding our losses close, though how much did they really have to do with the way we met the world? Whatever influences our mothers had on us, that work had been done long ago. And though we had our moments of tunneling into the past with hardhat and headlamp, for the most part, out of loyalty and love, fear and denial, we didn't want to think about it.

What I'd thought about a lot since my mother's death was the story of how she came to be my mother. That is, from a child's perspective, how she came to be herself. I knew the story from bits she had told me over the years and from the narrative license of my own imagination.

Elizabeth Rylant grew up on a farm in Idaho. She was the only child of older parents who were surprised when she finally came along. They'd resigned themselves to calves and chicks and kittens for babies. But Elizabeth was born, and she was a restless child, racing through her chores and startling the animals. She watched the Times Square New Year's Eve celebration on TV every year. "The Big Apple," she wrote for a fourth-grade social studies report. "It doesn't have apple trees and it's actually not that big. But seven million people live in it. When I grow up, I will be one of them." Her parents smiled at her fantasy. What she didn't know, apart from how impossibly expensive everything was in New York, was that big cities are horrible. The buildings close you in, the crowds push you down. The day is choked with smog and the night is shut off from the stars. Her great-grandparents had climbed aboard trains heading west the first chance they could. Elizabeth would be lucky to go to the University of Idaho.

She spent a year there, taking geography and history classes, memorizing the details of places that were too far away in miles or too far back in time to travel to. She met a saxophonist named Hollis who wanted to play in clubs. He had a little money and thought they could go to Chicago, but Elizabeth convinced him it had to be New York. After her last final exam, she packed up her suitcases and sold her beat-up Ford. On the bus heading east she wrote a letter to her parents, breaking the news as gently as she could. She told them she and Hollis were planning to get married. But they didn't marry. They lived far out in Brooklyn, and Elizabeth rode the subway two hours each way to attend City College. She got a job as a waitress, while Hollis smoked and drank and played music in the street. A year before I was born, when my mother was twenty-one, she was finishing her degree in accounting with a minor in history and working five nights a week, hoping that the few gigs Hollis was finally getting would lead to gigs that were actually paid in more than beer. She worked late at the diner, but he was out later than she was. They didn't explore New York together the way they used to, making fun of stores and hairdos, trying out whatever food was foreign and cheap and could be eaten while walking, stopping in parks to kiss on benches.

And then one day a musician friend told her that Hollis had been seen dancing with a slutty jazz singer, dancing too late at night and too often and too close. Elizabeth was furious, but before she confronted Hollis for this and other sins, she went out and cheated herself. A man several years older than she was came into the diner to drink coffee and flirt. Now she flirted back in earnest. By the time she found out she was pregnant, she and Hollis had split up, and she was back in Idaho, visiting her parents, who'd never liked him anyway. They missed their daughter, who had, after all, not done so badly. She'd graduated from college with honors and a BA in accounting, and she hadn't been mugged or raped or murdered or had the country glow knocked out of her. She was flushed and docile. She walked in the fields in the early morning, nauseous, and the moaning of the cows didn't help. She could stay with her parents and they would take care of her in their quietly efficient, only slightly disapproving way. She could return to New York and struggle on her own. I don't know if she considered abortion. Her family was Catholic, but religion didn't mean anything to Elizabeth. In the end, it seemed, she was determined to follow through with me, as she had been determined to make it to New York, and to support herself, and to make practical plans for the future, and to leave a cheating man—though not as the innocent wounded party, but guilty herself.

She left Idaho, keeping the pregnancy secret from her parents, and she went back to New York and stayed with a friend until she got a job at an accounting firm. She worked until they let her go on maternity leave. As for the diner customer, she never saw him again. But she was sure that he, and not Hollis, was my father, and she was glad of it. If I had been Hollis's child, she would probably have broken down and told him, which would have meant that her life would be forever entwined with his. One of the many beauties of New York City, a beauty shaded with disappointment and resentment, was that you could stay in it for the rest of your life, avoiding your past, living another life than the one you thought you were going to live.

What had never occurred to me until I was pregnant with a potential child I hadn't planned to have, and by a man I didn't expect to see ever again, was that my mother might have kept me for the company. Though of course she didn't know this at the time, she would never have another serious relationship. There were men who drifted in and out, whom she tried to manage along with the daughter she was raising herself, and her demanding job, and going back to Idaho when she could to care for her ailing and then dying parents. Of course if she hadn't had me, who knows what other company might have come along? And what if I hadn't demanded ballet lessons from the age of six on up; and if she had been able to pursue her love of geography and history instead of plugging away at people's taxes for reliable pay; and if her boss hadn't insisted she attend a training in Atlanta that she never made it to, because a taxi driver made the worst possible mistake? I was always aware of the sacrifices my mother made for me, and in little ways she didn't fail to remind me of those sacrifices. But to think of that was to tumble toward one of those tunnels, into which I had barred the entrance.

It was getting late, and Anne was expected at her in-laws'. Elaine was heading home to Nancy; they were in the middle of watching a TV series that I'd never heard of on DVD. Lara could look forward to a chat with any number of online guys. We settled the bill and went out into lovely May. It was hard to be in the light. Down the street a middle-aged woman pushed an older woman in a wheelchair. The older woman wore a corsage and her head was cocked to one side as if someone was speaking very strongly to her into that ear. The four of us hugged or kissed each other goodbye.

"We should see each other more often."

"Yes, let's do that."

"You're going this way, right?" Lara gestured toward our subway line.

"Actually, Karyn, could you walk with me a minute?" Anne's hand was firm on my shoulder.

"Sure," I said, surprised.

Lara looked surprised, too, but she said, "Well, take care, dears," and walked across the street.

"I should pick up some flowers. I think there's a place down here," Anne said. We turned away from the pub. A sign in the drugstore on the corner read "Remember Your Mother. Chocolate Hearts!"

"I remember her. I remember that she didn't like chocolate," Anne said.

"Really?"

"If someone gave her a box of chocolates, she'd break off the shell and eat the cream inside."

"My mom hated olives, so when I was little I thought I didn't like them either. In third grade a kid at school offered me one, and I told him my mom didn't eat them. *So?* he said. *So?* I realized the flaw in my logic, and I ate an olive. I couldn't believe how good it was."

We walked past a gaggle of parents and young children. Everyone, even the dads, was dressed in pastels.

"If this adoption thing works out, I guess my daughter will realize early on how different she is from me," Anne said. "I guess that's a good thing."

"I think it's really exciting," I said. I waited nervously for her to offer more, to explain why she'd wanted me to walk with her.

"Oh, there's the store," Anne said. The little market sold flowers under an awning outside. A few bouquets of roses remained, on sale, along with bouquets of their poorer cousin, the carnation. "I just don't think they're a beautiful flower," I said, pointing to the carnations.

"Yeah, they look raggedy. The roses are so tightly wound, and the carnations are just kind of splayed out there, trying but not making it." We laughed, and suddenly I was sorry for Anne in a way that I hadn't been before, not because I pitied her, but because I admired her. She put her hand on my shoulder.

"How are you doing?"

"I'm, well, I'm okay."

"You seemed to be mulling something over this afternoon."

I hesitated. What did she know, or think that she knew? Sometimes my mother had seemed fully absorbed in her own concerns, and then she'd come out with an observation about me that I couldn't deny, though I tried to, with the vehemence of a young person convinced that to be known, even in her graces and triumphs, was fundamentally an embarrassment. If my mother were here today would I persist in that evasion, or would I lay my sorrows and my tiny burst of joy at her feet?

"I feel weird telling you this."

"I'm a social worker, remember? Weird is all I know."

"Okay. I'm pregnant. Thirteen weeks. The guy is gone, but I'm going to have the baby." I looked down at the flowers, their colors kaleidoscoping in my eyes. I wiped my nose with the back of my hand. A little noise escaped my throat, like the squeak of a hinge. I couldn't look at Anne.

"What do you think of the irises?" she asked. "They don't last very long, but you can't beat that blue."

"They're pretty," I managed. I leaned down into a lilac. It seemed to me that the smell could knock me out. I didn't want to stand up.

"There's a bench down the street," Anne said. "Why don't I finish up here and I'll see you there in a minute."

I stumbled over to the bench. It was next to the kind of tree that is carefully doled out on well-tended New York City blocks, a tree with its own tiny plot of dirt, fenced off protectively and given its best chance to grow. Anne was coming toward me with two bouquets of flowers, irises and lilacs, wrapped up in paper cones. She smiled with the pride of a woman bearing something beautiful. She set her canvas bag down on the bench and gently angled the irises inside it.

"These are for me, though when my mother-in-law sees them, she'll think they're for her." The dizzying scent of the lilacs enveloped me. Anne placed them in my hands.

"And these are for you."

Tash Aw
Sail

1.

It was the shape of an arrowhead: sleek, sharp, fast. Thirty feet long, it sat on the ash-gray water, away from the other boats, aloof. "The only one in Hong Kong," the Frenchman said. "No one else has owned anything like this in Asia. This boat is *made* for you."

Yanzu looked out across the marina at the ranks of plastic-white yachts; the jumble of masts and ropes reminded him of the washing lines and aerials that clad the run-down apartment blocks in the New Territories. Shorn of their sails, the boats looked fragile, purposeless. Just beyond the last row, not quite in open water, lay this new toy, its nose pointing westward toward the dipping afternoon sun.

"Listen," the man continued, "there's no pressure. If you don't want it, no problem, okay? Someone will, how do you say, *snap it up*." He ran a hand through his copper-colored hair, streaked with lighter strands where it had been bleached by the sun. "Quickly, it will go. Some big guy here will buy it for his son. Or else I will ship it to Shanghai. They do sailing on a lake there—*pff*—but you know, they want it, I arrange it. Those Mainlanders have a lot of money nowadays."

Yanzu looked at the brochure. There was a picture of a yacht—this very yacht—sailing on the open ocean, tilted on its side, its nose slicing through the spray and swell. There was only one person visible on board, a lonely sailor battling the elements. The price was printed discreetly at the bottom of the second page, as if it wasn't important. Yanzu triple-checked—it was in U.S. dollars: one zero too many.

"I'll call you tomorrow," Yanzu said, packing the brochure into his briefcase. "I just need some time to think."

2.

He was, of course, seeking consolation for a failed love affair, a woman whom he had known for three brief months earlier that year. Twelve weeks over the course of that summer, which had been especially muggy and close—hardly long enough to count as a relationship, she had pointed out. She was English, as it happened, and loved boats, which is why he was here, negotiating the purchase of a fast yacht he did not know how to sail. Men do the stupidest things when they are in love, she had once told him, laughing high-spiritedly; but he did not agree: men do the stupidest things when they are out of love, because they think they have failed. This was something he realized now—now that she was gone and he was a failure.

3.

But Yanzu was a successful man. *Is* a successful man. From his office in Causeway Bay, he runs a number of thriving business concerns both on the Mainland and in Hong Kong itself—a paper mill in Jiangsu province that sells recycled paper to the U.S., a flour mill in Hebei that produces only organic wheat and rice flour for export to Southeast Asia, and, most recently, a development of eco-homes in Chi Ma Wan, built using the latest Swiss technology, which proved so popular amongst the moneyed, arty thirtysomethings in Hong Kong that Yanzu is now thinking of expanding this model to other countries such as Singapore and Malaysia. He has achieved all this at the age of thirty-nine, and sometimes, in a rare, self-congratulatory moment, he might allow himself to think: this is remarkable, given that I arrived in Hong Kong from Beijing, aged twenty, with no money and no qualifications, having been forced to abandon my studies.

He had been a timid student; chemistry was his subject. The alchemy of things: it suited him, this intricate study of change. Politics was not his thing, but a casual, almost blithe signing of a circular letter in support of the Students' Autonomous Movement had made him an "activist," or so he feared. There had been a girl, a semideclared passion and two or three acts of recklessness to prove his virility and enthusiasm, including his support of the Movement. He had not even spent much time in Tiananmen, except to see the girl he'd liked and to bring her food parcels. With two friends, he fled to Hong Kong that summer, knowing that he would never again see the city he was leaving behind, that if fortune ever brought him back to Beijing, he would be a foreigner, unable to comprehend the people around him, the people he had grown up with, eaten with, laughed with, slept with, and that he would wish that he had not been allowed back home, would regret ever returning.

He arrived in Hong Kong, a city of buildings and people that dazzled and shone and did not care about him. He could not understand Cantonese and had no English at all. Twenty years old and already a failure.

He got a job as a cub reporter at the *Ming Pao,* which he admired because it was sober, unemotional and anti-China. He hated China in that first year in Hong Kong and wanted to write articles that railed against the Party, against its treatment of students and intellectuals; he saw himself several years down the line, a serious, celebrated columnist who would write brilliant essays about the fall of the Communist experiment, tinged with anger but never falling prey to emotion. Instead, he was assigned to cover petty crimes—first at the police station, at the end of the evening shift, then, as his fortunes began to rise, at the courthouse. Bag snatchers, visa overstayers, classy call girls—those were the people he saw and had to write about, week after week, trying to spot something tragic enough to force its way into the three small paragraphs at the bottom of page six of the newspaper. At first he tried to string these stories together to construct a bigger story, something that made him feel like an investigative journalist exploring alarming changes in society:

Drug Use Among Foreign Backpackers in Chungking Mansions
Twelve Pakistanis Violate Visa Conditions
Louis Vuitton Knockoffs Gaining in Popularity

But even as he typed up these stories he thought they were pointless. There was nothing he could do to make these trivial events untrivial.

In his spare time he continued to write his brilliant commentaries on the state of society in China, arguing from the position of the exile, someone who knew his subject intimately but viewed it with the objectivity that distance afforded him. He was fair and analytical, he thought, exploring the changes in China and the direction he thought it would take. Once, he dared to submit a piece to the editor in chief, but the article was returned to him some time later, dog-eared and with an ear-shaped tea stain seeping through the top page, scrawled with the comment MESSY—*Your argument is . . . . .??* Undeterred, Yanzu continued to work on these little essays in private, half-believing that someday soon, someone would publish them and belatedly celebrate his wisdom, his eerie foresight and scalpel-sharp analysis of a nation in trauma. He worked on those pieces for most of that first year, and possibly most of the second too, immersing himself in their world of controlled bitterness, until one day he realized that he was bored and had nothing more to say. He had exhausted his well of rancor and he no longer cared. The people he wrote about were already beginning to feel unfamiliar, as if he had never really known them. It was strange, he thought: the more he wrote about Beijing, the more distant it seemed. When he looked out of the window of his narrow bed-sit he no longer yearned to see the landscape of his northern past: the fine dust that swept in from the deserts, settling on the rooftops and leaves, bleaching everything of all color; the steam rising from stoves in winter; the wide flat avenues that disappeared into the horizon. He no longer felt the flash of panic or sickly streak of anxiety at the thought of losing those images, no longer wanted to cling onto that scene. It was a still life that belonged to someone else's history, not his. Instead, he found himself looking quite calmly at the unchanging view, at the washing lines sagging with wrinkled clothes, the lazy whirring fans of air-conditioning units, the families who lived in the next building, so close that he could hear their TVs, watch their young children grow up, day by day; and everything suddenly shrouded by the sheets of rain during the downpours that would last all afternoon in this semitropical city. These were the things that kept him company now.

He knew he would never write again.

4.

He bought a book called *How to Be a Millionaire—Fast!*, written by a Chinese American who had made a fortune investing in Asian markets and now lived in Monte Carlo. Its numbered chapters had titles that were cheery pieces of encouragement. "Trust Your Instincts: You're Better Than the Pros!" "Change Your Life:

Move to Where the Money Is!" As he stood in the bookshop flicking through the pages of translated text, Yanzu marveled at the optimism of the writing. There was something odd about seeing so many exclamation marks on a page of Chinese characters; the tone was disconcerting, too—unfailingly positive, exhorting the reader to venture forth with courage, to act without hesitation, like a carefree child. Very un-Chinese. There were words that Yanzu had never heard before in Chinese, like *investment trust* and *hedge fund,* and occasionally the text would lapse into a phrase in English which Yanzu would not be able to understand. He knew that such energy and free-spiritedness could only have been expressed in English, and he wished he could see through the fuzzy screen of translation and appreciate the blitheness of this language in its original form.

He wanted to reach for the English version to see how many words in it he could understand, but there was a young woman standing in front of the shelf, leafing through the same book. She was about Yanzu's age, though her dark, fitted jeans and silky businesswoman's shirt lent her an air of sophistication that made her seem older, cleverer, successful. Yanzu hesitated. He felt embarrassed, as if the mere act of opening the book would betray his lack of English. The woman was carrying a slim briefcase with the name Violet K. M. Lau imprinted in small gold letters on its front flap, just above an oval embossed with an emblem: a racehorse in full flight. She was flicking through the book purposefully, lingering on some pages slightly longer than others: she did not have a problem with English.

"Sorry, am I in the way?" she said, lowering the book and stepping aside. Yanzu noticed the way the pale gold bracelet of her watch strap clung delicately to her wrist.

"No, not at all," Yanzu replied, reaching for a copy of the book. As he opened it and leafed through its pages he felt ashamed of his pretense. The words flickered past him—lines and lines of a language he couldn't understand. He saw her looking at him; he was certain she knew that he was lost, that he was a fraud.

"It's not as good as his last book," she said.

"Really? I didn't read it."

"Where are you from? I mean, your accent . . ."

"Beijing—originally. But that was a long time ago."

"Oh, a *Mainlander*. I should have guessed. I thought maybe you were an ABC or something. Your Cantonese isn't very good."

They ended up going for a coffee in the French café next door. There was music—old Parisian songs, Violet explained. She had been to Europe many times when she was growing up; her family went on holiday there once a year. But now her parents were old and needed their home comforts, and Violet herself no longer had the energy or passion for traveling long distances as she once did. It was harder now that she had a job and was at an age where, well, one starts to think about settling down.

After a couple of months of dating Yanzu visited her parents' home. The furniture was European-style, and there was a piano at one end of the dining room. There were framed photos of Violet and her family: on holiday in a snowy landscape, their faces obscured by woolly hats and sunglasses; Violet as a child, reaching out to touch a killer whale; and at graduation, dressed in black robes with a furry hood, standing on a jewel-green lawn.

The conversation was polite and unprobing, but the family often lapsed into English—one-line jokes that Yanzu didn't understand but smiled at nonetheless. Afterwards, over whiskey (which Yanzu found he liked very much), Violet's father chatted about business and Chinese politics. "At least you seem to have opinions," he said, refilling Yanzu's glass, "for someone who isn't that highly educated."

5.

Their marriage coincided with Yanzu's first business venture, the purchase of a small light-industrial unit in Wong Tai Sin, run-down to the point of near dereliction. There were pigeons roosting in the iron joists in the roof space, and their droppings were corroding the metal, already half-eaten by rust. He achieved the deal with the help of a generous loan from his new father-in-law, whose expectations Yanzu would later dash when he refused to accept the offer of employment in the family business (a dull affair consisting largely of luxury car franchises). Yanzu bought the place with ambitions of turning it into an independent printing press, something that would not make huge amounts of money but would publish thought-provoking books on the State of the World. But somewhere along the line this plan was modified and then dispensed with altogether. In the end, the block was turned into twenty-eight solid but spartan apartments, each one sold at a handsome profit. It was the mid-nineties: property was the way forward ("Spot a Big Wave Early and Surf It!").

6.

There are certain things that Yanzu is good at, as his first venture proved. Transformation: taking something unpromising, throwing in other elements and turning the original components into something shiny and new. His seamless progression into the new millennium illustrates this: burgeoning investment portfolio, bold, new joint ventures on the Mainland and even further afield, all achieved with just the right balance of bravado and prudence, so that the growth of his wealth is steady, never ostentatious. The chemistry of his work is, it seems, always right.

Even his look has changed in the last decade and a half. There is the wardrobe of quiet, classic clothes, of course—double-cuffed shirts and handsome brogues; but there is also the way he carries himself, as if he had been born into the island's long-established entrepreneurial class, the memory of money-making imprinted in his genes. Even he cannot now discern the aspiring young Beijing intellectual, born in the middle of the Cultural Revolution.

Neither the 1997 financial crisis nor the current downturn has hurt him unduly. His judgment is sound, the balance just right.

7.

When the first of the contracts with the American buyers were negotiated, his assistants interpreted for him. He sat at meetings, unable to participate beyond issuing pleasantries: the mute CEO, the stereotype of the smiling Chinese businessman, nodding now and then whenever he knew that he should do so, smiling every time he discerned a joke. His assistants, expensively educated at Western universities, laughed heartily, nodded, muttered asides and summed up huge tracts of conversation for him in a single sentence. He gave instructions and then returned to his smiling silence, his frustration bordering on shame. Sometimes, when the slanting sunlight fell on the large glass windows overlooking the harbor, he would catch sight of his reflection. A man like him should not feel the way he did.

Violet said, "Maybe we should try speaking only in English at home for a while. You can make as many mistakes as you like in private."

They tried this for a week, maybe less. Yanzu could not get through a single sentence without being pulled up for some fault or another. His pronunciation was off. His grammar was nonexistent. His vocabulary was tiny. His lack of progress and Violet's growing impatience made him anxious; he stumbled over everything he said. He knew that she resented this imposition on her time: she was a busy woman, nearly a partner in her law firm; her hours were long and even outside work she had plenty to think about, such as whether they should have a baby. All her married friends were starting to have babies. She didn't have time to explain the difference between *a* and *the*.

"Why don't you get lessons, darling?" she suggested after a

while. "If you pay someone to do something for you, there's never any embarrassment."

8.

Before she arrived, the woman with whom he would fall in love, there had been an earnest Canadian ex-Mountie, an Australian ex-accountant, and an ex-headmistress from the British Council: foreigners who float through Hong Kong for a thousand different reasons, some staying six months, others three years before earning enough money to go south through Vietnam or Laos, or back to their homes in temperate lands. They had TEFL qualifications and taught Yanzu the basics. In his head he would rehearse properly constructed sentences but when it came to saying them aloud he stumbled and failed.

After some time she came to him through an agency—a cheaper rate, they explained, because she had little experience. Only one previous tutee—but a senior investment banker, mind you, who had given her a glowing testimonial.

She was not deliberate like the others had been, not methodical or conscientious. Her folders were a mess, dumped on the table in a heap as she laughingly rifled through them for the first day's lesson. So embarrassing, she said, to be this disorganized on the very first lesson, oh my God, she was sure she was making a very bad impression. But she did not seem very embarrassed, Yanzu thought, as he watched her getting her things together, nor did she seem to be bothered about the impression she made.

"That's okay," he said. "I mean, that's fine."

She looked at him and squinted like a child figuring something out. "So you do speak English. I was told you had virtually no English. Well, this will go swimmingly, I think!"

She made him introduce himself to her, however he liked; he was not to worry about proper sentences or anything like that. And she wanted him to speak about anything he wanted, to forget

the formal introductions and talk about any aspect of his life—
just so that she could get an idea of who he was. For example, her
name was Liz, and when she was young her brothers used to call
her Lizzie the Lizard, such a childish name, thank God it didn't
stick. She loved the sea, which is why she liked Hong Kong, its
proximity to water. Water, water everywhere. Wonderful. She
loved boats—sailing. She was forty years old. Yes, very old by,
especially by, Chinese standards, and unmarried. *Remaindered,*
that's what they called women like her in China, ha ha. She was
born in Britain, on the south coast. When she was young she
could see the sea from her bedroom, sailboats on the water.

When Yanzu spoke she held his gaze, nodding. She did not
correct him, allowed him to stumble, said, "Really? Wow!" a few
times, her eyes widening with surprise at the things he told her—
things that he can't now remember, banal things. She had lines at
the edges of her eyes that creased when she smiled.

9.

They went on outings. It was better to practice your language in
real-life situations, she said; language isn't a dead thing.

She made him order cakes and coffees at the Starbucks in the
lobby of his office building. Yanzu felt strange speaking English
to the Chinese kids behind the counter; he could see them straining to understand him. Two coffees, please. What *kind?* Normal
kind. Their earnest frowns unsettled him. Why was a Chinese
guy speaking to them in broken English? One of them tested him
with pidgin Japanese, her expression brightening as if expecting
greater comprehension. He nodded, still without understanding.
The girl behind the counter was only a teenager, but he could see
her polite serving-staff smile turn first to bemusement and then,
swiftly, to scorn. From her vantage point midway between the
revolving-door entrance and the lifts, she would be able to see
him come in every morning, dressed in his expensive suits and

carrying the new calfskin attaché case Violet had given him; and she would giggle each time she saw him because she would know that he couldn't even say what *kind* of coffee he wanted.

He turned back to look at Liz; she smiled and nodded encouragement. They sat down at the little round tables and had their lessons there, away from his office, surrounded by teenagers surfing the net on their laptops. There was breezy music with guitars playing in the background, and Yanzu thought he could understand the words of the chorus.

She took him to a café, just off Hollywood Road, run by a friend of hers. His English was coming along in *leaps and bounds,* she said, but he needed to use it in new situations, speak to other people; he was getting too accustomed to her speech patterns. The owner of the place was there when they arrived, an Italian. "Darling," he said, his vowels expansive and confident. He leaned in to kiss her on both cheeks, his hand resting on her waist even after she had pulled away a little. "I haven't seen you for months— where have you been?"

"Franco, this is my new student," she said, moving aside to introduce Yanzu. "Actually, not that new anymore. We're going to have our lesson here today—isn't that fun?"

They were shown to a table in a quiet corner, from which Liz could survey the rest of the room. Yanzu could look only at her; the wall above her head was painted with a grapevine trailing through a pergola. She was talking excitedly, flitting from one subject to another—about things on the menu, how they reminded her of trips to Italy; about the impending typhoon moving across from the Philippines; the new scooter she was thinking of buying. Occasionally she would wave at someone but Yanzu did not turn round. He felt comfortable like this, visible yet unseen. He liked the idea of people wondering who Liz was having lunch with; the possibility of recognition emboldened him. As he watched her trace her finger down the wine list he realized that she, too, was excited by the novelty of being here with him in this shady alcove.

There was a glinting quality to her laughter, a sunniness he had not discerned before.

"It's been an eternity since anyone took me out to lunch," she said. "Although I suppose this is technically a lesson and not a social occasion!" She closed the wine list and then brought it to her chest, holding it against her as if guarding a secret.

"Why don't we pretend this is a date?" she said at last, smiling, the corners of her eyes creasing into crow's feet. "Is that all right with you? It'll be more fun that way. You're going to do all the ordering, communicating with the waiters—everything. Just take charge!"

He took his time studying the menu. Each item was accompanied by a brief explanation; it wasn't so difficult to understand what everything was. The waiter, another Italian, took the order without fuss. Liz whispered, "Your English is *miles* better than his."

At home that evening, he tried not to sound boastful as he related this triumphant episode to Violet, but there was no disguising it: he heard the pride in his own voice as he repeated what Liz had said, in English.

"Your English has definitely improved," Violet said. "She sounds like a good teacher. Is she old? She looks old. That's what your PA says."

10.

Yanzu cannot pinpoint the exact moment their affair began. Was it the accidental meeting of fingers—an awkward clash—over the bread basket? Or perhaps while waiting in the cab rank at rush hour, feeling the first heavy drops of rain that would soon become a thunderstorm, foreshadowing the typhoons that would come later in the summer. Or did it occur in the middle of a sentence, when, arranging subject, object and verb, he found that everything fell into place and he was finally *speaking?*

Beijing is a city that I miss. I miss Beijing. It is cold but beautiful in the winter. It is where I grew up.

Yes, I understand.

Really?

Yes. It's difficult being far from home. It's hard for me too. You're doing really well—carry on.

Hong Kong does not suit me neither. Hong Kong does not suit me either. I am not, not—sorry. I don't know the word.

As he fell into silence Yanzu recognized in the expression on her face a quality he knew too well: she was alone in a foreign place, and this is why she would fall into a relationship with him.

11.

"Come to my book club," she said one day.

They had slept together four or five times by then, usually in the afternoon when it was easy for him to be away from the office. They got together in her cramped apartment in Happy Valley, their ankles and wrists and elbows knocking painfully against the bookshelves that stood on either side of the bed, only a foot away. Her bed smelled of milk. They lay naked, on top of the rumpled sheets, listening to the air conditioner drip onto the ledge outside the window, a staccato *ta-tap,* a miswired heartbeat. When he looked at her, he thought he could see the same expression of solitude he had recognized at the beginning: she was adrift, and this comforted him.

It was July now and the air-conditioning was too weak to cool them properly.

At first their times together felt like a gift which he accepted gleefully, childishly, but like all children, he soon wanted more, and when she turned down his dinner invitations he was surprised by the strength of his disappointment, by how quickly he had outgrown the newfound thrills of their midafternoons together. He wanted to go out with her, *accompany* her. The excitement of their outing to the Italian restaurant remained with him, but that had not technically been a date, as she had pointed out at the time. He needed to correct that imperfection. In the rest of his life he would not have tolerated this lack of satisfaction. He thought of how he behaved in meetings, calmly insisting on the execution of every last detail, on the absolute nature of success. It was the only way he knew how to conduct himself. Yet now he was staring at a ragged mass of unachieved aims, staring at failure.

He wanted to know her foreign friends, wanted to risk being seen with her; he wanted to be part of her life. He tried to ignore the prick of annoyance he felt at her evasiveness and his inability to pin her down. "Restaurants in Hong Kong are such terrible value," she said, "certainly the ones you're suggesting. Bad French food at those prices? In this heat? I don't think so. Much prefer some back street noodle shop. That's more my style. No *gwailos* around."

When she had friends visiting from abroad, she never explained who they were.

Sometimes she promised to call but didn't.

He would text but get no reply.

She would forget to turn her phone back on, or fall asleep early—sorry, so disorganized, so tired.

When, therefore, she unexpectedly issued the invitation to her book club, Yanzu was not sure if it was a battle he had won, if he had bent her to his will, or if it was merely a favor she was granting. But it didn't matter. As she wrote the address down on a piece of paper and handed it to him, he tried to feign nonchalance. He kept the piece of paper folded in his wallet all week, looking at it from time to time to check that he had memorized the address. At the top of the torn-off fragment of paper it said "Conduit Road Ladies' Reading Group."

It was just to practice his comprehension skills, she'd said; he could just sit and listen, see how much of the discussion he could understand—an extended, relaxed lesson. But he knew it was not merely an informal class—it was a declaration of sorts, her way of showing that she, too, wanted a more public existence with him.

He arrived late that evening—a meeting that had gone on too long. Liz winked at him and raised her glass when he came in, but there was no space next to her, so he had to slump on a beanbag on the far side of the room. There were five women there, spread out over a sofa and two armchairs; four nearly empty bottles of wine stood on an Indian chest in the middle of the room. Yanzu tried to scribble down words and expressions that he'd never heard before, especially when Liz spoke. She was speaking with a freedom and rapidity he found unfamiliar—with him she was deliberate, careful, caring. Here she rushed ahead, talking over everyone else, which made him smile at first; but soon he found he could not keep up with what she or anyone else was saying. Sometimes one of them would raise her voice, insisting on a point; other times they would all break into laughter, sharp and brilliant as shattering glass, but Yanzu would never be sure of the reason for their disagreement or joy. He would discern individual words here and there, the odd phrase, but all of a sudden, Liz was no longer speaking a language he could understand—the language they had shared. Occasionally she would catch his eye and smile—a flash, here now, then gone—but then her attention was swept up again by her friends, the book, the wine: her life. None of the others looked at Yanzu, and yet he continued to pretend to jot down notes, and sometimes even nod as if in agreement. He looked at what he had written: lines remembered from his lessons, nothing to do with where he was now.

There was a lull in the conversation, someone flicking through the pages of the book. Liz looked at him, and he thought maybe this was the moment she would introduce him to her friends; maybe someone would ask him what kind of work he did, where he was from. Answers to imaginary questions began to form in his head. I am the CEO of a group of companies I founded myself. Yes, I suppose you could consider me successful. Our turnover? Oh I don't know, I'd have to check with my PA. No, no, of course I'm not a billionaire, but I'm *comfortable*. Property, mainly, and renewable energy, but I'm always open to new ideas. I am building a house in Clearwater Bay, designed by a famous architect. Right now I live on the South Side of the island. Yes, it is very agreeable there.

But the woman found what she was looking for and began to read. It began with "The passage of time . . ."

That was all Yanzu could discern before the words and the conversation began to slip away again.

The answers he had prepared remained poised on the tip of his tongue; he could feel the words rest there, heavy, redundant. He looked at Liz. She was talking loudly, both arms waving, her face flushed with wine. He had been wrong. She was not lonely in Hong Kong, she was bored. She was a foreigner, she was passing through, she was bored, she wanted adventure. That is why she was with him.

12.

"Is it safe?"

"Yes, of course it's safe to swim, you big sissy, just jump." She raised one hand out of the murky sea and tried to splash him. If her swimsuit had not been bright yellow he would not have been able to make out her body. The smog was thick and he could not make out whether her face was pulled into a smile or a frown. He hesitated, pressing his foot against the rope that ran in a low circle along the side of the deck. "The water looks cold," he said.

The yacht was anchored in the shelter of a small bay; the island was small, rocky, unapproachable; its vegetation a drab green. The water seemed dark to Yanzu's eyes, almost opaque. He looked at Liz in the quiet sea, bobbing gently, as she kicked to stay afloat. She was still waving at him, her arm popping out of the water now and then, like a toy, something inanimate. They were far from the noise of Central, far from all the *gwailos* she claimed to detest, even though she was one herself; far from all the things she hated. They were alone at last.

She had borrowed the yacht from a friend. "Oh, someone you don't know," she'd said with a merest shrug of her shoulders, a gesture that did not countenance further discussion of the matter. "Just concentrate—the sooner we motor off the better. God, you look adorable in your life jacket!"

He listened as she gave him the safety brief, how to turn the engine on and off, how to work the radio and fire the flares—he would need to know these things, just in case she fell overboard and drowned, she said, or if she got hit on the head and fell unconscious. It would be up to him, then, to keep them alive. They would float, undrifting, on the cold foamy water, swallowed by sea mists, the tops of the high-rises jutting just over the peaks of the steeply sloped islands around them, frustratingly out of reach. And when they perished—from dehydration and exhaustion—their story would be one of those freak tragedies that filled the nether pages of the *South China Morning Post,* sandwiched between world news and features, one of those chilling but faintly comic episodes that people would talk about in the office for days afterwards: did you hear, those people died, were *shipwrecked,* just five miles from Chek Lap Kok; and in the gutter press there would be speculation—maybe they were lovers, why else would they be out there, alone. And some people would wonder: who died first, and was he or she forced into cannibalism?

"Will you pay attention?" she yelled from the helm. "I said cast off *aft*. No, the back—the other end, at the back!"

He stumbled over ropes, bruised his knee on a hard metallic thing whose purpose he couldn't discern, felt his leg deaden, then tingle. He did not know where to place himself, whether to stand or sit. When they were clear of the harbor she gave the order to hoist the sails, but as he fumbled with them she darted beside him, nimble, her face flushed with concentration and he could tell that she was impatient to be free and on the move, impatient to be beyond the reach of land. The wind picked up, swelling the mainsail, and she let out a cry, a *woooo yeaa* as they cut through the waves. He wiped the spray from his face and turned back to look at the marina receding slowly into nothingness. He knew he ought to feel exhilarated, but didn't. Couldn't. He tried to remember what she had told him but still he wound the rope the wrong way round the winch. He was a smart guy; this shouldn't be happening, he thought. He had thought he understood her when she spoke, followed her crystalline vowels and steady rhythms, but now she spoke in a language that left him for dead. Tack, ready about, helm's a-lee. Let draw. She repeated things, cheerily at first, encouraging, then briskly, as if he were a hindrance, which—there was no point denying it—he was. "Never mind, I'll do it," she said, and he knew that her smile was a pretense, betrayed by the frown that cut deep ruts in her brow.

They sailed through the low cloud and smog that was especially thick that day, obscuring the cheap tower blocks that lined the shore, arranged in dense rows that backed on to each other in terraces. Stretches of mud lay exposed on the hills, bulldozers perched on the slopes. Pile drivers and pylons jutted from the indistinct landscape, but he could hear no noise, just the rushing of the wind. They were leaving all this behind now, sailing further into the fog. It was better like this, he thought, better that he could not see what he was venturing into. He realized that he was in her hands, that she could take him anywhere she wanted, and that would have to be okay with him. Maybe that had always been her idea.

It was his task to drop the anchor, she said; of course she trusted him. "You're doing just fine."

He watched it slither off the deck, disappearing noiselessly, serpentine, into the water.

"All gone?" she cried from the helm. "Is it holding?"

He shouted something—not really a yes, nothing committal, enough to make her think he had done his job, enough to assuage her.

The yacht took its time to settle, even though there were no waves in the inlet, just a low swelling of the sea now and then, never breaking the surface.

Of course there were things that he wanted to discuss with her, for example: did she think they could possibly have a life together; did she think about him when they were not together; whether she would stay in Hong Kong for much longer; the fact that he was planning to divorce his wife; all the places he wanted to visit with her, the countless lists of countries and sights he had drawn up, including Beijing, which he wanted to return to after all these years, now that things had changed there—now that he had changed. They were silly things that were not easy to say in the middle of an English lesson when he was trying to remember the difference between object and subject and clause and subclause. As they sat cross-legged on the deck eating their prepacked BLT sandwiches, she began to talk and he could not find an opportunity to interject. The fog reminded her of her childhood, she said, of all the times she went sailing with her father in the Channel. It wasn't fog, Yanzu said, it was actually pollution. But she ignored this, said it didn't matter, it looked like fog. She had learned to sail when she was very young, and her father would take her across to France, to places like Honfleur and Deauville and Le Havre. She could still remember those little towns of sheltered harbors and cobbled streets and shops that sold fancy chocolates that nowadays one could buy in Hong Kong. Tiny overheated cafés that served mussels and crepes, the damp mustiness of her cabin, the smell of seawater and creosote, the warmth of her sleeping bag. Back then it seemed so magical. She remembered, in her teens, sailing back from Brittany and getting lost in thick fog at night. All of a sudden the weather closed in, the wind rose violently and there was heavy rain. She couldn't see anything except for the occasional glint in the dark when the raindrops caught the light from the cabin below; but all the time she could feel the freezing spray on her face and her hands, numbing her fingers. Her father was getting older then, and was afraid. But she had not been scared, she had loved the sensation of not knowing where they were. It had emboldened her, made her sure of herself. She knew it sounded stupid but she loved the feeling of being between places, of being nowhere. It made her feel she could go anywhere, anytime she wanted, on her own. She would never be pinned down; she would always be her own woman, never dependent on anyone. Being on that yacht had made her realize she would always hate a sedentary life. Sedentary, it means, um, staying in one place, inactive, boring, that sort of thing. She could never stay anywhere or be with anyone for too long. She wanted constant adventure, moving from one place to another.

"Right, well, enough of all that—let's swim!" she announced, peeling off her T-shirt to reveal her yellow swimming costume.

He had never learned to swim properly but he could keep afloat, and he did not fear the water. She splashed inelegantly but powerfully, kicking up a froth, and occasionally she would call out to him, a whooping carefree cry of jubilation. He stayed near the boat, lurking in the safety of its shadow, hanging on to the foot of the ladder until she swam up to him and put her arms round his neck. She kissed him on the lips but her legs, treading water, bumped into him, so—gently—she wrapped her legs around his waist. The weight of her body pulled him gently away from the boat and she giggled as he let go of his grip and they sank-bobbled on the water, their wet embrace becoming half-submerged. He kept his head above the water as she clung to him, both of them kicking to keep afloat now. She was laughing. Her skin was very pale against the darkness of the water. He held her tightly, and suddenly he felt the weightlessness of her body in the water, felt the strength of his arms against her. He wrapped his legs around her, as she had done to him earlier, and felt her sink with his weight slightly, her tiny descent immeasurable to an observer standing on the shore, he thought. His placed his hands on her shoulders and pushed downwards, her head vanishing under the water, her grin swallowed by the sea; underwater, her shoulders felt bony in his armlock. He could hold her down there and she would never come up; he could do that for as long as he wanted. That would make the newspapers too, for sure; the gutter press would dig into his personal life and everyone would talk about it at work. There would be no doubt: everyone would know they had been lovers. What a way for it to end, it was so sad, but I told you, that guy might have been successful but he wasn't quite right *up there,* he'd been in Tiananmen, maybe it messed up his head. Anyway, he was a Mainlander, what can you expect—he never quite fit in. That's what people would say when his love affair became public. He felt her struggle, kick out against him, her arms pushing at his chest with the feebleness of someone who knows they are trapped, helpless. I was just playing, he would say later, just . . . fooling around. Like kids do. She would say, Jesus, what were you doing, you nearly drowned me, you idiot, and she would slap him on his buttocks as she sometimes did, an invitation to foreplay. He closed his eyes and saw her floating away, like a picture she had once shown him, a famous painting of a princess who had drowned herself after being rejected by her loved one, a crazed prince. He had forgotten the name of the painting, even though she had written the name of it for him; but he remembered clearly the milky-white skin against the black, unmoving water.

And now, months later, when he remembers those last moments with her—a few seconds during which, in a strange way, he felt closer to her than he had ever been—he still cannot recall the name of the painting, and this frustrates him.

Ann Beattie
Anecdotes

MY HUSBAND AND I were in Tivoli, and we went to the gardens at Villa d'Este. He'd been to Italy before, but it was my first trip. There were rails in front of the fountains because the water was so polluted, they wanted to keep you from being splashed."

"I went to Italy when they were almost giving shoes away—shoes made of leather as soft as gloves—and there were no tours being given of the Forum. I don't think there was one Japanese tourist in all of Rome. Maybe my trip was before cameras were invented."

Lucia and I were playing the Italy-One-Upmanship game in the back seat of a Carey car. I knew I was going to be the one to pay the fare. I was doing my friend Christine a favor. Lucia, her mother, had come in from Princeton on the train to hear Christine's talk at Columbia about Margaret Bourke-White. Christine would also be showing slides of newly discovered photographs, printed from Bourke-White negatives that had been mislabeled at *Life*. She was hoping to be hired full-time at Columbia and this was one of several talks she would be giving there and elsewhere, aiming to impress.

Christine had hoped to be a model when she came to the city, but she'd been diagnosed with diabetes shortly thereafter and hadn't been able to keep up the pace. There were still problems with her energy; she felt like she was having what she'd heard were classic menopausal symptoms at thirty-four. She was pretty, though, as you'd imagine. I'd met her in college when we'd been two-timed by the same guy, who also happened to be our professor. I overheard the tantrum she threw, late one evening. I'd gone back to school because I'd forgotten my raincoat, and the forecast was for a weekend of rain. Arthur was in his office; Christine was yelling, and as I came up the stairs, I heard my name mentioned. Loudly. She and I went to a bar when she'd finished confronting him. He went home to his wife. Christine and I lost touch, but met up several years later in New York, when she called to compliment me on an article I'd written for the *New York Times Magazine*.

Earlier in the week Christine had asked me to pick up her mother before she realized that my car was in the repair shop (hit from behind at a red light on West End Avenue), and she probably also called because I did better with her mother, generally, than she did.

"Let me ask you this, Anna," Lucia said. "Was there a moment you knew your marriage wasn't going to work, or was it more gradual, the realization?"

"He took the puppy back to the breeder. That didn't help."

"You always say something unexpected. That's why you're a good writer, I guess. Let me ask this: do you think Christine didn't marry Paul because all her women friends are independent, or do you think she just got tired of him? He sent me a Christmas card, and his heart is still broken."

I thought, for a moment, about poor broken-hearted Paul. Though ostensibly monogamous for the three-plus years he and Christine lived together, he'd given her herpes. Another thing I knew about him was that he'd put a pillow over his head and stayed in bed the night she had food poisoning. I also thought that when she stopped wearing make-up and pulled her hair back in a French twist, the little tendrils that escaped still didn't make her feminine enough for him. He'd kept a picture of her from her modeling days in his wallet.

"Lucia," I said, "I don't think women break up with their boy-friends because other women are without boyfriends."

"But think: the diabetes made her angry, didn't it? She wanted somebody to take it away. I find significance in the fact that she started to go out with her doctor."

"You're as funny as I am," I said. "Shall I recommend you to my agent?"

"Funny? Nothing funny about that awful disease," she said, missing my point, because she found it necessary to correct every-one.

"Which side?" the driver said.

"On the right," I said. "Far corner."

He gave me a quick look in the rear-view mirror; the light had just turned red, and by the time he got to the far corner, cars in back of him would start honking the minute he stopped.

The young man setting up the slide projector looked up, think-ing one of us must be the speaker. He held a clip-on mike, awk-wardly, as if courting someone with a little unwanted flower.

Lucia sat in a chair midway down the aisle. She looked vaguely irritated, or simply tired. She had not wanted Christine to be a model, but neither had she wanted her to be in the academic world, which Lucia felt was full of pseudo-intellectuals hiding from society. As far as I could tell, Lucia had some vague notion that her daughter should be working outside the system, to save the world.

"Wasn't this scheduled for seven?" I said. "Where is every-body?"

"I'm just here to set up," the young man said. "You've got noth-ing to do with this?"

I shook my head. That was so often my situation with Christine: she insisted I was indispensable, though I had nothing directly to do with what was going on. In school, I hadn't known she was seeing Arthur, but when I found out, she insisted that we have a drink, because only I could fill in the pieces of the puzzle.

Lucia had taken off her enormous scarf—cashmere, certainly—and folded it on her lap, her hands clasped on top. She looked at me with quiet attention, as if I might start singing. Her hair, streaked with silver, was windblown. The way the wind had messed up her part made her look less austere. Where Christine had gotten her cheekbones from, and her lips, I couldn't imagine. (Her father had left before Christine began school and I'd only seen him once in a snapshot she carried in her wallet.) Lucia was attractive, but in a quite ordinary way. Like many women her age, she diverted attention from her face by swirling scarves around her throat and shoulders, wearing big necklaces or turtlenecks that seemed like perfect soufflés just lifted from the oven. I was rummaging in my bag, trying to find the piece of paper on which I'd written the time and place. Yes; the talk was taking place here—that's what I'd written down—at 7:00 p.m.

Suddenly there were voices in the corridor, and students rushed in like horses spooked by firecrackers. There had been another lecture—this was part two of their evening. I stared into the crowd, hoping to see Christine. The person who'd set up the slide projector paced the aisle, talking on his cellphone. The microphone sat in a tangle of wires back on the table.

Lucia beckoned to me. I walked back a few rows, jostled by students—though I noticed none of them had disturbed the elderly lady who sat in the aisle seat, her garments piled in her lap. She had slipped out of her coat, which was a shade somewhere between beige and butter.

"Listen: you have always been such a good friend to Christine that I want to tell you something. Will you sit?" She patted the chair next to her.

Almost none of the students seemed to be wearing winter

clothes. A few had on unzipped jackets. I sat next to Lucia, carefully stepping over her elegant shoes.

"Here is what I want to talk about," Lucia said. "You remember Thanksgiving in Princeton? I pointed out my neighbor—the lady who had been so sweet on the visiting writer?"

"Vaguely," I said.

"Vaguely! I made an apple tart from scratch, with crème fraiche!"

"It was delicious. Your meals always are. I just couldn't remember the face of the woman who'd—what? She'd written love notes to him, or something? To the writer?"

"She wanted him to come live there. She said, 'Bring your wife, there is a whole separate house. Don't commute the way you do, it will wear you out. I love having young people around. I will teach your wife to cook—whatever she wants.' Which is true, by the way. Edwina cooks better than I do."

"I didn't know all that. I think you whispered to me who she was. That she'd made trouble by writing letters to him, or something."

"She wrote letters, and he finally came over to have a drink. They hit it off, and he decided he and his wife should take her up on her offer."

"So what happened?" I said.

"His wife got on a small chartered plane in Michigan, and that was the end of her. It went down in a storm, the pilot killed, everybody. Two other people, I think. And he came over to Edwina's house and picked up bricks from the new walkway that was being laid and threw them through her picture window. The police were called. He was completely crazy. He couldn't ever go back to teach his classes. And Edwina was devastated."

Christine had come into the auditorium. From nowhere, the man with the tangled microphone charged up to her, getting much too close, so that before she understood who he was, she jumped back. She had a bag bulging with things slung over her shoulder, and carried another bag. It must have started raining, because her hair was matted to her head. A clump of it curved down her cheek like the top of a big question mark. Her earring stud might have been the point that completed the punctuation.

"Your friend shouldn't feel bad," I said. "You're right. It wasn't her fault, of course."

"Yes, but she thinks it was," Lucia said. She did not follow my eyes to Christine.

I waved. Christine didn't see me at first, but then she did. "There she is," I said to Lucia, wondering why she wasn't turning as I waved.

"What I understand of the situation is that he'd slept with Edwina once. She's old enough to be his mother! She was offering her home anyway, so I don't think he was calculating . . ."

A girl and a boy pushed past us, trailing jackets. The girl had on pink Uggs.

I stood to walk toward Christine, who looked a little disoriented. When she saw me, she gave me a nervous smile. She said, "I washed my hair, and my dryer broke. Can you believe it?"

"That's awful," I said.

"Thanks for getting her," Christine said, squeezing my shoulder as she walked past, the microphone already clipped to her lapel, the receptor in her coat pocket. "Hi, Mom," she said, smiling, but not bending to kiss her mother's cheek. They were more affectionate privately, I'd noticed. In public, there was some awkwardness.

The row Lucia sat in was almost full. She frowned as more students pushed past her seat. It was a small auditorium, but this was a good crowd.

Christine stood behind the podium, her coat tossed on a chair, the bags slumped beside it.

"The person who was going to introduce me has laryngitis, so I'm just going to introduce myself—I'm Christine Liss, from the English department—and thank you for coming on such a cold night. There is exciting new work by the eminent photographer Margaret Bourke-White I've gotten access to as it's being catalogued, some of which you'll see tonight. Ms. Bourke-White was a fearless photographer who did the first cover for *Life* magazine—a very influential picture magazine of its time, with a reputation that still elicits great respect. She worked downtown, in the then newly built Chrysler Building—a building with a terrace where she kept two small alligators she was given as gifts, until they grew large enough to devour the tortoise she had also been given. Some people wouldn't visit the studio. She was married twice, the last time to Erskine Caldwell, whose name might not be as recognizable to you now as he would have hoped. Her photographs can be seen many places in New York—currently, at ICP Midtown. What you're going to see tonight are mostly aerial shots . . ."

I should probably have returned to sit with Lucia, but I'd trailed Christine halfway down the aisle, and when the lights began to dim, I sat, as if I'd been playing musical chairs. Down the row, someone was videotaping Christine, the little square of light distracting and mesmerizing. Rows back, a cellphone played music and was quickly turned off. The projection screen was filled with aerial views of destruction: Germany, after the war.

Christine's hair had begun to dry, and she looked different, with her hair down and her glasses on. Her earnestness made her look younger, and took me back to the bar where we'd sat in Pennsylvania years ago. Christine cursing Arthur, pulling a necklace with a lapis stone out from under the neckline of her blouse, pulling so hard she broke the chain, the gold puddling on the tabletop, the little stone flashing in the fluorescent light. She had scooped it up and later addressed an envelope to Arthur's wife and mailed it to her without comment.

Slide after slide, when seen from a high vantage point, the world was transformed into abstract art. The photographs were pattern and shape before they became slowly distinguishable as the landscape—the wreckage—they depicted then; as you stared, they devolved into abstraction again, making your eyes skate figure eights. Margaret Bourke-White had no fear of heights, Christine told us, and couldn't have worried about being in a helicopter when she thought nothing of crawling out on the gargoyles atop the Chrysler Building to photograph the city. There she was, bent over her camera, high up, like a steelworker. She photographed machines. She photographed Stalin, who didn't give her an inch until she nervously dropped her flashbulbs, and then he laughed.

Christine talked about industry, mass production. She talked about photographs in black and white, about silver halide crystals, and how photographs were processed. The images at the end of the talk were back in the world—dams and wheels, enormous things. When the lights came on, people applauded. Christine smiled, unclipping the mike, pushing her hair out of her eyes. A few people called out to each other; cellphones appeared immediately, hats and scarves were left behind, picked up by someone else who ran up behind them, like a relay race in reverse. I saw one of Christine's colleagues, whose name I couldn't remember, and said hello. "God, Bourke-White photographed Stalin's *mother*, you know. I'd think *that* was a dangerous assignment—unless the guy didn't like his mother. And since he didn't like anybody . . ." He shook his head as he passed by to congratulate Christine. The person operating the slide projector was removing the tray, putting it in a box, his cellphone clamped between his chin and shoulder. Lucia stood, her row empty.

"Why do they wear those boots like horse hooves?" she said, looking at the departing students. "Pastel-pink horse hooves."

"Comfortable, I guess," I said. "Sort of like big bedroom slippers. They love pajama bottoms, too."

"It used to be that every generation had its style. I guess this generation's style is what you'd wear if you spent your day in the bedroom. In my day, that would have been a negligee and makeup, which is just as silly, I suppose."

"What a fascinating talk Christine gave," I said.

"Too many anecdotes," Lucia said.

I looked at her, surprised. She was often hard on Christine, but the talk had obviously been so good, I hadn't been expecting such a remark.

"It doesn't matter how many husbands a woman has, or doesn't have. I don't know why she felt she had to mention that," she said. "I thought she was going to digress and tell us about the man she loved the most, a soldier she was going to reunite with, except that he was in a military hospital in Italy, and they bombed his wing of the hospital. The other wing was intact, but he was killed instantly."

"You know about Margaret Bourke-White?" I said.

"I read autobiographies, Anna. It's all there in her book."

"Well, I thought Christine did a very good job, talking about how Bourke-White got into the workforce, and—"

"Getting the job done is what's important. Not how you got the job."

"You're too hard on her," I said.

She looked at me. "Do you think so? I just don't have much patience with anecdotes."

"She was explaining that Margaret Bourke-White had a lot of sadness in her life, just like the rest of us."

"Yes, I think we could assume that everyone experiences sadness," Lucia replied.

I thought: why do you never offer to pay, like you're a princess? Why not arrange your own transportation in the city? Why don't you cook your own Thanksgiving dinner for fewer people, rather than having two Mexican women in the kitchen all day, and you making only your perfect apple tarts?

My face must have clouded over; she put her hand on my arm and said, "Sit down for a second. We're friends, you and I. I have something important to tell you."

I sank, rather than sat. Was she going to tell me she was sick?

She had seated herself one chair in, giving me the aisle, gesturing grandly, as if the seat were a gift. The last cluster of students stood talking to Christine.

"You're a writer. Writers have become celebrities, haven't they? Whether they want to be or not. Well, the visiting writer did want to be the center of attention, it seemed to me. Writers are so often insecure. So let me tell you: in my one conversation with him, it seems he'd never even heard that Bruce Chatwin hadn't told the whole truth, and nothing but the truth. Didn't know Chatwin had made things up—including the information about what killed him, we now know. If I'd talked about James Frey, I suppose I could have made some of the same points. From what the visiting writer revealed about himself, I thought he was a literary lightweight. I wouldn't have offered him, and his wife, my house. But that's neither here nor there. Edwina, my friend, has been taking one of those mood-altering drugs, and she's calmer now, so she understands she isn't responsible, but you know, she'd gotten to the point where she imagined him and his wife in her house. She imagined them sitting by the fireplace, she looked at her window and saw the shattered glass even though it had been replaced, she saw the dead woman standing in the kitchen doing dishes—she didn't really *see* her, she's not crazy, but she imagined her. I told her, Come to my house. Get out of there; get out of that environment for a while. I guess I did just what she did, didn't I, offering my house? But she was impulsive, and I was her friend of more than twenty-five years. So it came as quite a surprise to both of us that we fell in love. We did. Your eyes are as big as saucers, Anna. If we did, we did."

I nodded, registering the beginning of a faint headache as I narrowed my eyes.

"Writers like to surprise readers, but they don't like to be surprised, I've found." She grasped my wrist. "Here is why I'm telling you: I'm going to tell Christine about it and I think it's going to come as something of a shock for her, so I wanted you to know, before we have our drink. You knew we were going to the Carlyle, where I'm staying tonight, the three of us, to have a drink?"

"I don't think she told me," I said, though as I spoke, I vaguely remembered Christine saying something. More as a possibility, though. Her phone call to me a couple of days before had been on the run, pleading: "I've got to teach, then run home and walk Walter, then get back to give the talk, so can you please, *please,* meet her train and see that she gets there okay?"

Lucia could book a room at an expensive hotel, but not offer to pay for the car? She wanted . . . what? For me to be prepared, in case her daughter became (improbably) a basket case, when she told her? I wished she hadn't told me. I wasn't pleased about knowing this information before Christine did. It would make a liar of me if I pretended what I was hearing was news, and I'd be her mother's confidante if I let on that she'd already told me.

"This is private. It's between you and your daughter," I said. "I'm going to go home and let you two talk."

"No, Anna, you have to join us," she said.

"You want an audience, just like those writers you're so suspicious of," I said. "I'd wonder, if I were you, whether he ever slept with your friend, or whether that wasn't her imagination, too. You hear about it when a person has a reputation for sleeping around," I said. "I doubt that it's true."

I had met his wife at a fund-raiser. She'd quickly confessed she felt out of place, and didn't know what to talk about. Her pin had fallen on the floor, that was how we'd met. I'd bent to pick it up, and had helped her fasten it to the collar of her silky black shirt again. When her husband the writer saw us talking, he came up to us. I could tell by the way he put his arm around his wife's shoulder that he worried I might be too much for her, in some way. They'd both grown up in the Midwest, and I'd grown up on the Upper West Side—which was no doubt why Pennsylvania had seemed like Siberia to me in my college days. I'd liked the writer's protectiveness, and I'd picked up on the fact that he wanted his wife to talk to people on her own, but the minute she did, he wanted to make sure she was comfortable. When he saw that we were giggling and talking about jewelery, he'd gone away.

"Anna?" Lucia said. "You seem to have turned your attention inward. If I didn't know you so well, I might think I'd surprised you."

"I don't care who you have a relationship with," I said. "If you really care what I think about lesbianism, I approve of whatever relationship brings people happiness."

I walked away, up the aisle. When I was younger, I would have bought into it, assumed I was involved, just because someone older insisted I be. Now, I thought how nice it would be to listen to music I wanted to listen to, instead of the tinkling piano at the hotel. I wouldn't feel I had to offer to pay for my own drink, because I'd already paid earlier in the week, when I bought myself a bottle of Grey Goose I could pour from, into my favourite etched glass I'd bought at a stoop sale in Brooklyn. What would Christine think of me disappearing? Maybe that I was smart. I wondered how Lucia would lead into the subject. By criticizing Christine for being "anecdotal," then zinging her with an important fact? Lucia was self-important and manipulative, and if Christine didn't know that by now I could mention the obvious, by way of consolation, later.

Outside, I turned the corner and went into my favorite Chinese restaurant. There were only two tables, both taken, so I went to the counter for takeout. "Anna!" Wang, the waiter, said, turning the paper menu toward him, pencil poised delicately, like a conductor's baton, to circle what I wanted.

"You don't know she wants shrimp fried rice?" his brother, who was now known as James, said. James was taking night classes at NYU and sometimes asked me for help with his homework. "Once, twice a month she has chicken with broccoli, but tonight she doesn't want that. This is her look when she's in a hurry. In a hurry, always shrimp fried rice." He smiled a big smile and circled the correct item and handed the piece of paper through the opening into the kitchen. "Great reading in my course. The poetry of William Butler Yeats. Next time we'll talk," James said.

Wang had walked away from the counter and was standing at one of the tables, where a customer with his hands folded on top of his violin case on the shiny tabletop seemed to be giving him a bad time about the beer not being cold enough.

When I left, I held the paper bag away from my coat (I always worried I'd stain it). I'd splurged on the coat three years before, a mid-calf cashmere coat I'd resolved I'd take good care of and wear for years. Every time I slipped into it, it felt possible something good could happen.

In my apartment, no husband, no Walter the dog awaited me. Instead of a pet, I had a terrarium with small plastic knights inside, some on horseback, some felled, some still fighting on AstroTurf sprinkled with red nail polish—a gift from a boyfriend who'd been a disaster, though he'd had a great sense of humor. I took off my coat, reached in the pocket, ripped up the receipt for the car and threw it in the trash, so I wouldn't be tempted to do something mean, like send it to Lucia. Christine was still my friend, though I was free of her mother now. I'd been without a family for almost ten years, and I didn't want a replacement, with all the inevitable surprises and secrets. The more I thought about it, the more sure I was that the writer hadn't slept with Lucia's friend, but that Lucia's neighbor/lover was on the make, and if she couldn't have the writer, she'd decided to move on to Lucia. I was glad he'd thrown a brick through her window, glad she'd had at least a moment of fear, that someone had created a little havoc in her so-well-intentioned Princeton life.

I sipped the vodka, admiring the glass, enjoying the taste. And then—though this is merely anecdotal—I picked up the phone, called information, and asked for Arthur's number in Pennsylvania from an operator who said, "Please hold," followed by an automated voice that gave me the number. He still lived in the same place. Imagine that: he was where he'd been all his adult life.

Arthur's wife answered on the second ring. She answered pleasantly, the way people did years ago, when there was no screening of calls, no answering machine to kick in. "Hello," she said, and I thought: she is completely, *completely* vulnerable. The winter landscape of the little town outside Pittsburgh where she lived came back to me: the whited-out sky; the frozen branches always about to snap. If I hung up, she probably wouldn't even know there was such a thing as hitting *69 to find out who the caller was. Or maybe she would, and she'd call back. Maybe she and I would talk, and become fierce enemies, or even best friends— why not, if neighbors in their sixties became lovers? But that couldn't really happen, because she and I were just two voices on the telephone. I didn't have anything against her. Back then, all I'd had against her was that she had him.

"That necklace," I said, realizing immediately that I needed to raise my voice and speak clearly. "The one with the lapis lazuli. I was your husband's student—it doesn't matter who I am. I'm calling to explain. I returned it to you in 1994 because I found it on the floor of his office, and knew it must be yours. He didn't see me pick it up. I was poor, and I wanted to keep it, but I figured it was yours, so I sent it back."

I hung up, crossed the floor and reached into the terrarium. I bent the knees of one of the warriors and put him back in his saddle, atop a shiny black plastic horse. I slipped a shield over another's head, inadvertently toppling him. I delicately stood the figure upright. I decided against a second vodka.

The phone did not ring. I got into bed, under the duvet, then spread my coat on top, the soft collar touching my chin, as I listened to jazz I wanted to hear, long into the night. When the storm started some time after midnight, I imagined the sleet was hard little notes from a piano way across town that had come to pelt my window, telling me to come out. To come out and play, please.

L. Annette Binder
Lay My Head

BABIES WEREN'T FRIGHTENED OF her face. They didn't yet know sickness. They saw only her eyes, how big they were. There was a baby girl before her in the aisle. A little round-faced girl, no older than two. Her ponytail went straight up like a paint brush, and her mother had tied a pink ribbon around it. The girl stood up on the seat while her mother read magazines. Angela smiled at her. She set aside her book and covered her eyes with her fingers and uncovered them again. The little girl giggled at that. She grabbed the fabric of the headrest and squealed. She reached for Angela and for the stewardess who was pushing the drinks cart up the aisle. Her mother patted her on the bottom. *Felicia Marie,* she said. *You better hush. People are trying to sleep.* The girl squealed again, and her cheeks were dimpled and shiny like apples. The mother looked between the seats then. Her face went dark when she saw Angela. *Get down here, young lady,* the mother said. *Get down here right now,* and she moved quickly. She pulled her little girl away from the headrest. She held her baby against her. She held her there and didn't let her squirm.

The roundness in Angela's cheeks went first. Her skin went from olive to yellow. She'd spent all those mornings on her deck, but the sun didn't warm her, not even in September when L.A. was hottest. She'd shivered and watched the neighbor kids splash around in the pool. They worked their squirt guns and wrestled in the water, and they were happy even when their parents fought. How little children need to be happy. How little it takes, and still things go wrong. She watched them all summer and into fall, and the roundness was gone and from one day to the next the veins popped out on her forearms. Her hands were spotted like her grandma's had been. Liver spots, Grandma called them, and Angela had wondered why.

Her belly grew round like a pregnant lady's. Like Mr. Hogan from the old neighborhood who drank beer every morning and tossed the cans onto his wife's compost heap. In the last few weeks the bones in her throat had started to show. There was a hollow between them, and her mother would notice this right away. She'd see it and know. Thirty years married to a U.S. soldier, and her mother still thought like a German farm girl. She'd been right about Angela's father. She knew he was sick from the smell of his breath. *He's got the mark,* she'd said. She knew it months before the doctors did, and she'd see the mark on Angela now, too. Her girl who'd been pretty once. She should be a model, that's what all the people said. And what did it matter. Every day brought another loss, and her prettiness was the least of them. It fell away like the burden it was.

Her mother was waiting at the luggage carousel. She carried the same winter coat, the extra one she kept for guests because it was cold even in November. Angela didn't remember that old plaid coat until she saw her mother standing there in her winter boots. She'd brought it along every Christmas when Angela came home from college. *Look how you're dressed,* she'd say back then. *You're always in short sleeves. You need to cover up.* Angela would pretend she didn't feel the wind when they went through the sliding glass doors. She'd say she was warm in her sandals or those loafers she wore without socks. Anything was better than letting her mother be right.

The coat smelled like mothballs. It was years between visits now. Years when it used to be months. Her mother walked too quickly at first. Angela couldn't keep up, and the air outside was sharp in her throat. It squeezed her chest. She'd forgotten how thin the air could be up here. This was probably how fish felt when they were pulled from the water. She slowed and stopped and set her hand against the retaining wall where the juniper bushes grew. Her mother stopped, too. She came close and fixed the collar on the old plaid coat. She took her scarf off and wrapped it around Angela's neck, and her eyes were black when she spoke. "You need to cover your mouth," she said. "The wind's picking up. All those years in California and you've forgotten how it blows." They walked slowly to the car. Her mother always parked in one of the farthest spots, out by the long-term lot. There were patches of ice in places. Angela slipped and caught herself, and the mountains were dark already against the sky.

Her bed was the same and the feather quilt, but her books were gone and most of her posters and ribbons. Her mother had packed these things in plastic boxes and set them in the closet. The bookshelves were full with her mother's art books now and porcelain figurines, and up at the top there was the yellow book of fairy tales her mother had brought from Germany. She'd read it to Angela when she was little. She read to her in German, and Angela understood. Struwwelpeter with his wild hair and Hans im Glück who was happiest when all his gold was lost. She knew the stories and her mother's voice, and that was the last thing she heard that night and the first thing in the morning.

Her body was healthy in every way but one. She wasn't even forty and her heart was healthy and her lungs were clear and everything was perfect except for the thing that wasn't.

She held a cup of tea in her lap. Whitethorn and lemon balm because they were good for the circulation, that's what her mother told her. Her mother had set the redwood chaise in the middle of the yard. She'd brought out blankets, too, and wrapped them around Angela's knees. It was almost forty degrees out, and it felt even warmer. The sun was shining on her head. It was bright as California outside, mountain bright, and she should have worn her sunglasses. Two little girls played in the front yard at the old Meyer house. They tunneled into the melting snow. One of them was wearing a skirt without any tights, and even from across the street Angela could see the pink of her legs.

The Meyers had moved years before and who knew what happened to Patty, fat Patty who was round as a bowling ball but completely flat-chested. They called her Fatricia at school. Angela did, too. Only once but it was wrong and she knew it even then. She did things when she was young as if she had no choice. A couple of the girls painted Patty's face one day in gym class. *Close your eyes,* they'd told her. *Stand real still,* and Patty waited for them to make her pretty. Calm as a Buddha while she stood there by the mirror. She waited for them to melt the eyeliner. They used Bic lighters back then to get the flow just right, and Angela didn't want to look. She put her jeans back on, those extra-slim Jordache jeans that cut high across her waist. She combed her hair and waited by the lockers for the bell to ring. They were working on Patty's eyes. They nudged each other and laughed at the enormous arches they drew and the red circles they put across her cheeks, and Angela saw it all and she didn't stop them and she didn't say a thing, not even to Patty, who stood there with a crooked dreamy smile. She left before Patty opened her eyes. She went out of the locker room and into the courtyard where the smokers waited between classes.

The little girls were running circles now. They shouted and poked their fingers through the links of the fence. Their mother was looking out the living room window. She held a baby against her shoulder. Angela waved to be neighborly. She raised her hand and the woman waved back without knowing who Angela was and then she called her girls inside. It was dinner time. *It's getting colder,* she told them. *Quit your running and come.* She hustled them in and shut the door.

Angela leaned back against the chair. The lights went on in all the houses and she should be getting inside, but she stayed because the night air smelled like winter. Like pine needles and chimney smoke. Somewhere a dog barked and another answered, and she held her cup and looked at the old Meyer house, which hadn't been painted in years. The screens hung away from the windows in places. The house looked tired and the street, too, and the sky was pink above them with fading traces of the sun.

Her mother talked about transplants in the evenings. This was their routine. They sat together in the kitchen, and her mother said Angela needed to get on the list. *It's time,* she said, and she touched Angela's wrist where it was swollen. *We've waited long enough.* Angela leaned back in her chair. Look how small her hands were, her mother's hands with their bent fingers. She talked about transplants every week and then every day, and now she was holding Angela by the wrist the way she did when Angela was little. She talked about alternative therapies, about a tree in Costa Rica with medicinal qualities in its bark, about Chinese herbs that stimulated the liver. There were mysteries in the world the doctors didn't know, and Angela said *yes, yes, that's true and you're right,* and her mother held her wrist. Her fingers left marks, indentations like dimples that took hours to fade.

They'd taken peginterferon together three times a week. Peginterferon via subcutaneous injection and ribavirin pills because the combination worked in 50 percent of people. They soaked the sheets with their sweat. They shivered and nothing warmed them and they were burning from inside. Forty-eight weeks of treatment and they lay together in bed unable to wash themselves or change the TV channel. Forty-eight weeks sicker than they'd ever been and none of it helped and none of it mattered and it felt so good to stop.

Thanksgiving weekend they went together to see her father. It was time to change his flowers. The sun had no mercy, her mother always said. Even in winter it faded their colors. Angela wore her coat in the car. They drove out past the old high school and the Citadel Mall where she'd spent every Friday with her friends, and she'd stolen a radio once. She'd walked right through the doors. Past the city park and those red rocks in the distance where the Indians saw spirits. Clouds were blowing in from the mountains. She shielded her eyes from the blue of the sky. Things were beautiful, and she hadn't known. She'd thought only of leaving when she was young. She'd marked off the days until graduation because the coast was waiting. She'd follow the sun west and watch it set over the water, and all she'd done was trade one sort of beauty for another.

Her mother patted the headstone the way she used to brush his jacket. She was smoothing down his shoulders and whispering in his ear. She was someplace else, and Angela watched her from the car. She didn't want to walk that cemetery path. She never got out, not even in high school when her father was freshly buried. The markers made her uneasy, and his section used to be so empty and now it was almost full. There were soldiers buried there who'd died in Vietnam and in the Gulf, and they looked so young in their pictures. Earnest and sweet-cheeked as high school boys. Her mother set silk poinsettias in the pots on either side of the stone. She arranged them, and her scarf blew around in the wind. It wasn't like the graveyards in Europe. She'd said this many times. People didn't tend to their dead. The city didn't let the families grow roses or plant tulips for the spring, and the silk flowers were pretty but they weren't the same. Graveyards need something living and not just plastic and silk.

The car was getting cold. Angela rubbed her hands together and looked along the rows. Other cars were driving through. People were bringing pinwheels and fresh flags, and one lady had a plastic Santa Claus sitting in a sleigh. They decorated the graves and swept the snow off the stones, and she should have visited Gary more often. She should be more like her mother and set flowers on his grave.

They'd been sick together for three years. He'd stopped working first and then she stopped, too, and they stayed inside the apartment. They watched *Baywatch* reruns and old cartoons and anything but the news or medical shows. They shared their medicine and their needles, and none of it mattered. A hundred people had come to his memorial. They came from the studio and from his writers' group, and his fraternity brothers came all the way from Ohio. Everyone came, it seemed like, everyone but her mother, and they waited in line to step up to the podium. They told stories about somebody she didn't know. She'd lived with him for almost ten years without ever learning he could juggle or that he'd played chess in high school. His brother told how Gary had stolen a scooter once from the college faculty lot. He drove it down the town hall steps and landed in the fountain. People laughed at that. They clapped their hands and shook their heads, and their stories made her lonely. Everything he'd seen and done, he took it with him. She'd already forgotten the sound of his voice.

Her mother stomped her boots before climbing back in. "Next time you'll come out," she said. She drove slowly to the gate. She always drove slowly, even on Powers where the traffic was heavy and people were rushing to make the light. *You can't see the flowers from the car. You can't even read his name.* She turned on the defrosters because the windows were all steamed. They went past the matching stone benches where the city founders were buried. The Madonna stood between them, and her arms were open wide.

They walked the block at three o'clock most afternoons, and then they watched *Judge Judy*. Angela shuffled along. Even on cold days it was better than staying inside. The mantel clock made her nervous how it chimed every quarter hour. They were coming around on Brentwood when her right leg buckled. She felt no pain as she went down. She landed in a mound of freshly shoveled snow. It was soft as powder and not gray yet from the cars. Not like that Sierra snow that came down like cement. She lay on her back with her mother leaning over her. *What's wrong with your leg,* her mother was saying. *Did you slip on a patch of ice?* But Angela just lay there and looked up at the sky and her mother's worried face. She wasn't cold, and she wasn't frightened. She wanted only to lie back against the snow, to close her eyes and sleep.

Her mother brought out the wheelchair the first week in December, the foldable one from when she'd sprained her ankle in Boulder. It hurt worse than a fracture, her mother had said at the time. Sometimes it's better when things break clean. She took out the chair and wiped it down, and Angela didn't complain. What use was it when anyone could see that she couldn't walk, not even to the mailbox out by the fence. They went together around the block when the weather was clear because it was better than medicine to breathe in the air. Her mother talked while she pushed the chair. *What a shame about the Gerbers,* she said. *They've really let things go. Every Sunday they go to Red Lobster but they've got no money for ice salt to keep folks from slipping.* Angela nodded while her mother talked. She held tight to the armrests.

The neighborhood had changed. Her mother was right about that. The Danzigs were gone and the Lucas boys, too, and not even the snow could hide how the new folks had neglected their yards. And still Angela recognized those houses and the bare elm trees. Her mother struggled a little where the Cleymans' maple had cracked the cement. She pushed hard on the chair, and together they went over the sidewalk where Angela used to ride her bike. More than thirty years later and Angela knew it better than the streets she walked every day back in L.A. She knew its cracks and how it curved and all the spots she'd fallen.

Five houses up another pair was approaching. A figure with someone else in a chair. As they came closer Angela recognized old Mrs. Needleman wrapped in a plaid blanket. Her granddaughter was pushing her along. *Look how nice they've got her covered,* her mother was saying. *Last March she was a hundred. They showed her picture on* Good Morning America. *The governor sent her a card.*

Her mother waited in the Meyer driveway when Mrs. Needleman came close. "The sidewalk's too narrow for us both," she said in greeting. "Even when it's shoveled."

"Another day like this and the last of it will melt," the granddaughter said. She stopped the chair and stood on the sidewalk and looked up and down the street. "It's warm as April today."

"How are you, Mrs. Needleman?" Her mother reached for the old lady's hand. "It's a nice day for a walk."

Mrs. Needleman looked at Angela and at her mother and back at Angela again. "I remember you," she said. "You always walk that little dog and never pick up the poop." Her eyes were sharp. "You listen to that strange music."

"Mrs. Needleman," her mother said. "Angela hasn't been here in years. Not even to visit. She's been in Los Angeles. She decorates sets for movies."

"I want to go home," the old woman said. "I've got people waiting. My husband's waiting for me on the bridge."

The granddaughter shrugged as if to apologize. She held out both her hands and smiled. She's stopped making sense, she seemed to say, but Angela understood.

.   .   .

Starlings flew in formation just outside her window. At ten thirty every morning they went over the house and back again, and the sky was black with their passing. They moved as if pulled by some hidden current, and she leaned against the window frame to see. She wanted to take a picture of them. She wanted to capture them just as they were. She had the camera ready. She steadied her hands as best she could, but the pictures were unfocused and smudged by the screen. She just watched them after that. She leaned close to the windowsill, and her breath steamed against the glass. They went over the tree tops. Toward the mountains and back and around again, and she tried to remember them as they went. She tried to remember the sky and the snow on the peaks and those black winter birds. She wanted to take them with her.

Dialysis with the angry nurse who rimmed her eyes in liner. She wasn't gentle with the line. Dialysis until the dialysis would stop working. This is how it would go. One thing fails and then another and another one after that and the sky outside the window was beautiful as any she'd ever seen. A blue so pure it would burn your eyes and the wind lifted the snow from the rooftops and bent the naked branches.

We're just leaves on a tree. That's what Gary told her once. They were rockhounding in the Mojave. Looking for crystals in the trailings of old borax mines and the hills were pink in the distance. *Leaves on a tree,* and their hike wasn't even half done yet, and he closed his eyes the way he did when he was happy.

Sleep all day. Sleep from noon into night and then lie awake and listen to the heater fire up in the basement. Listen to the wind as it blows. Sleep and more sleep and it was never enough. It was sweeter than food. Sweet as liquor and she wanted more. She slept when her mother pulled open the drapes. She slept when the vacuum cleaner ran or the doorbell chimed. She slept when her mother read from the book, and she didn't dream. No, she slept the way babies do. Like someone waiting to be born.

Once there was a boy who wanted only to go home. His boss wished him well and gave him a lump of gold as big as his head to thank him for his service. But the gold was heavy and when a rider came along the road, the boy gladly traded it for the horse. But the horse galloped and threw the boy and when a man came by with a cow, the boy traded in his horse because walking was better than riding. And the cow became a piglet because beef was stringy but the piglet had sweet juices. And the piglet became a goose because there was nothing better than crackling goose skin and the fat beneath. The boy was happy with all his trades until he saw a scissor-sharpener working by the road. *How lucky you are,* the boy said, *to know a fine craft.* The kind man looked around for a good sharpening stone and found one in the field. *Here you are,* he said, and the boy took the stone in exchange for his goose, and he was happy again because fate provided. But the stone was heavy and he wasn't careful and it fell into a stream. And the boy thought how lucky he was, how truly lucky, to be free of this heavy stone, and he walked the rest of the way home.

Things were crawling under her skin. They lived inside her belly. The slightest touch raised bruises. They spread in clusters across her legs, and on Christmas Eve the whites of her eyes turned yellow. She scratched her arms and her neck until her mother threatened to put mittens on her hands. *Those cuts will get infected,* she said. *There's nothing wrong with your skin,* but Angela scratched anyway. She tried to find those things that turned circles inside her. She needed to get them out, but they were always faster.

Her mother washed her in the tub. She sponged water over her head, and it was peaceful in the house. The clock was chiming and the windows were dark, and her mother turned the spigot because the water was getting cold. *All these things will wash away,* she said. *You're the same as when you left.*

She combed through Angela's hair and braided it loosely down her back. She talked, and Angela followed the sound of her words. She listened to their familiar rhythm. Her mother was saying it was the devil's virus. The devil should take it back. She needed to be strong for another day and another and the doctors would know what to do. Her eyes were black in the bathroom light. Dark like her mother's had been and like Angela's, too. And if Angela had had a daughter her eyes would have been dark, too, and it was a ribbon running through them, this blackness. It bound them all together.

I'm sorry, her mother said. *I should have gone to his service. It wasn't right to stay away.* She held Angela's hand like a parishioner looking for a benediction. She held it and squeezed it and cried.

It was time to ride in the car. She knew it without her mother saying so. Her mother didn't struggle when she lifted her up. How could that be? She was almost seventy, and she carried Angela from the wheelchair to the car. Her mother let the engine warm up and turned on all the heaters. She tucked a blanket around Angela and pressed her palm against her cheek.

They were going to the hospital. They were going to the high school and the cemetery and the Citadel Mall. The radio was playing, but Angela didn't know the song. It was one of her mother's stations. Her mother was talking. She was saying something. She was reading from the yellow book of stories, and Angela was lying in bed and she knew all the words. Hans im Glück was going home. He was free of all his gold. The stepmother chased the princes from their castle, and they were swans when they flew. They were starlings, and the sky was full with them.

Donald Antrim

He Knew

WHEN HE FELT GOOD, or even vaguely a little bit good, and sometimes even when he was not, by psychiatric standards, well at all, but nonetheless had a notion that he might soon be coming out of the Dread, as he called it, he insisted on taking Alice to Bergdorf Goodman, and afterward for a walk along Fifty-seventh Street, to Madison, where they would turn—this had become a tradition—and work their way north through the East Sixties and Seventies, into the low Eighties, touring the expensive shops. He was an occasional clotheshorse himself, of course, at times when he was not housebound in a bathrobe.

And it was one or the other, increasingly. The apartment or the square! He should have bought a place when he could have—he and Alice rented in the Village—back when he worked all the time instead of only rarely. But, no, that wasn't the right attitude. Keep moving, he said to himself.

She was half a block ahead, across the street already, carrying her bags, which held the simple white blouse and the French lotions they'd bought for her. She was waiting for him to catch up. The light changed, and he crossed the street. He had a young wife. She didn't yet know what life had in store for her. Or did she?

He'd long ago been a competitive runner, and he sometimes thought about resuming his sport at the veteran level. He'd been worrying about his heart, and it would do him good. But he'd never do it. Or maybe he would.

She called out, "How do you get to stay so handsome?" and he was in love again. He trotted up the sidewalk and said, "Ha, that's nice of you, but I'm overweight."

"Who cares? So am I," she proclaimed. "Look at my ass! I need to get exercise!"

"I love your ass," he said. "What do you see?" They were standing in front of a boutique. She laughed. "We already have enough Italian *sheets!*" There it was, the volume rising on the last word, her shrill crescendo.

It was about the time of day when they should be choking down a few pills. "We'll need to find some fluids before too long," he said.

He put his arm around her shoulders and gently hugged her. She arranged her shopping bags in one hand and wrapped her other, free arm too tightly around his waist, steering him up the block. They didn't fit well, walking so close—she swung her butt, and their hips collided—and eventually they drew apart and held hands. She had long dark hair and round brown eyes, which, when he looked into them, seemed to have other eyes behind them. What did he mean by that? It was a feeling, hard to shape into words.

Thank God the money was holding out. He wasn't too worried about their shopping. It had been his idea, to begin with; it couldn't be laid at her feet, and, in fact, he wasn't always spending on her. To do so, as was his intention that afternoon, might implicate him in a father stereotype, it was true, but who cared? It was a bright, cold Saturday, the last Saturday in October—Halloween—and the light seemed already to be fading toward night. Stephen had got himself shaved and outdoors for the first time in two weeks, and women wearing heels and men in European clothes were showing themselves in the uptown air.

"Can we stop here?" she said. They'd arrived at the lingerie store where, every year, before Christmas—usually at the last minute on Christmas Eve, at the end of one of his eleventh-hour gift-gathering runs—he came to buy her tap pants or a camisole, just as he'd done for his former wife on Christmases in years past. Marina, how was she? Was she still with Jeff?

"Let's go in and get you a pair of fishnets," he said, and they went in—the store was narrow—in single file. Two salesgirls were there to help them. One walked around the counter, toward Stephen, who raised his hands in the air, as if to prevent her from coming too close. Alice could easily be made upset if she thought she saw intimacy springing up between Stephen and another woman, even an attentive shopgirl or waitress, and he had learned to play down these innocent encounters. He announced to the women that he was shopping for his wife, and then put his arm around Alice and pulled her up beside him. "We'll need a tall size," he said.

He charged a pair of black woollen fishnets and two pairs of regular black stockings, and then they crossed the street and detoured off the avenue to look at a window display of men's suits. He had no need of one, and in fact hadn't bought one in quite some time, not since the world economy had taken its downturn.

"Let's keep moving," he said. A beautiful jacket in blue worsted wool was making him feel sad over—what? His reduced opportunities in life, probably. "How're you doing?" he asked Alice. "Are you holding up?" She was leaning against him. Here and there around them, babies, pushed in strollers, came and went.

"I'm holding up," she said.

The problem—the *problem*—was that he was no longer getting cast in the comic roles that had become, over years of acting in plays and, for a brief spell, on television, his strong suit. Or, no, maybe that wasn't the root problem. In a way, though, it was, in part because the dropoff in work and income had increased his normal daily load of terror, but also because his heartbreaking difficulties onstage had amplified his sense of himself, of his *Self,* he should say, as somehow consisting in, or activated by—what was a fitting way to put this?—the willing community made by the laughter of audiences.

"Will you please let me hold those for you?" he asked, and reached for Alice's shopping bags, the things he'd bought for her. She backed away from him quickly—had he startled her?—and said, "You're too slow, *man!*"

"You're right about that," he said.

"Come on! You're not even going to try?"

"Oh, God. You want me to fight you for the bags?"

"Yeah. Fight me."

"Are you fucking with me right now?" he said, in the snarl of a stock comic-melodrama villain. But this didn't come out funny—it was far too unhinged-sounding, in tone and in volume—and her smile dropped, and she exclaimed, "Jesus, you don't need to freak *out!*"

She handed over the two purple bags and the one little black one, and they continued up Madison. They stopped for a light, and he asked her, "Are we skipping Barneys?" The entrance to the women's side of the department store was close by. Around the corner, over near Lexington Avenue, was the apartment of a hooker he'd visited in the nineties. Victoria.

What he hated about nice clothes was both wanting and not wanting to wear them. He disliked his own conspicuousness to himself, whenever he was out in the world expensively costumed. It was only the pleasure he felt in his tactile awareness of sewing and fabric, of the hands of the maker in the garment, that led him, again and again, to risk the danger of seeing himself— literally; reflected in the mirror of a bar, perhaps—as somehow faintly ridiculous.

It was an American problem, something that he felt only in America. He should have moved across the ocean when he had the chance, after his divorce from Marina. Though he'd never really had the chance. Where would he have gone? Rome? Berlin? London? How would he have worked? His old Neighborhood Playhouse friend Ned had decamped to the Netherlands some years back—when people still called it Holland—in order, Ned had told Stephen, to follow through on an artistic commitment to experimental performance, of which there always seemed to be so much in northern Europe; but then Stephen had heard through mutual acquaintances that Ned had married a Dutch woman, who'd helped him qualify for some form or other of enlightened state arts support, and that the two of them had taken to spending their days and nights smoking pot with expatriates in Amsterdam coffee shops, which sounded, to Stephen, both awful and wonderful.

"There's nothing at Barneys this season. Everything's got an Empire waist," Alice was telling him. She said, "That cut makes me feel like a little girl in an Easter dress. A giant little girl."

"It's not my favorite look," he agreed.

"It's all right on some people," she said, and he finished her thought for her, saying, "But not on you."

"Is it my tits? Are my tits too small? Is that the problem?"

"Take it easy. It's not your tits. Your tits are great," he said, and went on, "Those dresses are weird sometimes. You know what I mean? You're maybe a little too tall for an Empire waist, unless, I guess"—he made shapes with his hands in the air—"unless the skirt is very long."

It was how they'd met and fallen in love five years before—her absurd height. Alice and Stephen had been invited to the same dinner party, for which they'd arrived at the same time. They got into the elevator together, and he pressed the button for their friends' floor, and she said, "That's me, too, thanks," and after that the doors closed and they avoided making eye contact, but on the way up they slipped and *saw* each other in the same instant, and, in the shock of meeting her eyes, he exclaimed, in a whisper, "You're so tall!" and she blushed, and his face got red, too. Later that night, after they'd both drunk a lot of wine, while their hosts were clearing up, she confessed to him that, in the elevator, he'd uttered aloud her first, fleeting thought whenever she met anyone, which was that she was tall—her noticing of herself *being seen,* being taken in, was part of her appealing self-consciousness: it was her come-on, and it was working on him—and she'd added that (though Stephen had hardly been the first man to lead with a comment on her height) no one had ever read her mind in quite the way he seemed to have done.

That Halloween afternoon on Madison Avenue, she sounded mildly manic. "You're right! You're right, as always. It's not a big deal. I'm too tall for an Empire waist. It's as simple as that! I try it and it doesn't work, and I try it and it doesn't work, and I should know better by now, because it's *obvious!*"

They were holding hands again. But he had a strong feeling that she was beginning to sink, that she was anxiously coming to feel and believe that she would somehow never be right. "Let's get you something to eat," he said, and she sighed and said, "Yeah, I'm starting to spin."

"I can hear it," he told her.

"You can?"

"Your Southern accent is coming out."

"I don't want to be too tall for you," she cried.

"You're not."

"I'm a wee bit dizzy."

"I'll hold you," he said.

A baby carriage was bearing down on them. He gripped her coat sleeve. On the next block, on the other side of Madison, was a coffee shop. He would have preferred a bar, but the one that he and Alice liked lay many blocks ahead. It wasn't yet time for drinking, anyway. He guided her off the curb, between two closely parked cars, and directly out into the open avenue—there was a moment, he figured, before the light changed and traffic surged forward—where he maneuvered her diagonally across against the wind that funneled down between the buildings. "We're almost there, come on," he called. He heard cars rushing up behind them, and a horn from one blew loudly as he sped her across the final lane, onto the sidewalk, and then ten feet more, to the door of the restaurant.

He held the door. "In you go," he said.

At the booth, he counted out pills, his anti-depressants and her anti-anxieties—he carried and dispensed for her more often than not, ever since her suicide attempt—and he asked her, "How many do you think will do the trick? One? Two? Do you need two? Honey, can you talk?"

"Are those ten-milligram?"

"They are."

"Give me two. For now."

"Hang on."

"You're scattering them across the *table!*"

"Sorry. Sorry."

It was true, he'd dumped out a few too many pills, and some had rolled off toward the condiments, the ketchup and the sugar and the salt and pepper shakers and so forth, and he was missing— what was he missing? He had Alice's portion under control. And there were his pink-and-yellow anti-psychotics. Where had his beta-blockers gone?

He peered up and saw that Alice's hair was a mess from the wind. He could see the tension in her face—it always came on so swiftly and visibly. It was her terror of going back into the hospital. Her jaw had clenched; she was grinding her teeth, and the muscles in her neck were taut. "You're twisted up," he said, and reached across the table to help her adjust her clothes. Her cotton blouse had been pulled back over one shoulder when she'd taken off her coat, causing the shirt's brilliant mother-of-pearl buttons to look as if they were about to pop off at the collar.

He pushed two Valium tablets her way. Then he noticed Dr. Tillman, sitting alone at the counter, at the back of the restaurant.

The waitress arrived, and Alice said, "I'd like a Coca-Cola and a big piece of chocolate cake, but not the kind with raspberry filling."

Stephen said to Alice, "I think I see my former doctor over there," and Alice asked him rather too loudly if he was ready to order.

She told him, "You should eat something. If you don't, you're going to have a crash, and you're going to get all angry, and I don't want to be screamed at by you later on the street."

"Excuse me?"

He rolled his eyes at the waitress and blurted, "Ha, I don't know what to say to that!" But he felt embarrassed, and conceded to her, to the waitress, that he'd probably better have a muffin.

"Pumpkin, please," he added, and abruptly got up and pushed past her and escaped to the rear of the diner, calling, "Dr. Tillman? Dr. Tillman?" But the man didn't seem to hear him. Stephen came closer and got a better look at his old analyst, hunched over a plate of pancakes. Why was Dr. Tillman alone? Had his wife, whom Stephen had never met or even glimpsed, passed away? Dr. Tillman had to be in his eighties by now; he'd shrunk, of course, and his hair had finally gone fully white. And then Stephen remembered, shockingly, that Dr. Tillman had died six or seven or maybe eight years before. The man in the diner could never have been Dr. Tillman. Stephen marched off to the men's room, where he sat in a stall and checked his cell phone for text messages from his old friend Claire. Where was she? Had she gone to the country with Peter? He needed to talk to her—he needed her to calm him down—if only for a moment. It was a risky thing to do, with Alice so close by. Alice accepted as fact her suspicion that he and Claire had had an affair, several years back, during the months when Alice was hospitalized. They hadn't had an affair, actually, though for a while Claire had been important to him as a confidante. He'd fallen in love with her, a little, for her kindness, and, he told himself now, for her soft, deep voice, which always seemed to reassure him. He flushed, buckled, went back to the booth, and, thinking of Dr. Tillman, told Alice that he felt as if he'd seen a genuine ghost, and that he couldn't imagine how he'd forgotten the death of his psychiatrist of almost fifteen years, and that, although he understood that that time in his life, the time of his analysis with Dr. Tillman, was far in the past—or maybe because of this fact—he felt disoriented, weird.

"Welcome to the club," Alice replied. The Valium was doing its work. She already sounded slurry.

He said, "How's your chocolate cake?"

"Better than your muffin."

"You ate my muffin?"

"I didn't eat your muffin. It's sitting in front of you on your placemat."

"Right you are, there it is," he admitted.

He heard the sounds of a football game. Was there a television in the restaurant? It was the weekend of the Nebraska-Colorado game. Was it? Or, no, that game came closer to Thanksgiving.

"Are you all right?" she asked him.

He watched her eat. She'd scooped out all the cake and left a shell of frosting on her plate, which she'd saved for last. He watched her lick the icing off the tines of her fork. "Are you?" he asked her.

"I asked you first."

"I'm all right," he told her.

"Should I believe you?"

He picked up her medicine bottle, shook it gently, and dropped it into his sport coat's inside breast pocket.

"Are *you* all right?" he asked once more.

"I'm fine. I'm eating my lunch."

Later, back on the street, they made their way at a kind of wobbling pace uptown, toward the Whitney Museum. The sun was getting low in the sky. He said to her, "Alice, how many did you take?"

She was leaning hard on his shoulder, like a drunk date. They slowed to gaze at autumn scenery in the shop windows along the way. The first children wearing Halloween costumes had begun to appear on the avenue. Stephen saw a dragon, a skeleton, and several little princesses. He again asked Alice how many pills she'd sneaked while he was in the men's room.

"Five?" Her voice sounded like a young girl's.

"Five in all? Or five plus the two I gave you?"

"Five in all. Three more."

He shifted her shopping bags from his left hand to his right, and offered her his other shoulder. Supporting her weight, block after block, wasn't easy, and at Seventy-third Street he insisted that they get in a cab, go straight home, and tuck her into bed for the rest of the day.

But she simply apologized for letting her anxiety get the better of her. She said that she was also sorry for provoking him, in the restaurant, with her fear that he might yell at her if he didn't eat properly. She hadn't meant to shame him. She loved him. She wanted them to have a fantastic time out in the world. That was all that mattered.

More children, herded by parents and nannies, ran past them, trick-or-treating, hitting the boutiques. The costumes were good. A few—in particular, a spectacular lion suit on a four- or five-year-old boy—looked to have been sewn with care, showing a level of detailing appropriate to durable stage costumes, the sort meant for nightly scrutiny under theatre lights.

When Stephen was younger, when he was a young actor, working in his costume for the first time—putting it on before the call for the first dress rehearsal—had always been a revelation. This was the case for many actors, certainly. Wearing the garment was an acquisition of—why not say it?—humanity. A Victorian frock coat or a pair of Windsor-style stovepipe trousers or even Depression-era dungarees, worn *as* a character, could in turn produce character. When Stephen put on a costume, he could feel his whole nervous system, his muscles, and his bones, re-arranging themselves to form his character's body and posture. For instance, the heavy woolen overcoat worn by a foolish servant caused a slump in the shoulders and an itchy stiffness in the neck that might seem to an audience to be the symptoms of a master's beatings. The drama became palpable through tailoring. Maybe it followed that Stephen's life seemed to gain grace and substance when he walked at an even pace on a nice street in well-cut pants.

She wasn't letting him do this. Both of her arms were wrapped around him. Alice was hugging him tightly from the side, and they'd become like two people in a three-legged race at some county fair or family reunion. Neither of them had much in the way of family. She'd come to the city from North Carolina, as had he. They'd grown up in neighboring valleys in the Smoky Mountains, though he'd left home—he was gone before his eighteenth birthday—before she was even born. Their somewhat shared origins had, of course, been a crucial factor in their romance. (It wasn't her body alone that had attracted him, that night at the dinner party; nor had she truly believed, when he spoke to her in the elevator, that he was an actual mind reader.) For the first year or two of their relationship, they'd discussed plans to rent a convertible and drive south together through New Jersey and Delaware and Maryland, continuing around Washington and on through the Shenandoah Valley, in Virginia—there was a nineteenth-century inn near Staunton that he'd read about in a food magazine and wanted to spend a night or two at—and then from there into the southerly regions of the Blue Ridge, where, taking their time, they'd leave the interstate and get on the old two-lane, hairpin-turn state and county roads that would take them up and across the mountains, to home. But they hadn't done it.

They hadn't done it because there was no one there for them. His parents were dead, and he had no aunts or uncles left, either. He had only a sister, who lived in Minnesota. Stephen and his sister had less and less to do with each other these days; and it had been at least a couple of decades since he had heard from, or thought to be in touch with, any of their remaining kin, the more or less distant cousins, who (some of them, at least) were surely still scattered about the countryside around Asheville. Alice's situation wasn't much happier. Her father, an alcoholic, had left her mother when Alice was four, and the man whom Alice had grown up calling father had been killed in an automobile accident when she was sixteen. Her mother, in later years, had become one of those people who try new places again and again, endlessly relocating. Currently, she was parked outside Fort Worth. Alice had an unmarried, born-again brother who repaired computers in Sacramento.

Stephen turned to face her. Adjusting himself wasn't easy to do; they were pressed together, and his arms were pinned at his sides by her close embrace. Her clothes remained as they'd been in the restaurant, tugged slightly askew, and strands of her hair, caught between their bodies, were pulled when he moved. "Ouch!" she said.

She looked good—no, great. That she was so attractive while sedated troubled him. Did he like her best when she was out of it? "I know exactly the thing to do," he said, and she whispered, "What's that?"

"Let's go buy you a hat."

"A hat!" she said.

"Would you like that?"

"Yes."

"You'll have to let me move. Let go, all right?" he asked. But she didn't release him. The boy in the fancy lion suit bolted from a store's open doorway, and Alice said, "Oh, honey."

She wasn't talking to Stephen. She was peering down at the boy, who'd stopped short on the sidewalk in order to roar at them.

"Are you a *lion?*" Alice asked. "What kind of lion are you? Are you a fierce"—she paused; it was the Valium—"lion?"

"Yes," the lion growled, though not very fiercely.

Here came the father, calling, "Baby girl, baby girl, where are you going? Don't run off! Come take Daddy's hand. Leave those people alone."

The man was about thirty-five or maybe thirty-eight or -nine years old, forty or so, and his wife was coming up behind.

"Sorry about that, please excuse us," the lion's father said.

The man's wife looked plain, with short brown hair and a small chin, though, on the other hand, she was attractive. "Don't be a bother," she instructed her daughter. She was English. Both she and her husband were conservatively dressed. The man was frankly, openly appraising Alice. Did this entitled young punk think that greater age made Stephen weak? He said to the parents, "I was noticing what a finely made costume your little girl is wearing. She looks so ferocious in it, I was certain she was a boy."

"Girls can't be ferocious, then?" the mother said, and her mildly accusing tone made Stephen unsure how to take this. Was it a reprimand, and, if so, was it also a flirtation?

A low mood was creeping up on him. "Of course girls can be ferocious," Stephen replied. "My name is Stephen." He held out his hand and said, "And this is my ferocious wife, Alice." Alice was still leaning on his shoulder, with her right arm wrapped around his neck. Her body, against his, seemed to be sliding toward the pavement.

"I'm Margaret," the English wife said, and her American husband followed: "Robert. It's nice to meet you."

The mother said, "Claire, can you say hello to these nice people?" Stephen felt a sharp tremor in Alice, and he thought, Fuck, why *that* name?

Together, as if on cue, they all peered down at the daughter. The girl was slowly turning, spinning in a circle inside the cage of legs that had formed around her when the adults squared off to shake hands.

"Don't spill your candy, dear," her mother said.

The lion girl looked at her mom. She checked in with Dad. She seemed quite drawn to Alice, whose gaze she held a long moment.

"Claire, please say hello," her mother said again.

"Claire!" her father ordered.

Stephen could feel Alice clinging to him and pulling away at the same time.

"Hello," the little girl said, and Stephen loudly blurted, "And how old are you?"

"Five."

"Five!" he exclaimed.

"We're in kindergarten, aren't we?" her mother said to her, and went on, "It takes her a while to feel comfy with strangers."

"I understand," Stephen said, and wondered what Margaret and Robert were thinking of him and Alice. What picture did they make, this older man worrisomely buoying up his sedated young wife? His anxiety was on the rise, the sun was setting in earnest, the temperature was falling, and the wind was building. He might need to sneak one or two of Alice's Valiums. He spoke for them as a couple. "It's awfully nice to have met you and your lovely daughter, but we should get going."

And to Alice he proposed, brightly, "Hey, we're looking for a hat for you, remember?"

But before they could make their getaway Margaret announced to her husband, "Oh, Rob! I know who he is!"

"You were on that TV show," she said to Stephen. "Am I right? What was the show called? Was that you?"

"It may have been me, yes."

"You were that friend of the main character who was always causing mischief for everyone."

"Get out of my way," Stephen said.

"What?" the husband said.

"The show was called *Get Out of My Way*," Stephen explained, and added, "That was a long time ago. I'm amazed that you recognized me."

"You were very funny."

"Thank you."

To her husband, Margaret said, "Do you remember that show, dear?" And he answered, "No, I don't."

"He's not much for television," she said to Stephen, in a low, confiding tone. "Are you on something now?" she asked, and he thought to make a joke about his meds.

"No. I've been in a hiatus."

"Refueling the creative juices?"

"Something like that."

"And are you an actress?" Margaret was addressing Alice. Stephen said, "Alice, she's asking you."

Sleepy Alice replied, "Oh, no."

"My wife is also between things," he said, and then, stupidly, he remarked to Alice, "We're taking some time to enjoy our lives, right?" He gave her a squeeze, and she glared at him.

Later, after they'd finally got free and resumed their trek up Madison Avenue, she accused him: "You were flirting with her."

"What? I wasn't."

"She's the type for you. Refueling the creative juices."

"Come on, let's get you home."

"I don't have a *home!*"

"Yes, you do, you have a home with me."

They'd been lost in these woods before.

"How many pills did you take, Alice? Will you tell me how many pills you took? You took more than five, Alice. Please don't lie to me. How many?"

She wasn't talking. They passed shop after shop, but she didn't want to go into any of them. She'd pulled away at last and was walking faster, out ahead of him now, fleeing. He buttoned up his coat and pulled off his scarf—it was the blue scarf that she'd given him in the first year of their marriage; he loved it and wore it all the time in the colder months—and ran up beside her and wrapped it around her neck. He said, emphatically, "Alice, nothing ever happened between me and Claire. Nothing was ever going to happen," which was true, though Alice would not believe it. Alice had met Claire and found her to be very beautiful. She suspected that Stephen would be more comfortable, more at home, with a woman closer to him in age—Stephen and Claire had gone to college together. Alice had conceived of Stephen's betrayal in the days before her breakdown, and, once in the hospital, when she'd been unable to simply go to a phone in the night and call him, the idea of their affair had grown in her; to this day, he could not say with certainty whether she'd tried to kill herself over her anticipated abandonment or whether that deranging fantasy had been a symptom of some deeper despair. It haunted them still.

Alice said, "Don't blow up at me."

"I'm not."

"You're shouting."

"Alice, I love you! Please try to take that in!" he shouted, and then quickly glanced around to see if he'd been heard by people passing by. In a lowered voice he said, "Why must we always return to this?"

"You were sleeping with her when I was on a locked ward! I thought my life was over! Where were *you?*" she pleaded.

"I was with you every day, Alice. I visited you every single day."

"And then you went to her!" she said angrily. Now he could hear and feel her terror, and he, too, began to feel frightened, because he knew where this fight could take them.

"Alice, stop this," he commanded.

"Leave me, just leave me already," she cried, and he watched as she ran away, up the block and across Seventy-ninth Street.

"Alice!" he called. But she was still going, a dark shape charging unsteadily up the street with her shopping bags.

It was the time of day when the lights from apartment buildings and stores begin to shine brightly. Through the pools of light spilling out of shop doors came people in costume, not only children but adults, on their way to Halloween parties and bars. He forged ahead against a tide of ghosts and pirates and sexy nurses from the spirit realm. He passed a shattered Marilyn Monroe, but could no longer see Alice in the distance. With hands trembling, he took her pills from his coat pocket, opened the lid, and shook out two. Did he need one or two? It was the question he'd asked Alice earlier in the coffee shop.

He put one in his mouth and another in his shirt pocket, in case. His mouth was parched from his own medications. He held the pill under his tongue. Eventually it would dissolve. He had only to wait.

He would wait at their bar. Maybe she was there already, he thought, as he turned the corner and left the avenue.

The place was a carnival inside. Cardboard witches and crêpe-paper bats hung from the ceiling, and candlelit jack-o'-lanterns had been set out on the marble surface of the bar. Everyone inside was costumed, to some degree, but in his agitation Stephen imagined that it was actually he, in his soft windowpane jacket and pressed shirt and woolen pants—he and not the dead and undead thronging about him, blocking his way—who was wearing a costume. Through the crowd he pushed, searching for her. Finally he gave up and went to the bar, where he leaned into a gathering of wraiths and ordered a bourbon from a pretty bartender with a blood-red slash impastoed darkly across her neck.

The Valium was starting to help. He drank, and the alcohol burned his throat. When a seat became free, he took it immediately and ordered another bourbon, before locating his phone and dialing Alice's number.

"You can run a tab," he told the bartender, and added, "I could use some water, too, when you get a minute."

Outside in the night, he thought, Alice would be walking, disoriented. She'd be feeling scorned. She would hear her phone ringing in her purse, and know it was him, but she'd be unable to answer, though she badly wanted to. She'd be afraid of him pulling her back, afraid of going childless all her life, and winding up a widow, like her mother, running from place to place and never stopping. He'd heard all of this played out before.

Of course, he'd told her again and again that he wanted to have a baby with her. Why hadn't it happened already? Why hadn't they yet done it, like normal people?

He pictured her gathering her coat around her and slumping on a townhouse stoop, ignoring his calls, or, likely, though by now she knew better than to expect a helpful response, calling her mother.

When he dialed her number for the fifth or sixth time, Alice answered. He told her that he was in their bar and felt desperate. "Come back," he said. "Will you?"

"Are you having a drink?" she asked.

"I am," he said. He pressed his phone hard against his ear. Loudly, above the bar chaos, he asked her, "Where are you? Do you know where you are? Do you need me to come get you?"

"No," she said. She hadn't gone far; she was only around the corner from where they always wound up at the end of these days when he took her out and bought her gifts.

She said that she was on her way, and a few minutes later he saw her appear behind him in the antique saloon mirror above the bar. She peered over the crowd of monsters and ghouls, his statuesque, distraught Alice, until she caught sight of him, his reflection and hers making contact in the glass.

He stood and said, "Excuse me, excuse me," to some skeletons and ghosts who were clustered between them. He opened a path for her and led her back to his seat. The goblin who'd been sitting beside him at the bar, when he saw Alice in her very real anguish, said, politely, "Oh, here, please, sit," and Stephen said, "Thank you," and nestled in beside his wife and let her rest her head on his shoulder. Gently, she cried. He wrapped one arm around her shoulders, and with his other hand he stroked her hair, pressing her close to him, so that her cheek lay against his heart. The bartender approached, but he gestured at her to give them time, another minute, then picked up his drink and brought it to Alice's lips, saying, "Here, love, it's okay, it's okay."

"I'm scared," she said.

He let her drink, then put the glass on the bar and, with his fingers, softly massaged away the mascara that had run in streams down her cheeks. For a while, they stayed together like that. He ordered a drink for her, and another for himself, and, little by little, she regained herself and was able to sit up straight. "I'm sorry," she said to him, and he said, "I'm sorry, too," and she asked, "Can you forgive me for running away?" and he said, "Alice. I don't want anyone but you."

"Do you mean it?" she said.

"More than anything," he answered. He said, "I know what we need to do. We need to take a vacation. We need to take our trip to the mountains. Let's do it. If we go soon, we'll still be in time to see the autumn leaves."

They talked about the trip, what kind of car they'd rent—not a convertible at this time of year, certainly—and about how many days they might spend in this place or that; and they wondered together what they'd find, after so many years away, of their old home towns and the houses in which they'd grown up. He held her hand tightly in his as they spoke, and she remembered something she'd never told him before. There had been a spring that made a little swimming hole in the woods behind her house. It had been a secret place for her—she hadn't even told her brother about it. Would it still be there? Would it have been bulldozed for a strip mall or a retirement community or a new drive-through bank? Would she be able to find it again?

"Let's go there," he said, and with that he left three twenty-dollar bills on the bar and stood up and put on his coat and helped her to stand. He buttoned her coat for her and wrapped his scarf in a knot around her collar. He picked up her bags and took her by the hand and led her carefully through the Halloween necropolis. They were the only two regular-looking people in the place.

Outside, he hailed a cab. He held the door for her, then got in beside her and gave the address, and they rode down Fifth Avenue, past Central Park and the Plaza and Tiffany & Co., and Cartier and Rockefeller Center and Saks, down through the Forties and the Thirties and the Twenties, to Washington Square Park, the very bottom of the avenue, and west from there into the Village. She leaned on him as they climbed the four flights to their walkup. He unlocked and pushed open the door. He turned on a light and guided her through the living room and into their bedroom, where he turned on the little lamp beside the bed. He took her coat and sat her on the edge of the bed and knelt before her on the floor. He started tugging off her clothes—first her shoes, then her skirt and her stockings. "Raise your arms, baby," he said, and pulled her blouse up and over her head. He unsnapped her bra and took that, too. He helped her to lie down. He pulled the covers over her, and then undressed himself, switched off the lamp, and went unclothed into the living room, where he sat on the sofa, absently touching and spinning the gold ring on his ring finger. After a while, he got up and turned off the living-room light and made his way quietly back to her in the dark. He raised the covers and got into bed beside her and brought her close, spooning, so that he could cup her breasts in his hands and feel the length of her body against his.

In the morning, he told himself before falling asleep, they would sit naked beside each other, resting against pillows, drinking coffee in bed—his black, hers with milk—and he would speak to her openly and forthrightly about getting his acting career back on track; and before long they would kiss, and when they made love he would drive hard into her and come, hoping, hoping for her pregnancy, for the child, their son, perhaps—a boy like him!—and believing as best he could that their family was drawing close, was near at last.

Asako Serizawa

The Visitor

H E CAME AROUND NOON, this man, this soldier, who called himself Murayama. At first I thought he had come, like so many of them, to beg for food, or inquire after the whereabouts of someone I may or may not have heard of, but this soldier, this Murayama, had come clutching a piece of paper, claiming to have known our son, Yasushi.

I did not *not* trust him, my eyes wandering from the scrap of paper he had apparently followed here to the gaunt, downcast face fidgeting one step back from the entryway, a deferential gesture rarely seen these days. Clutching his satchel, he spoke politely, and as curious as I was about the paper, I did not ask to see it, his presence like a beaten dog's, weary and shamefaced, his whole shrunken person so darkened by what I assumed was the tropical sun that he appeared like a photograph negative backlit against the bright, busy street. He never once attempted to peer around me as I listened through the wooden gate, opened just wider than a crack, despite my husband's parting caution, and a few moments later I found myself leading him into the front room, excusing myself to rummage for some tea leaves and a small bowl of millet noodles, which was more than I could offer.

The paper was brown, shiny with wear, and I resisted looking at it as I poured the tea, embarrassingly weak, and nudged the noodles, taken from my evening portion, toward him. In this room, softly lit by the midday sun sifting through the fragrant osmanthus tree rustling outside the sliding glass doors, he seemed less shrunken than coiled, his ligaments and muscles wound by an inner tension that seemed to tighten the air around him. Looking at him, I wondered how and when I might nudge him out; the extra cleaning I would have to do further limited the time I had before my husband's return in the evening, and one thing I was clear about was that I did not want my husband to know of this visit. In retrospect, I understand that it was a guarding instinct at work, though I cannot say for whom.

Murayama did not speak right away. Instead he darted his gaze around the room, bare now, except for the pale, ornamental vase my husband had sent from China during his tenure there. Like everything else, I did not expect the vase to stay long, its delicate color soon to be given up for a sack of grains and a few stalks of vegetables, but for the moment it cheered the room, its quiet shape attracting the eye, settling the soul, though it did not seem to have this effect on Murayama. Seeing that he had withdrawn into himself, I got up and slid the glass doors open.

The air outside was still, the sky abuzz with cicadas clamoring as though to convince everyone that it was summer, a hot one, ripe for kites and watermelons, both of which had been conspicuously missing from the season for some time. In fact it was hard to believe it was already July, almost a year since surrender, with the flood of returning soldiers and refugees seeming only to be increasing, bringing new hopes and difficult tidings to those in perpetual waiting. Until now, I had steeled myself against any hope, knowing that even if Yasushi had survived, he may not choose to return to this house he had once found so intolerable as to run away. But now? I sat back down, glancing again at the creased paper placed at the edge of the low lacquered table.

Murayama, for his part, seemed to have forgotten me, and again I nudged the tea and noodles toward him. To my surprise, he looked up, our eyes meeting. This man, this soldier, had been where Yasushi had been; the knowledge, like a sudden jab, shifted a curtain of air, and for a moment I could almost feel my son, his presence as palpable as this man before me, his shape, his face, almost visible, until Murayama, perhaps disturbed by my intensity, moved, and the moment snapped, releasing me back into the room.

Murayama picked up his chopsticks. Bringing his hands together, he nodded thankfully and began to eat. He ate slowly, chewing the noodles, sipping the broth, his movements measured as though heeding the advice of someone who had once told him to slow down, eat with care, and as he replaced the chopsticks, he said as much, explaining that his mother had insisted on it. "The good thing is, I never get indigestion, and these days it helps with the hunger," he said, adding that the last time he'd eaten properly was two days ago, when he discovered that his home, his entire neighborhood, had been razed by the bombs.

"Were you able to find your family?" I asked, suppressing a suspicion that sent my mind scurrying to inventory the house.

Murayama shook his head. He'd searched for them, wandering through the shanties that had cropped up in the ruins, but nobody had seen or heard from them. "That's when I remembered Tanaka—I mean, that's what he called himself: Tanaka Jiro. Of course he never told me the reason, but I've always wondered why he'd chosen that name, you know, instead of something snappier. He never wanted to talk about it, and to be honest, I'm surprised I even found this house. Not because of the bombs, but I thought he'd made that up too."

I nodded, but I was reeling. Tanaka Jiro. That was a name we knew. It belonged to the police officer who had once interrogated my husband about his so-called anti-patriotic views. How Yasushi hung onto the name, I could not imagine; he had been so little, and we never spoke of it. "Did Yasushi mention anything else about us?" I asked, my pulse leaping.

Murayama looked away. "Tanaka was a vocal guy, but we all had something. We tried not to pry."

"Still, he gave you his address. You must have been close," I said.

Murayama glanced at the paper. "Honestly, I don't know why he did. We were about to be deployed. At the last minute I got pulled from my unit because I had mechanical skills they wanted to re-route. I kept the paper, thinking I'd come look for him afterwards."

"So it was your own decision? To come all this way?"

Murayama nodded.

"Where were you at the time?"

"Luzon. But I knew him from Singapore. Our units got merged there," he explained.

"So you knew each other for some time. You must have been close, if Yasushi confided in you," I tried again.

Murayama shook his head. "That's the thing. He never confided. He was always joking. It was hard to know what was what with him."

"But he told you about his name. He gave you his address. He must have had a reason."

"Like because he knew I was staying behind? Look," he said. "I even asked him if he wanted me to, you know, take care of his things if it came to that, but he didn't say anything, and the next day they were gone."

"But he gave you the address. You said he was evasive about himself. He was taking a risk, don't you see?"

Murayama did not reply, and for a moment I could not help but wonder whether Yasushi had given him the paper. Murayama could have stolen it—barrack life was communal, wasn't it? Or else he could have come by it by some other means—but what? Finally, I shook my head. "Murayama-san, you must excuse me.

As you probably guessed, we had no idea about Yasushi's where-abouts for some time. Of course we had our suspicions—he was always committed to enlisting—but our inquiries yielded no traces of him, and now I know why. Maybe you can tell me just one thing. Is Yasushi still—?" My voice caught.

Murayama lowered his gaze. He explained that Yasushi's unit had been part of a regiment assigned to garrison an island. "Given the conditions . . ." He gripped his knees.

I looked down at my hands, rough now because of the short-ages. Of course, like any mother, I had anticipated this, but the finality of the confirmation sank what hope had been plucking at me, and I began to shake.

Murayama placed his hands on the table. "Listen, the truth is, no one knows for sure what happened out there. And these days you never know who's going to turn up," he said, alluding to all the soldiers who had returned only to find their names written off on tombstones in the family lot.

I nodded, thankful for his gentle consideration, but I was exhausted. It was a weariness I had long been keeping at bay, and now it seeped into my flesh, burrowed into my joints, making me feel oddly afloat, as though the weight that had kept me tethered had been cut, my whole body, all the years it had shaped itself around Yasushi, collapsing in a heavy heap below me. I turned and looked at the sliding glass doors, the leaves of the osmanthus tree shimmering like coins, the evanescent cicadas chorusing to an emulous screech. I looked at the pale green vase to my right. Its demurely fecund shape now seemed only to emphasize its hollow interior, and I saw why it had not had a calming effect on Murayama. "May I?" I gestured at the paper.

Apologizing, Murayama handed it to me.

The paper was soft, the worn folds releasing a leathery smell, and at once I saw that it was my son's handwriting, his gruff script still slouching to the left despite his early determination to correct it, and this evidence, stabbingly familiar, pierced my chest, releasing a swell of memories that soon crested with gratitude for this scrap of Yasushi that had made it back.

I was about to say as much, thank him for the care with which he must have carried the paper, but when I looked up, I saw a strange expression cross his face, an odd, observing detachment as though he had been watching and noting the moment—a lone middle-aged woman in slow undress—and my stomach tightened. Of course, he was a soldier, I reminded myself, the various rumors that had been circulating in the streets suddenly murmuring close to my ear. What did it matter that he was polite, that he knew Yasushi, that he had been demobilized? I glanced at his hands, thick but sinewy, his long fingers fingering the teacup, a rich blue glaze, one of a four-cup set I had been holding onto, and my skin bristled. I leaned closer to the vase, knowing full well that I would be no match for a soldier, even a starving one like this.

Murayama did not seem to notice my alarm, and when he spoke, his voice was gentle. Once again he apologized for his presence, thanking me for my hospitality, repeating that he'd only come here hoping against the odds that Tanaka had made it back. "I just didn't know what else to do. Us soldiers, we're pretty unpopular these days. It's hard to know what it was all for," he said.

I did not reply. I took out my handkerchief to blot my face. Then I got up and slid the glass doors wider.

Outside, the day had mellowed, a light breeze beginning to loosen the air, the cool shadow cast by the eaves beginning to elongate on the ground, suggesting the presence of an awning we did not have but always wanted, a generous one, ample enough to cover the stone step placed at the foot of the sliding glass doors. Even Yasushi had smiled at the idea, most likely thinking that it would let him sneak his cigarettes even during a rainfall, and for a while, encouraged by the approval, my husband had put considerable energy into seeing it constructed, the two of them tentatively tolerating each other, until one night Yasushi failed to come home. That night the cicadas had been relentless just like this, and the pang of that memory clarified me. I sat back down and said, "People are tired. They're looking for someone to blame. You mustn't let them bother you."

This time it was Murayama who did not reply. Instead, he gripped the teacup, swirling it, and I noticed that a slight sheen had come to his forehead, betraying a nervousness that prompted me to wonder again how I should send him on his way. I did not want to provoke him, but I was beginning to feel imprisoned, his physicality, though not quite a threat, beginning to oppress me. Why had he come here? The question bloomed in my chest, and a vague sense of uneasiness fanned across my back. After a while, thinking that he had not heard me, I repeated, "You really mustn't take these things personally. People are nervous. And you had your orders to follow."

As it turned out, Murayama had heard me, for he looked up brusquely and told me that he appreciated my sympathy but he was tired of people, so-called civilians, rolling out the carpet when there were things to cheer about, only to whip it away when the going got tough. "You people have no right blaming people who risked their lives on the battlefield. What do you know? All the crap, the dirty business, the *shit* you sent us into. Do you think we liked it? Who do you think we were doing it for?"

"But we didn't know. If only we had known, if we'd been properly informed—"

"Then what? What would you have done?"

"Well, there would have been something, there would have been someone—"

"Like the Emperor, you mean?" He laughed. "The truth is, nobody wanted to know. All you wanted was someone to do the dirty work, and now you want us hanged."

"But how can you say that? Nobody can fault you for following orders," I said.

"Orders?" Murayama looked at me. "Sure, we were following orders. We were always following orders. What do you know about orders?"

"Please," I said, glancing at his hands again, grubby with dirt brought back from Luzon, Singapore, and who knew where else. "In a few months, things will settle, then it will be different. Would you like one more cup of tea?" I moved to comply, even though I knew I had none left.

Murayama glanced at his teacup. Then he leaned forward. "Listen, you've heard the talk, I know what people are saying. But do *you* believe it? Do you believe that your son—" He stopped.

A sudden fear sprang up my throat; I gripped the neck of my blouse. "What? What about Yasushi?"

Murayama did not move. Then he licked his lips. "Forget it. Tanaka was a model guy," he said, his voice turning dutiful and hollow.

Was this then why he had come? To confess a secret? I picked up the paper and again examined Yasushi's script. There was nothing there to betray him, but having assumed myself a mother of a soldier, I had not been immune to the rumors, the grisly anecdotes, the muddy details, all no doubt embellished by the time they reached me, collecting like secret pearls in the back of my mind. I smoothed the paper back onto the table. "You were about to say something. What were you about to say?"

Murayama sat up, surprised. For a moment his face was clear, his eyes wide. Then he glanced at the vase, his expression dimming. Looking at me again, he reassured me that Tanaka was an upright soldier, almost a stickler, but well loved by everybody. "The thing is, we had a job to do; we had to do what was necessary. That didn't mean we did *stuff*, all that craziness, hacking down innocents and eating each other. I mean, did you hear about that? Those guys in those remote—I mean, don't get me wrong. Tanaka was on an island, but his island had villages, jungles, the whole nine yards. Sure, there were bad guys. Sure, we had to secure our positions. But my point is, if they'd just coop-erated, told us what we needed to know, but those natives"—he laughed nervously—"would you like to see our album?"

My heart froze. I stared at his face, oily with sweat now, despite the breeze that had begun to visit the room, and I could smell his body, piqued by a nervousness that frightened me, his sud-den question like a mirror lake, concealing what could only be a murky depth. I squeezed my handkerchief. Yes, I nodded. Yes, I wanted to see his album.

Murayama wiped his forehead and reached for his satchel. Explaining that Yasushi, being initially from a different regiment, was actually not in his album, he assured me that military life was more or less similar everywhere. "See that?" He pointed at the first group photograph in the book. "That's me." He pointed at another speck. "That there?" A buddy who had enlisted with him. Page after page, he picked out key figures, rattling off facts about his division, the chief commanding officer, the number of battalions, platoons, and squads that made it up, his voice rising as the photographs showed fewer rows of soldiers, their individual faces becoming clearer, the background changing to show slivers of fields, runways, harbors. Coming to a portrait of his own unit, he told fond anecdotes, the hardships of training, all the work that went into steeling themselves, how they ultimately made them feel more exposed, more penetrable, their quickest reflexes always plodding against the speed of bullets. "At some point you just realize they're training you to be shot at. But the worst was the discipline," he told me, remembering each slap, each punch, the humiliation pumping him up so that by the end of it he couldn't wait to unleash himself. "This guy here?" He pointed at a scrawny boy. "He made us suffer the worst. They were all about group punishments, and that kid, he made us want to kill him." He laughed. "The good thing was, we had bigger enemies. See those officers?" He pointed at a row of decorated men. "They're lucky they had rank. Otherwise?" He drew a slash across his neck.

"Were there incidents like that?" I asked.

"Nah, not in our unit. That would've been suicide," Murayama said, chuckling as he remembered the more colorful characters in his unit, their small acts of rebellion, subversive but inconsequential, and again the feeling of Yasushi's proximity seized me, the topography of his life, suddenly vivid, filling in all the years of his absence that had faded to a mute canvas occasionally flushed by old memories but otherwise remaining silent, blank, defying imagination. How much had I wished for this, these details? The unfolding was beguiling, and I found myself yielding to these pages, letting myself indulge just this once in this reunion with my son.

At five o'clock, the hall clock chimed, its sonorous report startling us. Explaining that it was my husband's prized Gustav Becker, I seized the moment to comment on the yellowing sky, the quickening traffic flashing through the gaps in the wooden fence foretelling my husband's impending return. Murayama, to my relief, flipped to the last pages of the album. They had been officially left blank for personal use, and he had pasted in a few snapshots; he lingered over these long enough to locate them for me—Singapore, Malaya, Philippines, Java—identifying all his closest friends, explaining that Yasushi would have been there, in these pictures, had they been able to coax the camera from him. "He really loved that thing, a Leica, I think he said. He wanted to be a journalist," he told me, adding that the Leica was one of their best requisitions. "These here were his favorites," he said, pointing out several photographs Yasushi had been especially fond of. They were of small things—an ant on a crushed cigarette butt, a fish in a puddle of water held by an empty crab shell—but they were emotive, lyrical in their effect, and they provoked in me a surreal sense of pride and desolation. That these were Yasushi's vision, what his eyes had seen and moved his body to capture, show, remember, opened a space in me, and I breathed, swallowing a lump that came to my throat.

Murayama, seeing this, hastened to cheer me. He relayed stories about their arguments, legendary in their absurdity, the technical points of their disagreements turning like empty spits in the heat of their rivalry. "What did we know about photography?" He laughed. "Still, he ended up learning something," he said, pointing out a few more of Yasushi's photographs, mostly portraits in persistent repetition, some exhibiting a clear development, a growing promise I could not bear to witness. After a few more pictures, I reached out and touched the album. Murayama all but leapt up. He slammed the album shut, his gaze darting from my hand to the wall, finally settling on the vase, the pale shape now burnished by the afternoon sun. When he turned to look at me, I saw again that peculiar look, cool and assessing but also almost guilty now, and it struck me again that he *had* come for something, perhaps to burgle me after all, and I quickly apologized, explaining that I had meant no harm, that I had been overwhelmed, that his visit had been an invaluable gift, one for which I wished I had something to offer him in return. "It's really nothing, but would you like to take some of Yasushi's clothes with you?"

Murayama blinked. He looked confused for a moment, then his face furrowed, and he looked stricken. Vehemently shaking his head, he muttered what sounded like an embarrassed apology, and he stood up, stuffing his album into his satchel. Thanking me again for my hospitality, he apologized for the time he'd taken, the food he'd eaten. "You never know about Tanaka," he told me, pulling on his gaiters, hoisting his satchel, his voice edged now with a chattiness that seemed to rattle the house. "He really was famous for pulling things off." In fact, when he did show up, would I mind letting him know that he, Murayama, had looked him up?

Promising that I would, I unlatched the gate, asking if there wasn't anything more I could do. Telling me that he'd already inconvenienced me beyond measure, he bowed deeply and stepped away, turning once to wave before dissolving into the evening crowd.

Returning to the room, I shakily set about straightening it, gathering the chopsticks, nesting the teacup in the bowl, carrying them to the kitchen to be washed. Returning again, I wiped the table, swept the tatami, gently slipping the paper into my pocket. Closing the sliding glass doors, I locked them, vigorously testing the latch. On my way out, I stopped to wipe the vase. There in the bottom was a photograph, its white shape stenciled against the dark, and a sharp chill snaked up my spine. I picked it out. In the foreground was Murayama, his open smile revealing the sunny boy I had not seen this afternoon. Behind him, a field spread out, a few shrubs in the distance, the open meadow bisected by a diagonal line—a newly dug trench. Along this trench was a line of people, roughly clothed and blindfolded, their legs folded under them, their ankles and wrists bound by ropes tied to stakes hammered deep into the earth. Though diminished by distance, their faces were crisp, their flapping blindfolds clearly visible above their open mouths contorted by the imminent approach of the row of soldiers standing perhaps ten meters behind them, bayonets unsheathed. Like the prisoners, the soldiers' faces were also diminished but crisp, and as I stared, my eyes darting back and forth between the ferocious faces of these boys gripping their bayonets and the runny faces of the prisoners twisted in desperate fear, I realized that their expressions were in fact identical, both parties bound by a ferocious fear, the attackers anticipating the same moment of piercing anticipated by the victims who would receive them, and it was then that I recognized that what I was looking at was not, as I had first assumed, an execution, but rather a training session, the line of shrubs not at all shrubs but a row of chairs fattened by decorated officers observing the performance. Two questions sprung at me: Why had Murayama left this picture hidden here in this vase? Was this, like the others, Yasushi's photograph? Then it dawned on me that perhaps this whole visit had been a ploy, a cruel, subversive act, plotted perhaps by Yasushi himself, not only to leak the image, a clear indictment of the military, but also a signal to me that Yasushi, though uninterested in presenting himself, had in fact survived.

This last thought seized my imagination, and the more I thought about it, the more it seemed plausible. After all, that would explain Murayama's peculiar behaviors, and hadn't he, at the last moment, been careful to prepare me for Yasushi's eventual return? I brought the photograph closer to my face, its faint chemical odor penetrating my nose. Yes, those were indeed officers, and those definitely a row of training soldiers, one end eclipsed by Murayama's head, the other end cut off by the photograph's border, the last visible soldier a mere slice, one visible leg stepping forward, one visible arm raising the bayonet, his face, angled and therefore whole, sending a bolt of shock through me. Yasushi. I put down the photograph. Outside, the sky had cooled, the branching footsteps of the passersby beginning to thin, depositing one pair outside the gate, rattling it: the sound of my husband sliding the bolt. I snatched the photograph. Glancing around for a place to hide it, my gaze, like Murayama's, alighted on the vase, the coarse interior of which my husband was unlikely to examine. Carefully laying the photograph face up so that its darker hue might blend with the color of the vase's interior, I stepped back, my knees buckling. Outside, my husband's footsteps paused. Gripping the neck of my blouse, I braced against the sound of his key fitting the lock and arranged myself, straightening my back, smoothing the hem of my skirt, tugging the corners of my blouse, as all around me, the momentary quiet of the room, assailed once more by the cicadas, was swallowed up by the darkening summer sky.

Samar Farah Fitzgerald
Where Do You Go?

O NE SPRING, WHEN THEY had been married two years, when they both had good jobs they could do from home, they left the big city as they had always planned to and bought a house. The house had a two-car garage, so they bought two cars. In the attic—they'd never had one before—they stored everything they thought they'd outgrown. Kierkegaard, for one. Plus, her thrift-shop leather jacket, his music posters, their longhorn cattle skull.

They had found the skull—desert angel, dank bone picked clean in certain morning light—on a trip out West, shortly after they moved in together. It was expensive and awkward to carry on a plane but perfect for the front wall of their studio apartment. One year, before a party, someone painted the horns blue. Another year, someone stuck a dried corsage in a hollow eye socket.

Their new home was an hour from the old studio, in a town that was nothing like the boastful but forgettable suburbs nearby. More of a village than a town, set snugly on a pretty, wooded hill. A person might live five miles away and never know the place was there. But it was. If you took the right road and stayed with it around a narrow bend, then up the hill, eventually you'd come to a clearing with modest homes encircling a small lake. All of the houses were cottage-sized—no three-story colonial fortresses here—and yet remarkably distinct and intricate. Pointed turrets and steep gables, stick work in the Victorian gingerbread style and eaves extending over small rounded doorways like visors. Their three-bedroom stucco sat at the bottom of the hill. It had a prim stone walkway, two short chimneys, and a slim cast-iron balcony with enough standing room for one, facing the water.

Because they were so charmed by the setting and the architecture they were willing to overlook the fact that most of the residents were older, much older—retired couples, widows, and divorcees well into the winter of their lives. The evidence was everywhere. The nearest supermarket stocked blood pressure monitors at the checkout counter, and signs within a half-mile radius proclaimed street names in a colossal font. Wednesday nights, half the village gathered for card games in a community center at the top of the hill. They could see these tepid parties from their side of the lake, the large atrium windows giving up a dozen or so round, indistinct silhouettes. On weekends, a purple bus rumbled up the hill and idled in front of the center, waiting to carry the cotton-headed gamblers south, to the casinos and beaches.

It was sort of funny that they'd joined an outpost for the near-to-dying—that's what they were able to tell each other at first. They enjoyed themselves: "Next stop on the casino bus: diaper change in Freehold." At the beginning, anyway, they were too busy relocating to give much more thought to their new neighbors. When they'd moved into the studio years before, it had been a simple merger: his things and her things coming together. Now, although their total living space had more than tripled, nothing from the past seemed right—the painted longhorn skull looked kitschy in the foyer, adolescent in the master bedroom—and they were struck deeply with the desire to purge and start all over. Some of their belongings they posted for sale online, some they hauled to a Dumpster, and what they found themselves unable to remove entirely from their lives they relegated to the attic. They wrapped the skull in a large white sheet and set it on an old piano bench abandoned by previous owners. It wasn't long before the sheet loosened and pooled around the animal's brow, so one exposed eye socket loomed threateningly each time they climbed the attic stairs.

They took breaks from the purging to order a new couch, a dining room table, a kitchen table, and matching nightstands for their bedroom. Late at night, worn out from the effort of recalibrating the value of the things they owned, they made their way to the balcony. They stood, holding each other—the only way they could both fit—and contemplated the new scenery. It was high summer by now. When the moon was bright and a light breeze lifted the boughs, they watched turrets and gables undulating on the surface of the reservoir.

But it didn't matter how tightly they held each other. Henry and Vega were always alone with their thoughts. Taking it all in, he was often reminded of the porcelain Christmas village his grandmother would unbox every winter. He looked out at the water and swelled with nostalgia, a sweet and mellow sadness for all the things they'd discarded and for the days to come, which of course would one day be past, too. Vega, looking at the same scene, was mostly reminded of a movie—was it a documentary or some kind of supernatural drama?—about a group of little people living in a dense forest. Sometimes, though, all she could think of was Hansel and Gretel, the perilous cottage.

"You ever think," she said one night.

"Mmm."

"It wouldn't be that hard for me to do something really horrible to you, something really violent, Henry." His hands were clasped in front of her, and his chin rested lightly on her head. She twisted in his embrace and looked up at him. "What if I strangled you? Or stabbed you with our kitchen knife? It would be possible, you know. A little while ago, I saw you bent over the box in the dining room."

He shook his head. He took her slender neck in his warm hands and squeezed gently. "I think I might win that one," he said. This made her smile, and he let go.

In the city they would part ways on the front stoop, one of them going east and the other going south to their separate jobs. Now they shared an extra bedroom as an office. It took a little time and effort to arrange the furniture but finally they positioned their desks so that they sat with their backs to each other. And it was sort of pleasant working side by side, or back to back, on their projects. Henry courted Vega all over again. He sent her emails with subject headings alluding to the pattern or color of her underwear, which he noted each morning as he watched her dress.

> Subject: Getting my ducks in a row.
> Subject: Nothing but blue skies.
> Subject: Remember the Pink Panther?

They had sex instead of lunch some days. And as the summer grew melancholy with signs of fall, Vega threw out her pills—five packs of little blue pellets wrapped in foil sinking in the garbage. They found the added sense of purpose invigorating and kissed more, even when Henry was deep inside her, as if the kisses went straight to his sperm and her egg, pumping their future child with all this love. Nothing except love.

They slept with the windows open. In the mornings, without a commute downtown or crosstown, there was time to read the paper—the entire front section, plus one or two stories from a "silly" section—before they each had to dial in to the publishing houses where they worked. Some mornings there was even time for a spinach and feta omelet before the telephone rang and their inboxes filled up. They wondered aloud if their work was suffering, but nobody had complained. Still, because nothing in this world was given freely, they tallied their losses. They had to haul themselves into the car for the simplest errand; no longer could a whim, a pang for an apple or a baguette, take them down the block to the corner bodega. The independent movies didn't always show up in the local theater. And they missed their friends in the city, though not as much as they said they did when they had the chance to see these people for dinner or drinks. All in all, small things.

Meanwhile, the neighbors had taken notice of the young couple. They waved tentatively as Vega and Henry took the bend around the lake in one of their new cars. "Slow down," their nervous fingers seemed to say. They came by with gifts. Raisin pie, bran muffins, wheat cookies in holiday tins with wintry scenes.

Vega found their welcome gestures stale. Or, not so much stale but peculiarly flat.

"Really? Tastes good to me," Henry said, snapping a cookie in two and taking a bite.

"No, they taste like old people," she said, her hand on her stomach and her lips curling with distaste.

One afternoon, deep into October—the warm weather now far from everyone's thoughts—Cynthia Lippincott from next door knocked. She was a short woman, plump from the hips up and with a natural rouge in her cheeks. In the crook of her ample arms she cradled a tin of gingersnaps, like a mother with her infant.

"I've come to warn you about Gordon," she said brightly, handing over her gift and stepping nimbly into their home. Her husband—the tall, stooped man who never smiled or waved—was not well, and Cynthia didn't waste any time explaining his condition. It was emphysema: his heart was dangerously enlarged from the stress of breathing. She wanted Henry and Vega to know that Gordon would probably come around asking for cigarettes.

"The man who lived here before you, he was a young bachelor, and he liked to give my husband smokes. When I asked him to stop, well, Gordon started paying him to do it."

Henry did his best to assure her that neither of them smoked nor would they ever think of buying cigarettes for Gordon. Cynthia nodded, satisfied. Her presence was above all social and, once she was convinced that business had been taken care of, she wanted to know everything about Henry and Vega. How long had they lived in the city? Did they plan on children? What did they do on those computers all day? "You're both editors? Isn't that fascinating," she said, wistfully. "People work at home now, don't they? Not like when I was young. I suppose it wasn't his fault, but Gordon was gone such long hours."

Henry offered their visitor a seat on the living room couch and disappeared into the kitchen. Vega sat herself on the opposite end of the couch, her knees angled politely toward Cynthia.

"What does your husband do, Mrs. Lippincott?"

"Well *now* he's a full-time professional pain in my ass," Cynthia said and erupted into sharp laughter. Her hand extended, as if to pat Vega on the knee in recognition of some wifely bond, but her stubby arm came up short. She let it hang there a moment, then settled for rubbing the cushion between them. "You mean before he retired, of course. Oh, he was, you know, a manager over at Grayson. That large pharmaceutical just two or three miles north of here, closer to the highway? He was with them for a long time. Good pension. We could have moved anywhere, honestly, after he retired, but here we are. Still living up the road. People are funny, aren't they?"

Henry came back smiling and carrying a flowered plastic tray with the ginger cookies. The tray caught Vega's eye. It had been a thoughtless flea market purchase years ago. Where had Henry been storing it? The memory had almost escaped her mind, a last-minute trip to a bed and breakfast in Rhode Island. That night, they had their first shower together: her fingers and his mouth where they hadn't been before. And the next morning at the flea market, there was a sun so bright and warming that nothing, absolutely nothing except the day itself, entered their minds.

She forced her attention back on the old woman. Exactly how old was Mrs. Lippincott anyway? She seemed younger than Mr. Lippincott, but her husband looked so frail and pallid he could have been just a few days away from one hundred.

Not long after Cynthia dropped by, Vega went out one night to harvest her herb garden. Back in July a flare of ambition had driven her to till the small plot on the side of their house, and she had decided to plant more than the ordinary mint and basil—herbs like fennel, lovage, and dill. It was after eleven now. Henry was upstairs, his teeth brushed, in bed with a section of the paper. She was not accustomed to nights like this, black, suburban nights. In a childish way, it frightened her to think about all the small faceless creatures moving around the recesses of the yard, the nameless fish darting in the lake, an intruder skulking past the shadowy angles of the neighbors' houses. She crouched over her garden and began to fill her plastic bag with crisp, pungent stalks, setting the curve of her body against all of that unknown. Soon, the wind shifted, and the sharp, buttery smell of tobacco wafted over her shoulder. Or, she felt his eyes on her. She couldn't have said which happened first, but Vega stood abruptly and turned around, in the direction of the Lippincott house. She started.

There was Cynthia's husband, Gordon, standing at the edge of his property, under a leafy oak. He was wearing what Vega recognized as his usual outfit of gray pajama bottoms and a navy suit jacket. He was smoking and watching her. She gasped lightly and set her hand on her chest, but he did nothing to acknowledge her alarm. She wrapped her cardigan tight and stepped tentatively his way. She drew closer to his thin, decrepit form as she might have approached the apparition of a large animal, with a mix of fear and irresistible disgust. But just as she got close enough to see the slight quiver of his cigarette hand, he coughed softly. He became an old man again.

"Mr. Lippincott?" she managed to say. "Gordon?" She was about to add, "Are you all right?" but stopped herself. Henry had a tendency to slip into a ministerial habit with the old people. It bothered Vega, just as it did when he would unconsciously flex his vocabulary around their doorman in the city. "Julio," Henry used to say, "you are the best doorman we've ever had, inimitable." He hadn't meant anything terrible by it, of course. She understood that her husband was simply a man who was grateful for the things he had. But still, it made her squirm.

Gordon nodded "hello," or "fine," and reached into his suit jacket. He pulled out a cigarette. For her. "Don't go telling that husband of yours either. He'll tell Cynthia, I know he will."

She couldn't help smiling at this, but she shook her head. "I don't smoke."

"You? You smoke. I could tell it right away."

"Excuse me?"

Gordon shrugged. Then he started coughing again, this time more seriously. It was difficult to watch. Only when he finally brought the cigarette to his lips and took a long drag were his lungs tamed. Amazed, Vega watched him exhale. He lifted his head slightly, lowered his eyes, and basked in the release. Who knew, maybe the shortness of breath and coughing were a welcome substitute for words. Vega decided that he did not seem like someone much interested in conversation, emphysema or not. She knew the kind. Before Henry, she had been drawn to solitary and taciturn types. Her eyes drifted to his crotch, unprotected in his pajama bottoms. She wondered how much he could still feel. She looked up and his face flickered awareness of the direction of her gaze.

The truth was that she used to be a casual smoker. But she hadn't accepted a cigarette from a man in a long time, not since her years right out of college, first traveling as a journalist in Eastern Europe, then back in the city. "All right," she said, and felt herself smile coyly. Gordon lit the one for her, and as her dry lips closed around the lost habit, she pictured him briefly as a young man, when he must have been imposing in his new suit jacket. He was not unhandsome. He had an abundance of gray hair and a strong forehead and chin.

The cigarette didn't taste quite as good as she remembered, but the papery softness between her fingers was nice, and she welcomed the lightheadedness that came slowly. "Your wife doesn't like you smoking, you know," Vega said.

He frowned. "Well, it's got nothing to do with her."

When she asked him for another, he looked satisfied. Now she saw not the young man, but the boy he must have been—in his mouth and his eyes there were traces of a willful child. His thin hair sat stiffly on his head and she wanted to reach out and pat it down.

She brushed her teeth vigorously before climbing into bed with Henry. In the morning, she told him about the smoking anyway. To his patient "Do you think that was a good idea, Vega?" she only shrugged.

But that wasn't the end. A few weeks later she drove by a small park not far from the village and spotted Gordon sitting on a bench, cigarette poised between his lips, both of his hands placed formally on his legs. A light drizzle was falling. Before she could change her mind, Vega turned into the small car lot next to the park. She found an umbrella in the back seat and approached the bench. Beyond where Gordon sat there was a plastic jungle gym. A child squirmed in his mother's arms, pleading for another turn down the slide. Finally the mother relented and watched her triumphant son run up the slick ladder.

Vega shivered. Mr. Lippincott didn't look up when she greeted him, but he slid his hands slowly along his thighs and she took this as a sign that he recognized her. She sat down next to him and extended the umbrella over his head. "Do you need a ride, Gordon? Come on, I'll give you a ride."

He was far away. She waited for him to look at her and acknowledge, in some small way, their moment under the oak the other night. Finally, he started to stand. She offered her arm, but he managed fine without her. As she was pulling onto their road, she turned to look at his profile in the passenger seat.

"Do you have a cell phone, Gordon? You can call me, next time you get stuck."

"Cell phone? What for?" He explained that walking was his doctor's idea, but he hated walking one way and coming back the same exact way. So, sometimes he ended up wandering too far and had to rest a good hour before he found strength for the return. That's when Vega mentioned a nice path she'd discovered that meandered around the lake. "It slopes in a few places, but nothing too steep. It's pretty."

"Well," he said, when they were idling in his driveway. "Thank you for the ride."

The next day, he knocked on their back door. "I'm ready now," he said. "For the walk." And instead of blanching at the abrupt invitation, as she might have expected herself to, she grabbed her parka, called out to Henry she was stepping outside, and closed the door behind her.

After that, they walked regularly, every afternoon during the week at four, unless Vega had a deadline that interfered.

Sometimes Henry boiled tea and stood at the kitchen window. So he could watch Vega and Gordon embarking down the footpath that led first toward the lake and then veered off into a patch of wood. Gordon's suit jacket, usually unbuttoned, flapped in the wind, and his pajama bottoms clung indecorously to his crotch. Vega's compact frame, shifting slowly below the latticework of brittle branches and sunlight, looked ghostly. Henry was surprised to see his wife, always so quick and impatient in her daily routines, taking careful steps at the old man's side.

He loved her so much that it was okay to think certain things, as a rhetorical exercise. For example, he wondered sometimes, if he hadn't found Vega when he did, ten years ago, if he came across her now for the first time, would she still manage to captivate him? He was a couple of months out of college, without a job, without an apartment, wallowing in his own shiftlessness, when they met. She was leaving in two months on a journalism fellowship to Romania, after which she'd promised to meet him in New York. Their first kiss was in his parents' basement. He told his friends that she was intense. What he meant was that she wasn't afraid to ask a question directly, and nothing anyone could say seemed to make her flinch. Not even that unbelievable story she extracted one evening from the bartender on 86th, who hobbled around on a prosthetic leg. When Vega had asked him how he'd injured himself, he looked briefly like he was going to evade her question with a joke. Then he wiped his hands on his towel, folded his elbows on the bar, and told them—told Vega, Henry was just a bystander—his story. Which was this: four years before, having failed to convince at least half a dozen surgeons to saw off his healthy leg, he took a lifelong obsession to be an amputee into his own hands. He froze his limb in a cooler of dry ice as long as he could stand it, and then called 911. Though Henry was incredulous, Vega believed every word, including the bartender's claim that he had absolutely no regrets.

After her fellowship ended, she took an extra two months to see the rest of Europe. Eventually, she did meet up with Henry in the city, and later they found an apartment together. She spilled into his world, bled into his clothes, and stained his skin. With time, though, he saw what he hadn't been able to see right away: that she would leave for long stretches, turn into herself for days. She never faltered in the ritualistic ways of couples, a hand rubbing a shoulder, fingers exploring the nape of a neck. But her gaze grew distant, less direct, and she lay awake in bed for hours at night. If he tried to reach her then, to pull her back with his desire, she recoiled as though he were violating some agreement.

He learned to accept that Vega was a proposition. He could have her, shroud himself in her good looks and borrow her passion and her brand of fearlessness, but in return he wouldn't ask about her silences.

Now there was something new. Since leaving the city, Vega was having inexplicable episodes of disorientation. Her face would go sallow and she'd grip his arm tightly. This happened at the supermarket, even at home. Henry researched and printed up a diagnostic list of symptoms for panic attacks. He talked with her about it. She agreed to see a doctor but never made an appointment. She started going on these lake walks with Mr. Lippincott, with the old man, the two of them disappearing down the footpath. And Henry started having dreams that he was looking for his wife in crabby caves under the lake. He worried that if he could properly assemble everything in his head, wrap his mind around all of Vega, there might be reason to think she might really, physically, vanish for good one day. He waited for the packed suitcase on the bed, the note on the credenza, and felt, more urgently than he had imagined he could, the desire for a baby.

Where they lived now, the smallest excursion brought new risks. Vega went out for the mail one day and saw Mr. Jenkins from across the street on a gurney, his eyes wide and alert, but his body limp and ineffectual as an EMT lifted him into an ambulance. She stepped out to pick her dill and saw frail Mrs. Wallsterson, folded over the railing like a banana peel as she climbed her front steps. She stopped at the pharmacy for stamps and overheard Mrs. Height asking for more steroids for her cancer.

When she reported these things to Henry, he would shake his head sadly. Sometimes he shared similar observations. But he had no trouble returning to the shopping list in front of them or the unedited manuscript on the computer screen. She didn't fault him, but for her it was harder.

Sweet, but not terribly interesting—that's what she'd thought, dismissively, the night she first met Henry, at a party. He was introduced to her as the friend from the suburbs who was crashing on the couch. He wore khaki pants and a polo shirt. He held a napkin under his beer. He was, that awful phrase, *clean cut*. And easy to talk to. He asked a lot of questions about her, and when she answered, he looked right at her. Meanwhile, her eyes drifted, searching out someone grumpier, more aloof—more mysterious, she thought. Henry didn't say or do anything that night that made a powerful impression on her, but over the next couple of months she found herself accepting his invitations to go out—the first time because why not, and after that because . . . because on their first date he had gripped her forearm so firmly as they crossed an intersection that it actually hurt. The gesture had stunned her. She rode back to Jersey with him one night, to his parents' house, and they kissed in the basement like furtive teenagers. Her friends called him naïve and simple, and she found herself defending him. He wasn't those things, but he lived by a secular faith that he could keep himself and those he cared about safe. And despite what she'd believed for years about herself— that she was unshakably independent, empathetic with strangers but cruel and indifferent to those she was intimate with—she found herself moved by the idea. No one was more surprised than she was. Except for, perhaps, Henry himself. And at some point, Vega's unlikely reaction to Henry's attention—the very fact that she didn't anticipate falling for anyone like him—became more exciting, more arousing to her than the adventures she could have with a man who was uncaring, unkind. She thought she would forget about him when she went to Romania, but he was the first person she called when she returned.

In the early years of their relationship she would occasionally have a passing concern. Had she tricked herself into falling in love with Henry? Had she merely inverted one set of expectations for another? But she didn't worry much anymore about her love for him; time had successfully argued against her doubts. Still, as they got older, her husband's protective manner affected her less and less. Her anxiety had worsened since they left the city. Sometimes this anxiety was diffuse, like a dull headache. Other times it was overwhelming and sharp. Once, the two of them were waiting in line at the supermarket, their cart brightly loaded with tomatoes, detergent, peanut butter. Henry was talking about an irksome writer resisting fixes on an article, while she shifted their groceries onto the conveyor belt. There was no one thing that could have caused it, but the air in the room reconfigured suddenly, enlarging certain discrete facts to an oppressive size and pitch: the familiar thickness of Henry's voice, the beep of the bar-code scanner, the pointed finger of the woman in line, disciplining her daughter, and the ripe, earthy smell of tomatoes. It was enough to make her gag.

"Henry, stop. Just stop for a second," she heard herself saying, because she couldn't ask the mother or the checkout clerk to stop. By the time Henry had guided her outside, one hand on the small of her back, the other pushing the cart, she was better. But it was only a matter of time before that feeling, the knowledge that something was coming for her—and for Henry too, coming for them both—would return.

Henry helped Cynthia prune her bushes one weekend and after that she spread the word that he was "handy." Other single old ladies and widows in the village began calling on him for assistance with odd jobs—setting up a new computer in order to email a grandson or replacing a dead bulb. He did not in fact consider himself a handy man, or even a man who really liked to roll up his sleeves. But he didn't mind these odd jobs they found for him to do. They always served him cake and coffee or tea afterward. Or they insisted on making him a peanut butter and jelly sandwich. And it was so easy to make them laugh! He'd flex his arm and make a little joke about his overpowering strength and they girl-giggled. Oh, it was pathetic, blushing at the flattery of old women. Vega would have teased him. But she wasn't there. And besides, flirting was a good way to avert his eyes from some of those living rooms and kitchens.

For the most part, the homes he saw fell into two categories. Some were excruciatingly clean, the fear of bacteria and viruses sitting in for the fear of death. Mrs. Height, who had just finished a round of chemo, kept fresh paper towels on every surface that a guest might come into contact with: the armrests of a chair, the top of an end table, the seat of her toilet. She asked Henry to gather up and throw away any that he touched at the end of his visits. Other homes were layered with the dust and sour stench of a life gathered under one roof. These homes were cluttered with tarnished mirrors and milk-glass containers filled with stale candies.

But the women cheered him with their modest flirtations and touched him with their gratitude. They looked almost teary-eyed when he stood, ready to leave. They never forgot to mention how lucky and appreciative Cynthia was to have him next door. He found himself developing a mild protectiveness toward Mrs. Lippincott, and when she complained to him that her husband's breathing was getting worse and worse because he was smoking more and more, he offered to talk to Vega. It was wrong, Mrs. Lippincott said—and Henry agreed—that Vega was smoking with him. Vega's reply was that she only smoked with Gordon sometimes. She was getting him walking, and wasn't that a good thing? But Henry felt sorry for Cynthia. He sensed a sadness in her that Vega seemed unwilling to recognize.

He went to talk with her one afternoon, when his wife and Gordon were taking their walk. She didn't seem at all surprised to see him—pleased, rather, as if she'd been waiting for someone. She wore a jumpsuit with a pattern of yellow daisies on the breast pocket, and a plastic barrette clasping together a few gray hairs above her ear. A line of pink lipstick teetered across her thin lips. He thought of a child's sincerest efforts to color within the lines.

He recalled that she had asked him to fix a squeaky hinge on the medicine cabinet.

"Don't worry about that now," she said. "Come have tea with me."

He followed her to the kitchen. She was very short, and Henry guessed she probably came up to Gordon's elbow. He wondered if Gordon wasn't stooped from years of bending to hug and kiss her, and then thought of Vega, a few inches shorter than he was, and hoped—foolishly, he knew—that his own body would start to curve over the years.

She took his mug to the table. She herself was not having any. He sat next to her.

She patted him on the knee and then folded her hands on the table. The sun threw long bars of light across the cabinets. A small sapphire stone on her finger refracted the light, but the band was swallowed up in the creases between her knuckles.

Henry asked after Gordon's health.

"Better this week."

"That's good."

He could tell she didn't want to talk about the emphysema. "He's just, well, you know, he's always been Gordon. He does things his own way," she said.

"I know a little about that," Henry said tentatively, unsure where her thoughts were headed. He wondered if it made sense to put a hand on her shoulder. "Is there something else?"

She let her hands fall into her lap. She drew her shoulders together, took a deep, shaky breath, and said, "It's been years since . . . now he goes on these walks every afternoon. He didn't used to. He always hated me for nagging him to walk. I always said—" She paused and then sat up a little, fortified by her frustration. "I'd ask him, 'Gordon, want to take a walk today by the lake, together? It's nice out,' I'd say, 'it'll be good for you.' And now of course he walks with your wife every day and I'm grateful, because it is good for him, even though they do smoke. But I don't know where they go. And, well, I always wanted us to walk together."

"Mrs. Lippincott," Henry said, softly. He decided it was okay to touch her shoulder. Her smallness surprised him.

"You're a nice man, Henry," she said. "A good husband, I bet. Your wife is lucky." He felt an immense pity that he didn't want to feel, for Mrs. Lippincott, for himself.

Before he left, she pulled out a small envelope from her purse and handed it to him. It was an invitation to the annual Labor Day dance at the community center, featuring *Live! The Funky Monkey Jazz Quartet.*

"Bring your wife, too," she said. "Everyone is hoping you'll both go."

Vega knew that Henry was worried about her. And that he didn't know what to think about her afternoon walks with Gordon. The old man wasn't as sweet or solicitous as his wife. He probably cared for nothing as much as he cared for his cigarettes. But Vega thought there was something honest there. Better than the old people buzzing and twittering in the community center Wednesday nights. As though it weren't true their hearts could stop at any moment.

She decided not to tell Henry about the time she and Gordon took a break from their walk, stopping to rest on a stone bench near the lake. Thanksgiving was behind them at this point, Christmas still a few weeks ahead. A few neighbors with helpful and available children had strung lights across the backyard trees and set up mechanical reindeer, for the benefit of those across the lake. But in the thin daylight the effect was more broken and sad, and as she took this in Vega thought she could feel Gordon next to her thinking the same. She turned so that he could light her cigarette and he cupped his hand around hers, to block the wind. She inhaled deeply, his rough hand still touching hers. When she pulled away, she saw that he was eyeing her chest.

She was wearing a scarf wrapped around her neck, a snug parka. Underneath, a loose silk blouse. She hesitated only a moment. "Here," she said, and unzipped her jacket. She took his hand and guided it under her parka, over her right breast. His fingers tightened; he squeezed her like a child might squeeze a ball. This made her smile. She wanted to give him more.

It was December, cold, but she unbuttoned the top of her blouse and shifted her bra up, revealing both breasts. Gordon watched with a cigarette dangling in one hand. Then he raised his other hand back to her right breast and ran his thumb over her nipple, till it hardened. A silent sigh escaped his shoulders. He tugged on the silk of her blouse. She reached up and touched the crown of his head. His hair was stiff, as she'd imagined.

That was it. Their conversations never went too far. She didn't confide much in him, though occasionally she would ask questions, easy questions. He was born in upstate New York, and he had been an engineer for decades, but he'd always wanted to be an architect. He had one child, a son, who lived in Florida. Mostly, she just liked watching him inhale—the recklessness of it.

Henry had to coax Vega at first but she canceled their dinner plans in the city and they went to the dance.

They went a little drunk from a bottle of wine they shared at home. They went with ironic smiles, determined to record absurdities. In their tipsy walk up the hill, they joked about a fiber cake, prune-flavored vodka martinis, door prizes including monogrammed heart monitors. They even dressed up a little. Vega wore a chiffon skirt and Henry found a bowtie.

The room—the large atrium they'd only seen from across the lake—was dolled up with streamers and balloons in red, white, and blue. "Overstock," Vega whispered. "From the Fourth of July." And Henry squeezed her hand.

They stood near the door for a few minutes, feeling shy, feeling like a new couple. Plastic platters of pigs in a blanket and chips and dip were arrayed along one wall, soda, beer, and wine along the opposite. In one corner, the Funky Monkey, four reedy men in rented tuxes, were already on their first break. Mrs. Height—a blue silk scarf tied snug around her head—was sashaying their way with a plate of Ritz crackers and cheese. Someone's grandson was using the band intermission to play a CD on a laptop, and "Chattanooga Choo-Choo" strained the small speakers. In the open space between food and drink, half a dozen or so couples two-stepped hand in hand.

Cynthia found Henry and pulled him into a ring of her friends near the alcohol. Vega followed. "Look who made it, look who made it," she cooed. Gordon was sitting in a chair not far away, a beer in one hand and in the other, a carrot stick that he rolled between two fingers.

One of the women took Vega's hand and Henry's and clasped the two together. "You kids have to dance at least two songs," she said. "That's the rule for us, and don't think you're getting out of it. No one does." They waited for the Funky Monkey to start up again, and then they did join the swaying hips and shoulders. For Henry, there were winks and nudges from the ladies on the floor. The quartet included a flutist, and when he played a weeping solo at the end of a peppier number, everyone slow danced. Henry bent his knees so Vega could rest her chin on his shoulder. As they danced, their ears touched.

When the time came, it was going to be different for each of them, they both knew that. Vega would become unreachable, impatient and sullen as a teenager. Henry would cry and, if his wife was still alive, he'd draw her into his weak arms.

They stayed at the party maybe an hour, no more than two. They both felt something pulling them home. In the kitchen, they shed shoes and bowtie and chiffon skirt, and kissed each other deliberately, thoughtfully. Upstairs in their bed they took their time. They brought each other along. In the morning, Henry placed a hand on Vega's stomach and looked at her hopefully. She nodded "yes," although it was impossible to know yet for sure.

Ruth Prawer Jhabvala
Aphrodisiac

Kɪsʜᴇɴ's ᴜɴɪᴠᴇʀsɪᴛʏ ғʀɪᴇɴᴅs ᴀᴛ Cambridge completely understood when he talked to them about the sort of novel that should be written about India—the sort of novel that he wanted to write. The thing was, he explained, to get the integers right, to be sure that these were sunk into the deepest layers of the Indian experience: caste-ridden villagers, urban slum dwellers, landless laborers, as well as the indecently rich of commerce and industry.

His own integers were sunk in a prosperous gated colony in New Delhi. Here he returned from Cambridge to live with his mother and his elder brother, Shiv, in the villa that his late father had commissioned in the International Style, which was prevalent at the time. During Kishen's absence, Shiv had got married—in a big, traditional wedding, which Kishen couldn't attend because he was in the middle of his finals. So he didn't meet his new sister-in-law until his return. He hadn't meant to stay in India. He'd wanted to go back to Cambridge and maybe study for another degree until he felt himself ready to start on his life's work. But then this happened, she happened: his sister-in-law, Naina.

It hadn't been an arranged marriage; Kishen's mother was too modern to arrange marriages for her sons. A respected economist, she had always been at the forefront of educated Indian women. Sometimes she and her elder son even served on the same committees, for Shiv was a high-ranking bureaucrat. He had met his bride at a reception in honor of her uncle, a member of parliament, who had brought Naina from her father's estate in their native province for her first visit to New Delhi. She was very young, shy, scarcely educated, though she had attended an élite girls' boarding school in Jaipur. After her marriage, her mother-in-law tried to encourage her to study at some New Delhi college, but Naina claimed to be too stupid—yes, even for domestic science.

Although Kishen couldn't help agreeing that she was, to some extent, stupid, she was the only person in the house with whom he was eager to discuss his projected novel. She took no interest in it at all, yet somehow she casually disposed of one of his greatest problems: how to communicate the nuances of Indian life in English, which was the only language in which he could truly express himself. Naina simply jumbled up her languages, English and Hindi. When he tried to talk to her about his work (because he wanted to talk to her about everything), she didn't even pretend to listen. Instead, she said, "I'm meeting the girls—coffee *pina hai. Aoge? Chalo bhai* we'll have some fun—*mazza ajaiga.*"

She had formed her own circle of girlfriends, and Kishen soon became a source of entertainment for them. Naina was proud of the way he amused them and humored all their concerns. They valued his opinion in matters of style, and also of culture, though he laughed at their taste, which hadn't changed since they were schoolgirls. They held morning coffee parties in the smartest Connaught Place restaurants or watched pirated films together on the giant screens in their giant living rooms. When they cried at a heroine's onscreen plight, Kishen would murmur some remark into Naina's ear, converting her tears into giggles, which soon spread to all the weeping girls.

They liked attending polo matches and pretending to be in

love with the contestants, who were princelings from the President's Bodyguard. These young women were all married, but mostly to rich, paunchy businessmen who in no way resembled the polo players. Only Shiv was tall and handsome (the opposite of Kishen), and Naina's friends sincerely appreciated her good luck. So did she, though she was, or pretended to be, critical of Shiv: of his absorption in his work, which didn't leave enough time for her; of his lack of interest in the romantic films and books she adored. She often laughed about him—she imitated his walk, the way his feet splayed outward, so busy, so important— and Kishen laughed with her. If his mother overheard them, she rebuked them but couldn't help smiling with pride in her elder son, which she knew Naina, for all her mockery, shared. Only Kishen's laughter was genuine.

Mother and Shiv, both busy with their work, were glad that Kishen and Naina were such good company for each other. But sometimes Mother would ask, "And your work?" For she was waiting for Kishen to become as successful in his field as Shiv was in his. "Coming along," Kishen answered, and he considered this to be true. He felt that, with Naina and her friends, he was immersing himself in his material. *They* were the integers with which he would build his world—the India that he knew, not what others thought he should know. The girls, too, were waiting for him to become published and famous. When they asked what he was writing about, he said, "You." That made them laugh, and they clamored for a percentage of the fortune he was going to make with their lives.

Meanwhile, he entertained them with stories, anecdotes from their New Delhi social world—hungry kites swooping over an open-air banquet, new, palatial apartment buildings without electricity or water, the Ayurvedic doctor poking his tented patients through their burkas, the dire results of a homeopath mixing up his aphrodisiacs with his laxatives. "You should write it down!" the girls exclaimed—and, at their urging, he began to do so. They snatched the pages from him and sent them to the editor of a leading English-language newspaper, who was a friend of all the girls and the lover of one. These writings—these tongue-in-cheek anecdotes—became the basis of his local fame. A magazine commissioned a weekly column; he was read everywhere. Mother returned from her meetings reporting the chuckles of her fellow committee members; Shiv quoted a cabinet minister who said that Kishen "had hit the nail right on the head." Everyone was proud of him.

That was during his first two years back in India. Then things began to change in the house. Actually, physically, they had begun to change soon after Naina's arrival. Mother had originally furnished the house with the newfound enthusiasm of the intellectual classes for indigenous Indian handicrafts—vibrant textiles from Orissa, village women's silver anklets turned into ashtrays. Now another layer was added, for whenever Naina went home to see her family—which she did often in those first years—she brought back precious objects of her own. These were not village handicrafts but something differently indigenous: the gaudy taste of the maharajas' palaces, which had drifted down to her own family of feudal landowners. She installed multicolored chandeliers, oil paintings of hunting parties and court ceremonials. Mother's bright hand-loomed rug was replaced by the pelt of a recently killed tiger. Naina was so proud of these acquisitions that Mother even allowed the head of a water buffalo to be nailed to the wall, though it had to be taken down when, having been improperly embalmed, it began to decay and disintegrate.

Then came Naina's first pregnancy, for which, in accordance with custom, she went home. When she reappeared, it was not only with a baby but with his nurse. This nurse, known as Bari-Mai, had been Naina's mother's and Naina's and was now very old. She spoke in a dialect that only Naina could understand, and she made it clear that no one in the house was of any importance to her except Naina, whom she called Devi (goddess), and the baby, Munna. But with Kishen Bari-Mai did establish a peculiar relationship. From the first moment she saw him, she wheezed so much that she could only point at him in derision—but for what? Naina said, "It's because she's never seen anyone like you."

"You mean, anyone so ugly?"

"*Aré,* gosh, darling, *yeh kya baat hai?* What are you saying?" She stroked his cheek, and, although he liked this affectionate gesture, it made him aware that he was short, squat, and balding: ugly, no doubt, to both her and Bari-Mai.

"*Dekho, Baba—Papa hai!*" Naina called out when Shiv came home from the office, and she thrust the bundled baby into his arms. Shiv held him nervously. No one in the family felt comfortable holding the baby. There was something disconcerting to them in the many little amulets he wore around his neck and wrists, each guarding him against a disease or the Evil Eye. He was also greasy from the oil that Bari-Mai smeared on him for the health of his skin and hair. And he had a peculiar smell, which was not that of a baby but more—though no one said it—that of Bari-Mai. For not only did she clutch him all day but she slept with him at night, on the floor of the nursery that Mother had furnished for him with a new white cot, a playpen, and a mural of Mother Goose rhymes.

After Munna's birth, Naina abandoned the outings with her girlfriends, and Kishen stayed home with her. She was very free in his presence, suckling the baby at her great round brown nipples, while Kishen sat near her, scribbling a piece for his column. He was a chain-smoker, and sometimes she had enjoyed a cigarette with him. Now she returned to chewing betel, and one day she ordered Bari-Mai to prepare one for Kishen as well. "Open your mouth," she told him, and he was about to obey her when he saw his mother's cook making warning gestures at him from behind the door. "*Aré*—open—*kholo, bhai,*" Naina said impatiently. Ignoring the cook, Kishen allowed her to pop the leaf into his mouth. He disliked the taste and the feel of it. He asked, "What does she put in it?" Naina laughed. "*Khas cheez hai*—something very special to make you love Munna and me forever."

It was Kishen's birthday, and Mother had a gift for him. She watched him unwrap it: a slim volume tastefully bound in hand-loomed cloth, containing reprints of his newspaper and magazine articles. Full of her own excitement and pleasure, she said, "It's all there. All your beautiful work." He thanked her, kissed her, but he thought, Is this all you expect from me?

They were interrupted by the cook, who burst in on them, wailing, "With my own eyes!" He had seen with his own eyes how she—the witch, Bari-Mai—had stirred a powder, a poison, into Kishen's birthday *pilao*. Naina came rushing in, shouting that Bari-Mai had wanted only to add her own touch with a pinch of saffron. "*Zaffran,*" the cook repeated angrily. "As if I don't know *zaffran*." Naina had already turned from him to Munna, riding on her hip. "*Bolo*—Happy birthday, Chacha-Uncle!" She thrust him forward to greet Kishen with sticky caresses.

But later, when they were alone, she said, "It's all lies. Don't believe them."

"No," Kishen said. "I don't believe Bari-Mai is trying to poison us."

"They're all crazy. *Pagal hai sab.* They think she's a terrible witch."

"It's you," he said. "You're the terrible witch." Before she could say anything, he went on, helplessly waving his arms, "I'm twenty-seven years old today and I haven't done a thing. No! No, I have not written a beautiful book. Only Mother thinks so."

"Munna thinks so," Naina said, nibbling Munna's ear.

"When Munna grows older, he'll laugh at me as I'd laugh at anyone who wrote this sort of rubbish. But what's the use of talking to you? You don't listen to anything I try to tell you."

"Oh, yes. I'm very stupid."

"You are—no ideas, no theories—thank God! If you had

them, if you drove me crazy the way I drive myself crazy, thinking and theorizing and doing nothing all day but sitting here with you and all night thinking about you—it's you, you who's poisoning me. No, don't go away!" To keep her from leaving, he put his arms around her waist. At first too surprised to resist him, she then did so with ease. Not only was he shorter than she; he was overweight and breathless with lack of exercise. She gave him a push that sent him staggering backward to the floor, then stared down at him with angry, kohl-rimmed eyes. He stared back, partly in fear of her, partly in fear of himself and the sensation that had filled him when he touched her hot, soft flesh. The next moment, she put out her hand to pull him up; she was laughing, and he tried to laugh, too. It was all just a game between them.

When a second boy was born, Bari-Mai decided that only she could provide the nourishment her Devi needed to breast-feed two babies. She pushed aside the cook's stainless-steel vessels for her own blackened cauldron, into which she stirred spices unwrapped from little twists of newspaper. Noxious cooking smells—asafetida, like a gas—pervaded the house. Naina moved around her urine-and-milk-soaked kingdom with one child on her hip and another sucking at her breast. Shiv's study was moved out of earshot of the rest of the house, and as far as possible from what had been his marital bedroom and was now inhabited by both children and Bari-Mai, who stretched out on the floor, bundled in the single cloth she wore day and night.

Shiv began to come home later every night; Naina was always waiting for him. They spoke in low voices, but not intimately. Naina's initial passion for her husband had changed into some other kind of passion, charged with resentment. Kishen, in his bedroom, willed himself not to hear, and he guessed that his mother was doing the same. When he went into her room after a restless night, he found her sitting up very straight, with her hands folded in her lap. Mother said, "Of course he comes home late—he's very busy with meetings and conferences with the cabinet, with the Prime Minister. He's important to the whole country." Her voice rose. "She should be proud!"

"She *is* proud."

"She doesn't understand. She understands nothing."

A modern woman, Mother had set herself against the stereotypical role of mother-in-law. She was determined not to complain about her daughter-in-law, or about the encroachments, the ruin of her ordered household. So she said nothing, not even to Kishen. Instead, she stayed out of the house at meetings of her own. Kishen suspected that she was no longer elected to the offices for which she had once been the unquestioned candidate. But still she forced herself to be present—trimly dressed, her short, stylishly cut gray hair brushed back, even a dab of lipstick and rouge applied to simulate an energy that was no longer required of her.

Meanwhile, the boys were growing up. They were no longer attached like limpets to their mother's body. And then they grew up more and were sent off to boarding school in the hills. Kishen had expected that Bari-Mai would be sent away, too, but that didn't happen. She still spent her nights rolled up at the foot of Naina's marital bed while Shiv slept on the couch in his study. He was at the height of his career now, and there were photographs of him in the newspapers, hovering beside the Prime Minister at the signing of an agreement that he had helped negotiate. However late he came home, Naina waited up for him. Her voice had become more strident and desperate; Kishen listened in spite of himself, and he knew that Mother, too, was awake and listening.

During the day, he could no longer sit quietly writing his column by Naina's side. She kept interrupting him with complaints about Shiv; and when Kishen tried to defend his brother by saying that he was working late, she brought out the newspapers with photographs of Shiv and the Prime Minister and pointed to some female under-secretary in the background. It might have been a different woman in each picture, but Naina sneered in outrage—

"Is this his work? Fine work!" Once, she dragged Kishen to the room where Shiv now spent his nights; she picked up his pillow and thrust it into Kishen's face. "It's *her* smell. Her dirty smell he brings home with him after he does what he does with her." She made a sound of disgust and Bari-Mai echoed it with a splutter of saliva. More and more it seemed to Kishen that Bari-Mai was not a person at all but an emanation of something in Naina herself: something that had been bred for generations in the stifling women's quarters of their desert home.

It was June, and the days were hot, cruelly hot. Kishen warned Mother not to go out, but one afternoon she said she had to—if she didn't, goodness only knew what those new committee members would get up to. An hour later, the driver had to bring her back, and she was an old crushed woman. She lay on her bed and Kishen sat beside her; when he tried to get up, she clutched at his hand in a pleading gesture that she had never used with him before. She did it again, moments later, when they heard Naina's voice outside, with Bari-Mai's wild echo. "How do you stand it?" Mother whispered, and then he told her what he hadn't quite told himself—that he was thinking of returning to England.

At once, she rallied. She said that he should take another degree, or at least some sort of course. "What—now?" he said, for he was almost forty. "A course in writing," she said vaguely, and he said, teasing her, "I thought you liked my writing the way it is." But he knew that she wanted him to leave for other reasons—in fact, for the same reasons that he wanted to go.

He looked into a writing school in Bristol, and Mother eagerly sent away for the application forms. She knew that it would take some time for these to arrive, but when six weeks had gone by she said that they would have to request them again. Although she and Kishen were alone in her bedroom, she lowered her voice: "I'll write for them today, this time by express mail." He nodded his consent, as though he, too, suspected that someone might be listening.

The next day, Naina invited him to go out with her. She drove with abandon, so fast that he feared for the rickshaws and the wandering animals that she kept missing by inches. His timidity amused her, so he tried not to show it and sat there tense and silent, his hands clutched between his knees.

She took him to an open-bazaar stall that was reputed to be the best for a kind of very spicy Delhi snack food. Kishen, with his delicate digestion, had never wanted to eat there, but Naina seemed perfectly at home. He watched her as she scooped up the little messes with her fingers in a trance of enjoyment; she soon sent him back for a second helping, which she finished just as quickly, and then—"I shouldn't!"—for a third. At last she was sated, spread out on a rickety little bench as a tattered servant boy with a rag wiped the ground underneath it. She seemed oblivious of the looks of urgent desire directed at her by other customers and passersby, and by the proprietor himself, perched up on his platform stirring a vat of fly-spotted cream; or perhaps she was used to them, as she was used to the way that Kishen was looking at her across the table.

She was almost middle-aged now, her body widened, fattened by pregnancy, by excessive eating, and by long hours of deep sleep in the hot afternoons. Yet he talked to her as he had done in her youthful years, though he knew she wasn't listening—not in the way his mother listened when he spoke of his work, or of himself.

And suddenly she interrupted him: "Why are you wanting to run back to England?"

He tried to explain it to her. He told her that it was better sometimes not to be too close to one's source of inspiration. And, as if he were talking about her as that source, she said, "But if I don't want you to go? If I say *mat jao?* Please stay?"

"Try to understand." And he repeated it all—about being detached, about recollecting in tranquillity—everything that Mother and his friends in England understood and Naina didn't. But as he talked he thought of a painting by an elderly English painter who was a friend of his mother's; the painting depicted a giant hand caressing a mountain and was titled *I Have Touched the Breast of Mother India*. It had always made him laugh, and now Naina was laughing as though he had said something just as ludicrous.

"When will you send off your application?" she interrupted.

"As soon as it comes," he said.

"It hasn't come yet? No? *Sachmuch?* Really?" She suppressed a smile as she opened her handbag and dug around in its messy contents. An envelope emerged; she held it out for him to see but not to take. He realized that not only did she listen at doors; she lay in wait for letters to purloin.

Now she smiled at him openly, teasing him—and how could he help smiling back at her? "Shall I?" she said. "Tear it up?"

She held it out, pulled it back, held it out again. It was a game now—one that he was determined to win. He leaned forward and snatched the envelope out of her hand, quite easily, because she let it go as if she knew what he would do with it: tear it in half, then in half again, all the time gazing at her for approval, which she gave.

The next time Mother asked him about the application forms, he told her that he had filled them out and sent them off. She seemed satisfied, but a day or two later she fell ill. Instead of going to her meetings, she lay in her bedroom with the curtains shut and the air-conditioner on. Her face was drawn, and because her partial denture had been removed her mouth was sunken. The doctor came—he was a friend and contemporary who had worked with her on health-care reforms. He prescribed medicines, but when those didn't work Kishen and Shiv called in other, younger doctors. Still the sickness failed to subside, and now Mother mostly lay on her bed with her eyes closed.

Once, Bari-Mai, quick and agile as a monkey, clambered onto the bed and began to press down on Mother's legs. Mother cried out in shock and Kishen, too, cried out, so that Naina removed Bari-Mai and both left indignantly, protesting good intentions.

Alone with Kishen, Mother apologized; she said she was aware that it was unfair to see anything but a poor old woman in Bari-Mai, sunk in the rites and superstitions of a backward part of the country.

But the cook saw more than that. He came into Mother's room and, whispering just loud enough for her and Kishen to hear, told them how all day he was on duty in the kitchen, and even at night he stayed up to watch. But who knew—worn out by his vigilance, he sometimes dropped off to sleep for a few moments, during which Bari-Mai must have insinuated her powders and potions into his pots. How else was it that Mother had been laid low by a sickness that the greatest doctors in the world were unable to cure?

"It's unhygienic," Shiv said, after discovering the cook asleep in the kitchen one night. When Kishen and Mother told him the reason, he said that it was psychologically unhygienic to allow such thoughts to enter their minds. Still, they continued to feel uneasy, though they were ashamed to admit it, even to each other.

It was the summer vacation, and the two boys, Munna, now fifteen, and Chottu, fourteen, came home from their boarding school in the foothills of the Himalayas. It was the same school, modeled on Eton and Harrow, that Shiv and Kishen had attended in their time. Shiv had been very successful there, Kishen less so. Both Munna and Chottu followed in their father's footsteps, played all sports, were popular; Munna already had Shiv's confident voice and his pompous walk.

Naina couldn't stop petting her two boys, stroking their downy cheeks, though they frowned and pretended not to like it. They bullied her, told her she was getting too fat, and did she have to chew that disgusting betel? They made her play cricket with them in the back garden; she flew like a young girl between the wickets, flushed, her hair coming down, but they kept getting her out before she could make a single run. Bari-Mai was appointed fielder; she squatted, motionless as a stone, only her jaws moving in their perpetual mumble.

Shiv tried to come home from work earlier and, instead of shutting himself in his study, he sat with the boys to discuss their future. Munna wanted to join the Administrative Service, like his father, and Chottu was thinking of the Navy. Shiv considered their choices, the three of them serious together. Naina hovered around them with unwelcome interruptions—"Did you finish your milk, Munna?"—until he shouted at her that his name was not Munna but Raj Kumar. "Oh, big man," she said, her angry stare directed not at her son but at his father, who tried not to meet it. That night, for the first time since the boys' arrival, he and Naina fought again.

The older boy was especially affected by what he overheard, and the next day he sought out Kishen. Trying to answer Munna's questions about his parents, Kishen had to admit that he knew nothing about marriage—how could he? All he knew was that there were bound to be clashes of personality, especially between two people as different as Shiv and Naina. The boy nodded. "So you think they shouldn't be married?" he said. Kishen avoided a reply—not because he didn't have one but because he suspected that Naina or Bari-Mai might be listening behind the door. The boy repeated his question, and when Kishen was still silent, he gave his considered opinion, as judicious and balanced as his father's would have been: "Maybe they should get a divorce." The next moment, Naina came flying through the door. "Divorce!" she cried. "You dare say that in this house!" She abused him in her native dialect and then she raised her hand and slapped him. The sound of the slap echoed through the house, and remained there, ineradicable even after the boys returned to school.

Shiv invited Kishen to lunch at one of the new hotels, a grand palace with slippery marble floors and hothouse blooms in man-size vases. The prices here insured that only the richest Indians could gain admission. But the richest Indians were no longer the old style of businessmen, the ghee-fed descendants of milkmen and moneylenders: they were younger men, better traveled, almost cosmopolitan. Several of them came over to greet Shiv, with the respect that was due to him as a member of the administration that controlled permits and licenses. When they returned to their tables, Shiv informed his brother of their positions in the corporate world, the multi-*crore* companies over which they ruled. Kishen noticed his almost wistful glances at these men—and at the lively young women who accompanied them. He guessed that these were their secretaries, or perhaps their lovers, but Shiv said that they were their wives: yes, these slim, youthful women were wives, many of them mothers, too, and at the same time helpmeets, social assets to their important husbands.

Here Shiv changed the subject. He said that he had now reached the highest rank of the bureaucracy; his next posting would be as an accredited ambassador, and his success in that role would depend to a large extent on his social skills, and those of his wife. "Naina wouldn't be happy," he said.

"How do you know that?" Kishen said. "You don't know. You know nothing about her."

Shiv, too, grew more heated. "And she knows nothing about me. And cares nothing, about my work, my career—what sort of marriage is that?" He changed the subject again. "What about you? And if you don't mind my asking—you and the Great Indian Novel?"

"I thought you liked my little pieces."

"You shouldn't be hanging around the house so much. You should be getting out, meeting people. The middle classes. The new generation of businessmen. The entrepreneurs."

"And their suitable wives," Kishen said.

Shiv's voice became more intense, charged with suppressed anger. "She has this mad idea that I have some grand love affair going." He laughed without laughing, cut up his meat, chewed violently.

"And is it true, her mad idea?"

"Of course not! And, if it were, who could blame me? Living in that house, in that atmosphere—no wonder Mother's sick. We're all sick. The stench of those beasts alone is enough to poison the lot of us." He put down his knife and fork and stared at his brother, shocked at himself, though presumably he had been referring to the buffalo head, long since disintegrated, and the tiger pelt, which was going the same way.

Alone with Kishen in her bedroom, Mother whispered, "Have you heard from Bristol about your application?"

"They turned me down."

He lied without a qualm, and was amazed by her reaction. She covered her face and rocked to and fro. When he caught her in his arms, she clung to him and wouldn't let him go. How thin she was, how worn away. When she released him, he tried to smile. "I didn't realize you were so eager to get rid of me."

She stroked his head, regretting perhaps all the hair he had lost. Then she kissed him. "Go to England," she said. "You'll have peace of mind there."

"And if I'm far away and you get worse?"

"When I know you're writing your book, I'll be well."

But the next day Naina told him, "Six months, that's all. Three months, six, a year. At home we can always tell. My uncle had a mistress, Mrs. Lal, *moti-taazi,* plump and nice—oh, he liked her very much! But Bari-Mai knew, and others knew, too. In six months, it was all gone, like a balloon, *psssst,* no more *moti-taazi.* It was God punishing her."

"Mother has done nothing to be punished for."

"She wants my husband to leave me. She's even set my sons against me! You think that such thoughts would come into my child's head if she hadn't put them there? I slapped him, God forgive me, but now God himself is slapping her—*aré, sunno,* where are you going?" He had got up to leave. She caught hold of his shirt, and it ripped in her hand. That made Naina laugh—her old playful, girlish laugh, like clear water running.

Kishen began to take Mother to various specialists. She enjoyed driving with him from one clinic to another; he held her hand the way she had held his on the first day of school. Whatever the doctors said, she claimed to be perfectly well—a little pain here and there, but what was that at her age, compared with what others had to suffer? Still, she grew more and more gaunt, while Kishen looked on helplessly; and every morning Naina and Bari-Mai sat on the front veranda and watched them drive away.

Finally, Shiv decided to send her to England, to consult with a Harley Street specialist. Kishen would have to take her. If at all possible, Shiv would join them, but meanwhile he made the arrangements for his mother and brother—the plane tickets, the hotel, the appointment with the doctor.

Mother was glad to go and Kishen knew that it was for his sake. He wanted to leave, too, he thought, to be in a cool green place, to collect and recollect everything in its complexity, which was impossible here with it all pressing down on him. Yet, at the same time, he felt guilty—maybe he had no right to go, maybe his place was here, even if he hated it.

"When are we leaving? Have our tickets come?" Mother asked Kishen so often that he began to believe there was some weakness in her mind. "Let them be sent by courier," she said, and then, every day, "Has the courier come?"

Kishen called the travel agent, who assured him that the tickets had been sent—yes, by courier. Kishen told him to cancel those and have duplicates sent to Shiv's office. Shiv brought them home and Kishen at once hid them in the inner pocket of his waistcoat, where he could check several times a day and know they were safe.

Naina had one of her great fights with Shiv. "Why are you sending them away? What use are your wonderful English doctors? It's written! Written here!" Kishen, listening from Mother's bedroom, imagined Naina drawing her finger across her forehead in the place where one's fate is inscribed.

· · ·

"She won't last the journey," Naina warned Kishen. "And no one there will know the ceremonies. All they have is the electric crematorium; they'll give you the ashes and you won't even know whose ashes they are."

"Why are you saying all this?"

"If you go, that's what will happen. Did your tickets come?"

The way she was looking at him, through him, it was as if she could penetrate right to his heart. But he knew that she couldn't see even as far as the contents of his waistcoat pocket, and for once he felt he had the upper hand.

Maybe she felt it, too, for she said in a different, cajoling voice, "When you're gone, will you remember me? Will you remember me as I was?"

He looked back at her: no, she was not as she had been. She was heavy, her complexion spotted by the spicy pickles she consumed, her mouth stained red by the betel. Even her tongue was red—like a demon's, he sometimes thought when he was angry at her. But at this moment he was not angry; he said, "No. Now. I'll remember you as you are now."

She threw back her head and laughed with a deep-throated pleasure that could swallow him whole. "Will you write about me?" She took a newly prepared betel from Bari-Mai, and asked, "What will you write?"

"All the bad things you do."

"Yes, I'm a bad woman." She translated this for Bari-Mai, who broke into excited chatter. "Bari-Mai says she's making you a very special *paan*."

"Oh, yes? What's she putting in it?"

"You'll see—very special." Her eyes were dancing over his face, looking to see whose turn it was to make the next move and win.

Bari-Mai handed her another betel, and Naina instructed him, "Open. *Kholo*."

Kishen drew back slightly, and she said, "There's nothing in it that you haven't eaten a hundred times."

He thought, Well, whatever it is—an aphrodisiac or whatever—it's as superfluous now as it was all those other times. He opened his mouth and soon it was full of betel juices. "Good, isn't it?" Naina said, and he affirmed, *"Badiya."* Superb.

She said, "Come on. Show. *Dikhao.*"

He didn't even pretend not to know what she was talking about. He took the tickets out of his waistcoat pocket. He handed them to her like a forfeit that he was called upon to pay.

She held them. "Shall I?" She waved them at him. "Or will you?"

"My turn," he said.

She pouted. "You did it last time." But she let them dangle loosely in her hand so that he could take them from her and begin to tear them in half—first his mother's, then his own.

Joan Silber

Two Opinions

WHEN MY FATHER WAS in prison, my mother took us to visit him. I was nine when he first went in, and my sister was six. Some of my mother's friends thought taking us there was a mistake. "The girls have to know," my mother said. "They're not too young. And why would I do that to Joe?"

My father was in Danbury, Connecticut, which my mother said was nicer than a lot of places, and he was there on principle. I knew what principle was. He was against the war, despite his despising Hitler and Hirohito as much as anyone ever could; he was against all wars waged by governments. He was against governments. He was an anarchist. Other people my parents knew went into the army as medics or did service at special camps, but not my dad, who wouldn't register for the draft before the war even started. I had a fair idea what registration was, but my sister didn't get it.

My mother dressed us nicely for these two-hour bus trips, in pleated skirts and Mary Janes, as if we were going all the way from Manhattan to visit a relative, which we were. We had never, of course, thought of our father this way, and Barbara, my sister, shrieked when she first saw him in those brown clothes that weren't his, with his mouth a tight line in his face. "Get her shushed," the guard said. "Or get her out of here. I'll say it once."

My father had an expression I'd never seen before, a wince of mortification. I made a zipping motion over my sister's lips, sealing them. "Hey, muffins," he said to us. We were in a visitors' room with a bunch of wooden chairs and several other families in dramas of their own. Our mother made us tell him what we'd done in school—Barbara had learned the state capitals, and I had come in second in a spelling bee, after Maxie Pfeiffer, who thought she was the top of the world. "Second is good," my father said.

We couldn't bring crayons or pencils or toys into this room, so when my mother wanted adult talk, she had me take my sister into a corner and tell stories to entertain her. "*Thank* you, Louise," my mother said. We sat on the pitted linoleum and I made up a story about a blue elf that made no sense. Barbara pretended to like it.

"Behave yourselves, kitten-heads," my father said when we left. On the bus going home, my mother opened a bag with special treats—celery stuffed with cream cheese, ham sandwiches with relish, homemade brownies and date-nut squares too, and a thermos of lemonade. We were very excited, the whole trip seemed to have been so we could have this food.

We learned to expect treats on every trip, donated by friends or baked by our hardworking mother at night. My dad was allowed an hour of us a month, which could be broken up into two half-hour visits. The visits had creepy aspects—our mother had to go behind a curtain to be searched; one of the prisoners had a face like a panther; the guards blocked us and made us go home the time we were four minutes late. All the same, we mostly looked forward to going. Our father was quieter there than at home—no rowdy games, no tickling—but he could tease us about our big feet or tell us we were more beautiful than Lana Turner; his voice was still his voice.

The kids in school were the problem. My father didn't care

if the enemy bombed and burned and shot everyone in his own country. He didn't care who died among all the brothers and fathers who were fighting for all of us. I heard this all day every day from kids I didn't know and kids I did. "He's my *father*," I said. Maxie Pfeiffer dared another girl to punch me in the stomach. I had been taught not to hit, and my hands trying to shield myself just made everybody laugh. A teacher broke us up and sent the girl into detention (Maxie went free), but I was never safe at school. Barbara didn't have it easy either. Once they threw a bag of dog shit at her back.

My friend Ruthie's family wouldn't let me come to their apartment any more. Ruthie said, "Does your father *want* Hitler to kill us? We're Jewish, you know."

"*I* know," I said. "I've only known you since you were five."

Her parents wouldn't let her in my house either, but we were old enough to go to the park in Washington Square ourselves, where we continued a game about cowgirls and runaway horses that we'd played for years. There was a grassy spot across from the fountain that we especially liked, and we met in all weather, out on the range in earmuffs.

None of this got easier as time went on. My father was sentenced to a year, and when he came home, my sister kept sitting on his lap every time he sat down, and I was always tap-dancing for him. I pursued him nonstop with the shuffle-off-to-Buffalo. There was a big party to celebrate his return, with music on the Victrola and my mother giggling. She kept working at the job she had now, sketching ads for a department store in Brooklyn, and our dad was mostly home, where he read a lot. I didn't understand what happened next. The law still wanted him to register for the draft—hadn't he already told them? He had to tell them again. He was home for six months and then he was back in prison.

My sister Barbara was a mess, so I had to be not a mess. I ignored her stupid whining and I acted very upright and prissy, which was a good idea—after a while she tried to imitate me and stopped being such a pill. My mother started to visit the prison more often without us. And in my dad's second year there, he was part of a work strike because he didn't like it that colored men had to sit separate in the dining room (my father told the *guards* he wouldn't work) and this went on for months, and none of us could get in to see him.

I was a teenager and the war was over by the time they let my father out. He had been a jovial, talkative man before he'd gone in; he came out shadowy and subdued, a phantom father. But then, week by week, he grew more distinct and animated, he spoke to us more often and more loudly. Sometimes he was newly bossy, checking to see if we'd made our beds, making us wait to eat till our mother sat down. We were a little afraid of him now.

In the meantime, I was starting to think about boys. In high school people still knew my father had helped the enemy, but some boys decided it wasn't my fault. I liked almost any boy who liked me; I couldn't get over the thrill of their interest, though I had been raised to be a serious person.

Various boys joked around with me after school or leaned over me on the subway ride home, but nothing came of it until there was an argument among the staff of the school newspaper, about whether we needed another article about prom etiquette, and this boy and I were on the same side (against it). He was a broody, sharp-edged guy, with a nicely developed sense of irony, which allured me greatly. Walking on the street after the newspaper meeting (our side had lost), we did our own spoof of a student boob presenting a corsage and stabbing the girl with its pin. I clutched my chest and leaned against a stoplight, to act out my wound. He pretended to half-carry me across the street, and all that horsing around was extremely interesting.

What was his name? Ted Pfeiffer. He was Maxie Pfeiffer's older brother! This twist of fate was not as jarring as the other known fact that came with it: the father in that family had been killed in the last year of the war. "I know your sister," I said.

"She's a complete pain," he said.

. . .

It wasn't until our third time at the movies, when he made a move to start necking and I absolutely didn't stop him and we emerged from the theater with pink, blurred faces, a tickled-to-death couple, that he told me on the way home that he really hadn't wanted to start dating me because of my father.

"But you're not him," he said. "Are you?"

I didn't even pause. I didn't resist or explain or defend my family. "No, I'm not," I said. "Definitely not."

I would've said anything to keep him with me, to make sure he didn't change his mind, and perhaps I was lucky he didn't ask anything worse, but that was the beginning for me, and I knew it, of a different life. When I got back inside the apartment, I looked at my mother, who had fallen asleep on the sofa waiting for me, and I thought, *This apartment is really shabby.* And in the room I shared with my sister, I hissed at Barbara when she woke up, "Stop looking at me. I despise your looking at me."

For a long time, I'd held what I thought of as two opinions. With my parents, I was entirely against the war and all wars. What could be gained by millions of people marching out with the sole purpose of killing as many of each other as they could? I couldn't believe this butchery was *allowed.* Had always been allowed. The ugliest of all insanities. I was proud of my father for not going along with any of it. On the other hand, we all saw the photos of the concentration camps in Europe, after our soldiers went in, the living skeletons lying among piles of corpses, and what if our side hadn't won? Could people who did such things ever be stopped by peaceable means? I didn't mind having two viewpoints—it made talking to my friends easier (especially Ruthie), and it showed that I was advanced enough as a thinker to hold more than one idea in my mind at a time. Wasn't that a sign of a higher intelligence?

"It's okay to have two opinions," my mother said, "if all you have to do is have an opinion. If."

I thought my mother, typically, was making everything harder than it had to be. Meanwhile, Ted and I were getting along extremely well. We cracked each other up at the newspaper meetings, we talked about what a bunch of yahoos most of the school was. We argued about whether Tolstoy was better than Dostoevsky (I said, "Tolstoy is *fuller*") and we agreed about William Dean Howells being really boring. And he walked me between classes at school, a sign of major attention. *This is what real life is,* I thought, at his side in the hallways, *and I have it already.* Even Maxie started being nicer to me.

Once, when I was complaining about a sudden streak of sultry weather in May, Ted said, "My father always liked the heat." I had stopped feeling that he held his father's dying against me, and I had gone over to another feeling, an envy of what Ted knew about death.

"You should like hot weather then," I said. "As a tribute."

He nodded at this, he liked my making room for his ceremonies of memory.

We did a lot of necking. I was only sixteen, I didn't think—and he didn't demand—we would get into actual sex, but we hovered in an exquisite border area, became adepts in its every shading of excitement. How slow and patient we were then, how attenuated in our efforts. It was the sweetheart desire of innocents, for all its shocks and grunts and revelations.

He was two years ahead of me in school, and I did not have a good feeling about his graduating, though I gave him a very nice edition of Tolstoy's *Resurrection* for a present. I didn't like the way he thanked me for it by saying, "I only hope I'll have time to read it." He was going to City College, just a subway ride uptown, but I had reason to fear he'd slip away from me.

And I wasn't wrong. He took up with some female from his Western Civ class, and then, more fatally, with a blonde who worked in the library. He decided that we should no longer "fence each other in" and I was "free" to date other people. During this speech, he looked stern and aggrieved at having to speak at all. "Thank you for the blessing of liberty," I said. Sarcasm was not even slightly effective.

What could I do? I wanted to fight for him, fight hard and dirty if I had to. I had my pride and my upbringing, but I wasn't above using Maxie. Nothing sneaky, but I goaded her into inventing mean nicknames (Frog Eyes, Miss Dainty) and using her gifts of mimicry after the poor girlfriend paid a family visit. Maxie claimed the girl had actually said, "I *adore* pot roast," and Maxie loudly adored everything in sight for weeks after.

My job was to be the true-blue one. If I ran into him (Maxie aided this), I was friendly, forthright, calm. "Great to see you, Ted. Everything okay?" Ever loyal. Very, very warm.

My mother did not admire my scheming. "What can you gain by trickery?" she said.

"It's not tricks," I said. "And all is fair in love and war."

"Oh, Louise," she said. "Can you hear yourself, can you?"

I spent two years of my adolescence gutted by the outrage of being without him, eaten up with agonized guesses about my future. It was constantly clear to me what I had to have, every cell in my body was fixed in certainty. I had no way to know whether I would win. All the nights of imagined raptures, could they be for nothing? My friend, Ruthie, who didn't have anything going yet, envied my suffering, and probably thought it was better to have loved and lost than never to have loved at all, but I didn't. And I didn't have a Plan B. When Ruthie said, "You could get Alan Brody to like you if you wanted," I said, "No! Thank you, no." No halfway measures, no compromises. I knew what I knew. I shouldered my burden, I had been bred to staunchness.

Senior year I worked after school at a bakery in the neighborhood. It was called Mrs. Plymouth's, a homey place with mile-high coconut cakes and fudge-filled yellow layers. People still remembered when butter and sugar had been rationed in the last war years, and they liked the party-prettiness of what we sold. My earnings went to our ailing household budget; my father had found a job at a printshop, but we were always behind on our bills.

I told my mother I could bring in more money as a file clerk, once I was out of school. Plenty of girls as smart as I was had jobs like that, and (I didn't say this) I hoped to get married very soon anyway. Neither of my parents had been to college, but my father had his heart set on my getting a degree, and his bloodied heart was sacred to all of us. My mother thought I should go to Hunter (all girls) and not City, where I would run into we-knew-who.

I ran into him anyway, in the bakery, where he pretended to be surprised to find me. "Hey!" he said. "What's up?"

"Couldn't be better," I said. "This is *such* a good time for me. I think I'm going to Hawaii. To help with the big dock workers' strike."

"Hawaii! How will you get there?"

"There are ways. I have friends."

"What friends?"

"Oh, you know. So school is good?"

I had been raised to always, always be truthful, and I refused to say more, knowing I was not a skillful liar. "Forget I mentioned it," I said. "Okay? Please."

"Hawaii, huh?" he said.

"Forget I said it." I gave him my sunniest, sweetest look. "Everything good with you?" And I went off to wait on someone else.

I didn't have wiles, not really, but I knew that woe and suppli- cation had no sex appeal. He phoned me that night, trying to find out who I was seeing. I let him talk me out of my fake Hawaii plan, and that was the start of our revival.

No triumph could have been purer, more glorious, than those early days of having him back. I was smug with victory, I went around giving my sister the most platitudinous advice about love and life—"if it's meant to be, it happens," "when you know, you know." His mother was less than pleased about me and tended to refer to my parents as Reds, no matter how many times I explained they were anarchists, not Marxists—the black flag, not the red flag!—and their actions these days were mostly down to picketing with labor unions, which was perfectly lawful. I did go out on picket lines with them (we'd always done this as a family), but I wasn't big on chanting. "They're just slogans!" I said.

"What *do* you have faith in?" my mother said.

The truth was that I wanted to be ordinary. I wanted the coziness of private life. Why should that be out of reach, why couldn't I have that?

"I have faith in *people,*" I said.

"What does that mean?" my mother said. "You think you can do without ideas but you can't."

I lasted through a year and a half of college, and then Ted and I were married. It was his idea as much as mine—his dating life had scared him about the risks of ending up with someone shrill or cloying or shallow or stupid. I was at the very least none of those things. Once we were engaged, we had sex of a lavish and reverent kind. He looked at me very intently afterward, his eyes deep in their sockets, without his glasses, and his features softened and slightly swollen, an almost-naked face. I was dazzled myself, but I had been dazzled before we even did anything.

My parents were against my marrying Ted—my mother said, "You're selling yourself to the first bidder," a surprisingly bitter thing for her to say—but they put together a decent wedding for me, not fancy but with bouquets of pink carnations and a real cake from the bakery. Everyone was crowded into our living room, and we had a Unitarian minister, which satisfied no one, and I wore a dress I'd sewn from a pattern, with a scalloped neck and a gathered skirt, in dotted swiss, white on white. I looked good in that dress.

Ted had managed to graduate a semester early, and the city was in bleak winter. We moved into a tenement on the Lower East Side, with crappy heating, and I worked very hard to make it nice. We paid the rent from Ted's new job teaching English in a high school, and I liked all the budgeting and household cleverness.

No one in my family admired the drapes I made for the windows, a tasteful slubbed weave in creamy beige. "I can see a lot of effort went into this," my mother said, not that nicely.

"Isn't everything you fight for," I said, "the peace and the fair wages, for the sake of each family?"

"We fight for *freedom*," my sister said. "Not for cornflakes."

But I fooled them all by being happy.

Ted came home every day from being a "permanent sub" teaching five English classes—oh, God, five—of ninth and tenth graders in deepest Brooklyn, and he could be very funny. We'd crack up over their misapprehensions of *Silas Marner* and their hilarious sentences, and I'd get indignant on his behalf when the principal made absurd decrees, and in this spirit of teamwork we ate my excellent meals, and by dessert I was explaining why I thought Pearl Buck wasn't that great a writer or how Tolstoy could get into any character's head. I had plenty of time to read.

We were happy in bed too. I had a life of considerable animal pleasures, a day of simple tasks easily done, and a husband who treated me well. I felt very elemental, in our fifth-floor walk-up, with its clanging pipes and lopsided walls—I was a person who'd guessed right about what was essential. I had what I wanted: how many people have that?

I didn't even mind the summer, when our small, boxed-in rooms were airless ovens and we slept on the fire escape. Ted was teaching summer school to make more money, and in the days alone, I'd go dunk myself in the municipal pool on Carmine Street, near where I used to live. The pool was so crowded it was like swimming on the subway, but I'd see Ruthie or other girls I'd known in high school. I felt older, calmer, less worried than they were. I'd lie on a towel in my bathing suit and be very aware that my body was not a virgin's body.

Ted's summer school had all the students who'd flunked, and he was stuck with seventh grade (which he wasn't even licensed for), a nightmarish age. Squirming, untamed creatures. He could not get them interested in the poetry of Oliver Wendell Holmes or the need for verb agreement. They were always talking, eating candy, passing notes, exploding into illicit laugher over who-knew-what.

One evening, Ted said he had worked out a "plan for dominance." He'd told the class that any student who reported on another student eating in class or passing a note would be rewarded with an extra tenth of a point toward his or her grade.

"You're training them to rat on each other?" I said.

"I'm teaching them to be loyal to me above all."

"That's fascism," I said. He laughed.

In my family, ratting was the lowest of the low. My father had survived in prison by not breaking solidarity with other inmates and refusing special favors from the warden, lest people think he was a spy, and in the years since, more than one friend had gone to prison (and not for just a few months either) rather than give names of people who belonged to so-called communist fronts.

"So you bribe them to turn each other in," I said, "and you're going to give them a false grade, with padded points?"

"You know absolutely nothing about keeping control in the classroom," he said. "You have no idea. Do you?"

Ted came home the next day and said, "Hah! It's working." Three boys were turned in for eating a bag of Tootsie Rolls. He'd sent the three to the principal's office while Ricky, the kid who reported them, crowed in his seat and was full of himself all day.

When the boys came back to class the following day they stole Ricky's shoes, ripped his shirt, and then claimed to find a half-eaten Milky Way on his desk. "Here's the evidence! You said we had to have evidence!"

Ted walked all four of them, whining in protest, to the principal. All was calm, except the principal came by after school to ask why Ted was having so much trouble.

"Uh-oh," I said.

"I have to think of other punishments."

He had to what? I saw that I didn't know him very well, which made me feel extremely stupid. I hadn't seen him this way before because I hadn't seen him up close when he was losing. He was losing this class, I could tell.

The punishment he "invented" was docking their grades, and the summer became a tournament of shaved points up and down, a mess of calculations and pettiness and futile warfare. He explained its progress often, and I could never follow what he was saying. I felt sorry for him, with his bluster and his vain efforts. Who was he kidding?

I felt increasingly sorry for me. Not that there was much to do about it, but why did I wait at the end of every day, with dinner on the stove, for a conversation I only wanted to get away from? The system didn't work if I didn't believe in him. Everything seemed ridiculous, including the drapes I'd been so tickled with.

And who did I think I was? Feet of clay, anyone would've said if I had complained about my husband. A mere bump in the long and winding road of marriage. My mother guessed (and I didn't want her to guess), I could tell by the way she peered at me and patted my hand. I told my mother I wasn't pregnant, if that's what she was worried about.

We were still having sex, and I didn't hate the sex either. It was now a more private set of excitements, as if I were crying out to myself. What a liar I was becoming, on all counts, scared and selfish both. Ted half-knew, but only half. Some women stayed in love with their husbands long after the men began to beat them or cheat on them or publicly shame them. Ted was hardly guilty of anything worse than being a new and incompetent teacher. I knew that, I told myself that.

Once summer school was over, Ted had a brief spell of holiday in the hottest part of August. He dragged a kitchen chair out to the fire escape and sat in his undershirt, reading. Didn't he want to go to the beach? Maybe just uptown to Central Park? He didn't want to do anything. "What's the point?" he said. He read the newspapers all day, he read magazines written for stupider people. "Go swim with your friends," he said. "I'm fine here."

When the pool closed for its annual week of maintenance, I sat with Ted on the fire escape, but he didn't want any chatting. And he didn't want the radio blaring from the kitchen either. No Tchaikovsky, no Fats Domino. "I guess that job really made you tired," I said.

"What do you care?" he said.

I had brought about this state of irritated sorrow, this defeat. He did know.

I'd always been taught the truth sets you free, but it wasn't doing that here. Here was a man who could hardly move from the weight of the truth. His sweating body was hunched over the page as he read. Hours passed when he didn't raise his head. Who had made him suffer? I wanted to punch this person in the nose.

"Didn't you used to fish in the park with your dad?" I said. "Don't you want to go to the lake some time?"

"I bet your dad never fished. I bet he didn't want to kill a single minnow."

"Anarchists *used* to be very violent, some of them. My father is an evolved form."

"Why didn't you marry him then?"

I gasped and stared at him. "Very funny," I said.

"You think he's this great hero," Ted said. "But he let my father die. He didn't help him."

I was furious then at Ted's father, who'd been killed at Anzio—a hearty man with boorish tendencies, in Ted's stories. It was just as well I had nothing to say against him because I might've said it. A decade had passed, a whole other inexplicable war had happened since then—the "action" in Korea was just over that summer—what was making Ted bring this up now?

"What do you want from me?" I said.

"Admit he's a failure."

"Who?"

"Your father."

"Failed how?" I said.

"To do anything. Ever."

"Like what?"

"Did he stop the war by getting arrested? Did he bring an end to all governments?"

"It isn't *about* that," I said.

"It's all gestures," he said. "Showing off."

"It is not."

"You sit on your can all day and you think you know about the real world, but you don't."

"Who do you think you're talking to?"

"The queen of fake purity."

I went inside the apartment to get away from him, and then I kept going, out the door, down the five flights to the street. How far away could I get? The street had the summer smell of ripe garbage and incinerated soot. Our sweltering block was at its quietest, with all the Jewish shops shuttered for Saturday, but on one stretch of sidewalk the Puerto Rican kids were playing, yelling and chasing each other and calling out dares. I'd made a great mistake in marrying Ted. Nothing could be clearer. What was I going to do now? I walked east, block after faded-brick block, till I got to where the streets ended, and past the bank of seared grasses, the glaring water of the river rose like a mirage. I'd fought so hard to get him. There were clues all along but I had no use for them, I might've paid attention but I didn't want to. I thought the world was love-love-love.

And if I left his bed and board, how would I live? Back to the bakery? I was so dazed and stricken that I sat thinking about Boston Cream Pie and peanut butter cookies, soothing thoughts, brainless dreams, until the fading light scared me and I walked home.

When I got back to the apartment, Ted was lying in bed, face down. He turned when I came in. "If you want to leave, just leave," he said. "You can go back to your parents. That's the simplest thing."

How reasonable he sounded, how hoarse and desperate.

I could be free in an instant if I wanted to be. As I was taking this in, I heard myself crying, loud as an infant; I made horrible sounds of real anguish. "Don't make me leave," I managed to say. How choked and pathetic my voice was. I said weepy things about how I loved him, I said we were meant for each other and he knew it too, didn't he?—I knew he did. The words flew out of me, as if they were true. Was I lying? The whole time I was speaking, I felt that I had to put this over, I had to act with as much conviction as I could. Did I believe it? I did and I didn't.

And I made Ted happy. Under my wails and moans and tears, he softened. His eyes lost their stunned, dead look and took on their old, intelligent shimmer. I was pulling us back from a very dangerous precipice. We could be safe, we could be. A bliss of relief went through both of us.

All that suffering had a good effect on us in bed, as if we had been through a battle together as comrades, not enemies. Our natures were more fully bared to each other. We had only to take off our clothes to be our more audacious, less naïve selves. We knew more, we went further. It startled us both, and we laughed in astonishment after.

When Ted went back to school in September, he was given an extra class—could his day be any fuller?—and I was outraged for him, which he liked. When he had to appear at Meet the Teachers Night, I decided to be eager to be in the audience. I sat with other wives in the big wood-and-linoleum auditorium, surrounded by a sea of parents, while our spouses stood and explained their educational goals. Ted said he hoped to bring students to an understanding of the power of the English language. A Mr. Sloan, whose wife was next to me, said he believed that algebra refined all thinking. "Well, they have to say *something*," she whispered.

"Or take the Fifth," I said. A Latin teacher in the school had been fired for taking the Fifth Amendment when asked about communists in the teachers' union, and I suddenly thought this was not my best joke. Not funny to me. But the woman smiled.

"At least they're not talking about locking the bad students in the closet," she murmured. "They used to do that when I was a kid."

"Some of them need it now."

"I'll say," she said.

"My husband bribes them to rat on each other," I said. "He gives them rewards for it."

"Does he?" she said.

Someone shushed us, and I flinched in my seat—it was right to shut me up. What sort of person had I become now, with spite leaking out of me? If Ted had started baiting and buying off his ninth graders, what did it matter to me? I had to hope she would forget my words, why would she bother to remember, and I got away from Mrs. Sloan when we all filed into the gym for punch and cookies. "You were excellent," I said to Ted.

"Aw, shucks," he said.

. . .

But I knew what I was. At the slightest opportunity, at the first instant that offered, I'd informed on my husband, just like that. Speaking against him had been very easy. Every day people were hounded for refusing to bear witness against someone—they were fired or arrested or blacklisted for being un-American and still they kept their mouths shut, on principle. And me? I leaped at the chance to spread a small bit of damage about the man I slept with every night.

Mr. Sloan was, in fact, the vice principal, I later found out. This was not good news. Ted was on a one-year contract, and if they dropped him, what school would take him? I had never been like this before I knew Ted. Who knew what I would blurt out next? *Look what love has done to me,* I thought.

One night, after we'd had perfectly good sex and Ted fell asleep and I lay awake for hours, it struck me with horror that I had never been a good liar but now I was. I could scarcely take off my clothes and turn to my husband without some degree of fraudulence and calculation. I, who'd been raised to be always truthful, had somehow taught myself to be one of those women who lure and lie for their survival. How had this happened? *This is what gives carnal relations a bad name,* I thought, cracking a joke to myself about it, a bad joke.

Maybe all marriages, if you looked too hard at them, were riddled with corrupting compromises. Maybe other people had a higher tolerance for the bargains they struck, and that was just the way of it. I was going to have to live with this particular insight. It wasn't something I wanted to shout from the rooftops to anyone. I had a long, bad night, with Ted's steady breathing next to me in the bed and the noise of trucks going by in the street below. In the books I liked to read, and in the politics of my parents, people changed once they got hold of a new way to see things, but I wasn't going to change. I wasn't.

. . .

In the spring Ted got official word that his contract wasn't being renewed. No reason was given—they would only say another teacher was filling the spot—and a number of people thought it was because my parents were communists, even if they weren't. Someone said the vice principal had been especially against Ted. I was so upset I could barely tell people, my voice broke when I gave the news—while Ted, to my complete surprise, went in for cheerful irony. "We don't need to eat, what's so great about eating?" he said, and "I love a character-building experience," and (his favorite) "Exploited today, fired tomorrow."

How little I knew him. This wisenheimer flintiness, this hearty valor, was not at all what I might have expected. I was the vile, small-minded, petty, treacherous one. I was the one who had burned our ticket to a decent, straightforward life. And now I gave long speeches about how we lived in tainted times, with goodness smeared by fear, and how all the higher-ups were jealous of Ted's star teaching. "Hey," Ted said. "We'll get by. Not the end of the world." He comforted me, my husband who'd been robbed.

What could I do? I kept seeking him out in bed, trying to lavish myself on him and to dower him with oblivion. I hardly let him rest, I kept drawing him back and wanting to begin again. It seemed the very least I could contribute to our dreary situation. The spell of it worked on me too; I'd emerge still half-delirious, bruised and spent, out of myself. I whispered to him, "Best of all husbands."

"You're my girl."

"They have no idea who you really are," I said.

"Forget 'them,'" he said. "Nobody's here. Just us."

In our room, a single light flickered from a candle I'd set by the bed.

"My father's a failure," I said.

"What?"

"He is."

"Why are you saying that?"

"I want to."

"Shush," he said. "Be calm, okay? It's all right."

If he no longer wanted to hear any such thing, there were other things he wanted. He wanted complete silence while he read for hours, he wanted to win any argument about any topic, from Tolstoy's translators to the post-armistice in Korea, and I let him. When my parents fed us nourishing suppers, he kept up his darkly blithe quips about his prospects. "Exploited today, fired tomorrow," he said (yet again). They all laughed. They liked him better now. My sister said, "I wish you were a teacher in *my* school." My father poured beer for him and talked to him about purges and backlash and touched his shoulder, which Ted seemed to like. He didn't, after all, have a father of his own.

But what were we going to do and what about me? My mother let me use the typewriter in her office to tap out Ted's job-seeking letters to states where he wasn't known. What a mess I had made. Ted's paychecks stopped in June.

I told him I was going to ask if they needed anyone at the bakery, and I was a little surprised when he didn't object. It was humbling to return to Mrs. Plymouth's as a married woman— "Didn't think we'd see *you*," customers said—but I still liked the buttery smells, the doilies on glass shelves, even the striped aprons and the silly hairnets, that orderly, sugary version of home.

My mother said there was no dishonor in being short of cash. *"Au contraire,"* Barbara said. I brought home crumbled cookies and soggy Danish that stuffed us and made us feel poorer.

Ted suggested I bring boxes of day-old cake to the Ramirez family down the hall, and their kids adored us after that. I liked my poor husband better than I ever had. He was oddly improved by being broken—I'd read of that happening, but I'd never seen it before in real life. He told Maxie, "I couldn't pick a better girl than Louise to be unemployed with."

But I told Ruthie I wasn't, actually, sure I could get through this part on love alone. I was having a Popsicle with her in the park, near a grassy patch we'd always liked. "What if I have to follow him into exile in Siberia?" I said. Ted had just sent an application to Provo, Utah, which we could not resist calling the Steppes.

"You would ditch him when he was down?" she said. Nobody we knew did that. In Hollywood, in trashy magazines, but not in our neighborhoods.

"No," I said. "But I'd hang on without my heart in it. I'd be one of those sour wives, all martyred and sarcastic."

"*No*. Not you. You love Ted," Ruthie said. She had a boyfriend now and hoped their dating would end in marriage, and I was alarming her.

I thought of my mother saying, "sold to the first bidder," when she wanted to warn me against leaping too fast into love. But if love didn't make the world go around, what did?

A month later, I found myself packing, not for Utah but for Okinawa. The one job that came through for Ted was teaching English to American kids on an air force base in Japan. Ted said all the Americans liked it over there, and there were thousands of Americans still in Japan. With children who needed my husband's attentions. My mother was very upset.

"You'll be living *inside* the U.S. military," she said. "Do you want that? You don't want that."

"I'll learn Japanese!" I said. Although they said people hardly left the base, I dreamed of myself making new sounds. "I have to be with my husband," I told her.

"He doesn't have to go."

I wanted to go. I felt superior to everyone I knew because I was going.

"You stuck with Dad," I said.

"Do I have to say how different that was?"

My father didn't say much, but he was clearly very disappointed. He'd look into my face and then turn his gaze away.

My sister said, "Do you know where you're going? They used to send planes from out of there to bomb Korea. For Christ's sake."

Ted and I were in wonderful spirits. Japan! We talked for hours about what to bring, we read *The Chrysanthemum and the Sword* and a book of haiku the library had. I found a recipe for sukiyaki and I stirred bits of beef in a pan with canned bean sprouts. "Sometimes bad luck turns into good luck," Ted said. We both thought we'd fallen into a wildly suitable fate: everything would be taken care of, and everything would be beyond what we'd imagined. We were making a great escape. We fell asleep holding hands.

My sister, Barbara, said, "I never thought you would be like this."

We were going by ship from California, and we had to send everything in trunks and crates. What was the weather like? Like here except warmer in Okinawa. And I read that the Japanese believed theirs was the only country that really had four seasons, which seemed sweet of them. I was sorting out which books to give to Ruthie when Ted came into the room, shouting, "I don't believe it!" Papers had come with an official seal: Ted had a security clearance to reside on the base, but family member Louise Buckman Pfeiffer was refused one.

"Did you know about this?" I wailed.

I'd never heard of such a thing. But what, really, had I heard of? "Maybe I can get work as a janitor in your bakery," Ted said, grimly.

I hated the goddamn government. My parents were right. Had always been right. "You should go without me," I said. I was angry with Ted for having wanted to go in the first place. "You should just go as if you really were in the army."

Ted was hugging me. "You're the most amazing person." We were both sticky from the summer heat, and the scent of his skin was such a sharp, familiar smell as he held me.

He was ready to get on the ship to Japan without me, and he thought I was noble. I felt quite crazy.

I could have stopped him from going, but I didn't. He kept saying, "There aren't many wives like you," as if I were a paragon of enlightened sacrifice. "I am just so wonderful," I said, but he didn't mind my tone. Why should he mind? He was going to have his adventure. I was the one cheated and defeated. Ted, in those last weeks, seemed to have decided he had a treasure in me. He'd watch me move around the house and say, "You are something." He'd hold me close for minutes at a time, and I'd feel my heart in my chest beating for him. He would miss me. I was scared and said so, but he thought this was another sign of my valor.

The first months without him were atrocious. I had to move back to my parents' apartment, and I'd lie awake in my old room, with Barbara rustling around in the next bed, and everything was intolerable. The absence of Ted was like a weight in all my limbs, and my poor body was beset with useless longing. Ted made one expensive phone call to me on arrival—"The base is ugly!" he said, and sounded very thrilled. It was three weeks before a letter reached me ("I went into town and bought a grilled sweet potato on the street, very smoky. The students are easy—I don't have to bribe them!"), and I wrote to him every day ("The autumn weather is still very warm" and "Barbara wants to be a French major, very practical"). My father said, "I can't get over having a son-in-law on a military base," and in truth I agreed with him. The whole thing was a humiliation.

My work at the bakery was not very taxing and the hours felt

very, very long. I ate too many cupcakes and got sick of them.
My mother suggested I bring some of those eternal leftovers to
the Catholic Worker place on Chrystie Street, which their friend
Dorothy ran. Dorothy wasn't there most of the time, and the
House of Hospitality was full of sad, wacky, life-damaged people, roaming the rooms of an old building, with crucifixes on
the walls looking down on all of it. They were exactly the people
no one else wanted to bother with. Everybody—staff and residents alike—was thrilled by the boxes of pastries. "It's Louise!"
they would yell, when I walked in the door. One woman jumped
around in circles until she had to be calmed by someone.

What did I ever believe, where were my principles? My mother
used to say my politics were driven out by my hormones, an
insulting version of my history. Serious thought, as well as lust,
had made it plain to me that love was truer than all the other
weak notions in the world, and that justice could never be served
by anything you did (what was the use), so there was no satisfaction serving it. Now I was in a different spot.

Ted wrote, "I wish wish wish you were here." Well, I wasn't.
His contract was for two years, and he had one free trip home in
a year. How could I be lost in bedroom fantasies of someone I was
so outraged with? At the bakery I had a hazy, distracted look a lot
of the time, too much of the time. We were paid very little, and
some of the women had families living on this pay. "Wake up,
Susie-Q," they would say.

Ted thought I was being "rash and shortsighted" when I moved
out of my rent-free home with my family and got a one-room
apartment on East Third Street—tub in the kitchen, toilet in the
hall. "By yourself?" Ruthie said. "No one else?"

My mother said, "I thought you wanted to save money."

Nobody thought I was smart, and maybe they were right. But
how many months could I stay in that room with Barbara? How
hard I tried to make the new place interesting, how earnest my
attempts at décor—the one wall painted coral-orange, the poster

of Picasso's *Guernica,* with its twisted figures. I was not really at home there at first, but I thought that I would be, and I was right. I'd been raised to love freedom (of another sort, but this sort had a meaning) and my pride took me a long way. Sometimes the sight of my own table, where I read whatever I wanted to while I ate, put me in a kind of rapture. No one believed me.

At Thanksgiving, my father took all of us to join a small march downtown in support of the United Auto Workers' strike at the Kohler steel plant in Wisconsin. My mother brought a thermos of hot cider to make sure Barbara and I stayed warm. The Thanksgiving weather was sunny and not so cold and we knew a lot of the people marching, so it was an okay afternoon. "Be wise, don't buy Kohler plumbing supplies," my picket sign said.

And how was Ted's holiday, with his fellow Americans in Japan? Not bad, but he missed me. His voice sounded underwater when he called. He got to go to the Officers' Club, where they all drank enormous amounts of whiskey and sang "Over the River and Through the Woods" together. A staff sergeant kept imitating a turkey. Gobble, gobble. Yes, yes, I missed him, but I was secretly glad I wasn't there.

And so it went. We longed for each other in raging fevers and we nursed our resentments. My youth was being wasted, and Ted said he was in exile because of my parents. Clearly he kind of liked his exile. ("Just tried buckwheat noodles. And bits of pigs' ears!" he wrote. "Very tasty!") To distract myself, I went and took a night course at Hunter College, on Love and Money in the Victorian Novel. I was older now and spoke more in class, I had opinions about Becky Thatcher.

Arrigato meant thank you in Japanese, Ted wrote, and *konnichiwa* was hello. In the spring Ted was coaching a school softball team. I'd never seen the man play baseball in my life. We stopped squabbling in our phone calls but I didn't always know what he was talking about. I was friendly with two girls from my class at Hunter and we'd go for tea afterward and have ideas about Rochester's blindness. And then how nice it was to come back to my room, the stillness at the end of the night. Ted was in my thoughts but it wasn't so bad being parted. I could tell he felt that, too.

"How'd you come up with this?" he said, when he saw my apartment, on his big trip home in August. We'd already embraced long and hard at the door, but he was a little thrown by the coral-orange wall and the desolate sink. "*I* like it," I said. I was still tasting the feel of his mouth, the fresh surprise of it. "I pictured something different," he said.

But we did very well, in our odd circumstances. Once we got over a few preliminaries in bed, we were back as familiars, lolling in the luxury of actually really having each other. I had forgotten the Ted-ness of sex with him, the specificity of it. All my craving had not been a true memory. How weak the imagination was.

Ted said, "In Japan they take baths at night, they think we're weird with our showers in the morning." He enjoyed slipping in these reports. I was curious, but not as curious as he thought. "They eat raw horse meat, not just raw fish, can you believe it?" he said. "But they're very clean. The base is immaculate." My friendly imperialist of a husband. I didn't talk much about school, I didn't want to hear what he thought he knew about Dickens.

The clock was ticking, we only had two weeks to be happy together. It took concentration, but we did all right. I cried at the airport—I felt so bad for myself—but I said, "Don't mind me, I'm silly," as if I really were a soldier's wife.

At the bakery, one of the older women teased me about those geishas over there and how the smart thing would be to have a little bundle of joy to keep him tied to home. People really said these things? I couldn't tell her: I love my husband and I don't. And everybody knows, you can't be a little bit pregnant.

· · ·

I'd long since lapsed out of writing letters every day, and in the second year I didn't always remember every week. When his monthly checks arrived, I'd write, "Thank you for your lovely contribution to the ever-popular Louise Likes to Eat Fund." I did need them for the rent. Was this what made us married, that he still sent me money? Sometimes he'd say, "I know you can always use it," as if it were extra. "I love your taste in checkbook paper," I wrote. "The green tint goes with everything."

I had a preposterous flirtation with one of the bakers on the night shift at Mrs. Plymouth's—he came on during my last hour of work, and sometimes we kidded around in the kitchen. His name was Trevor, he was from Trinidad, and I told him he looked like Harry Belafonte (he did). He was very careful around me, but when I complimented him on his way with the dough he gave me an appropriately merry look. My fantasies of him began to block out my fantasies of Ted, which was a peculiar feeling. And what did it matter, if it was all in my head anyway? But one evening I asked Trevor what his days were like, did he sleep all day, and I somehow invited him for supper on Monday, when the bakery was closed.

He dressed so nicely for that dinner, in a pressed shirt of dazzling pale blue, and we talked about the winters in Trinidad— "oh, yes, gets up past eighty degrees"—over my fried flounder and mashed potatoes. "I like the colors in your house," he said. "Little, little place but you make it pretty."

I had to give him a sign—I brushed against him on the way to the stove—and after that it was simple. We were in bed! I'd never thought I would have any other lover but Ted, and I was astonished at myself, even after all the rehearsals in my mind. He was different from Ted—more full of flourishes, and also more jolly and confident. I thought that I was a reckless person but I had chosen a kind man. I can do this, I thought, I'm lucky.

· · ·

This went on for several months, and then Trevor became more afraid he was going to be fired if the bakery found out. This was perfectly true—we didn't have a union—and we both knew that ugliness might be waiting for him. We rarely talked about race, that most delicate of topics. "Happy but going nowhere," he said of us.

"I know, I know," I said.

We never went outside together, we never went anywhere except my place. The kids in the building tittered at us in the hall and sometimes worse. They were just kids but I hated them. We kept ourselves out of sight, like the scandal we were. "You know what I have in Trinidad, near Port-of-Spain?" he said one night.

"No," I said.

"You know. A wife."

Why are you telling me this? I hadn't known but I wasn't stunned for more than a minute. I had a husband, didn't I?

"Her name is Hyacinth," he said.

This was not a good sign, that he wanted to invoke her. Some dopey little girl of a wife, who sat home in a tiny kitchen all day, waiting for his MoneyGrams.

"That's how it is," he said.

Oh, was it? He wanted me to let him go before there was trouble for either of us. He wanted me to be a good sport.

"Time to call it a day, isn't it?" I said.

"I am so sorry," he said. He did have manners.

In the bakery, for weeks after, we hardly spoke when we passed each other. When we moved around the kitchen and made sure our gazes didn't meet, I felt that life had insulted us both. I tried not to hear his voice in the room, the tune of his English.

One evening I didn't see him on his shift, and one of the counter girls said he'd left for another job. "When?" I said. "When did he go?" None of them had the name of where he'd gone—

"How would I know?" they said—and I couldn't keep asking every single person.

Ruthie said, "Is your heart broken? I'm worried about you."

"I would say no. Not broken. Do I look devastated to you?" I said. "A little the worse for wear maybe."

"Do you have a heart?" Ruthie said. "Just kidding."

Ted wrote, "And you know what is interesting about the Japanese? Their single-mindedness at any task. How hard they concentrate. I like their sake too!"

It wasn't really that much of a surprise, near the end of the second year, when Ted began to say in his letters that he might be staying on. What did I think? What kind of man wants to live on an air base? I thought. I still thought of Trevor every day, but I'd gotten sort of interested in a guy I'd talked to about getting a union into the bakery. He worked for the CIO, traveling to their member unions, and was on the road all the time. We hadn't done more than have conversations, but he called from Duluth and Sioux Falls and told me goofy jokes. So it was clear that life had possibilities. "If you really feel you're needed there," I wrote to Ted.

"You are such a rare wife," Ted wrote. "This is hard on both of us but I will be getting a raise and sending a little more money."

"How can he keep you on ice like that?" Ruthie said. I thought Ted probably had a Japanese woman in town or maybe some secretary on the base, somebody he wasn't about to marry. I wasn't angry at him for this. I told people he was staying because the salary kept getting higher, and sometimes I said it was because his work was so rewarding. People could never make sense of the ways we'd redistributed the affiliations of our union, and you couldn't blame them.

My mother said, "It's very unusual."

"Is that a crime?" I said. "Unusualness? I thought you were on the side of that."

. . .

Ted came back in July that year, in time for Ruthie's wedding. I had to bring him, I couldn't leave him home. There we were, sitting together in the synagogue, with Ruthie in white silk organza marching toward this Bob guy she was so crazy about. It made me as tearful as it made everyone else, at the same time I felt it was all a poufy fraud. Why would you vow yourself to an unlikely ideal? I snuck a look at Ted, dressed up in a navy-blue suit I'd never seen, and to my amazement he took my hand. We had been getting along at home, but not saying much. Now he was rubbing my fingers, an old sweet gesture. *He's grateful to me,* I thought.

And so it went. Once he was gone, I did take up with Mick, the union organizer, who was really a very charming guy and never in town for more than a month at a time. He was used to talking to all kinds of people, and once you got him off his rhetoric, he had great stories. The guy whose dog always knew what time it was, the woman who sang in two languages at once: Mick could tell about all of it.

He was very taken with me, and he didn't like it when I neglected him for my night classes or my homework, but I pretty much stuck to my guns. He'd say, "Sweetie, just tonight," and I could say, not too meanly, "Honey, I'm not your wife." Ted paid the rent, such as it was, and I had no reason to take off my wedding ring. I had the protection of a husband without the nuisance of him being there. Everybody thought I was kidding myself.

Meanwhile, Mick and I, after a lot of work, got the Bakery and Confectionery Workers' International Union voted into Mrs. Plymouth's, much to the disgust of the burly old owner (Mrs. Plymouth was a fiction). The owner was very disappointed in me and would've fired me if he could've (not legal!), but I was leaving then anyway, because I'd actually managed to graduate from college.

My mother wanted to make me a dress to wear to commencement, a touching but terrible idea. My father was immensely pleased. One of his kittens was getting a diploma. "We did okay, didn't we?" he kept saying. Mick, who was not a secret from my family, sat with him at graduation. They were great pals.

Ted wrote, "Congratulations to my brilliant wife."

I got a silly English-major's job as a proofreader at a women's magazine, where I read pap all day ("twenty smart tricks with paper towels") and was good at finding mistakes about baking, which I did know about. My proofreading skills catapulted me into a much better job at the National Maritime Union (okay, Mick knew someone), where I copyedited their newsletter and eventually sort of rewrote most of it and was, in time, listed on the masthead as an editor.

And what about Ted? When I moved to a better apartment, he wrote, "Don't make it so nice I don't recognize it." How long could this go on? "Have unpacked your favorite sheets," I wrote, "and they lie waiting for you." "Miss those sheets like crazy," Ted wrote. Did I mind that Ted didn't come home that year? I thought I did. He said he was saving his money to improve his housing, or something like that. He stayed faithful in his monthly allotments to me, whatever that meant. Mick wasn't around then either—he was working in Idaho for a few months—and it was a long, bleak summer. "Don't take this personally," Ruthie said, "but I think you're an idiot."

"It's okay now, but what if you get sick?" my mother said. "Later on, I mean. What if you need help and there's no one?" My health stood every chance of staying excellent for a while, Mick had once made me a hot toddy when I had a cold, and we all knew women lived longer than men anyway. "Someday," my mother said, "you're going to have to decide."

. . .

Lots of people at the Maritime Union knew Mick, but my name was still Mrs. Pfeiffer to them. I never lied about any of my life, when asked, and because of that I was considered very frank and outspoken. Imagine that. The job suited me—the old thuggish union guys in their rumpled suits, the seamen getting their papers, the no-nonsense women in the office. And every day I was glad to have something to do with keeping the boot of heedless profit off the necks of workers. The newsletter was a little hokey, but I did my best.

A number of people pointed out that I wasn't going to be young forever, but I was young for a really long time. Mick and I went hiking in the Grand Canyon, and another year we went snowshoeing in Utah, which turned out to be a handsome state. Mick, who'd once worked as what my mother called a "stevedore," tended to like physical stuff. I liked it more than I expected, and for a while I even took ice skating classes at a rink on a roof in Midtown. "You always surprise me," Ted wrote. "I'm thinking of you in a little twirly skirt."

"I wear slacks," I wrote.

Okinawa was subtropical and never got below fifty. Ted claimed to miss the snow but I didn't believe him.

Well into my thirties, people thought I looked much younger. Ruthie's kids called me Aunt LouLou, as if I were a cartoon auntie. They loved coming to my apartment—much bigger than the last, with blue-painted floors and *Guernica* replaced by a Matisse—but they could never believe I lived alone. No one else here, really? I wasn't just making up a story?

What I didn't like, actually, was when Mick showed up out of nowhere without letting me know in advance. "I have rules," I said, but he ignored them. I was always glad for the sight of him, so I gave way, but it leaked out in other ways, my sense of injustice. We'd quarrel over how much hamburger to buy or which store was a rip-off or who was really a very self-centered person.

Once I had to announce to him that Ted, my husband, was showing up again in August. Ted only came back to the States every few years and he stayed with me when he did. It was, as they say, a given. And Mick had to know to keep away. How difficult was that?

"I think you're telling me to go jump in the lake," Mick said. "Very friendly."

"Don't sulk like a girl," I said.

One remarkable thing about Ted was that he never seemed any different, no matter how much time went by. Oh, there was always a moment when I was surprised at how old he looked, and he'd start in about things I'd totally forgotten from his last visit, but we got used to each other at once. We'd hop into bed right away (the same bed, with the maple headboard), and then we'd lie around having a conversation we might have begun only the day before. He'd hold my hand and stroke my fingers. "Hey, Louise," he'd say. "What's up?" It was all very sentimental.

Ruthie was always asking me, "Does he just think he owns you?"

She knew I'd been brought up with much talk about property— property is theft, property is the exploitation of the weak by the strong. "What you really mean," I said, "is that I should exert my ownership rights on *him*. Reel him back in, make him mine."

"You could." Maybe.

"For freedom there is no substitute, there can be no substitute," I said. It was an old quote from Rudolf Rocker, an anarcho-syndicalist my father loved. I didn't think it was all that interesting or true—it was a slogan!—but it had become true for me. Or true sometimes. My mother would've cringed at that qualifier. I used to always tell my parents I was *not* an ideologue. "So what are you?" my mother would say.

"Not a hypocrite."

"That's minimal," my mother said. "That's not an answer." But I thought it was. I liked how I'd turned out. Through trial and error.

Ruthie said, "Oh, you just think you're too cool for the way anyone else does it. You want to make everything up as you go along."

"So?"

"Oh, please," Ruthie said. "How can anyone trust you then?"

"Well, they can," I said.

When I was close to forty, I had a major quarrel with Mick, about the usual. He wanted me to fly out to see him in St. Louis, for a four-day weekend. "I happen to be employed," I said. "I can't just take off."

"I'm paying, darlin'," he said. "It's on me."

"So? Please. Not the point."

"You know what it is?" he said. "I'm the one you don't take seriously."

A man I saw five or six times a year was talking about serious? "If your hubby wagged his finger to invite you to Japan, you'd hop on a plane and go."

"I don't want to go to Japan! I don't!" I mostly didn't, not any more.

"St. Louis is a great town. Got the Arch, got the Cardinals. Only needs you."

And I went for those four days, to placate him. St. Louis was fine, but right away he pestered me about staying an extra day, and I got indignant about the sneakiness of that. Why would I neglect my newsletter for him? It was not a good trip, and Mick started to call less often after that.

My father was disappointed to lose sight of Mick. They'd been fans of each other, all these years. "Pussycat," my father said. "I thought things were going to turn out differently."

"You did? I didn't."

"Some men are always on the move," he said. "That's just how they are." Listen to my father, trying to sound worldly. People were always feeling sorry for me for the wrong things.

And Mick didn't disappear altogether. In the middle of the night he'd need to talk to me, or I'd let him slip over when he was in town. So I wasn't entirely single. My solitude had a flavor to it, a tint of distant admiration. It wasn't bad getting those phone calls out of nowhere, kisses on the line. Then I'd stay up late, reading in bed, with his company in the air around me but a pure silence in the room. My room.

Ted was not really that old when he decided to sort of "retire" from his teaching career in Okinawa and set himself up over there as a private tutor of English. He could make a decent amount by the hour and he was looking forward, he said, to living in Japan in a different way. It was really not that expensive for an American to get by, and he would continue sending money home, but less money.

He didn't exactly ask what I thought. Really, the amount he mailed had not changed much over the years and was by now pretty puny. My own salary had moved forward by the usual decent increments, so the change wouldn't break me, would it? My mother was hotly outraged and would've sued him if she'd believed in governments. She actually said, "He owes you more."

Ted was moving into the town and out of the gated and guarded base (which my mother always said sounded like a prison). I sent him a set of curtains for his new house, a very sharp geometric print I thought he would like. I didn't entirely know what he liked any more but I knew something.

Afterward I worried that I'd picked the wrong fabric. "You are so weird," Ruthie said. "Go buy yourself a new sofa instead."

We were on the phone at the time, and I looked around at my house. I liked everything in it, from the floor I had painted a clever shade of blue to the chrome lamp to the bowl of oranges glowing on the table. I was secretly enchanted with my own cruddy décor and its history. What did I need? Nothing wrong with my sofa, which had been in my parents' living room. My stubborn dear parents. You don't know what you're going to be faithful to in this world, do you? It was true I didn't have what other people had, I knew that, and yet I couldn't think of a single other life I envied—no, I couldn't—though I knew better than to try to get anyone to believe it.

Melinda Moustakis

They Find the Drowned

HUMPIES
Oncorhynchus gorbuscha

A river loses strength, loses water. Scientists catch the humpies and put them into tanks and drive to the Kenai River. The humpies are released near the mouth when the reds are running. The humpies don't know where to go—they don't know the Kenai and they don't follow the reds. They don't recognize the currents of the river, or the smells, or the way the light refracts into the water and bounces off the bottom. The reds run up while the dead humpies float down. They die because they have the wrong memories.

OUTHOUSE

A woman with long, dark hair falls asleep with throbbing shoulders from fishing all day. She sits up and rummages in the cabinets for aspirin. She can't find the bottle and doesn't want to wake the others. But her daughter wakes up and tugs her shirt.

The woman takes the girl's hand and they tiptoe out the cabin door. The girl forgets and the door slams shut.

They wince and wait for the others to stir, but no one does. They walk the short trail to the outhouse and the girl goes first, the mother standing outside. She hears a rustle and a low, throated moan. And then nothing.

The woman looks around. The girl takes a long time, so the mother raps her knuckle on the door. "Shouldn't take this long."

The rustle comes closer. She sees a large, dark creature in the woods. And then nothing.

Did her daughter think this was a game? She knocks hard on the door. "Are you in there? Answer me." She stops knocking to listen. "I said answer me."

The rustle creeps closer. "Open this door." The woman kicks the door in with her unlaced boot. The wood splinters from the force.

"Stop," says the girl from inside. She opens the door. Her eyes marvel at her mother.

An animal bursts out of the bushes and the woman shoves the girl behind her. A grizzly charges toward them, running as if he's going to knock them over. The woman holds her ground. Then he stops. Sniffs the air. Walks toward the river. The bear wades into the Kenai, crossing water to reach the mainland. When they see him climb the bank on the other side, they hurry back to the cabin.

The woman remembers the first aid kit has packets of aspirin and swallows two tablets. She puts the girl back to bed. "Don't do that again."

The girl, thinking of the broken door, is soon asleep.

LOON
Gavia immer

A loon drifts down the current. The bird has a daggered beak and with his black, black head, red eyes, and white-striped wings, he's easy to spot. The loon dives down and disappears and the scientist times him, scanning for the breach. After a minute and eleven seconds, the loon reappears upstream, shakes the water off his head. There are loons and there are ducks. Ducks are never alone.

STORM

The woman's husband knocks on the door. They were looking for him. He has blood soaked down the front of his shirt. They hadn't heard a gun. Maybe the axe, but there wasn't a wound. A thick, familiar smell calms them.

He stumbles over the doorway and falls. Two of his buddies carry him to the boat and he's vomiting red into the river. The woman watches the boat leave her and the island and the blood behind. "This is the last time," she says. She nods as she's nodded before, lays towels over the mess, and wipes the blood with the toe of her boot. Then she dips the towels into the river, wrings them out.

The woman sits on a stump near the bank. In the stillwater, the smolt move like a storm of comets. The terns swoop down with their pitchfork tails and scoop up small fish. Seagulls on the gravel bar bicker over scraps.

THE SCIENTISTS

The scientists sit in a boat and dip tubes into the river.
"Turquoise," says one, noting the color of the water.
"Green," says another.
"Glacier blood."
"Crushed sky."
"Kenai Blue."
They test levels of sediment from the ice fields.

LIFE JACKET

The neighbors across the river have a big family. Grandma has a whip of a cast, a fluid flick of line into the water. Grandpa wears his white underwear to swim—his barrel of belly hanging out. The grandchildren scream and splash about in their life jackets. There are five boys and their shouts echo and amplify through the spruce, scaring away the moose and the mosquitoes, if mosquitoes could be scared away. The boys swim out past the dock and let the current carry their floating heads downriver. They stay in the shallow, where they can put their feet down and climb the bank. But if their feet miss, they can grab the net rope fixed to an orange buoy. Sometimes they swim farther across and spend an afternoon on the gravel bar with the gulls.

SPRUCE BARK BEETLE
Dendroctonus rufipennis

The scientists call it the plague—the outbreak of spruce bark beetles that has infested the forests of the Kenai Peninsula for over ten years. A couple of warm summers and the beetles became a blight. They have eaten through two million acres of white, lutz, black, and sitka spruce.

They are the length of a small bullet and they thrive in dryness and heat. The scientists hope for a summer of rain to contain them. The beetles burrow through the bark and chew a path to the cambium layer, the only part of the tree that is alive. They tunnel a gallery inside the host tree and lay eggs. The scientists set pheromone traps and watch as the forest turns into firewood, the dead outnumbering the green.

ROLL

The woman hunches over the reel and her long hair falls forward. Her hip's bruised blue from fishing, but she's got to anchor down with the rod. Boats move out and make a clear path as they drift down.

"Everyone wants to be you with this big ol' fish," says her husband.

They pass the end of the drift and he takes a side channel to avoid the backtrollers.

"Let's get this one in," he says.

She reels in slow and steady. The spinner flashes and he strikes with the net. The king thrashes. He slips to one knee, loses the handle. The king rolls, fifty pounds of fish wrestles out of the net. He steps in and grabs the handle, then grasps at the mesh. She reels but the hook springs loose.

"A hen," she says. "Could've used those eggs."

"Don't jaw me," he says. He throws down the empty net. "I know."

MOOSE
Alces alces gigas

The scientist has a favorite—he calls her Al and every once in a while he'll sit on the river near Bing's Landing and look for her. She has twins now and crosses to the island at night when the river is quiet. He found her on the side of the road after she'd been hit by a truck on Sterling Highway. The driver died and he didn't think she was going to pull through. The scientist visited her when she was bandaged and bruised—he'd talk to her. "Listen," he'd say. "You're the first thing I've been good to in a long time."

YELLOW PATCHES

He and his buddies cut the trees that were turning brown from the blight, where bark beetles eat and weaken the tree from the inside. The diseased trees are yellow patches in a quilt of green. They are also dangerous. The woman is afraid the closer trees might fall over and crash into his cabin. But they're laughing and she calls them a bunch of idiots with axes.

One by one, the trees crack and fall away from the cabin. They splash into the Kenai and the current pushes them toward the bank. But one won't fall. His axe wedges into the diagonal cut.

The tree teeters toward cabin and land, not water. Women and kids scatter. After the boom, the cabin stands untouched. They stand unharmed. He raises a bottle of beer to his good fortune.

RAINBOW TROUT
Oncorhynchus mykiss

Rainbows are the shimmering litmus, the indicator fish. If anything goes wrong in the Kenai, the rainbows tell the scientists. If there is pollution, they die. If a feeder stream stops feeding, they die. Kiss a rainbow, the scientists say, and you'll know all the river's secrets.

A SIXTY-POUNDER

Across the river, Mom and Dad and Grandma and Grandpa play rummy and drink beer from an ice chest. They don't see the boy slide out of his life jacket on a dare. There's struggling and a shout. Dad dives in and emerges empty-fisted. Grandpa, in his white underwear, jumps into the boat and Grandma follows. They drive to the sinking boy and Grandma holds out the king net to him. When the boy doesn't grab, she scoops him with the net. He's a sixty-pounder and Grandpa has to help heave the net aboard. Grandma pinches the boy's nose—her nails making moon indents into his skin. She forces air into his icy mouth and presses his chest. The boy chokes on air and Grandma turns his head to the side. She brushes her tears away. "You little shit," she says. She pats his back. The boy spits the river.

EAGLE
Haliaeetus leucocephalus

The eagle is perched up in the tree, singing. His call jumps octaves, runs with scales. The scientist records the eagle's sounds and writes down the time of day. A boat drifts down Super Hole and stops near the scientist.

"Isn't that something?" says the fisherman. He and the woman both wait for an answer.

The scientist holds up his recorder and points. "Shhhh."

"Well, if you knew anything, you'd know they sing all the time." The fisherman's boat starts downriver. "They sing opera."

THE WALTZ

Her husband has sprawled in her absence. She lies on her elbow and hip in the narrow space and unbraids her long, dark hair. The bed is high—there are storage cabinets built underneath. Blankets and waders are stashed in the gap between her side of the mattress and the wall. He rolls closer and gains inches of mattress.

"Move over," she says. "I don't have any room."

He moves, but he rolls toward her and knocks her off the bed.

The gap is narrow enough to be a problem. "Help me up," she says.

She pats around in the shadows and feels fur. And a snout. Teeth.

She screams and scrambles to dislodge herself. He grabs her legs, pulls her up and pulls her up. She finds footing on the mattress and runs out of the room and then outside. The whole cabin wakes with the commotion.

Her husband stands on the deck with a bear head. "I was saving it for the teeth and claws." He unfolds the skin. "Harmless," he says and puts the bear head over his shoulder and fanfares off the porch. Then he waltzes, hand to paw, around the campfire. Man and bear nod in rhythm, in step.

HALF LIFE
Oncorhynchus nerka

The red swims a slow, stilted speed as if worming through sand. He swims outside the current, keeping to the edges with the smolt. His tail is white with rotting and layers of skin hang in silken scarves. A bite? Raked by the claw of a bear? The fish should be dead. The scientist steps closer and wades into the water, aiming with the net. The fish darts away.

BEETLEKILL

"We survived the oil spill and now this," says the scientist. There's division—no one agrees on how to separate the living from the dead. The canopy has thinned by 70 percent and everything under it is changing—a beetle gnaws through the bark of a tree and the salmon count drops and then a fisherman drinks himself into a ditch.

LOGGING

The boys swim strapped inside the life jackets. The jackets float up near their ears. The river brings a tree to them and they swim to the uprooted trunk lodged near the gravel bar—the amputated branches silky with moss. Three boys straddle the tree as if they were riding a horse. The other boys grab the broken-off branches and shove and push. The river catches the tree and the boys shove more. "Go," they say. "Go." The three riders wave their arms when the current takes the tree. Grandma and Grandpa clap. Mom and Dad grab the camera and start the boat. The boys are waving for the picture as they ride downriver. The fisherman starts his boat, drives fast, and waits below Mom and Dad. Naptowne Rapids waits behind him.

"One snag," he yells. "And the tree will roll."

HEN
Oncorhynchus tshawytscha

The scientist hovers over the dead hen, a female king, with twee-zers. He pinches a scale from the head, the side, and the tail, measures the length and girth.

"Ain't she pretty?" says the fisherman.

The scientist holds one scale up to the light—the sheer skin of a pearl. Kneeling, the fisherman leans over the scientist's shoul-ders, puzzled about the lengthy examination. "It's a fish."

"Yes," says the scientist.

CRUTCH

He breaks things—doors, glass, plates. He breaks bones, but only his own, and punches the walls of the cabin. Most of the time he comes home wobbly and soft and puts his arm around her and she crutches him to the couch, hoping he doesn't wake their daugh-ter. "I love my girls," he says. "I love my girls."

BODIES

The scientists come across a body while doing research. They need to count salmon and a human disrupts the day. A human can last six minutes to six hours in the water, depending on the temperature. They find the drowned don't have liquid in their lungs—they gasp in the cold water until their tracheas collapse.

CPR

The woman and her husband walk a trail along the edge of the Kenai. The husband watches her long, dark hair swoosh across her back as he follows behind with two poles and a tackle box. She stomps ahead not thinking about where they are going. He follows because he has always chased after her. This is what they do. He has not touched her hair in two months. She has not wanted him to touch her in two months. They have no children, not yet. They have a cabin and two trucks and a long-standing argument about who should drive which truck. The woman trips over a root and there is a little blood on her knee.

"Are you okay?" he asks.

"I'm fine," she says and keeps walking. Her jade ring feels tight on her finger.

The man's hand begins to sweat around the handle of the tackle box. "Pick a spot so we can fish," he says. He wishes that her hair wasn't beautiful, with tinges of red, in the sun.

She walks a minute to make a point, and then stops. "Here."

A low, throated call makes them look upriver. A moose calf is struggling against the current. His head sinks and then pops up, then sinks again.

"He's drowning," she says.

"No he isn't," he says.

The calf gains footing for a brief moment and then falls.

"He's being swept away." She starts to walk up the trail.

"Where are you going?" he asks.

She runs. She wades out into the river. He's still holding the poles and the tackle box. The calf isn't struggling anymore. He's floating. "Please," she says. "Bring him this way." She goes in up to her waist. She grabs the calf by the neck and finds the riverbed with her feet. "Help me," she says to her husband.

They both haul the calf to the shore.

She puts her face near the moose's nose. "He's not breathing."

"He's dead then."

The woman covers the moose's nostrils with her hand. She puts her lips on the moose's mouth and blows air. "Where's his heart? Where do moose put their hearts?"

"I don't know," he says. "The chest seems right."

The woman compresses the chest and tries more air. "Go get help," she says.

The man runs up the trail. If only she were willing him to live, pressing her mouth to his. Her hair falling over his face. He finds another fisherman and the fisherman tells someone to call the rangers and Fish and Game.

The calf's mouth feels like a stubbled cheek. She cups the jaw and focuses the air stream. One. Two. She crosses her hands over the chest. The ears twitch. She pumps and hears a gurgle and water spills out. She tilts his head to allow the water to drain.

When the man returns to his wife, there is a crowd. The calf's side heaves with signs of life.

His wife looks up at him and says, "I think he might be breathing."

Fish and Game comes with oxygen. "You saved the calf's life," they say.

"We saved the calf's life." She looks directly at her husband. Then someone hands her a bottle of water and she swishes out her mouth.

The man and woman gather their gear. They walk the trail as before. But when they're away from everyone else she turns to face him. He's holding the poles and the tackle box, so he stands there and she wraps one arm around his neck and puts her mouth on his. She kisses him and he kisses her and she puts one hand on his chest where his pulse quickens under her palm. This is what they do.

DEGREES OF NORTH

Here, the scientists know north is eighteen degrees on a compass. Not zero. They don't wander into the woods without a map. Or directions. Walking from camp, following the trail of moose—they don't lose their way. Losing, as they say, is not scientific.

George McCormick

The Mexican

THE ORANGES WERE NAVELS, from Redlands, California, packed in refrigerator cars, and they were four days on the Southern Pacific crossing the desert—re-icing only in Clovis—before arriving at midnight, here in Waynoka, Oklahoma. The oranges were yellow, and would ripen somewhere in Illinois or Ohio before arriving the next week in New Jersey. Yellow, they smelled yellow, and I imagined that must be what California and Redlands were like, yellow. Places unlike Oklahoma. Places not of constant wind but occasional breeze. A nearby ocean. Vast orchards of orange trees, their limbs swaying, barely, silent. Yellow. All of it under an afternoon moon.

I stepped off the platform and onto the top of the boxcar, and in so doing I was clear from the co-op's high overhang and had a sudden view of the hot, inky night. Town was a couple of miles west, but it was invisible at this hour, in this darkness. I walked along the top of the boxcar opening cooling hatches. I could feel the day's heat rising, could feel the heat of the desert, contained in the boxcar, rising. Beyond the co-op the tracks curved toward town, and above the curve was the moon, rising. *This* moon, a hard thing, seen clearly through the sky like a white stone in a river.

I kicked at the hatch clasps and opened them by hooking one of the prongs of the bident into the hoop and pulling up. On the platform, Chicken fastened the skids that connected the platform to the train. Behind Chicken, Uncle Alton pushed one hundred pound blocks of ice into the chute. We'd been doing this for three months and most times it was easy. The trick was to guide the blocks onto the skid where Chicken and I—mostly Chicken because he was older and stronger—would guide them with our poles into the open spaces of the cooling hatches. If the blocks came off too slow from the chute they'd stall and we'd have to manually create momentum, but if they came too fast they risked sliding over the side of the boxcar altogether. Ice wasn't expensive, but the labor to cube, sled, and skid it was.

We stocked the first three reefer cars fine, about ten minutes per, but on the fourth the blocks began to soften, absorb grit, and move slow.

"We're just going to have to lift the sonsabitches in," said Chicken. He stepped from the platform onto the boxcar with ease. He moved gracefully on top of a train, could leap between boxcars—a thing I was too afraid to try—and he was fast. He could hop an empty flat at twenty miles per hour, and the year before he'd stolen thirty-two bases for American Legion. I stepped across the platform and got on one end of the ice block while Chicken, straddling the gap, was on the other.

"Drop this mother on my toe and I'll kick your ass," he said. Chicken suffered chronic ingrown toenails, which Uncle Alton blamed on a lack of vitamin D, but Chicken knew was a result of his baseball cleats being a size too small.

We lifted the ice block and sat it across the open hatch. Then we guided it in where it dropped the foot or so into the ceiling's carriage. I closed the hatch with my boot and secured the clasp.

"I got my boot packed in gauze," he said.

"Go see a doctor?" asked Uncle Alton from the platform.

"Don't need a doctor. Just need to get in there and dig the sonsabitch out."

"Why haven't you then?"

We worked through the night with the soft ice, skidding when we could, but mostly having to lift the blocks in ourselves. Beyond the co-op was a cottonwood-lined wash that ran parallel to the tracks. In it were thousands of frogs, and on that night I remember their sound. But later, when I tell this story, I talk about coyotes running through the wash and yipping and singing at the moon. I say the night was full of coyotes and even though it's not true I know why I say it. But know now, here, the night was full of frog song.

That summer wasn't the first summer where I'd worked for pay—I'd already spent three summers on the road with Chicken and Uncle Alton and some others on a threshing crew—but it was the first summer I got paid regularly, every two weeks, in checks. Each of which came in a long, beige envelope that bore the name of my employer in black type: Waynoka Cooperative, PO Box 11, Waynoka, OK. The checks were blue and their edges were decorated in silver filigree. I had never imagined anything could feel more important than cash, not the way my father talked about it, but they did. And I kept the small paystubs in a tin box not as a way to file them away for some later official importance, but because they fit alongside some of the other things there: a chert arrowhead, several blue and yellow kestrel feathers, a Mexican coin, a page from a diary I'd stolen from a girl's desk at school.

Uncle Alton had gotten Chicken on first at the co-op and then, when the summer citrus business was peaking, convinced Mr. Abernathy to hire me. It felt good to work a summer near town, to not have to live out of a truck like we had, taking bathroom sink showers in gas stations; not having to walk all day behind a slow two-gear thresher, in godforsaken Nebraska, swallowing chaff in the heat under a white sky. When our checks came at the co-op they came in a bundle that was clipped together and hung on a pegboard outside of Abernathy's office. Every other Monday: $98.75.

At the end of the summer I would be back in school, ninth grade, and Uncle Alton would go on to work back at my father's restaurant and motel. Chicken was three years older than I was and had already dropped out of school. At the end of that summer he'd end up—despite all the talk about going to Amarillo to play ball—working at a Texaco in Custer City over the next decade. Or rather, some town near Custer City, I've forgotten the name of it. It had been on 66 and now it, and the Texaco, and Chicken, have long since disappeared.

Uncle Alton was a big man with enormous, quiet hands. He loved summers because he felt like he fit the kind of work that that season provided. But the rest of the year—when he ran the front desk or worked as a short-order cook for my father—I think he always felt like he was doing the kind of work one does when they've failed at something else. I don't think he thought it women's work, necessarily, though he did work alongside my sisters and my mother, but it was a kind of labor I think he felt to be small and tedious and inconsequential. Changing fryer grease after a three-dollar day, he said, you begin to feel like an asshole. You don't feel like that when the 10:10 SP comes blazing in, he said. Two hundred coal hoppers rolling to a stop. A moving mountain. You feel a part of something bigger, he said. Much, much bigger.

The string of reefer cars we iced that night were twenty-eight long, and on the second-to-last car Chicken and I pushed a block and watched it disappear through the hatch without a sound.

"Oh fuck," said Chicken.

"What," said Uncle Alton from the platform.

"Snag me that lantern, Jess," Chicken said to me and I hopped from the boxcar onto the platform and unhooked a lantern.

"What is it?" asked Uncle Alton.

When I handed the lantern to Chicken he knelt beside the open hatch and lowered the light in.

"What's wrong?" said my uncle.

"No carriage. All rotted through. Block went straight through and landed on the oranges."

Uncle Alton ran his hand through his beard and said, "Oh boy."

"Fuck it," said Chicken.

"No."

"Just melt off tomorrow anyway. Nobody'll ever know."

"No. There is product in there that, in all likelihood, is now damaged."

"Say it happened before it got here."

"No, Chicken. Abernathy has forms for this. I'll speak with Abernathy, I'll fill out the forms tomorrow."

"Goddamn it, we were just about fucking done, too."

I stood in the silence and watched Chicken and my uncle.

"We're pulling that thing out," said Uncle Alton. "Get in and unlatch the door. I'll get tongs and we'll skid it out." The boxcars were locked from the outside, and we weren't supposed to open them unless it was an emergency.

Chicken raised the lantern and handed it to me. He dangled his feet through the open hatch. Then he tried lifting himself in, but after a moment it was obvious he wouldn't fit. He took the lantern back and lowered it through the opening.

"Fuck. I can see the sonsabitch right there. I just can't get in."

"Jess," Uncle Alton said. "You try. You know how to open a boxcar from the inside?"

Uncle Alton knew I did, he'd showed me, but he was cautious and protective of me, as he always was with his brother's son, and by asking me the question out loud he was giving me a way out if I needed it. I nodded and went over to the hatch and looked in. Chicken handed me the lantern and when I lowered it I could see, instantly, the hills of oranges five or six feet below.

"Just shimmy through and hop down," he said, and I thought about the space—four feet—between boxcars that I'd never jumped. Four feet, so easily jumped on the ground, but which was impossible up in the air.

"I'll toss the lantern down to you when you get in there."

As I lowered myself I could see the serial number on the inside of the hatch. MADE IN SHEBOYGAN, WI. I rested a moment on my forearms, then lowered myself and hung by my fingertips on the lip of the hatch. Then I let go.

Inside, the boxcar was nothing but heat and darkness. The oranges were hard, but had broken my fall. I got to my knees and everywhere I could feel the day's heat contained in the fruit.

"You all right?"

"I'm fine."

He lowered the lantern. "Can you see if I just hold this down?"

"Yeah."

"I don't want to drop it down there and have it go out."

"I can see."

In the flickering yellow lantern light the drifts of oranges cast dancing shadows on the walls.

"Can you get over to the door?"

"Yeah."

I crawled over oranges to the bulwark and pulled myself over. There, in a small space beside the door, was a man. He sat with his knees pulled toward his chest. I inhaled so quickly I lost my voice. The man stared straight through me and stayed perfectly still. We stared at each other, then he looked up toward the hatch, and when our gaze met a second time I could see the fear in his hard face.

I tried to yell but there was no wind in me. I choked and, trying to scream, moaned instead. Then I coughed up a mouthful of bile that ran down my lips and onto my chin. In the silence I could hear him breathing. Then the man—he was a Mexican, I was sure—got up from his crouch and walked past me to the bulwark. He crawled over it and disappeared into the oranges like a snake into a river.

"Jess, you got it?" said Chicken.

I could hear Uncle Alton shout something I couldn't make out.

"Jess, you find the door?"

I moved toward the door, pulled the emergency handle, and slid the boxcar's door open. The light of the co-op spilled inside and I looked back and saw nothing. Uncle Alton came down the platform stairs with a length of burlap and his set of heavy ice tongs.

I stepped out of the car and walked toward him. I could feel the bile still burning my throat. The Mexican's white eyes. The way they moved *behind* the hard mask of his face. I walked toward my uncle and stopped and looked back. Plainly seen now, in the open door lit by the co-op's light, was the ice block resting on the oranges.

"I'll grab it and slide it onto the burlap. Then we'll just haul the whole thing back to the icehouse," Uncle Alton said. I watched as he stepped into the car.

Years later I'd move to Amarillo, have boys of my own that I would raise in a world very different than the one I had been a child in. I would tell them this story. Only I tell them a version where there is no ice, no oranges, no Mexican man. In it we're watering cattle cars. A string of thirteen holding Mexican steers, up from Hermosillo. The steers are colorful, I say. Very different than the ones we see in west Texas. The Mexican steers are marked blue and green and yellow, I say, like lichen on granite. And they are wild, and buck against the sides of the wooden cattle car, making it rock. Their horns are like swords and their eyes are black and their breath, God their breath, is awful. I tell them about how Chicken just avoided being crushed when they broke free from the car, how they'd kicked their way through the slat boards, and how Chicken scaled the outside of a boxcar and climbed to the top. I tell them about how I hopped from the platform onto the boxcar's roof and from there the two of us, safe, watched as the Mexican steers ran. How they scattered into the wash, through the cottonwoods, and out onto the night plain. Running, all of them running. I tell them this story because in the West what we love most are lies. What we love are images of a stampede, of animals running; of what we think are the right stories of stealing away.

Nalini Jones
Tiger

THE TROUBLE WITH THE cats, Essie believed, was entirely her son-in-law Daniel's fault. They first turned up on the day that Gopi was expected to come shake the coconuts down from the trees. It was mid-morning, a January day without too much Bombay haze, and early enough for the children to play outside without Marian worrying about the heat. Still, she insisted on hats for them. Essie said nothing when her daughter called the girls to the front veranda steps, just sat and helped Marian rub their limbs with lotion to protect them from the sun. Both were fair-skinned, though darker than Daniel, whose pale, pinkish skin reminded Essie of chicken not cooked long enough.

Marian went upstairs to help the servant Ritu wash the children's clothes, but Essie stayed to keep an eye on the girls. They were five and six only, babies still by Essie's reckoning, and it was her belief that Daniel did not pay close enough attention. She knew better than to approach him directly, of course; he would only turn to her with his blank American look and smile his blank American smile. It was all too soft and spongy for Essie, who had wondered when she first met Daniel whether he fully understood her. Who was this man her daughter had married?

Did he know proper English? Were his mental faculties intact? She had adjusted her speech in his presence, talking loudly and slowly, using smaller words. But her efforts had no effect and eventually she realized that conversation with her son-in-law would always have a shapeless quality, like sinking her fingers in a lump of dough.

She had prayed for guidance and patience, as she had once prayed for her daughter to come home again and marry an Indian Catholic boy from their own neighborhood. Such nice-looking boys! Essie had kept her eyes open to suitable possibilities. And then, the shock of this Daniel and his soft American answer: "Well, not exactly Catholic." There is no exactly in this matter, she'd informed him. A person is Catholic or not. She had confessed her disappointment to all the parish priests. But one after the other, they disappointed her too. What to do, they said, but accept?

Now when Essie was troubled by his American ways, she took her concerns straight to Marian. But her daughter, so clear-eyed in her girlhood, so close to Essie that they had seemed two limbs of the same living thing, had gone a bit soft herself after so many years in the States. When Essie pointed out that Daniel was too relaxed with the girls, Marian looked down, or away, or said, "Oh, Mum," as if Essie were one of the children, acting up and tiring her.

For a little while, the girls practiced badminton, a game their grandfather had played when he was young. Daniel, Essie noted, did not have good form with his swing. But everything had to be cleared away before Gopi arrived and coconuts came pelting down into the compound. Daniel pulled up the stakes of the net and the girls were collecting shuttlecocks. Nicole, who was older, flung her racket onto the lawn and ran up and down the garden wall, checking under leaves and behind the roots of trees as though hunting for Easter eggs. But it was Tara, a year younger, who found the cats behind a thick clump of bamboo and called everyone to come and see.

"Look at that! Kittens!" Daniel peered into the corner where a mother cat and two half-grown kittens had been hiding. All three were alert and staring.

"Don't touch!" Essie said quickly, drawing Tara back. "They'll scratch."

"No, they're nice," Nicole decided. She squatted on the ground and held out her hand. One of the kittens made a tentative move closer and Essie inhaled sharply, a sound meant as a warning.

"So dirty, baby! See their fur? They don't live with people."

"They don't look too bad," Daniel said. The mother cat was thin and dingy, with white fur that reminded Essie of yellowed muslin and patches of gray and ginger. One of the kittens was spotted, half its face shadowed in gray, and the other was ginger-striped, as if the mother had poured some part of herself into each of them.

Nicole extended her arm as far as she could and Daniel put a hand on her shoulder.

"Not too close, you'll scare them." He began to call the animals with a whispery noise.

"These aren't your American cats," Essie said. "They could carry disease."

But Tara was spellbound. "One kitten for each of us . . ."

"Your grandmother's right. These cats don't like to live inside with people."

Nicole looked up at her father, stricken. "But we have to take them inside. Gopi is coming!" The danger of the falling coconuts had been impressed upon her all morning; she must hold someone's hand when Gopi did his work, she must stay safely beneath the veranda roof. Otherwise, tuk! Her grandfather's fist had knocked against her head. (Essie had watched this display with disapproval and scolded her husband. "Such a thing to clown about, Francis! Have some sense.")

Now she hastened to reassure Nicole. "These cats are wild, darling. Like tigers. They like to look after themselves. See the mummy cat? She won't let anything happen. She'll hear Gopi and they'll all go running."

"Where?" Tara was solemn, all eyes and wonder.

"They have places they like to go." The girls were clearly unconvinced, Tara's eyes reproachful. Essie spoke brightly. "Maybe they'll go to the fish market, for a nice piece of fish!"

"Maybe Ritu has a little fish she can give them," Daniel suggested. "Let's see if they want something to eat."

"Not in the house," said Essie at once, but the girls were already scrambling up, naming the cats, begging them not to run off, promising to be back in another minute, *stay, stay,* their voices high as fevers as they called from the staircase and Essie watched while Daniel followed, letting them run up the steps without holding the railing, not saying a single word to slow them down.

The next hour was given over to the cats. They were easily lured into the garden with pieces of cheese, and step by step, the girls coaxed them up to the outdoor landing with saucers of milk. This was the main entrance to the upper story, by means of a staircase that began on the far side of the veranda and ran up the side of the house beneath a narrow wooden roof. The small square landing at the top led directly into the front room, and the heavy wooden door was kept open all day long to let in light and air. The cats, Essie thought grimly, were literally at her doorstep.

It was some small satisfaction, at least, that Marian greeted this development with dismay.

"Babe, what could I do? Their father told them to feed the cats. I cannot contradict him. All I can do is tell him the way we live here, but . . ." Essie paused. "What could I say?"

"Well," Marian said. "At least they don't look like they have fleas."

"Fleas are too small to see. We'll only see the bites."

The girls were alone on the landing, the kittens playing near their feet while the mother cat perched a few steps below. Daniel joined Essie's husband Francis, who had switched on the test match the moment he returned from a morning at his club. Daniel was new to cricket. He leaned forward to ask a question, a glass of beer in one hand, and Essie eyed him sharply to be sure he didn't put it down on the wooden arm of the chair.

She raised her voice to be heard over the television. "Marian, you were scratched by a cat when you were small—you don't remember. A bad scratch, on your cheek. I had to rub oil every day so you wouldn't scar."

Daniel did not turn from the screen but Marian sighed. "The kittens seem harmless enough." One had been lured into Nicole's lap. Tara, warned to be gentle, was stroking the other with exaggerated softness.

Essie grunted. "They've been eating in rubbish piles, God knows what they might pass on. And what is keeping Gopi? Maddening, these fellows! *Yes, yes, I'll come,* he says, and what? I've let the whole morning go waiting for him!"

"Let them play awhile," Marian said. "When Gopi comes, the girls will want to watch and the cats will run off on their own."

But Gopi never came. By lunchtime, the girls had names for all three cats—even the mother, a wild, skittish creature who kept her distance until she saw a chance of food and then came creeping up the stairs, low on her haunches as though she were hunting.

"That one is Tiger," Nicole told Essie. "She's the mother."

"What is this one called?" Essie tried to enter the spirit of things. "Is this Panther?"

"No," Tara said. She was squatting, perfectly balanced on her heels. "That's Smoke."

"And the little ginger one is Fire?"

"That one is Ritu."

Essie felt strangely dissatisfied. She had never liked cats, all hiss and tooth and claw, slinking like vermin among the market stalls. She would not want the girls to name one for her, but it did not seem right that Ritu should be singled out.

The real Ritu was bringing plates of food to the table, a chicken dish from the day before, a new fish curry. She heard her name as she was setting down a steaming bowl of rice.

"Who is Ritu? Oh! See, *bhai, chota* Ritu! Thank you, Baby, thank you, *Chota* Baby." She laughed, using the same sing-song the girls used when they remembered their manners. Ritu called both little girls Baby, but Tara, smaller, was *Chota* Baby. "Baby is taking care of *Chota* Ritu, and Ritu is taking care of *Chota* Baby. Come, food is waiting." She stooped to pick up Tara but Essie stopped her.

"Have you brought the curds to the table?" she said, picking up Tara herself. Ritu made fresh yogurt daily, which the little ones ate with their meals to cut the spice. "Come, darlings. Come and eat."

Nicole held one of the kittens to her chest, her voice pleading. "Can't we eat out here?"

"Girls." Marian used her warning voice. "Grandma says lunch is ready. Let the cats be, they've had enough."

The girls did not disobey but dragged themselves to their feet.

"Come," said Essie. The men had got up from their seats near the television but were still focused on the screen, standing as though anchored. She spoke in a loud, ringing voice. "We'll clean your hands first, lots of soap. Those cats must have been filthy."

That was the beginning. The cats returned the next day, just as lunch was being served, and again the day after. By the third day, Essie had agreed that the girls could leave milk for them on the back balcony. "At least let them be out of our way," she said. She could not have people coming up and down with stray cats on the landing, and the days were filled with visitors, neighbors, tradesmen. But even after she had banished the cats to the kitchen balcony, they seemed to creep into her days, pushing from one minute into the next, curling around the arms and legs of the children as though they were entwined. There were ten days left, a week, five days. Already the children had gone to the market for the last time, and the beach at Juhu. The banana man had come on his weekly round and had given the girls a full bunch as a present; he would not meet them again. Marian had begun to arrange all her packing in piles, and Daniel had taken the suitcases down from the tops of the wardrobes. The cases lay on the floor, flopped open like wide hungry mouths. Francis began to stay home from his club in the evenings, waiting for the girls to be bathed so they could pad out in bare feet and flowered gowns and say goodnight. Essie read to them from the Bible at bedtime, longer and longer stories, until they had collapsed against her shoulders or across her lap. Still the girls went running whenever the cats appeared, no matter what other treats Essie planned for them. In the late afternoons, while she and Marian entertained guests in the front room, she could hear the sounds of the girls' voices drifting in from the kitchen balcony as though from someplace other than her house, as though the balcony had torn free and no longer belonged to her but to the cats—the pirate cats with their patches and hooked claws, their grinning white teeth, their narrow eyes, floating slowly away with Ritu and the children, who were laughing as they left her.

Four days before Marian and her family were set to depart, Essie was soaping herself and felt the lump, a hard knot where her breast sloped toward her underarm. She checked again and again, feeling the way it seem to roll beneath her fingers. Then she checked her other breast: nothing. She stood for a moment, still and dripping, in the afternoon sun. They bathed out of buckets, one hot and one cold; now both faucets were off and instead of running water, Essie could hear the clear bright calls of birds. She leaned against the tile wall, slick but not cool. It was a thick afternoon, unseasonably warm, and she had come for a quick bath before the girls woke from their naps. She had not intended to wash her hair so she'd caught it back in a braid and flicked it over one shoulder or the other, out of the water. Now she pulled the damp tail of it to the front, over her breast, and slowly removed the elastic. She kept her hair carefully dyed, a flat tarry color that did not quite take on the living quality of her youthful black, but she was not yet willing to be gray. She had only two grandchildren, after all; her sons, one living abroad, one posted in Delhi, had not yet married. For the first time, she thought of letting the dye fade. She poured a dipperful of water over her head. Another. Another. Then she seized handfuls of her hair and wrung them like fruit, imagined the dye running down her chest and thighs in rivulets, staining the floor, pooling at the drain where a rubber stopper kept the cockroaches from climbing up the pipes. Slowly, carefully, she washed her hair. She did not rush, even when she heard the children wake and call for her.

She waited until the girls were asleep that night—dinner and baths and wet hair combed, heavy heads against her chest, both children in her lap, one last story, a moment's pleading, one more last story. Grandma, tell us about trains, tell us about Gopi, tell us about Mum when she was little. She went with Marian to tuck them into bed and pull the mosquito netting down like drapes.

She waited until Daniel had taken her suggestion and accompanied Francis to his gymkhana, Francis puzzled but with the same foolish bland smile on his face as Daniel's. Off they went together, to cards and whiskey and long-running tabs and friends Francis didn't bring to the house. Essie leaned out the front window and watched them go with relief. What help could the men give her? Let them at least be out of the way.

She waited until Marian sat quietly, writing letters to aunts and cousins in other parts of India, letters Essie would post for her. Essie watched her daughter. Even now, folded into a chair, no proper jewelry, Marian was a beautiful girl. She had lovely skin, a delicate jawline. She might have married anyone, might have had her pick of the best neighborhood boys. She might have lived all her life only a few steps away.

"You must cancel your ticket," Essie told her.

Marian stopped writing, looked up briefly. "We can't, Mum. You know that. Don't make it harder."

"I'm not making anything!" Her voice rose against her will; she wanted to stay calm, a woman prepared for whatever came next, a woman with her daughter beside her. "I have something here." She put a hand near her breast.

Marian's voice sharpened. "What do you mean, something? A pain?"

"Not a pain." Essie considered. "Perhaps it's a little tender. But not a pain only. I can feel something hard, under the skin. This is just what happened to Aunty Ann, you remember? One day she was fine and six months later she was gone. Totally diseased. Nothing the doctors could do."

"You have a lump? When, Mum? When did you find it?"

"Today only." Essie's eyes filled with tears; here, at last, was the daughter she had been missing, Marian alert and focused keenly on her, Marian sharing her secrets. "What to do, babe?"

"We'll go to the doctor. I'll take you tomorrow, we'll go first thing."

"But I have no appointment—"

"We can wait until he sees you. Daniel can watch the girls."

"No, babe, no need. We can make an appointment properly and go later in the week, you can extend a week or two and take me."

"Mum." Marian came to sit next to Essie on the couch, put an arm around her shoulders. "We should see him right away, okay? It could be nothing. But let's get it checked as soon as we can. I don't want you to worry."

Essie felt Marian's arm tightening around her, Marian's head resting softly on her shoulder. The letters lay abandoned in Marian's chair. Essie wondered, she truly wondered, if she was dying. She believed she was. But it was a distant idea, more faint than she expected. The more palpable question was how long her daughter might stay.

. . .

The doctor pierced her with a needle, extracted fluid, sent it off to the lab. "In a few days we'll know more," he told them. Marian sat next to Essie, holding her hand, her face tight.

The plane tickets could not be changed without exorbitant fees. Daniel had to go back to work. The girls could not miss another week of school. "We may hear from the doctor before the flight," Marian said, a limp offering.

Essie did not bother to answer.

"Mum, let's sit down with Dad and tell him."

Essie shut her mouth firmly, again said nothing.

"I can tell him if you're nervous. But he should know what's happening. Maybe he can help."

Essie snorted. Marian crouched on the floor before Essie's chair, looking up at her like a child. "The doctor says there's a good chance nothing is wrong. But listen"—she held Essie's knees—"I don't want you to feel alone while you're waiting."

Essie could think of nothing to say to this beyond the obvious. So she said nothing.

Marian put her forehead on her mother's knee. "You understand I have to go? I wish I didn't, Mum. I wish I could stay."

"What good is wishing?" Essie asked, and her daughter didn't answer.

The night Marian and her family flew home, Essie hired two taxis to take them to the airport so that there would be room for her to see them off. She held Nicole in her lap until the last moment—after Daniel had unloaded all the suitcases, even after Daniel said, "Come on, girls," and Marian counted all the tickets and passports.

"Check again," Essie told her, kissing the top of Nicole's head, her arms tight around the child's chest. "Check the date to be certain."

The girls were dressed in blue jeans and long-sleeved shirts, as though they had already left her for another climate. It was nearly eleven o'clock, long past their bedtime, and in the harsh lights flooding the airport entrance, they looked pale and drawn. They had already said goodbye at the house: to neighbors who had come to wish them goodbye; to their grandfather; to Ritu. *But where are the cats? Where are the cats?* Both began to cry. It was no good explaining that cats come and go, that the mother cat must put the kittens to sleep, that Grandma would find the cats tomorrow and deliver all their messages. "We have to say goodbye to the cats!"

They had stopped crying by the time they reached the airport but their faces seemed strangely hollow and serious, as if the past few hours marked the onset of a wild acceleration and they had already begun to grow older—girls Essie would hardly recognize in a year or two when she saw them again, if she saw them again. Did she have a year or two? They had not heard back from the doctor. When Marian called his office that afternoon, she was told the results weren't yet back from the lab.

"Mum, you'll be fine," Marian kept saying. "I'll come back. I'll come back if anything happens."

"Something has already happened," Essie told her.

"Just see what the doctor says, Mum."

Essie shook her head, a parrying motion. What was the point? She knew where things could lead. Daniel, she noted, said nothing.

"I'll come back."

Her daughter was crying, the way she cried sometimes as a girl, streaming tears and silence. For a long while she clung to Essie, shoulders shaking, then she moved away, a sleeve to her face. Essie's spectacles were useless, the airport lights blurred and flaring through the wet lenses. She took them off and tried to rub them dry. She must have a last good look at her daughter. By the time she put them on again Marian and her family had moved the few steps from the curb to the departure hall. No visitors were permitted inside but Essie watched the doors swallow them up, the girls looking small and forlorn, Marian still in tears, turning to wave a final time. After a few minutes, Essie climbed back into her cab.

At home the mosquito netting was still draped over her bed, where the girls had slept with her for their last nap. The cotton cover was rumpled from their bodies. Francis had slept in another room for years but Essie could hear him snoring and the evidence of his peaceful rest at such a time filled her with bitterness. The windows were thrown open and outside she could hear cats brawling, a tangle of raw-throated screeches and howls.

A few hours before dawn she switched on the light to begin a letter to Marian. She tried to chronicle all that had happened in the scant time since they had parted: the impatient cab driver, rushing her departure from the airport, the vacant hours sitting up by the telephone in case the flight was canceled. She described the dark house and Francis's useless snoring, the cramp in her hand from writing, her prayers for their swift return; she described the way the knowledge of her own death was stealing over her, a certainty she could feel in her bones and her muscles and yes, in her breast—she did not have to wait for the doctor to tell her what her body already knew—and even then she could not stop. Here was the way to keep Marian tethered to her, a stream of confidences no one else could share, a comfort mother and daughter might only find in each other. Words poured from her, a spill she could not check—her fear that she would slip away before seeing her daughter or sons again, her dread of disease, of her body rotting away from the inside—did Marian remember visiting Aunty Ann in the nursing home, did she remember the rattling cries, the smells? She wrote about the solace she found in placing herself in the Virgin Mary's hands. *You too might have done this, my girl— place yourself at the mercy of Mary and not worry so much about the costs of things. Who knows how God would have provided if you had decided to stay?* She wrote about her faith in being reunited with both her parents, the father she had lost when she was only a girl, the mother who had raised her; she leapt ahead generations and wrote about all her hopes for her granddaughters. *You must bring them up in the Church, so that they too have a light in these darkest times.* Eventually she began to reprise the terrible shock of Marian's decision to marry an American—the fainting spells, the long nights of weeping, the visions of this very moment, sick unto death with no children beside her. *Even now I can hardly believe you are wrenched from me at this crucial hour,* she wrote. *We may never see each other again. But these are the nights I foresaw when you married, which you did not.* She filled twenty pages before her eyes began to ache, and even when the room was dark again, Essie lay in bed, her mind turning with what she was too tired to write.

The late night at the airport had upset Essie's routine and she woke later than usual, the departure lingering like a hangover. Her ankles seemed swollen, her calves like rods, her limbs so heavy they might have been waterlogged. The world made its swollen turn, slow and stupid, senseless with miles. The day throbbed with hours. Everywhere she looked, something needed cleaning or putting away, but she sat in her chair, a pad of letter-paper in her lap, and watched dust tumble through dry shafts of sunlight like tiny shavings of wood. She imagined that splinters, fine as hair, worked their way into her skin every time she pushed through the air of the empty house.

She was alone. Francis had disappeared to his club, frowning at nothing. Ritu had dressed in *salwar kameez* and gone to the shops, viewing this as a treat since Essie usually insisted on going herself. Essie had intended to continue her letter to Marian but her efforts in the middle of the night seemed borne by a feverish energy, a kind of blood-letting. She sat in her chair now, depleted and drained, and listened without interest to whatever passed beneath her window, the mild traffic of a morning underway. Women's chirping voices, cars moving slowly past the rut in the road, a stiff volley of barking from the dog next door. Birds screeched like policemen with whistles, squawking over nothing; a motorcycle stuttered past, the sound loose as a chest cough. Essie ignored the long drifting calls of vendors, flung out like fishing line. She ignored the bell at her gate which set off the neighbor's dog again, and eventually she jotted down a few desultory lines. But the letter began to seem flat and useless. It would not reach Marian for two weeks at least. Marian herself would not arrive home for another day—that's how wide the world was. And even in her passion the night before, Essie found she could not express the full sweep of her thoughts. Each memory had eight or ten more at its back—a dozen, a hundred—too many to record so that anyone would understand how quickly and powerfully they came upon her. She could write and write, letters enough to span the globe; she imagined the lines of longitude and latitude in her own handwriting, floating gently over green and blue. And still it would not be enough to record the longings of even a single moment. Everything she hoped for was connected to everything she remembered and everything she had lost—a web spreading in all directions. Words moved in single file.

Essie pushed the letter aside and closed her eyes. She fell briefly to sleep, upright in her chair. When she woke she was still alone but light blazed in the window. Francis would soon be home and she was not up to cooking. *I have very little appetite,* she thought of writing to Marian. *This may be a sign of what is to come.* She must see what could be warmed for lunch.

The refrigerator was old, full of jars she had not labeled, but on the top shelf was a glass of fresh yogurt. *The house is full of reminders that you are gone,* the letter in her mind continued. *Everywhere I look I find something that pains me—even the curds I made for the girls.* She paused, wondering how best to convey the pathos of the uneaten yogurt. *I should not have made more with so little time left. But it is so difficult for a mother not to feel hopeful. Up to the last minute, I felt certain, in the circumstances, you would change your mind. Daniel had to go back to work, that is one thing.*

But would a few days more have been such a sacrifice, knowing what I am going through? She imagined the way she would describe her pleasure in seeing the girls eat, how much she already missed pulling chicken from the bone to feed them by hand.

Now here is the chicken dish they liked. I've shown you how to make it but I don't know what spices you can get there. Last night, you remember, Daniel took three big pieces, so there is not enough for today. Never mind, I can go without.

A faint scraping jolted Essie from her thoughts. She turned, expecting to find a rat. Instead she saw the ginger kitten, scratching an empty sack of rice. The gray was close behind, sniffing the whisk broom Essie had left in the corner; the mother was nowhere to be seen.

"And what are you doing back again?" she said aloud. "No one wants to see the likes of you," she told them. "All your friends have gone." Still she made no move to chase them away. The gray cat abandoned the broom and began to investigate the rough black surface of the grinding bowl. The ginger, the cat named Ritu, stood perfectly still and stared up at Essie, one of its claws still hooked in the burlap. Essie had the strange and unwelcome impression that the cat was awaiting instructions, or perhaps the opening of negotiations.

A sudden soft leap, and the ginger perched on top of Ritu's grinding stool.

"Tcha! Get down from there."

The cat drew its legs together on the small surface.

"Go on. Get down." Essie clicked her tongue and after a moment's hesitation, the cat dropped to the floor. The gray sidled closer, reminding Essie of the way Tara sometimes reached for Nicole's hand.

"Such nonsense," she said, but in a warmer tone. The gray stretched up its head on its thin neck; the ginger made a plaintive noise. "Little beggars, the both of you." The cats watched as she returned to the refrigerator and snipped open a container of milk.

"Outside," she told them, and they followed her onto the balcony, crowding near her heels as she stooped to leave the bowl for them.

For the next several days Ritu was permitted to feed the cats. The kittens always turned up first, leaving the mother cat to brood below in the shady corner of the garden. She would only join them after a slow, stealthy advance. Essie would not admit to her own part in this uneasy truce; she refused to pay any attention to their comings and goings and made a point of complaining about the price of milk. When Marian called to say they had arrived safely, Essie reported that the cats were sleeping on the balcony.

"You see, babe, what happens? Every day they come, bold as you please."

"What about the doctor? Have you called the office again?"

"Why should I call? He can call when he has his results. Until then, I know what I know."

"Mum—"

But she refused to discuss the knot in her breast, refused to give Marian that satisfaction. Birthdays, anniversaries, feast days, school concerts, sports matches—the parade of moments she might have shared with her family if they lived near—all thinned to voices on a phone line. But she was not willing to accommodate such distance in the matter of her dying. Marian had left; very well, let her feel the consequences. The Marian of her letters, the Marian to whom she revealed all the movements of her soul, seemed a different person than the Marian on the phone. The Marian of the letters was the daughter Essie thought she had raised, the daughter who would have stayed.

"The girls miss you so much," Marian told her. "They loved being in India. On their first morning home Daniel made them tea but both girls cried. They said the tea didn't taste the same."

"Use the tea I packed for you," Essie urged. "Make it yourself. Your husband doesn't know how to do it properly."

They could not talk for long; the rates were too high.

"Wait, babe—so much to tell you! Daddy is up to his old tricks, every night at the gymkhana, so everything falls into my lap. Even the coconuts—this fellow Gopi still hasn't come."

Marian had begun to say goodbye, her voice hollow.

"Just let me say a quick hello to the girls."

But Marian had put them to sleep. The connection was scratchy with a slight delay; words tumbled into their echoes. "Tell them I send tight hugs. I pray for them every night. Tell them to read their Bibles. The breast is paining a bit, but only slightly. Pray I'll be taken quickly, without too much pain."

"Please call the doctor, Mum. Don't put yourself through this."

"Ask the girls to pray for me."

"The girls will write soon. Lots of love."

Essie's voice rose, high and cracking over the static. "Tell them not to worry, Grandma is looking after their cats. Only they must come back soon."

"Goodbye, Mum."

Essie held the receiver until she heard the click. "Hallo? Hallo?" she said loudly, just in case, but the line had gone dead and after another moment she put down the phone. She went into the kitchen, where Ritu was washing up with a bucket of hot water and where Essie could see the cats on the balcony, napping against the balustrade. The mother shot instantly to her feet, whisking down the stairs, but the kittens only yawned, showing small sharp teeth, and stretched up their heads to greet her.

Days passed slowly, sagging with heat. Blossoms dried to soft brown skins and trees hung heavy, fruit swelling like goiters. Essie bathed her limbs each night with cold water and slept on top of her bed. *This heat wave has given me a rash. You remember your brother used to have them as a baby?* By now addressing her thoughts to Marian had become habit, as though all that passed through Essie's mind was part of a letter she was composing to her daughter. *I should stay out of the sun but then who will do the marketing?*

A batch of notes came from Marian and the family, all in a single envelope. Marian's was rushed and glancing; she was busy with programs for the girls' school, she would call again soon. Daniel had enclosed a postcard he wrote during their layover in the Frankfurt airport, which Essie examined but decided was not pretty enough to save. Nicole wrote on colored paper that was printed with flowers, each word with round, careful letters. *How are the cats?* Essie read. *We have no cats here. We love you.* Tara drew a picture of the cats with sharp triangle ears and whiskers stiff as bristles.

A week later, another fat bundle arrived from Nicole's first grade class. Marian had just visited their classroom, wearing a sari and telling the children about life in India. The teacher hoped Mrs. Almeida would not mind if the children wrote to her with some of their questions.

Essie emptied the packet onto the dining table. All the letters were written on rough, grainy paper, scored with solid and dotted lines to guide the children's pencils. Essie sifted through them, looking for Nicole's and picking out a line here and there.

What do you eat for breakfast?

How many languages do you speak?

Do saris [printed over a streak of grimy erasure marks] *ever fall off?*

Dear Grandma, she found at last. *Have you ever seen a real tiger?*

Essie put down the letter. *Yes,* she thought. Once when Marian was nearly two, they had gone to visit Essie's uncle, a conservator of forests in the south. They were driving through a protected stretch of jungle with six others packed in a small car, moving slowly, cautiously, around the blind turns. *Do you remember, my girl?* Essie sat with Marian on her lap, hot and sweaty, tired of jolting along bad roads when they suddenly rounded a corner and saw a tiger reclining in the center of the road. It lifted its huge head to stare at the oncoming car. *Quiet! Everyone, quiet.* They braked, not daring to pass. Essie could still remember the feel of Marian struggling to stand on her lap and see. She had caught the child's fists in her own hand, preventing Marian from thumping on the window. For three hours they waited while the tiger slept. After a time Marian fell asleep, her skin sticking to Essie's. The tiger had stretched in a shady patch of the road, protected by a thick canopy of trees until the sun bore down overhead. *See,* Essie's uncle whispered. The tiger remained in the sun a few minutes, so still it seemed dead, then suddenly, with a lazy roll, it stretched, rose to its feet, and ambled back into the trees, out of sight.

You only woke up when we were driving again and then you wanted to go back and find the tiger! It seemed to Essie that she could still feel her daughter sleeping against her chest, the hot breath against her neck, the sure damp weight of one who belonged to her.

That evening the phone rang while Essie was in the kitchen with Ritu. Marian, she thought at once. Her fingers were oily; she looked for a rag and couldn't find one, then tried to hold the receiver against her ear with just the palm of her hand. "Hallo?"

It was the doctor. "So sorry for the delay, Mrs. Almeida. The results were misplaced in the lab. But they've come at last and it's good news. Nothing malignant, totally benign. Come back in again this week and we'll drain the fluid. You see, Mrs. Almeida, I knew you'd be a good patient!"

She shifted the phone against her ear and nearly dropped it. "But the pain, doctor? And you don't know the history. This very thing happened to my aunt and she—"

"No, no, I'm telling you. You're in perfect health. The pain is from the fluid only. It's very common. There's no danger at all, you mustn't worry. Okay? Right then, come by this week. That will be that." He laughed and rang off.

Francis had drifted to the table, the way a dog might sniff at its empty bowl. Essie found she could not bear his expectant air. "Dinner's not ready," she snapped. "Another twenty minutes at least."

"Who was calling?"

She shook her head, too annoyed to answer.

"Was it the doctor?"

She stared at him.

"Marian said you had a . . . pain of some kind. A lump. What did the doctor say?" When she didn't answer, he moved closer and put a hand on her arm.

"I'm covered in oil." Her voice was frayed; she was on the verge of tears she could not explain. "The doctor says it's nothing serious. I have to go back next week to remove fluid, or some foolishness, I don't remember exactly."

He grasped her arm for a moment, then let his grip loosen and patted her gently. He kept his eyes on the place where his fingers touched her skin. "I can go with you."

"No need," she said. They stood quietly. When he released her she moved past him to the kitchen. "Twenty minutes," she said. "Go find something to do until then."

The phone rang again after Francis was in bed. Essie had been waiting in her chair. For a while she had watched television, then she turned it off and waited in the dark. It was all over, she would tell her daughter. A fright, nothing more. They had prayed and their prayers had been answered.

"Have you spoken to the doctor?" Marian asked.

Essie paused. She felt the phone lines between them like tight ropes, felt the moment sharpen to a single shaved point upon which she must balance. She felt herself falling.

"There's no news, babe. He hasn't called."

"Oh, God, Mum. It's been two weeks! Give me his number, let me call him myself."

"No, no! No need! I—" But she stopped. "I'll go myself next week. He's out of the office now, on leave, but after the weekend I'll go myself and ask."

"You promise, Mum? I mean, this is crazy, making you wait so long. I'm sorry I'm not there to go with you. Maybe Dad—"

"Stop pulling your father into my affairs," Essie said. "I'm perfectly capable of going on my own."

"Mum." Marian's voice was suddenly so small, so close to tears, that for a moment Essie imagined Nicole or Tara had come to the phone. "Mum, tell me honestly. Do you think it's serious?"

Later she wished there had been time to pray, time to beg Mary for an answer or for the strength to answer. How badly she wanted to reassure her child, to promise, no, no, nothing will happen— but how badly she needed to say yes, to show her daughter some part of the strain she had endured alone. "I don't know," she said, and her voice broke, and she began to weep.

It would only be a little while, Essie told herself after they had said goodbye. In a few days she would tell Marian all was well, and nothing more need come of it. But she felt jittery, agitated, a churning in her stomach. She went to the kitchen for a glass of water, moving quietly. Ritu slept on a roll of bedding in one corner of the kitchen balcony, just beyond the spiral steps that led to the garden.

She heard the cats before she saw them, a dark rustle, and flicked on the light. Blinding yellow for a moment, then the kittens twining near the empty rubbish pail, sniffing the rich dark stains. She could not see the mother at first, but then the cat leapt from the counter to the floor with a soft thud and stared up at her, so impudent, so fearless that Essie felt a surge of unaccountable fury. She caught up a whisk broom and beat the cat away with it.

"Out, go on, out! Back you go!"

"What, *bhai*? What, what?" Ritu had woken, lifting her head from her pallet and rubbing her eyes in the moonlight, but Essie kept after the cats—"Away with you!"—poking the broom until she had driven them onto the metal stairs. The mother cat dropped down two steps, turned, and hissed before she retreated, her tail lashing, her body curling sinuously around the central pole of the staircase, her half-grown kittens close behind her. At the bottom she leapt softly into the damp patch of earth where wash-water was thrown and stalked slowly, fearlessly into the garden.

The next day only one of the kittens appeared. It sat, thin and piteous, near the threshold of the kitchen and made a noise that sounded like crying.

"The mother is gone," said Ritu, looking worried. But by midday Tiger had emerged from a tangle of undergrowth. She could not, however, be lured up to the balcony.

"Offer a bit of chicken, she'll come."

But the cat remained in the garden. Finally Ritu took food down to her, moving slowly down the spiral steps. The cat hissed when she ventured too close, but ate hungrily once Ritu had gone back up to the balcony.

"See, *bhai,* Mummy is hurt." Ritu pointed to a fresh wound on the cat's shoulder.

By late afternoon, the ginger kitten had curled to sleep in the corner where Ritu kept her bedding but the gray kitten had still not returned.

Essie felt a dull certainty that there was nothing to be done and that she herself was culpable. "Just go and look for it," she told Ritu. She waited until the girl had gone down one side of St. Hilary Road before she set off toward the shops in the other direction.

The sun was still unseasonably hot and St. Thomas Road was in a state of upheaval. Men were shoulder high in pits, putting in new pipe, while women carried away baskets of rubble. Shoppers clambered past as though on river banks and Essie had to slowly pick her way past clots of clay and bits of broken pavement. At the juncture near St. Jerome's, three cows were ravaging a rubbish pile and she thought of what the girls would say to that, the funny, loud, slow, American way they would say "cows." She walked as far as the market and back along the shore where the

Varuna fishermen lived, narrow winding streets that teemed with cats. She searched the next day and the day after that, but they never saw the gray kitten again.

At the end of the third day, she sat in her chair and tried to answer Nicole's letter. She described the tiger in the road, other tiger hunts she had seen with her uncle, and then she stopped writing, not certain how to continue. The evening had rusted to night. Marian would not call.

She had given her daughter the good news. Perfect health, Essie said, and listened to Marian's flood of love and relief. She had tried to take pleasure in her daughter's words, tried to catch and hold them, to savor them later, but whatever Marian said had slipped away. The whole episode hardly seemed real. Essie felt empty and drained, as if the doctor's needle had taken more than he intended.

I never saw a tiger family, she wrote in reply to Nicole's question. *A tiger likes to live alone.*

Ritu came from the kitchen to clean the front room. Usually Essie would leave her to her task, but she felt rooted to her chair. She watched as Ritu brushed the dust and crumbs into cottony piles and flung them from the stair landing. Then, with a damp rag in one hand and the tail of her sari draped over the other, Ritu squatted on her heels and began to swab the floor. Essie sat in silence, listening to the soft kiss of the rag dipped into her pail, the trickle of water as it was wrung, the whisper of cloth sponging over the tile. The wet floor met the dry floor in a scalloped line, lapping forward as Ritu advanced on her toes. She crept just behind the slick edge, pressing it further along the tile, fanning her arm in wide swaths before her. Essie thought of the tiger hunts she had seen as a girl, with beaters who tamped down the grasses for the rifle-bearers.

Once I saw a tiger killed, but that— She stopped. What could she tell a six-year-old about population control?—*was a big and old tiger. A naughty tiger who liked to frighten children.* Would she give the child nightmares? *There are no tigers in America. And none in Bombay, so you can come back soon. Only in the jungle.*

Dip and wring, dip and wring. At times, the scratch of the bucket as Ritu dragged it behind her. Her toe ring clicked against the floor like a fingernail tapping; past the table, the sofa, Essie's own feet in slippers, all the landmarks of the room until she had reached the kitchen and then she peered onto the balcony.

"*Chota* Ritu is staying, *bhai*. But Mummy is gone."

Ritu hung the rag over her wrist and picked up the bucket to swab downstairs, her bare feet leaving cloudy marks on the floor which had already begun to dry in streaks.

Essie wrote, *The only tiger here is* your *Tiger.*

Not true, of course. *What to do, babe? I've looked and looked.* But there was no one to witness all her searching, no one to appreciate her effort and penance, no one to share what she had always imagined she would share with her daughter. It came to Essie then, as she had not felt since she was a child, that there were parts of her nobody would know or understand, thoughts too numerous to record, adrift and orphaned, with no one to hear them. She closed her eyes and tried to pray, to imagine God the keeper of all her secrets, but all she could think of was the sleeping tiger. She had wondered then if God could see her and what exactly He saw: the light picking through a tangle of trees, her uncle's hands, tense on the wheel, her own gold cross at the base of her throat, the child asleep in her arms. She wondered if He saw all that would happen once the tiger had awakened, if He knew now where the gray kitten had gone, if the mother had died.

A few minutes later she picked up her pen again. *Your cats are well and happy, darling,* she wrote to Nicole. *All three are fast asleep, happy here with me.*

The next day, nearly a month after he'd promised, Gopi turned up at last to harvest the coconuts. Essie had been sitting upstairs, replying one by one to the letters from Nicole's class, when he arrived: a small, dark-skinned man from Kerala, his leather strap slung over his shoulder. He waited until she had finished scolding him and then he lifted his hands. His wife just had a baby, he told her in Hindi. The baby came early—so small. Gopi held his hands apart, the size of a breadfruit. For three weeks, no one knew what would happen. But now—he smiled suddenly, a flash of light in his dark face—the baby was fine. A son, his first son. A son will stay, he told her. Daughters grow up and marry and go, but a son will stay with his family.

A few minutes later Gopi climbed the first tree. Essie had imagined standing with the girls beside her, watching the way he shimmied up, the strap looped around his waist, his bare feet curved around the trunk until he was lost in the thatch of palms at the top. She had already counted out the money she would give Gopi as a gift for the child.

For the first time in years, she did not oversee the coconut harvest. Instead she went to the back of the house, down the narrow winding steps of the kitchen balcony. The sun never penetrated that one shady corner of the property, and she sat on the lowest stair, elbows on knees, feeling the cool soft mud on the hard skin of her feet. In the front yard, she could hear Gopi climbing, the leather strap slapping against the tree as he hoisted himself up. The gray kitten, Smoke, was gone, the Tiger-mother nowhere to be seen, but the ginger, Ritu, was picking a delicate path along the garden wall, and Essie had brought a piece of fish down from the kitchen especially. She lured the kitten right to her, caught safe in her lap when the coconuts came raining down.

Lily Tuck
Pérou

THE YEAR IS 1940 and I lie fast asleep under a fur blanket in a Balmoral pram. The Midnight Navy Silver Cross pram, with its reversible folding hood and hand-sprung chassis, glides smoothly and silently down rue Raynouard. (Until recently, I thought rue Raynouard, located in the 16th arrondissement in the area of Paris known as Passy—as the names sound almost exactly alike—was named after the painter and spelled *Renoir*. Instead the street is named after a dull French academician, François-Juste Marie Raynouard.) Jeanne, my nurse, pushes the pram. Over her heavily starched white uniform, she wears a blue wool coat that is nearly the same Midnight Navy as the pram and that reaches unstylishly to her midcalf. She also wears thick cotton stockings, a pair of white lace-up shoes, and a coif. The coif, again the same matching navy blue, is secured to her forehead by a white bandeau and entirely covers her hair. Jeanne is pale, plain, and nearsighted. She wears glasses and, if ever I catch a glimpse of her without them, it takes me a moment to readjust to her face. Jeanne, whose last name I don't remember or, worse, never knew since to me she was always simply *Jeanne,* comes from a village in Brittany. She is nineteen years old and will devote five years of her life to looking after me—years she will spend in Peru.

Peru of all unimaginable places!

Jeanne, we have to leave Paris. Leave France, is what I imagine my mother says to her.

You'll have to get a passport. A visa.

Oui, Madame.

Does she have a choice? Could she instead say:

Non, Madame. I have to go back to *mon pays*, to *ma famille*.

A large family: the men fishermen, the women uncomplaining, hardworking. Mother, father, grandparents, aunts, uncles, brothers, sisters, and cousins.

Peru? Except for when, long ago, they went to Mont Saint-Michel on their honeymoon, neither one of her grandparents has traveled any farther than the city of Brest. As far as they are concerned Jeanne has disappeared off the face of the earth.

Where in God's name is that? Again and again Jeanne's father, a large man with an appetite for food and life, asks his wife, Jeanne's mother, Marie-Pauline. But, in the end, he looks it up for himself in one of the children's school atlases and he sees how far away Peru is from Brittany. He shakes his head sadly; in his heart, he knows he will not see Jeanne again.

Pérou, Annick, Jeanne's younger sister and the prettiest, says with a huge sigh. How I envy her. I would do anything to get away from this boring, stupid place. And, in a few months' time, on a warm summer morning, wearing her best dress, a sleeveless, red-and-white flower print, and bicycling quickly, without giving the village a single backward glance, she does.

What is Jeanne thinking? Handsome, blond Daniel, the cleverest of her brothers, thinks.

Or is she so attached to the child in the pram that she cannot be parted from her? Catherine, another sister, Jeanne's favorite, who is a young schoolteacher and has started to cough up a little blood, wants to know.

Unlikely.

Probably, Jeanne, a simple girl, feels it is her duty.

A Catholic, Jeanne is deeply religious.

But Peru?

Maybe she has simply misunderstood.

Misunderstood the way everyone else at the time has.

The British call it the "Phoney War."

The French, *la drôle de guerre.*

For eight months, from September 1939 to May 1940, nothing much happens. Although the European powers have declared war on one another, none of them has yet launched a significant attack. Everyone is waiting—waiting for the German troops to march into Belgium, the Netherlands, and Luxembourg. Nonetheless, the Atlantic Ocean is already mined and ships no longer cross it with an assurance of safety—take, for example, the HMS *Courageous,* sunk on September 17 with a loss of most of her crew, 518 men. A month later, on October 14, the HMS *Royal Oak* sunk as well, with an even greater loss, of 833 men.

We three cross the Atlantic in July on board the SS *Exeter.* A ten-ton single-funnel cargo liner built by American Export Lines, the ship makes several risky round trips in 1940 and 1941 between Lisbon and New York, transporting thousands of refugees. Like, no doubt, the other refugees, we have left behind most of our belongings—the silver, the china, the paintings, even the elegant pram, which, in any case, I will soon outgrow. (Interesting to note, however, that during the war, the main part of the Silver Cross factory was requisitioned by the Air Ministry and, instead of making prams, it produced over sixteen million parts for Spitfire airplanes.) Photos taken on the deck of the SS *Exeter* show my mother, dressed in white shorts, leaning against the ship's rail; on her head, tilted at a jaunty angle, is the ship captain's cap. In another, wearing an adult life preserver that covers me from head to toe, I sit on the lap of a young man who, obviously, is not my father. There are a few snapshots of smiling passengers—unknown women and children—and finally a photo of the captain himself. He, too, is smiling, because, perhaps, he has only just recovered his cap from my mother, and he is wearing it. There are no photos of Jeanne.

No one knew how long the war would last.

Jeanne cannot have the faintest idea how long she will stay in Lima, Peru, a city she has never heard of and where, during that entire time, those very, very long five years, she will be completely cut off and receive no letters nor, for that matter, any news from her family and where, by the end of the war, she will not have a clue whether any of them are alive or dead—imagine! A city where it never rains, a city where it is always hot, exceedingly hot; a city where there are frequent earthquakes (a particularly devastating one—8.2 on the Richter scale—which causes massive damage to the city and nearly destroys the principal cathedral in Lima, occurs in 1940, only a few weeks before she arrives), and where most earthquakes occur in the middle of the night so that Jeanne has to quickly get out of bed with just enough time to put on her glasses but not enough time to get dressed or put on a dressing gown, and run into my room to wake me and get me out of bed so that, together, we can stand in the doorway of the room, said to be the safest place in the house; a city, a country, where she does not speak the language—Spanish—a city and a country where she knows no one. Absolutely no one. Not a single other soul. A country and a city where, during those five years, she will not learn to speak much Spanish—only a few rudimentary phrases to get by—and where she will not meet anyone except for perhaps a few other foreign nannies and the Spanish servants in the house—the cook, the gardener, the maid, the part-time chauffeur, all of whom look down on her. Or, if they do not look down, make fun of her. Her timid ways, her pale skin and thick glasses, her starched and spotless uniform, all of which they construe as unfriendly and snobbish, her not joining in with their jokes and complaints in the kitchen which, anyway, she has difficulty understanding, her not eating their spicy food, the fried beans, the tough roasted corn, her keeping herself to herself.

How lonely she is!

To compensate, she looks after me with a concentration and an attention that I still vividly remember and can almost physically feel, like a presence. She hardly ever leaves my side—only at night, while I sleep, and on her day off, Wednesday.

We live in the upscale Miraflores district of Lima, in a rented house that has a large garden surrounded by a high stone wall, topped with sharp bits of broken glass. The garden is full of tall red flowers—gladioli. I once lop off all their heads and although, initially, I lie and blame the rabbits, in the end I confess and get a hard slap in the face from my father, then almost a stranger to me. By then, too, I am five years old and I should know better. The war nearly over, my father has only recently joined us in Lima after spending time—not by choice—first, in a French internment camp for German and Austrian nationals in the Loire Valley, in France, then in North Africa, in the Foreign Legion—this last move inspired not by any spirit of derring-do or romance but rather made out of desperation and to keep from being deported back to Germany—but that is another, very different story. Now, he and my mother argue a great deal. I can hear their angry voices in the bedroom.

No one knew how long the war would last.

True, in the back of the garden, next to the kitchen, there are rabbits. A cage full of them. The rabbits are unusually large and belong to the cook and she raises them to sell and to eat. She feeds them leftover food and dandelion greens. I become fond of one rabbit, a brown one, and name him Pépé. Every day, I take Pépé out of the cage and fondle and pat him. One day, of course, Pépé is gone.

The cook, the maid, the gardener, and the chauffeur always

talk about thieves—how, here in Lima, all the thieves need to do is climb over the garden walls, at night, to rob the houses of the rich. They give examples: Only two weeks ago, so-and-so only two houses down, the gardener says, pointing, was robbed. All the jewelry, all the silverware was taken. Another house, one directly in back of ours, the maid joins in—the people were out—out at a movie, for only a few hours—but when they got home, every piece of furniture, the paintings, the curtains, everything was gone. My mother and her friends talk about how unreliable the servants are and how they are certain the servants are robbing them.

I am more afraid of thieves than I am of earthquakes.

Jeanne! I call out, crying, in the middle of the night if I am having a nightmare, and she comes running into my room.

Ma petite chérie is what she calls me as she takes me in her arms and rocks me until I am comforted. It is then, too, in my darkened bedroom, that she talks about her family in Brittany and describes her brothers and sisters to me.

Tell me again about Annick, I beg her.

Annick is the naughty one, Jeanne begins. One day, instead of going to the *boulangerie* to buy bread the way she was told to, Annick . . .

Close your eyes, Jeanne says to me.

And tell me about Daniel, I say. I don't admit to having a crush on Daniel.

Oh, Daniel, Jeanne whispers to me, you should see him. All the girls are in love with Daniel. . . .

Jeanne even kisses me, once, twice, on the cheek, before I fall asleep.

But most of the time Jeanne is strict rather than affectionate; she is a disciplinarian. Rarely do I dare disobey her. If I try to play a trick or fool her in a silly way, she is not amused. For instance, I remember how once—and looking back, this event is so out of character I am tempted to think I have made it up—while walking in the street with her one day, I notice a dog turd lying on the ground, brown, fresh, still steaming and perfectly formed. Look, I tell Jeanne, *une saucisse,* and, leaning down, I stretch out my hand as if I am going to pick it up. Yanking me hard by the arm—so hard she leaves a red mark—Jeanne says she is going to tell my mother.

Looking back, I think Jeanne is humorless.

But then what does she have to laugh about?

Those Wednesdays?

What is there for a young French nanny who speaks little Spanish to do by herself in Lima on a Wednesday?

In the morning, first thing, dressed in a dark skirt, a cotton, long-sleeved blouse, sensible brown shoes, Jeanne leaves the house to go to Mass. She goes to a red stone church called La Ermita, located in the Barranco district of Lima a few miles from Miraflores, which means that she either has to take public transportation, the crowded, dirty bus, or, if the part-time chauffeur is not occupied with driving my mother and, later, my father, beg a ride from him. The church, originally a fishermen's shrine, feels right to her. A miracle occurred there—something to do with fishermen lost at sea in the fog who see a light. The light came from the cross on the church steeple and it guided the fishermen back to the safety of land. On her knees, on the cold stone floor, surrounded by burning candles, faded flowers, and the ornately decorated plaster statues of saints, Jeanne, a scarf tied around her head, her eyes closed, prays for the safety of her family back in Brittany. Such a long time since she has seen any of them, she often has a hard time trying to imagine what her brothers and sisters look like. The younger ones, especially, Jacqueline, Didier, and Nicolas must have changed and grown a lot since she has last seen them. No longer children, they are teenagers—Jacqueline is sixteen now, and Didier fourteen, and—do they do well in school? Are they obedient to their parents? Do they help out at home—milking the cow, feeding the chickens? And what about her father? Is there enough petrol for him to still take out the boat named after her mother—*Marie-Pauline*—to fish? And the others? Has Daniel married Suzanne as he hoped to? Perhaps they have a child already—Jeanne smiles to herself at the thought. Is Catherine still teaching school? She can almost hear how the little village children call out excitedly when they see her—*maîtresse, maîtresse!* And Annick? Has she dyed her hair red the way she always threatens she will? Again, Jeanne smiles. She also thinks about her mother, Marie-Pauline, whom she loves very much. All these questions and she prays hard to soon get some answers for them. Getting up from her knees, she lights a candle for each one of them.

Then does she go to confession?

Mon père, j'ai péché . . .

What sins can Jeanne possibly have to confess?

That she lost her patience with me, when, instead of getting out, I was splashing around in the tub, the water already gone cold, and she spanked my fat little *derrière?*

She pretended not to understand when the cook told her to keep an eye on the water boiling for rice on the stove while she stepped outside to feed the rabbits and the water boiled over?

She let the part-time chauffeur kiss her last Wednesday on the way back from La Ermita but stopped him when he tried to touch her breasts.

Non, non, Hermano, she tells him as she pushes away his hand.

Laughing, Hermano leans past Jeanne and puts his hand against the door handle, thus, forcibly, not letting her out of the car.

Un beso, Hermano demands in return for removing his hand and allowing her to open the car door.

Does it happen again the following Wednesday?

No.

It happens again in another way a month later, on a Saturday while my mother is away for a few days visiting Machu Picchu with her North American friends. My father has not yet arrived in Lima and the other servants may or may not be in the house. It is night and I am in bed and again, I am asleep. Jeanne is sitting in the room we call the nursery, which is on the ground floor, off the kitchen; she is knitting a sweater for one of her brothers, for handsome Daniel—but Daniel, unbeknownst to her, has already been dead for quite some time from the typhoid fever he contracted in a German prisoner-of-war camp; and not just him, but also her favorite sister, Catherine, who hemorrhaged to death several months ago; and last year, Jeanne's father, too, died—as she listens to the radio. The program is in English—it could be the BBC—and Jeanne only understands a few words—a word here like *invasion* or a word there like *bombardment*.

Hola! Hermano, the part-time chauffeur, says to her as he walks into the nursery.

Looking up from her knitting, Jeanne opens her mouth but does not answer him.

Hola, Jeanne! he says again and starts to laugh.

Is he drunk?

She is afraid all of a sudden.

Hermano walks over to where she is sitting listening to the radio and, bending down so that his face is directly level with hers, he makes a loud kissing sound with his lips. Then Hermano shouts something she does not understand.

Not quite true. She understands the word *puta*.

His breath reeks of *pisco*.

Jeanne holds the knitting needles tight against her chest, and Hermano, as if he could read her mind, grabs them out of her hands and throws the needles, the ball of wool, and the half-finished sweater for Daniel across the room. She hears the steel needles hit the wooden floor at the same moment that Hermano, with a backhand blow of his hand, knocks off her glasses and they, too, fall on the floor. And they break.

More things tear and break.

Poor Jeanne.

The only school I remember going to in Lima is a small private kindergarten run by an English lady that, after only a few weeks, shuts down because one of the students has contracted scarlet fever. Instead, Jeanne teaches me how to knit, how to sew and embroider. I embroider lots of doilies and half a dozen shoe bags for my mother who, in Lima, has acquired many pairs of high-heeled, open-toed sandals that show off her pretty feet. (Later, my mother likes to tell the story of how she was at the movies in Lima one night, and how sitting in the theater she had taken off her shoes when all of a sudden there was an earthquake and everyone got up from their seats and ran out of the theater while she still sat there groping in the dark with her feet trying to find her shoes until the man she was at the movies with shouted at her, "Anna! Come on. Leave your shoes," and she had had to leave off trying to find her shoes and had to run out of the theater in her bare feet. Then, the funny thing, my mother continues, is that when the earthquake was over and she and the man she was with returned to their seats in the theater, the very same seats they had before, she still could not find her shoes. She looked everywhere for them but the shoes were nowhere to be found. The shoes were gone.) All year long in Lima, my mother's legs are tanned and she paints both her finger- and toenails red and wears a matching bright lipstick that leaves a stain on the cigarettes she smokes as she talks on the telephone, making arrangements to meet with her friends—most of them Americans. North Americans who are stationed in Lima. Her best friend is from Miami and the wife of a Panagra pilot. Like my mother, she is tall and blond. My mother and the wife of the Panagra pilot, I hear people say, could be twin sisters. Gorgeous twin sisters! My mother's real sister is a doctor and during all the time my mother lives in Lima, she, like Jeanne, receives no letter nor any news from her family. Only when the war is over and she returns to France does she learn that her sister is dead.

Nearly every day, my mother plays golf and bridge at the Lima Country Club. On Sunday afternoons, she watches the polo matches there. One Sunday—a few weeks after my fifth birthday and a few weeks before my father is due to arrive in Lima—because Jeanne is not well—all morning, she has been vomiting—and it is both the cook's and maid's day off, and since the alternative is for my mother to stay home, she takes me to a polo match. I have to behave, she warns, and not wander off but stay next to her at all times. I have to hold her hand, she says. We watch the match standing directly on one side of the polo field, the side where the wives and friends of the players stand and where the grooms hold extra horses and equipment while, at times, no more than a few feet away, the game is being played. Horses gallop toward us, charge us, or so it seems, until, at the very last possible moment, snorting, their hooves clattering, the riders shouting, the horses stop short, wheel around, do an intricate quick dance of balance and of changing leads in midair on their slender bandaged legs, and gallop off again in another direction as their riders swing their mallets dangerously close to our heads. It is a hot day, the sun shines directly overhead, and my mother and I are wearing hats—she, a large straw hat and I, an ugly cotton one. Once or twice, when the horses come galloping over to us, I am sprayed with flecks of sweat from their necks and, for some reason, this pleases me and I try to lick the sweat off my face with my tongue. Looking down, my mother frowns and says something I do not catch. Then she takes a handkerchief from her purse and hands it to me but, instead of using it, I let the handkerchief drop to the ground and stand on it so my mother won't notice. Each time, between games, when the riders ride over to where we are standing to change their horses, one of the riders, before dismounting, stops briefly and leans down to speak to my mother. The rider's arms are dark and muscular and his teeth are very white.

Sí. Bueno, my mother answers, laughing.

After he dismounts, the rider takes off his helmet and wipes his forehead with a red kerchief, then, taking the bottle his groom hands him, he drinks a swallow from it and spits out another. I watch, shocked—spitting, I know, is forbidden—but I don't say anything to my mother. He is wearing a green shirt and on the back of it is the number 1. Taking the reins of his new, fresh horse—a gray one this time—he mounts it with a single leap—a leap like a cat—and before he is settled in the saddle or has his feet in the stirrups, the horse is already turning, moving toward the field in anticipation at the same time that the rider waves his mallet at my mother.

This happens three or four times.

When the game is finished, the rider again rides over to my mother but, instead of dismounting, he reins in his horse and, pointing to me with his whip, says, *la niña.*

My mother starts to shake her head but I have already let go of her hand and am reaching up to pat the horse's wet neck. Leaning down, the rider picks me up and, in one effortless motion, sets me down in front of him on the horse's neck. The horse, sensing a foreign presence, shakes his head up and down, and the rider speaks sharply to him at the same time that he gives him a slight flick with his whip as we trot off onto the empty polo field.

Manuel! I hear my mother call out.

Manuel has his arm firmly around my waist as I bounce uncomfortably on the horse's neck, but I don't mind. I laugh.

Also, my cotton hat has come untied and falls to the ground and I am secretly glad that he makes no move to retrieve it.

Manuel! my mother calls out again. Already, she sounds far away.

Soon after, Hermano is arrested for drunken driving and spends a couple of nights in jail and I overhear my mother, on the phone, tell her North American friends that it serves him right because, anyway, she never quite trusted him or his driving and she hopes that this will teach him a lesson. My father arrives in Lima and, to keep busy and out of argument's way, during the last few months of the war, he takes up golf. One day, he manages to hit a hole in one, apparently, a cause for celebration, and, in accordance with the customs of the Lima Country Club, he is obliged to buy everyone in the clubhouse a glass of Johnnie Walker Scotch Whisky—including one for Manuel who, that day, happens to be standing, still wearing his jodhpurs and mud-caked riding boots, at the bar. When, at last, the war is over and it is time for us to go home, Jeanne who, by then, is no longer able to properly button up her starched and spotless uniform—instead, she wears a loose, rough cotton housecoat she has purchased at the outdoor market located a few blocks from La Ermita—tearfully tells my mother that instead of going back to Brittany, she will stay on in *Pérou,* and thus, as, years earlier, her grandparents thought more than likely, she disappears.

Jamie Quatro

Sinkhole

WHEN THE CAMP DIRECTOR introduces God, he reminds us the man is just an actor.

"His real name is Frank Collins," the director says. "He lives in Knoxville and has a wife and three grown-up children." He looks down at the little kids on the benches up front. "I want to make sure you know this, so you don't get scared."

God a.k.a. Frank Collins comes out from behind a screen set up at the front of the open-air gym. He's wearing a dark navy sheriff's costume. He's short and muscular with a thick gray beard and buzz cut. He asks the little kids to get off the bench—they scramble onto the wood floor—then drags the bench forward and stands on it. He pulls a sheriff's hat from behind his back, molds the brim, and sets the hat on his head. From where I'm sitting, fourth row, I can see the tips of his white sneakers sticking out from beneath his pant legs.

"The name's God," the sheriff says. "You all don't need to tell me your names, cause I got 'em written down in my book."

He hooks his thumbs over his belt. "Will you look at me up here on my cosmic cloud? A-peerin' down with my eagle eye at all of *you*."

On "you," he quick-draws a pistol from inside his waistband. It's a cap gun, silver paint flaking off the barrel. He makes a show of opening and inspecting the cylinder, then snaps it into place and squints, his jaw moving like it's working tobacco.

"You there, sister," he says, aiming at a girl in my row. "How'd you like to have the flu, honey?"

He fires. Bodies jump.

"And I got cavities for *all* you all," he says. "This'll teach you not to mess around doing your homework on the Sabbath." He waves his gun over us like a wand, opening fire.

In my head I repeat the line my therapist gave me: I am my own Great Physician.

The tingling in my chest starts up anyhow.

I look around to try to spot Wren. Sometimes even just seeing her helps. I can't find her, so I move my hand up to the airspace in front of my pecs, in case I have to do the Gesture. It looks like I'm doing the air Pledge of Allegiance. This is my ready position.

This is not the Gesture.

Doing the Gesture = failure.

Doing the Gesture = letting the sinkhole be the boss of me.

Frank Collins twirls the gun around on his finger, then shoves it into his waistband. "Remember," he says. "I got your names written in my big ol' book. And lemme tell you something: I wrote most of you off a long time ago."

He steps off the bench and backs away, frowning, until he's behind the screen.

The camp director says that Frank Collins—an actor, you remember—will be a bunch of different Gods this week. Campers in grades one through six will vote on which God is the real one. The older campers will talk about the faulty theologies behind the fake Gods. I'll be a sophomore this year, so the faulty theologies group will include me.

During the closing prayer, the tingling goes away. I keep my hand in the ready position, just in case.

. . .

I'm an amazing runner. The most amazing runner in our city, the absolute best the city of Chattanooga has ever produced. Benjamin Mills, one of our own, the newspapers say. We've never seen the likes of it. The length of his stride, his ability to process oxygen, form and function melding in thrilling new ways. Whatever it is, it moves in him the way wind moves in trees.

And to think he's only fifteen!

I'm supposed to get even more amazing. I'm supposed to get so amazing that people will say, We have never seen this before in a human being, there has never been another distance runner like Mills, he's the best in the state of Tennessee, and when he goes to college, we'll say best in the nation, and someday, when we see him on television with the American flag wrapped around his body (look how amazing, he's not even sweating!) we'll say, We knew it, we've always known it: Benjamin Mills has given us a glimpse of the limitless perfections of God Himself.

The thing that will stop me from being amazing is this dime-size spot of skin between my pecs. This spot of skin is like a scar that cannot be touched by anyone or anything. If anyone or anything puts even the slightest amount of pressure on this spot—if I even think about someone or something touching it—the sinkhole opens. The sinkhole is black and spirals down and open like a whirlpool: first through my skin, then through the tissues and pectoral muscles and on into the bones of my sternum, and if I don't lie down and do the Gesture to make it stop, it will get all the way to my heart and wrap around it and clamp down until my heart stops beating and I die.

What I do to make the sinkhole close is, I press my fingers together the way swimmers shape their hands into paddles. Then I lie down and massage the airspace an inch above the spot of skin. I move my hand in what you would call clockwise circles if you were standing above me, watching. It's like wiping down a counter. The faster I wipe, the faster the hole shrinks back into the dime-size spot.

The first time my parents caught me doing the Gesture I was twelve. I was bringing in the garbage pail and trying not to think about the spot on my chest. But trying not to think about something is the same as forcing yourself to think about it, and I ended up lying down in the driveway.

My parents took me to the emergency room, where the nurses hooked me up to heart monitors that showed everyone I wasn't having a heart attack. But because of my little brother Sam—born with a hole in his heart that four surgeries in eighteen months couldn't fix—they did all kinds of tests. They taped wires to my chest and attached them to a monitor I hooked onto my belt. I had to wear it around for a week. If I felt anything funny (*flubbing,* the doctor said, or *racing*) I was supposed to push a button on the monitor to start recording. When I got three recordings, I was supposed to unhook the monitor from the wires and dial an 800 number, then hold the phone up to the monitor and push "playback" so the monitor could send the sound of my flubbing and/or racing heart into a computer that would write down the patterns with one of those jittery robotic arms.

I never called the 800 number. I never felt any flubbing or racing.

I felt the sinkhole opening, but the doctor didn't say *spiraling* or *clamping down.*

For another test, I had to run on a treadmill set at a steep incline until my heart rate was two hundred beats per minute. It took me a long time to get there. Dr. Logan, the cardiologist, kept calling me Lance Armstrong. "Faster, Lance," he'd say. "I'd like to get out of here before next week."

When my heart finally reached two hundred, I had to jump off the treadmill and lie on my back on a padded table. Dr. Logan said this is the most taxing thing you can do to a heart: take it from 100 percent exertion to 100 percent inertia. A nurse injected a dye into my arm. The dye made me taste metal and lit up all the pathways running in and out of my heart. An EMT was in the room, holding a defibrillator, just in case.

Dr. Logan said my pathways were clear as crystal. He said, "I've never seen a heart resume its resting rate that quickly."

My resting heart rate is forty-six beats per minute.

In my prime it could drop into the thirties.

After the sheriff-God, on the way back to our cabins, I see Wren at the snack table with some other freshman girls. She's wearing a tank top and jeans. Her bare arms start out in the darkness, white and smooth as the inside of a shell.

"Benjy," she says. She says my name like she wants to keep it inside her mouth; I imagine the letters all curled up together on her palate. Wren's hair is the kind of silky blond that shouldn't be thick but is, so thick it's like a sheepskin rug you want to dig your toes into. When she goes back to her cabin, I imagine she'll put on a white nightgown and kneel beside her cot to pray. Her prayers at Ethos are always humble and straightforward: Help us to see others as you see them. Give us your kind of love for people.

"So that sheriff's a no-brainer," Madeline Simpkins says. Madeline's one of these girls all the guys like—big chest, heavy eye makeup, obviously ready for whatever it is you want to do with her. "You'd think they'd want to, like, challenge us."

Wren is holding a little Styrofoam cup filled with popcorn. "I imagine him that way sometimes," she says. "Like he's just . . . I don't know. Waiting to fire."

I don't say anything. Neither does Madeline. Wren and I have lived on the same street on Lookout Mountain since we were five, the year her parents found out she had a tumor in her uterus the size of a grapefruit. Some weird kind of cancer with a name like *mezzanine*. They had to take out all her reproductive parts plus her colon. After her surgeries, her dad got her a new bike with training wheels. She'd ride around our neighborhood, bald-headed, a catheter bag dangling from her wrist. The next summer, she pulled me into the empty girls' bathroom at the Fairyland Country Club and lifted her T-shirt to show me the cloth-covered bag sticking out of a hole in her side. "This is how I go," she said. "I don't even have to sit down." Every summer after that, her parents were flying her somewhere to get a new surgery to try to fix her insides so she could at least have that bag taken off. None of the surgeries worked. I'm pretty sure they've given up. When we were in seventh grade, everyone started asking everyone else to go out. No one asked her. She told me that if Protestants had nuns, she'd sign up.

To look at her, you wouldn't know a thing had happened if it wasn't for the compression stocking on her leg. Something to do with the radiation killing all the lymph, or messing with the mechanism that makes the lymph move around. When she walks, she has to kind of drag her leg along with her, one swollen foot pointing out to the side. That foot makes me want to lift her up and carry her anywhere she wants to go.

"A bunch of us are going down to the waterfront at midnight," Madeline says. "Swimsuits optional."

I look at Wren and raise my eyebrows up and down a few times, like, hey baby *hey*.

"Right," she says, laughing. Which is exactly what I thought she'd say. Wren's the whole reason I came to camp. I'm in love with her. She doesn't know it and wouldn't believe me if I told her, because of her missing parts and her swollen leg. But I'm so in love with her that I've decided to ask her to do a faith healing on me.

This is called being the boss of my sinkhole.

Because of the sinkhole, I've never been with a girl. Never even hugged one close. Wren's the only girl I know who I think might be safe, who would treat me the same, even if she saw me doing the Gesture, because of what she's been through. Here's how I'm hoping things will go. I drop hints all week, tell Wren I'd like to talk to her about something. The last night of camp, I ask her to meet me somewhere private, maybe down at the waterfront late at night. She agrees. I tell her everything. She says she wants to help if she can. I take off my shirt and lie down. I say, Please don't touch my chest until I ask. She starts praying. I imagine she'll get her mouth down next to my chest, right above the dime-size spot. Her breath will be warm and moist, a sweet citrus smell to it.

When I tell her I'm ready, she'll take a drop of the oil I brought in a tiny Advil container and place it, lightly, with just the tip of her pinkie finger, onto the spot. The most delicate laying on of hands. She'll say, In the name of Jesus I command you. I might ask her to say some Latin I found on a Catholic website about exorcism—*In nominus Christos, Dominus vobiscum.* When she's finished, I'll touch the spot with my own finger, to be certain it worked. And when I'm certain—when I can tell the sinkhole isn't going to open—I'll lay my entire hand on top of my chest and take a few deep breaths. Then I'll place Wren's hand over mine to prove to myself I can handle the added weight, and to show Wren what she did for me.

The Presbyterians wouldn't tell us for sure if Sam went to Heaven when he died. I overheard the pastor telling my parents that it depended on whether or not Sam was one of God's chosen people.

"But I can tell you that the Scriptures are full of promises to children born into covenant families," he said. "And you are a covenant family, so in all likelihood Sam is with the Lord."

"Are we talking percentages here?" my father said.

"All I know," the pastor said, "is that if I get to Heaven and see every baby that ever died, I will say, God, you are so good. And if I get to Heaven and see only some of the dead babies there, I will say, God, you are so good. And if I get to Heaven and see not one dead baby there, I will say, God, you are so good."

We found another church. It's called Ethos. As in: the church needs a new ethos because the old one is screwed.

At breakfast, the camp director rings a brass bell hung up above the dining hall porch.

Most of us line up long before he pulls the rope. We can see the food through the screens, already laid out on the tables: pan-cakes, sliced cantaloupe, scrambled eggs, grits. Above the tables are chandeliers made out of wagon wheels. Just inside the doors is a big speaker with a microphone. After the director rings the bell, he asks one of the high schoolers to step inside and say grace into the microphone so that everyone waiting on the porch can hear. The prayer is like this bribe: be quiet and listen and you'll get food.

This morning—our second morning at camp—the director asks Wren to say grace. The kids waiting in line move away as she walks toward the doors. Dragging her leg with her. When she gets close to me, I see that she's wearing cutoff shorts and has her swollen foot stuffed into a flip-flop. Her toenails are painted pink.

She takes the mic and says one of her simple, direct prayers: Thank you for the hands that prepared the meal, use the food to strengthen our bodies, be present in our conversations around the table, Amen. Maybe I should let her wing it when I ask her to pray for my sinkhole.

Inside, I sit at Wren's table, beside her. She's with Madeline and a couple of the guys on the McCallie cross-country team. They're talking about James, a freshman wrestler who's supposed to win state in the 103-pound class next year.

"Doesn't he normally weigh, like, 130?" Madeline is saying.

"He was going to be six feet," Ransom McGuire says. "Now he might not make it to five-eight. He's stunting his growth."

"Have you seen him eat?" Quentin Jenkins says.

"I hear he *doesn't* eat," Madeline says.

"I mean after a match," Quentin says. "He'll finish off two pizzas, then go home and put on this plastic suit and ride a bike in his living room. Dude's crazy."

Ransom looks at me.

"We're running the ridge at four," he says. "You coming?"

"I think I'll do my own thing," I say. Quentin and Ransom exchange a look and I can tell they've been talking.

I turn to Wren.

"You doing the ropes course this morning?" I ask.

"Not the cat pole," she says. "Maybe the V-swing or zipline. Are you?"

"No," I say. "I need to get a long run in." I take a deep breath. "But I was thinking, maybe we could take a walk later? Like, after lunch?"

"Sure," Wren says. "As long as we don't, you know. Hike." She tucks her feet under the bench and I feel her thigh press up against mine. She doesn't move it away. She probably doesn't even realize it's there, because of the stocking. My sinkhole tingles a little.

"Just a walk," I say. "Meet me at the waterfront at one."

"How far are you running today?" Madeline asks.

"Whatever I can do in two hours," I say.

"For Ben that's like twenty miles," Quentin says.

"A-ma-zing," Madeline says, blinking, her lashes black and clumpy. "The discipline you have."

"More like addiction," I say. What I don't say is that for approximately half the time I'm gone, I'll be lying on the ground, panting, making air-circles above my chest.

When I'm running, I feel God wants to tell me something. I feel he wants to tell me the Big Thing he has for me to do. It's like this secret mission that only someone who has been touched by the divine could possibly understand.

Writing down the words I hear during my runs is my assignment. Not God's assignment, the therapist's. My parents made me start seeing him every week when they found out about the Gesture. So far, I've only written down one word: *you*. And I keep trying to tell my therapist that "hear" isn't right. I don't say "hear" because the sound isn't in my ears. It isn't a sound. It's this pulse or rhythm just below the prickling in my chest that I know has some meaning, and one of these days—if I can figure out the rest of God's words before the sinkhole takes over—I will know exactly what it is God wants me to do. The important thing is not to think about it. When I feel the words start to pulse in my chest, if I think about them, they disappear and I feel the sinkhole spiraling into my sternum, getting ready to wrap around my pumping heart. I have to figure out how to listen sideways, out of the corner of my eye.

My therapist says the worst thing I can do is fight the sinkhole or pray that God will take it away. He says the way to be the boss of my sinkhole is to a) accept it; b) have compassion on it; and c) *let it happen*. He says if I do this, I'll find out the sinkhole doesn't have the power I think it does.

Sometimes my therapist has me play out my worst-case scenario: what do I think will happen if I don't do the Gesture?

"Easy," I tell him. "The sinkhole will squeeze my heart to death."

He says that is my surface fear.

"Okay," I say. "Then my deeper fear is dying, period."

"Too easy," he says.

"So you tell me what it is," I say.

"I don't know what it is," he says.

"Then how do you know what I'm telling you isn't the truth," I say.

"It's like lasagna," he says. "It's steaming on the table in front of me, and from where I'm sitting, I can see mostly cheese and sauce. A little bit of noodle poking out. And because I have experience with lasagna—because I've eaten lasagna many times in the past—I can make a pretty safe bet that when you cut through the top layer, there will be more layers underneath.

"But you're the host. You're the one holding the knife, and until you cut in and pull up a slice, I have no idea what's in those layers."

"More cheese," I say. "More sauce and noodles."

"There are always surprises," he says. "Zucchini, for example."

After breakfast and the morning assembly, when the high schoolers head out to the ropes course, I go back to my cabin to change. It's only ten, but already the heat is radiating up from the grass on the soccer field, the sun reflecting off the aluminum cabin rooftops. Inside the cabin are nine beds: eight twin cots plus a double for our counselor, Daryl, a philosophy major at Westminster, who has an earring and a goatee and smokes pot inside his sleeping bag when he thinks we're all asleep.

I put on my running shorts and a singlet and lace up my shoes. Then I set my watch and start out at an easy 7:00 pace. By mile two I'll pick it up to 6:30; mile four, 6:00. These early minutes are the gray space, the bland miles I have to run through before the prickling starts and the God rhythms pulse in my heart and I have to trick myself into not listening.

My therapist says when this happens, it's the first hit of endorphins. It's not God, it's biology, he says.

My therapist is not a runner.

I head down the dirt access road, past the entrance sign with letters molded out of horseshoes. I reach the paved highway and run a mile and a half down a long incline, then turn left into the Little River Canyon National Preserve. We used to train out here in middle school. Two miles and I'll hit the footbridge that crosses to the trailhead.

I run beside the river. The water's shallow and mostly shaded, a few coins of sunlight on the surface. When I reach the bridge, I sidestep down the embankment and kneel beside the water for a drink. Then I dip my whole head in. Best way to keep from overheating is to keep your head cool.

I cross the bridge and start up the trail. I'm feeling strong. Invincible, even. I'm thinking, Best of the Preps newspaper article, scholarship to Stanford, Olympic trials. I don't picture myself getting these things—I picture other people *watching* me get them. Admissions committees crowding around my file, fans waving flags, my parents opening the *Times Free Press* to a full-size picture of me on the front page of the sports section. My father saying, We knew it, we've always known it.

Delusions of grandeur, my therapist says. Classic endorphin rush.

The trail hairpins back and forth. I'm going fast. My shoes kick up dust, leaves, small rocks.

Any second now, I think.

I focus my thoughts on the spot of skin between my pecs. Nothing happens.

I push myself harder. The incline makes my calves burn. Along the side of my knee, all the way up to my low back, I can feel my IT band tightening.

Now, I think.

Now.

No prickling, no tingling.

I picture hugging Wren, her chest pressing against mine.

I imagine wearing a tie made out of lead.

Now.

I reach the top of the ridge and still nothing's happened. I stretch, then walk up to the cliff overlooking Trenton. I pull off my shirt and feel the sun fire up my back. My stopwatch reads 58:13. It should be happening.

I pull up a tall grass weed, feathery at the tip. Knowing what I'm about to do creates a little buzz in my skin.

I rub the tip of the weed on my lips first, to test the pressure. Then I turn it over and, with the firm end of the stalk, poke the dime-size spot.

And then I'm on the ground. The sinkhole is spiraling open. It's whirling fast, faster than usual, and it's as if something is reaching up from beneath me, through my low back and spine and ribs, tugging down.

I get my hand in the ready position. I am my own Great Physician, I think. I am the boss.

The sinkhole widens through my skin, numbing everything it

touches. I start to move my hand in tiny circles. Not too much. I want to hear God first.

Here I am, I say. Tell me.

The sinkhole twists around in my pectoral muscles. I feel my throat start to close and I have to gasp a little for air.

Please, I say.

My heart sort of pauses, as if it's thinking. Then I feel this giant flub: *You.*

You what? I say. My voice is dry and wheezy as an old man's.

You. You. You. The word repeats with each heartbeat. The sinkhole moves into my sternum and I hear a crackling noise, like breaking ice. I move my hand faster.

You what?

The sinkhole is turning into a sphere, the size of an orange. I feel it fingering around, looking for my heart. *You you you.*

The corners of my vision are turning fuzzy gray. My chest burns. I've never let it get this far before.

You what?—in my mind I fling the words up to God.

I feel the sinkhole grab my heart.

YOU you. Squeeze, release, like a handshake.

You what?

You   you   you

You—

My brother is lying in a clear plastic bassinet in a hospital room. I'm allowed to see him one last time, and in my mind I know he's dead, but while I look at him, I feel this electricity jumping around inside my hands, as if any second blue lightning is going to shoot out of my fingertips, which feel burnt. And I think, if I touch him and say sit up, he will. I reach out my hand. Then I remember how God strikes people down for trying to mess with his decisions: Adam and Eve kicked out of Eden, Pharaoh and his army drowned in the Red Sea, Herod eaten up by worms.

When the nurse comes in to get me, I pull my hand away and walk out. I don't even say goodbye.

You could have.

. . .

When I wake up, I'm on my back. My T-shirt is crumpled beneath my head. I don't know how long I've been asleep. I can tell that the sinkhole is still open, stuck inside my sternum, sitting there like an open wound. No pain or tingling, just this eerie numbness.

I stand up, dizzy. The sinkhole spirals around in my chest, slowly, like an old record.

I turn and sprint the downhill back to camp.

Wren, I think.

Wren Wren Wren.

When I get to the cabin, Ransom and Quentin are just leaving.

"Dude," Ransom says. "Daryl went to the staff lodge. I think he's calling your parents."

"You guys knew I went for a run," I say. The sinkhole is so wide I'm sure if I take off my shirt, they'll see it gaping there, black and empty.

"Like, five hours ago," Ransom says. "We were heading out to look for you."

"I got turned around on the trails," I say.

"Your face is fried," Quentin says.

I grab my towel from the nail beside my bed, then kneel down and root around in my duffel, as if I'm looking for my shower stuff. But I'm gathering my faith-healing supplies: oil in its tiny Advil bottle, small New Testament bound in red leather, three votive candles, matchbook, flashlight. I wrap everything up in the towel, then go to the lodge to look for Daryl. I find him watching something on the staff television. He doesn't seem worried or mad when he sees me.

I tell him I got lost on the trails. I tell him I'm sorry and that I won't run alone again. I tell him I'll call my parents if he wants me to.

Daryl tilts his head back so he's looking at me down the bridge of his nose. "That girl came to find me," he says. "Wren. Said you guys were going to take a walk and you never showed."

"Like I say, I got lost," I tell him.

"She seemed genuinely worried," Daryl says.

"I'll talk to her tonight," I say. "I'm going to shower up and rest."

His eyes narrow. "Right on," he says. "Listen. I don't know what you've got going, but don't mess with that girl. She's good, you know?"

"I know," I say. He watches me walk out, so I turn toward the bathrooms. Then I circle around behind the lodge, take the rolled towel down to the waterfront, and stuff it deep in the bushes beside the canoe dock.

At the evening session in the gym, I find Wren sitting in the back row. She smiles and moves over a little when I walk up.

"What happened?" she says. "I waited till two."

"I'm sorry," I say, sitting beside her. "I got lost on this trail."

"Are you okay? You're all splotchy." She touches my cheekbone, just barely brushes it with the tip of her index finger. The sinkhole spins around a few times. I suck a little air in between my teeth.

"There's something I need to ask you," I say.

Her eyes go wide. She looks down into her lap.

"I was thinking we could go down to the waterfront—" But before I can finish, Frank Collins comes out from behind the screen. He's wearing black pants and a white shirt with a bow tie. A kitchen towel is draped over his forearm; in his hands are a pencil and leather notepad.

"My sincere apologies for being late," he says, using a British accent. "I hadn't expected to come to work this evening."

Wren nudges me with her swollen leg. "A thousand bucks he's the Genie God," she says. Again she leaves her leg against mine, and the sinkhole deepens, *you, you* humming faintly.

When she looks away, I move my hand up to the ready position.

"Beg your pardon?" God says to no one in particular. "Ah, the menu. How silly of me to forget." He hands an imaginary menu to a little boy. "Now, sir, the last time you were here, you ordered a win for your baseball team. Would you like another?"

The boy stares up at him.

"My apologies, sir, that item is not on the menu. But I'll see what I can do." He pauses, listening. "I know you can take your business elsewhere, and believe me when I tell you how much I appreciate your loyalty. It's just that I'm not entirely certain I can do what you're asking. No, please, sir, don't walk away. I rely on customers like you to stay in business. I might have to close up shop if I can't keep producing. I understand. No hard feelings. Know that I'm here, at your service, any time you'd like to return."

The waiter sighs.

"My restaurant used to be so busy," he says. "Then again, there were far fewer restaurants to choose from. And people used to listen when I made recommendations." He walks back to the fold-out screen, then turns to face us.

"I suppose I can't blame them for leaving," he says. "After all, I *am* just a waiter."

When he's gone and the camp director starts talking, I pull my hand down from the ready position and turn to Wren.

"Can you come to the waterfront with me?" I say. "I need your help with something."

"Can I meet you? I want to stop by my cabin first."

"Let's go now. I'll walk you to your cabin and wait." Wren's knees bounce; she keeps swallowing.

"And now," the camp director is saying, "before the music team comes up, we have another God."

"I'm going to stay and see this one," Wren says. "I'll meet you down there, okay?" As soon as she turns away, my hand starts moving.

Frank Collins scuffs out in slippers. He's wearing Bermuda shorts hiked way up with a belt and has a pair of reading glasses down on the end of his nose. He keeps gumming his tongue, which rests on his lower lip. He sticks a pipe in his mouth, then takes it out, looking around, as if he's expecting something.

"Hold on," he says. "Lemme turn up my earpiece." He pretends to twist something in his ear. "My name?" He digs around in the pocket of his shorts. "This is why I keep my ID with me." He pulls out a card. "My name is . . . Blue Cross Blue Shield!"

Laughter.

"That ain't right," he says, feeling in his pocket again. "Ah, here it is. My name is Blockbuster Video!"

More laughter. God smacks his lips. "Well, never mind who I am. It's more important what I do. And what I do is . . . eh . . ."

He inserts and removes his pipe a few times.

"I guess I don't know what I do. Ha! Mostly I just sit around here. Where's here? I don't know. It's not important. I'm here and that's all there is to it. Wherever this is, it's pretty boring, truth be told. I used to be busy. I remember this one time I created a whole universe. Took me a week! That was some hard work. But I liked that seventh day. I got hooked on that seventh day. After that seventh day, I decided I was going to just keep on having seventh days for the rest of eternity.

"Every now and then I peek down at what I made, poke around in a few of the old hangouts. Cathedrals and such. But it's discouraging. People don't like me, cause I'm old. But if I ignore what everyone is saying and just sit up here real quiet, I can remember the days when I was busy. And that makes me happy."

Frank Collins shuffles out while the music team starts to set up.

"That was him," I say to Wren. "The real God."

"Sure," she says, sort of laughing. Then she looks at my face.

"You figured this out, right," she says.

"Figured what out?" I say.

"None of them are God. That's the point." She frowns. "I wish he would be the real God, though. So I could picture who it is I'm mad at."

I stand. The room tips sideways, the sinkhole is squeezing, I'm trying to take sips of air between my lips.

"Meet me at the canoe dock in half an hour," I say.

It's dusk. Tree frogs tuning up, fireflies drifting just above the grass. My sinkhole is on slow rotation, *you you* vibrating in my ribs. An accusation, not a request.

I walk past the elementary cabins and dining hall to the staircase leading down to the water. I unhook the rope and lay the slack end on the hillside, then walk down and take the path to the canoe dock, which is tucked beneath a rocky overhang surrounded by bushes and trees. The dock is totally hidden; you can't see it unless you're on it, or approaching it from the water.

I find the towel. Unroll it and remove the supplies. It's completely dark now. I light the candles and set the Advil bottle, New Testament, and flashlight beside the towel. I take off my shoes and sit on the edge of the dock, let my feet hang down into the water while I wait for Wren.

When she comes around the bend, I can tell something's different. She seems sort of stiff, hunched up in her shoulders. Her hair is pulled back, and she's changed into a short white skirt. I notice that one of her legs is brighter than the other—it takes me a minute to realize she's not wearing her compression stocking.

"Ohhh," she says, looking at the candles. "That's pretty." She twists and untwists a section of her ponytail.

"Thanks for coming," I say.

"No," she says. "I mean, sure. I wanted to." She stands there, shifting her weight, then comes over and sits beside me. She smells good—summery—a mixture of grass and sunscreen and something like cake frosting. I feel myself start to get hard. The sinkhole picks up some speed. I need to get this over with, I think. I realize I never thought about how to get things started.

"So I'm super nervous," Wren says, turning to look at me. She's blinking a lot, keeps plucking at her skirt.

"Me too," I say. "I've been wanting to tell you about this, thing, for a really long time. Something that happens sometimes, in my chest—"

Wren's not looking at me. Her hand is moving around in one of her skirt pockets.

"When the doctor told me about the buildup of scar tissue, I knew I'd have to find out," she says. She draws this long, shaky breath. "I was hoping you'd be the one."

I feel her shove something into my hand. It's a wrapped condom.

Wren's crying now. "It's because of all the surgeries. The doctor said he wasn't sure if it would, you know. Fully *work* for me."

She takes my hand. "Please," she says. "I need to know."

The sinkhole is rooting around, expanding, making it hard for me to speak.

"You don't have to wear the condom. I don't even know why I brought it."

"Wren," I say. "There's this thing in my chest—"

But she's pulling at the hem of her skirt, getting it higher and higher above her knees. Her breath is coming in sharp sucks. Then she's lying back on the towel, and the sinkhole is huge, it's squeezing my heart. *You, you, you.*

I lie beside her, take off my shirt, start to do the Gesture.

"Listen," I say. "I need your help."

She moves my hand away and starts kissing my chest all over, quick, light presses, and the sinkhole is squeezing my heart, but now she's kissing my mouth and I taste salt, some kind of peppery spice. I reach for the Advil bottle.

"Use this," I say, handing it to her. "Pray for it to stop."

"For what to stop?" Her voice sounds far away, like I'm talking to her on the phone. She sits up and looks in the Advil container, sniffs. "Is this olive oil?"

"Say, *In the name of Jesus*," I tell her. My hand is circling, fast.

"Why do you keep doing that?"

"It's right in the middle," I say.

Wren reaches up and sort of smooths her bangs. Her hand is shaking.

"I thought you wanted—you brought candles."

"Even if you just breathe on it—" But she's pouring the oil out on her hands, she's reaching down inside my shorts, beneath my boxers, moving her fingers around till she finds the tip. I feel myself getting harder, and the sinkhole is squeezing my heart so tight there are long pauses between beats. *You. You. You.* I hear a wail, the voice high-pitched like a girl's. I'm terrified the voice is mine.

I feel Wren sliding onto me, the tight squeeze of it. A door swinging open.

The sinkhole contracts, moves toward the door, starts to go through it.

"Don't let it get inside you," I say.

"But I want it to," she says, crying hard now.

"You don't understand," I say, but it's too late, I am *letting it happen,* the sinkhole is spiraling into a thin funnel and exiting through the door.

"I think—I think it's working," Wren says. She lets out a sob.

The sinkhole, narrow as a pencil, turns from black to gray to white, like rising smoke. And then everything is clear, the *you*s are gone and I can hear my heart beating in my ears.

I take a few deep breaths. I open my eyes and see Wren's face, eyes closed, mouth open. Behind her the sky is a dark bowl pocked with stars.

"I think it's gone," I say.

Wren lifts up and falls onto her side, then curls into a ball at my feet. Her whole body is quivering like she's cold.

I sit up. The river is flat and still as a lake, all that power churning just beneath the milk-spill light on its surface.

I put a hand on my chest.

Both hands.

"Wren," I say. "It worked."

"I knew you'd be the one," she says.

She covers her face with her hands. "I'm so sorry," she says.

"No," I say, touching her leg, the one without the stocking. "That was amazing. You didn't even have to pray."

She sits up. "What are you talking about?" Her eyes are all squinty, her face so pale it's almost green, like a glow-in-the-dark toy.

"My sinkhole," I say. "You healed it."

Wren just looks at me. Her chin is shaking, and she has a dark smear going down one of her cheeks.

"I thought you wanted to," she says. "I thought you liked me, even though you knew about my surgeries."

I reach out to touch her hair, but she moves her head away.

I scoot closer to Wren, till we're sitting within inches of each other, face to face.

"I need you to feel something," I say.

I take one of her hands and lay it on the dime-size spot of skin.

I cover her hand with both of mine and press.

Ayşe Papatya Bucak

The History of Girls

WHILE WE WAITED, WE were visited by the ghosts of the girls who had already died, those who were closest to the explosion, in the kitchen sneaking butter and bread when the gas ignited, the ones who died immediately, in a sense without injury.

The dead girls waited with us, amidst the rubble, our heads pillowed on it, our arms and legs canopied by it, some of us punctured by it. The rubble was heavy, of course. The weight of it made us wonder what happened to the softer things. Our sheets and blankets, our letters from home, our Korans, our class notes, the slips of paper we exchanged throughout the day expressing our affections and disaffections for each other, for our teachers, for the rituals of our contained life. What about the curtains on our windows? we thought. The stories and poems we wrote to read to each other at night or the ones we wrote and kept private, folded in our pockets? What about our pockets? Our uniforms, our gym skirts, our head scarves and stockings? The too-soft pillows we always complained about? The ones the oldest girls hoarded, sleeping with three or four stacked under their cheeks even though their heads sank into the soft centers and their necks ached in the morning. The explosion, it seemed, turned everything to stone. Except us. We were soft then, softer than we ever were.

Have you ever seen a buzzard? They are all feathers and fat, not like skeletons at all, but soft like cushions. Except for their beaks and claws.

There were day girls and night girls. Day girls went home at three o'clock, swept their mothers' houses, helped their mothers cook *köfte* and *pilaf,* slept in beds with their sisters, with their brothers and mothers and fathers in nearby rooms. There were more than a hundred of them. Sometimes we confused the names of the younger ones. But there were only fourteen of us: older girls in the room on the right, younger girls in the room on the left. Not a door to close in between so all night long we heard each other giggle and snore and cry and dream and sometimes we shouted into the dark, goodnightgoodnightgoodnight!

They were curious about us, of course, and we about them. But there was always a difference: at night, day girls had mothers and night girls had each other.

There was Acelya and Seda, Samime and Hamiyet, Rabia, Turkan, and finally Fadime, the baby, seven years old on the day she came, only two months earlier. Ghosts.

And then there was Mualla, Latife, Zehra, Sahiba, Nuray, Gul, and Celine. Waiting.

How could we all hear each other? It was like we were on our own radio channel, the shared signal clear.

The dead girls were from the room on the left, the oldest only twelve. Usually we were the ones to sneak into the kitchen, usually they were the ones to sleep through. How many nights had they copied us without our noticing? How many nights would we, could we, bear the guilt?

We could not see them, and yet there they were. Among the darkness of night and the building's collapse and the bright ring of the explosion still sounding in our heads, we could not see much. Instead we felt the light fingertips of the dead girls' touch and heard their high voices saying, "Does this tickle? Won't you laugh? How about this? Does this tickle?"

"Stop it," we said. "We don't want to be tickled." But they wouldn't stop it and it did tickle just a little. So we laughed, and they did too.

"Help is coming," the dead girls said. "People are waking."

"Who?" we asked.

"Help," the dead girls said.

We called out the names of the night janitor and his wife and even their fat baby, but they did not answer.

"What happened?" we asked one after another until finally the dead girls told us. Naturally it was expected they would know things we didn't.

But how could we not know? It was what we long suspected. The gas. The dormitory was always too hot or too cold depending on what had gone wrong with the gas. Something was always wrong with the gas, and the teachers would adjust it only to turn the heat to cold or the cold to heat. At night when the teachers went to their homes and the day girls went to their homes and the cooks and the cleaners and the gardener went to their homes and we were left with only the night janitor and his wife and their fat baby, we curled under our blankets, sometimes three to a bed as if our bodies had any heat left to share. Or we slept on the tiled floor of the hall with our limbs slung out, as if we could separate from ourselves and become cooler.

First it was dark and quiet, later it was bright and loud. First there were dead girls and living girls; later there were girls in between. We would have lingered even there, stars poking through the rubble, cold ground beneath us, cold air creeping in, blood in our hearts and air in our chests. We would have stayed there as long as we could even with the dead girls saying, "It's not so bad. I didn't feel a thing. And look, now I can fly."

. . .

The youngest was seven, the oldest nineteen, though most girls left school before that age, to return home, to the east or the west, before marrying. Sometimes a husband they knew, sometimes not. Some girls went to university, abroad or at home. You shouldn't think they didn't; we were not the girls that you might assume. We did not wear our head scarves over our eyes. Some girls went to work. Some girls stayed on as teachers. The school had a long line of girls who did many things deep into the past and far into the future.

Some of us cried, of course. The dead girls tried to comfort us, but our tears were no longer ours to control. And when the dead girls tried to unpin our arms and legs, to move the rubble that held us in place, they found they had only their ordinary strength. And when they tried to hold our hands, stroke our hair, in the way we so often comforted each other after our petty fights, we found their touch had grown as hot as a lit match tip.

"Stop it," we yelled. "That hurts." "Sorry," the dead girls said. "We didn't know." "Sorry," we said back, "we didn't mean to yell." How courteous we all became while we waited.

"Are they still coming?" we asked. "When are they coming?"

"They're coming," the dead girls said. "As fast as they can." "Hold on," they said. "They're coming."

"Look how pretty you look," they told us. "I can't believe it. In the middle of such a disaster, you still look so pretty."

"Thank you," we said. Or, "Don't be ridiculous." We blushed and we giggled; we did all the things we always did. They were our best friends.

"How do we look?" the dead girls asked. "Are we wearing clothes? Do we have wings?"

But we didn't know; in the dark, we couldn't see a thing.

"I see a light!" Mualla yelled. "Look at the light." And first we thought she had been rescued, or had dug her way out as some of us had been trying to do, but then she died.

"Hello," she said, and the dead girls chorused back, "Hello, Mualla."

"Where did you go?" we asked her, and "What is it like?" But all she would say was "I saw a light." She was just the kind of girl to tell you what you already knew.

Have you ever had a hawk's shadow cross over you? It happened sometimes when we were in the garden with our potatoes. It is like death's cape sweeping swiftly over your head. Every time we screamed.

The searchers, when they came, turned on a spotlight. It shone through the rubble, a moonlight spotlight, leaving us blinded by light rather than dark. It was a light so sharp it should have cut through the rubble like a laser, and yet it was as heavy as a stone. We felt pushed into the earth like seeds poked too far underground.

The searchers called our names, the living and the dead—they didn't know the difference yet. Sometimes we recognized their voices: our teachers, the school nurse, the doctor that came to check us twice a year. Others were voices we had rarely heard: the baker who made the cookies we liked to buy when we were taken into town, the men who came and collected our garbage, the repairmen who fixed our leaks and painted our walls, the old man who delivered the ill-fated gas, accidental executioner. Then there were the voices of the day girls woken from their beds, and the voices of their parents and their brothers and sisters. How happy they sounded, how excited. How could they help it? Our mothers, of course, lived far away. Perhaps they knew what was happening, perhaps it was on the news already, perhaps they woke in the night and felt that something was not right.

Would we be mothers? we wondered. Or would we always be girls?

"Precious, precious," we heard someone wail until they were all saying it, "Precious, precious."

We called back at first, a chorus of the dead and the living, but the searchers never seemed to hear, and soon there was only the sound of shovels and machines, and digging that never came closer.

We were like diamonds waiting to be dug out.

"Precious, precious," one of the dead girls mocked until we begged her to stop.

"Oh," Celine said, a minor expression of surprise, uncharacteristically quiet, as she joined the dead girls.

"Hello, Celine," they said.

"I told Allah I was angry," Fadime, our baby, called out. "I told him he was evil for killing the Chinese boys and girls who had no brothers and sisters. You are all my punishment," she cried. "Allah got angry with me because I got angry with him."

After the earthquakes in China we wrote letters expressing our sympathies and sent them to the newspaper. After the Indonesian tsunami we wrote letters too, but we did not know where to send them so we buried them in the earth next to the potatoes. After the earthquakes in Greece, we prayed every night and when there were earthquakes in Istanbul we gathered the small sums of money we had saved to buy cookies and mailed them to the government.

"Oh, Fadime," we said. "Allah forgave you right away. It's not your fault, nor his."

"I don't believe, and you shouldn't either," Celine said. "I'm dead now and I see no signs of heaven. You should all do what you want and not worry about being cursed."

She was always in trouble anyway, we thought to ourselves. What would she have done differently if she knew there was no heaven?

"I heard that," Celine said, and we cried out, "You see, you are a miracle. This is no time for doubt."

"This is exactly the time for doubt," Celine said. "Why didn't anybody fix the gas?"

She was only half Turkish. Her mother was French and she sent Celine to a boarding school in Switzerland, but her mother died and her father brought her here. He did not think to sort her things, and so she brought Tintin and Madeleine and a book with dirty pictures drawn in ink. Also a Superman comic. Maybe she brought the devil, too. What did it matter to us then?

Why didn't anybody fix the gas? Surely that did not require an act of God.

"Maybe we're angels," Fadime said.

"Maybe we aren't dead-dead, only in between," another of the dead girls said.

"I just want to be dead-dead," Acelya cried. "I feel so tired."

"Me, too," the other dead girls said. "I feel so tired."

"Where are the rescuers?" we asked.

"Coming," the dead girls said, quiet again. It was always up to us to keep them from getting hysterical. "Can't you hear them digging?"

We were quiet, but we couldn't hear.

Have you ever pulled a potato from the ground before it was ready? It looks like a thing that has been alive too long.

"I see my mother," Celine said.

"Where?" the other dead girls cried.

"Inside of me," Celine said. "She is an angel inside of an angel."

"Celine," we said. "Stop it. They are only little girls."

"Tell us what she looks like," the dead girls said.

They never were ones to know when they were being teased.

"Don't, Celine," we warned.

"She has one eye hanging out of her head and there are rotten worms coming out of her ears and she has a broken leg. I can see the bone sticking out of her rotten skin."

The dead girls were hysterical then. They could not be contained. "I see her, too. Oh, she's hideous. Oh, I'm scared."

Last year they all got rashes. Last month they all saw UFOs. Before long the ghosts would all be seeing ghosts.

"Celine," we said, "we told you not to."

We had been taught the history of girls. In Hiroshima, hundreds of schoolgirls were clearing homes and roads to make the widest of fire lanes when the bomb came. In China, in India, some girls weren't allowed to live a day. In Russia, in Uzbekistan, in Georgia, in Ukraine, girls were sold once, then shipped abroad to be sold again and again. It was how we learned our geography. The history of innocents.

But we learned, too, the history of sinners. Girls who were stoned by their villagers. Burned by their brothers. Killed by their fathers. Cast out by their mothers. Our lessons were full of girls who died. Stoned for this and stoned for that. More geography. In Afghanistan in Somalia in Florida in Iran and Iraq and Egypt and Syria. Be good, we were told. Legs tight, lips tight, eyes open, mouths closed.

Gul was sent to school because her brother threatened to kill her for having a boyfriend. Acelya was sent because it was her best chance to go to law school. All of us were sent to school to be girls, to be protected until we were women. Girlhood, we were taught, was something to be survived.

Maybe, we thought, the world needs enemies it can love, enemies who are no threat at all. Maybe, we thought, that is the story inside the history of girls.

"We are virgin sacrifices," Celine called out.

"Oh hush, Celine," we said.

Nights, we used to tell tales. The Somalian girl turned to steel before the attackers' stones hit her, and as they bounced to her feet, flakes of metal rose from her, and when she turned back to flesh, she had only cuts and bruises and aches and pains. The Egyptian girl shot lasers out of her turned-to-ruby eyes and blinded her attackers. The Syrian girls turned to water, drowned their attackers, turned back to flesh, laid out the drowned bodies to dry, and lit them on fire. The Afghani girls rose up to the sun and hid it from the sky until their attackers turned to ice.

But don't think we wanted to be boys. Boys seemed lonely. Boys seemed helpless. Eventually, if we were boys, we would be expected to be cruel, at least once, if not every day.

We just wanted those girls to be strong.

"Celine, tell us about the dancing princesses," the dead girls said.

If we had never stolen snacks in the night, then they never would have copied us.

"I won't," Celine said. "I don't like that story anymore."

"We need it. We're scared. We're tired. We need it," they chorused.

They were so much as they ever were.

"You don't."

"We do."

"You don't."

"Oh, Celine," we said. "Can't you just humor them?"

"Why should I? They aren't babies anymore."

"Then do it for us," we said. "We are scared and tired, too. We need it, too."

"Well, then you're all babies," she said. And then, "Fine. Once there were twelve sisters and they never wanted to sleep and so they didn't, they danced. They danced all night and wore out their shoes and their father never knew why so he killed a bunch of princes trying to find out until one got help—totally unfairly of course—from some old hag and that prince followed the princesses and he danced and drank their drinks and had their fun and then he told on them and ruined everything."

"Celine!" the dead girls chorused. "Tell it right."

"Please, Celine," we said. And, "Where are the rescuers? Why can't we hear them?"

"They're there," Celine said softly. "They're coming. For you," she added.

What was the fairy tale future we hoped for? That we would turn to metal and be protected? That we would shoot lasers out of our turned-to-ruby eyes or that we would turn the world to ice and kill our enemies? Who would want such a thing? Those stories were no help to us then.

All we hoped for were lives of promise and fulfillment and to be released into heaven at the end of time. What we wanted was to live just a little longer. What we wanted was to be together.

"Please, Celine," we said.

"All right, are you ready?" Celine asked.

"Yes, yes," we said.

"All right. Once there was and once there wasn't, in the time of princes and princesses and genies and jinn and boys turned to men and girls turned to women, in that time there were twelve sisters. And they loved to dance. Each night their father, the Sultan, would lock them in their room—twelve beds, twelve sisters, all in a row—and each morning, he'd turn the key to find them still sleeping, but with twelve pairs of shoes worn through at the feet of their beds.

" 'Your shoes,' he'd cry each morning. 'What are you doing to your shoes?'

" 'Good morning, Baba,' the girls would say, each in turn, youngest to oldest, and they would run, barefoot, to kiss him and hug him and not ever answer his question.

"Then one morning he said, 'You must stop this. Your mother is weeping. The princes are weeping. The cobbler is weeping. He has threatened to kill himself if he has to make any more shoes.'

" 'Tell him not to cry, Baba,' the oldest daughter said. 'We don't even like shoes. He need not make us any more.'

" 'Yes,' her sisters echoed. 'He need not make us any more,' and the youngest daughter started a pirouette on her bare toes, but the oldest caught her in her arms and stopped her feet. 'Not now,' she whispered in the youngest daughter's ear."

"Celine, you're still not telling it right," Fadime said.

"Shush," we told her. "Let us find out what happens."

"The cobbler killed himself," Celine said and we could hear her lips press tight.

"Oh, Celine," we said. "He didn't."

"I don't want him to," Fadime cried.

"Fine," Celine said, "he didn't kill himself but he refused to make any more shoes and so the girls had to dance barefoot and the next morning when their father woke them he found their sheets soaked in blood and their toes worn down to nubs."

"Celine!" we cried out.

"The daughters could not walk so they spent the rest of their lives in bed where nurses brought them food and drink and they peed in pots that were kept under their beds and they even got married in bed and their husbands, all princes, lay in bed next to them. Twelve big beds all in a row."

"I don't want to grow up!" Mualla cried out.

"Don't worry, you won't," Celine said.

"Oh, Celine," we said. "You don't have to be so mean."

"I'm not mean," she said.

"You're selfish," we said. "We all know it."

"I'm not selfish," Celine said. "Say it. I'm not selfish."

"Celine," we said.

"Please, I'm not," she said.

She was and she wasn't; we all knew that.

There was a pause and a stifled hiccough or sob and Celine said, "Tell my brother I'm sorry I stole his Fenerbahçe jersey."

We were quiet, until Gul said, "I'll tell him."

There was another pause and another stifled hiccough or sob.

Then Sahiba said, "But are you sorry?"

Celine often wore the jersey under her uniform or slept with it in her arms as if it were a stuffed animal. We had even named it Mehmet after her favorite player.

We giggled.

She giggled.

"Maybe not," she said. "Maybe you should tell him it was a comfort to me."

"We will," we said. "We'll tell him."

"Yes, yes," the others said. "Tell my brother my sister my mother my father my aunt my grandmother my best friend from when I was five the boy I never talked to the boy I never met the husband I would have had the children I would have had tell them we are sorry we love them we are all right we will never forget them never forget us. Tell them."

"Yes," we said. "We will tell them."

"Everyone be quiet," Celine said, and we could not help but smile. "Once there was and once there wasn't," she said, "in the time when genies were jinn and boys remained boys and girls remained girls and nobody was born and nobody died, in the time when the earth stood still and the sun shone bright, in that time, there were fourteen princesses. And they loved to dance. They danced all night when they were meant to be sleeping, and then in the morning when they slept they dreamt of dancing. Night and day, they spun and spun, circling round and round, arms out wide and arms at their sides, spinning wider and wider until they could not even be seen.

"'Aren't you tired,' people would cry at the fourteen dancing princesses, but inside the dance the fourteen princesses saw only each other and heard only each other and they spun and they spun and they never stopped spinning and their feet never hurt and their heads never hurt and their hearts never hurt. Inside their circle, they spun and they never stopped, not ever, not to grow old and not to die and not to work and not to marry and not to have children and not to eat bread and butter or sleep in the cold or the hot, not to do anything but spin. Together. Always."

She was quiet and so were we.

"Thank you, Celine," we said.

"I don't care," she said, but we knew she did.

"You're not selfish," we said. "We didn't mean it."

"We're spinning, we're spinning," the dead girls said.

"Watch me," Fadime said. "Can you see me spinning?"

"Yes," we said, though of course we couldn't.

The history of girls is always told as a tragedy. Growing old is a tragedy and so is dying young.

What, we had always asked each other, could it be like to be stoned? Were girls pelted like the stray dogs we saw being chased away with rocks by shopkeepers? Was it like dodgeball, which our American teacher made us play in the yard until only Celine was left standing and we all refused to play ever again because she was so vicious? Was it like the snowball fights we read about in books? Or was it more like being hit with a hammer, close and bloody? Maybe it was the weight of human hatred that knocked girls from their feet.

Once we tossed rocks at each other just to see, but we missed every time.

Sometimes we fell quiet. Sometimes another girl died. She would let out a small sound or a loud one, death still a surprise, even under the circumstances.

"Hello," the other girls would say, as if she had entered a room they were in. There were so many more of them then.

How hard it is to explain, what it was like. We were together, as we were so accustomed to being. We made our present worth living, as we so often had. But then the rescue took so much longer than we expected.

"Oh, we're on television," the dead girls said. "There are cameras and reporters and even Americans."

"What can you see?" we asked, but the dead girls wouldn't say.

"Are our parents there?" we asked, but the dead girls wouldn't say.

"Are you still there?" we called out and they did not answer.

What is the heaviest thing you can imagine? A boulder? A house? An airplane? In all of the world, what is the heaviest thing? Can you even imagine it?

"Where are you?" we asked.

But they did not answer.

How quickly it happened then. One girl, then another. Gone.

"Please," I said, "don't leave me."

"Where are you?" I asked. "Can't I come too?"

"Please," I said. "Precious," I said. "Precious."

But they did not answer.

"I hate you," I said. "You are all mean."

"Take me with you," I yelled. "Please take me with you."

And from somewhere I could not see and in voices I could barely hear, they said, "Oh, Zehra, don't be silly," and, "We'll miss you. Don't forget to tell them," and, "Goodnightgoodnight-goodnight."

"I don't want to grow up without you," I said.

But they did not answer. And though my arms were at my sides, and my legs were beneath me in a way they never should be, and my voice could not be heard, and my eyes could not see, I felt twice over that I always would be—and I never would be—without them.

Have you ever seen a girl?

She is my history.

Andrea Barrett

The Particles

ONCE HE WAS IN the water, it was easier to see what had happened to the ship. The stern already low in the waves, the empty lifeboat davits and twisted rigging and the blackened, shattered wood on the deck, where the exploding hatches had blown deck chairs and people to bits. They'd been at dinner, spoons clicking on soup bowls, cooks poised over pots, Sam Cornelius thrown from his chair as he pushed aside a bit of carrot. Now it was past nine and fully dark: September 3, 1939. The searchlight picked out bodies floating near the boat, and when the woman crouched behind him gave her life belt to her wailing son, Sam gave her his and then was even more frightened; despite his age—he was thirty-four—he could barely swim.

In the distance a shape, which might have been the guilty submarine, seemed to shift position. The moon disappeared behind a bank of clouds and then it rained, drenching those who weren't yet soaked; more than eleven hundred people had been onboard. When the rain stopped, the moon again lit the boats scattered around the slowly sinking ship. The three of the *Athenia*'s crew in Sam's boat took oars, as did the three least wounded—Sam was one—of the four male passengers. The others, just over fifty women and children, bailed with their shoes and their bare hands, scooping out the oily water rising over their shins.

As the two dozen lifeboats separated like specks on an expanding balloon, one pulled toward Sam's boat to let them know that several ships had responded to the *Athenia*'s call for help. Soon, in just a few hours, they'd be saved. Those hours passed. Not long after midnight, a faraway gleam, which might have been a periscope caught by the light of the moon, caused two women to shriek. A U-boat, one said, the German submarine that had torpedoed them rising now to shell the lifeboats. But the last beam of the searchlight, just before the emergency dynamo used up its fuel and the *Athenia* went completely dark, revealed enough to convince Sam and some of the others that this was a rescue ship.

Steadily, Sam and his companions rowed toward the Norwegian tanker *Knute Nelson,* which, in the light of occasional flares, popped sporadically out of the darkness. A little string of emptied lifeboats tossed in the swell beside the tanker, the boat closest to the stern still packed with people. Some grabbed at rope ladders while the bosun's chair went up and down, hoisting those not agile enough to climb until, in the grip of a heavy woman who pushed off too vigorously, it overturned and left her suspended upside down. The crew struggled to retrieve her, but before they were done another boat nudged in behind the one still being emptied.

The man rowing next to Sam muttered, "They should stand out, that's dangerous," and when Sam drew his anxious gaze away from the faces he was searching, he could see how little space separated the last boat in line from the tanker's huge propellers. He turned back to his oars. The sea was rough, the boat's seams were leaking, many of his fellow passengers were wounded or seasick or both, and Sam was working so hard to keep their boat steady that he failed to see exactly what happened a few minutes later. By the time he heard the screams, the broken lifeboat, impaled on one of the propeller blades, was already rising into the air.

"Row!" said the seaman in charge of Sam's boat. "Row, row, row, row!"

Sam, the tallest but not the strongest of those at the oars (he was out of shape), lost his grip and banged into the man beside him, who shouted at him; then all of them were shouting at each other while women wailed and children cried. Unbearable to think about what must have happened to those drawn into the propeller. The boat sped into the darkness, headed, once the assistant purser spotted it, toward an enormous, brightly lit motor yacht that had appeared from another direction. Before they were close enough to hail her, Sam saw two lifeboats tangle at her stern, one crowding the other under the angled counter—the swell had increased, making everything more difficult—which, after rising unusually high, crashed down on the gunwale of the inner boat and tipped it over. Suddenly, struggling figures, too small to identify, also dotted the water.

That was enough for the seaman in charge; Sam's boat pulled away until it was clear of everyone. "Let's wait," the seaman said, "until sunrise, when we can see more clearly what we're doing." The swell grew heavier; dawn finally broke and three British destroyers arrived. The little boy whose mother was wearing Sam's life belt pointed at them, smiled for the first time since the ship had been hit, and said, "Ring around the rosy!" Sam couldn't see what the little boy meant, and then he could: two of the ships were racing after each other, herding within an enormous circle the remaining lifeboats, the tanker, the white yacht, and the third destroyer, which was plucking boatloads of survivors from the water. Twice, he thought it was turning their way, but each time it moved toward another, even more crowded boat.

The sky was red and then pink and then blue; Sam's hands were numb; he hadn't been able to feel his feet for hours. Once or twice he either fell asleep or passed out. Once, he lifted his head just in time to see an old woman in a lifeboat not far away leap toward a lowered rope ladder and miss, slipping into the narrow space between the boat and the destroyer's hull; the boat rose on a swell and the space disappeared. He was barely conscious when, in the middle of the morning, a U.S. merchant ship arrived, cleaned out one boat before taking in a crowd transferred from the motor yacht, and then waved over the boat that Sam was in.

The injured and frail went up in a bosun's chair, but Sam, jolted awake by the prospect of safety, scrambled up a rope ladder with the other men. A person reached out for him, grabbed his arm, and heaved him over the side—not a stranger, not a sailor, but someone Sam knew: Duncan Finch. Part of him wanted to jump back in the water. Duncan, here? But there was the ship's name, *City of Flint,* mocking him from the smokestack.

"You're all right!" Duncan shouted as Sam dropped onto the deck. "Are you hurt?"

Sam flexed his elbow, which he'd cracked on a thwart but which still seemed to work, and then inspected his shin, where all the blood appeared to be coming from one long scrape. "Nothing serious," he said.

Duncan pulled him toward a dry corner. "Is anyone else with you?"

Anyone, he meant, from the meeting; they'd been at an international genetics congress in Edinburgh, cut short by the situation. Sam shook his head. Families had been broken apart, siblings had ended up in different boats, and friends had been randomly assorted: where was Axel? Eight other geneticists had been on the *Athenia* with Sam. One by one, in the thick, dark smoke, they'd climbed into lifeboats, dropped down to the water, and then disappeared.

Duncan said, with apparent enthusiasm, "But at least *you're* here. You're safe."

Omitting, Sam thought, the fact that on their last day in Edinburgh, Duncan had asked Sam grudgingly, and when it was too late, to join the small group he'd finagled aboard this American freighter loaded with wool and Scotch whiskey.

"I did warn you," Duncan added now. Still, after eighteen years of annoying Sam, unable to rein in his red-faced, bullying self. "I *warned* you not to take passage on a British ship."

Anyone else would have understood how few choices existed. Sam's booked passage had been canceled, the other ships were quickly commandeered, and on September 1, as he boarded the *Athenia* in Glasgow, it had still seemed likely that they'd get away safely. They'd had to pick up passengers in Belfast and then more in Liverpool, both ports packed with Americans and Canadians trying to get home, but by the afternoon of the second, the ship was heading north up the Irish Sea, rounding the coast early on the morning of the third. By the time the declaration of war was radioed, they'd almost cleared the most dangerous territory, their ship overbooked but still comfortable and, Sam had thought with a twinge of pleasure, less crowded than Duncan's. Before Duncan left, not only his handful of stranded friends but also a group of college girls caught midway through a European tour had been stuffed into the *City of Flint,* making thirty instead of the normal five or six passengers. Now it bulged with another two hundred people, some freezing and still in shock, and among them—

"Is Axel here?" he asked.

Duncan turned, reached back to steady an elderly woman coming over the railing, and then pointed her toward a man who was giving out fresh water. "Of course not," he said, inspecting Sam more closely. "Did you hit your head?"

For Duncan, Sam realized, Axel was still in Edinburgh, where he'd stayed to visit a friend despite Duncan's frantic urging that he board the *City of Flint.* When the situation grew so dangerous that Axel's friend cut the visit short and delivered him to the Glasgow docks, Duncan had already been at sea.

"He was with me," Sam said. Two teenage boys tumbled onto the deck, their hair matted with oil; a girl in a tidy jacket rushed over to them. "The *Athenia* was the only ship that had a berth."

In another situation he would have enjoyed seeing the color drain from Duncan's cheeks.

"He *wasn't.*"

"He was," Sam said. "We were eating dinner with that couple from Minnesota when we were hit." One of what should have been many meals; what luck, he'd thought, to have Axel aboard! An unexpected benefit of letting Duncan sail without him. They might walk the decks, share quiet conversations, sit side by side in reclining chairs, and repair what had gone wrong in Edinburgh. At the dock, the sight of Axel's battered gray hat and unmistakable nose in the crowd had suddenly made everything broken and ruined seem hopeful again.

"But then," Duncan said, "how did you lose track of him?"

The smoke, the darkness, the wounded people, the babble of different languages as passengers crowded boats already full, launched half-empty ones too early. Sam drew a breath. "We went where the crew told us to go, and they assigned us to separate boats. Then the boats scattered. Can you find out if he's here?"

Duncan disappeared with a curse, leaving Sam to be herded down below with the newest arrivals. In a long room lined with barrels, they dripped into a growing puddle, which the crew and the freighter's original passengers tried to avoid as they ferried in spare clothing pulled from their luggage. A plant physiologist from Texas, transferred from the motor yacht, slipped an old sweater over his head as he said that these merchant seamen were a lot more welcoming than the Swedish billionaire who'd originally rescued him. Sam tied his feet into a pair of slippers a size too large, thrilled to find them dry, while his new acquaintance described the smartly outfitted crew who'd handed out soup and hot coffee and blankets and then—the sun was well up, the *Athenia* had gone to her grave, and the destroyers were making their rounds—told the rescued passengers that the owner couldn't interrupt his planned trip and needed to transfer everyone who'd been picked up. "To here," the Texan said, stepping out of his oil-soaked pants and into a seaman's canvas overalls. "Oh, that's *much* better."

Where was Axel, where was Axel? Maybe he'd been on that yacht, or maybe . . . he tried not to think about the huge propeller. Around Sam, coats, blankets, overshoes, shawls flew toward wet bodies, something dry for everyone. So many people, everywhere: bodies racked like billiard balls in every corner and companionway, babies calling like kittens or crows as women tried to comfort them. Among them, Axel might be hidden—or he might be in the water still, or safely headed toward Galway or Glasgow on one of the destroyers. Sam pushed through the mass, some faces familiar from the *Athenia*'s decks and dining room but many not and none the one he most wanted to see, until, when he came out near the galley, he heard his name and looked behind him. Duncan, who'd always had this way of proving himself astonishingly useful just when he was at his most annoying, waved his hand above the crowd. Beside him, his front hair pushed forward into a kingfisher's tuft by a gigantic square bandage, was Axel.

Of course Duncan had one of the actual berths; of course he turned it over to Axel, who, after touching Sam's face and saying, "You're here. You're all right," disappeared into the deckhouse and fell, said Duncan later (himself now modestly moved to the floor of his cabin, where he'd already had two roommates), into an exhausted sleep. Sam, who stayed awake for a while after Axel left, slept that first night on a coil of rope, surrounded by women in men's shoes and torn evening gowns, men wearing dress shirts over sarongs made from curtains, children in white ducks shaped for bulky sailors. A little girl whose parents had ended up in a different boat—Sam hoped they were now on some other ship—lay on a pile of canvas nearby. Earlier, he'd seen the two women looking after her piece together a romper from two long woolen socks, a pair of women's panties, and a boy's sweater. Now the women curled parenthetically around their warm charge.

Sam's trousers were still intact, and between those, his donated slippers, and a wool jacket generously given to him by one of Duncan's cabinmates, an old acquaintance named Harold, he was warm enough to sleep. The next morning, after a chaotic attempt at breakfast, he and Harold, along with everyone else who wasn't injured, helped the ship's crew spread mattresses in the hold, suspend spare tarpaulins from beams to make rows of hammocks, and hammer planks into bunks until everyone had a place to sleep. Harold had helped the captain organize seatings for meals—eight shifts of thirty people, they'd decided—and as he and Sam cut planks to length, they talked about supplies. Harold's friend George, also sharing Duncan's cabin, joined them an hour later and described the list he was making of those who'd been separated from family members and friends; first on it were the seven congress participants still unaccounted for. The captain would radio the list to the other rescue ships, which were returning to Scotland and Ireland—only theirs was heading across the sea, on its original course. But what about allocating medical care and pooling medications? What about basic sanitation? If we had rags, Harold said, we could tear them into squares. If we had a *system,* George fussed, gathering scraps of paper for the latrines.

If, if, if. Sam tried to think of them as amiable strangers helping to make the best of a hard situation—as if they'd not just been together at a conference where the two of them had looked on blandly as Sam's work was attacked. As if Duncan, elsewhere on the ship that morning, hadn't been the one attacking.

He worked all day, as the ship steamed steadily west and the passengers pulled from the water continued to shift and sort themselves, the sickest and most badly wounded settling in the tiny hospital bay with those slightly better off nearby, the youngest and oldest tucked in more protected corners, and the strongest where water dripped or splashed, layering themselves as neatly, Sam thought, as if they'd been spun in a gigantic centrifuge. He claimed one of the hammocks he'd hung himself, glad that at least Axel had a berth and a bit of privacy. Glad too to find, when evening came, that Harold and George had fit him and Axel into their dinner shift, which also included Duncan and the group of college girls.

The big square bandage bound to the top of his head made Axel, seated when Sam reached the table, look unusually defenseless. He smiled at Sam and tapped the seat next to him, but before Sam could get there, Harold, George, and Duncan swarmed in, leaving Sam seated at the corner. The college girls, already friendly with Duncan's group, filled in the empty seats and introduced themselves to Sam and Axel. One, who had smooth red hair a few shades lighter than Sam's, pointed to Axel's gauze-covered crown. "Is that bad?"

"Not really," Axel said. "A long jagged tear in my scalp, but the doctor said it should heal."

Not nearly enough information. Sam imagined Axel under water, trying to surface through the debris. An oar cracking down on his skull, a fragment from the explosion flying toward him. When did it happen, who was he with, who took care of him? He leaned forward to speak, but another of the girls, annoyingly chatty—Lucinda was her name—said, "How do you all know each other, then?"

"We work in the same field," Harold said. His doughy cheeks were perfectly smooth; of course he had a razor.

"Genetics," George added. Also clean-shaven. Briefly, Sam mourned his lost luggage. "The study of heredity."

"These two," Axel said, gesturing first toward Sam and then toward Duncan, "used to be my students."

"Really?" said the one named Pansy. "That wolf-in-a-bonnet disguise makes you look the same age as them."

It was true, Sam thought as the others laughed; the bandage covered Axel's bald spot, his sprouting beard concealed the creases around his mouth, and he was trim for a man who'd just turned fifty. Duncan, ten years Axel's junior, boasted a big, low-slung belly that, along with his thinning hair, made him look like an old schoolmaster. Straightening up, sucking in, Duncan turned to Lucinda and said, "We were all at the genetics conference I told you about."

"Where everyone was arguing!" Lucinda said brightly. "See, I *do* listen. Which side"—she turned to Sam—"were you on?"

"Lu*cin*da," said a girl named Maud.

"Actually," Harold said, rubbing his cheek with his thumb, "it was Duncan and Sam here, who were having a disagreement. But that's all behind us now."

Sam tried but failed to catch Axel's expression, while Duncan changed the subject. But as they were clearing out for the next shift of diners, one of the quieter girls approached Sam and said, "Were you really all quarreling about some experiment while the soldiers were gathering? I would have thought . . ."

" . . . that scientists aren't petty? That we're not as childish as everyone else?"

"Something like that," she said, with a surprising smile. "Although I don't know why I *should* expect that. I'm Laurel," she reminded Sam.

Straight brown hair, solid hips, pleasant, but, in Sam's opinion, unremarkable-looking except for her eyes. Up on deck, amid a crowd of people he didn't know and safely away from the ones he did, he watched the water move past the hull and listened to Laurel talk about what they'd heard on the radio. The Germans were smashing through Poland and had occupied Krakow. An RAF attack on German naval bases had gone awry. Each wave took them farther from what was going on in Europe. On the *Athenia*, along with the Americans and Canadians bolting for home, had been refugees from Poland and Romania and Germany who'd managed to get to Liverpool and then fought for berths, only to end up floating in the water before, if they were among the lucky, being rescued by a ship that would bring them back to Britain to begin the process of trying to flee again.

The sky was streaked with mare's tails to the south, dotted with little round clouds to the north; the last edge of the sun had vanished but some color remained. The open deck was so crowded by now that each of them touched at least one other person. Duncan pushed through like a fox through a field of wheat, nodded when he saw Sam, and kept moving. Duncan wasn't stupid, Sam thought; he knew some things, including what it meant to be part of a field of science still in its infancy. But he didn't know the new and enormous thing that Sam and Axel now shared. Sam in one boat and Axel in another, but the same sky, the same rain, the same flares and fears and darkness and dawn. Laurel said something about the windows of a church in London and Sam pretended to pay attention. Why was it, he thought, that even here Duncan seemed able to keep him and Axel apart?

In 1921, when Sam went off to college in upstate New York, he was sixteen years old and six feet tall, trying to conceal his age behind his size and so lonely that he might have attached himself to anyone. His father, an astronomer at the Smithsonian, had died when he was four; Sam remembered his smell, his desk at the observatory, his laugh. Afterward, his mother had moved them to Philadelphia to live with her parents, who seemed to be nothing like her. He slept in a bed his great-uncle had once used, near a shelf on which, between two photographs of his dead father, a mirror reflected back a face framed by his father's thick red hair but otherwise very different. His mother's mouth, her father's heavy lower lids, two moles on a jaw that must have come from someone on his father's side. When he touched that face with hands his father's size but his grandmother's shape, he felt a huge, hazy, painful curiosity that he couldn't put into words. Like his mother, he was good with numbers, but otherwise his mind seemed to leap and dart where hers moved in orderly lines. Perhaps, he thought, like his father's? He could only guess.

When he turned eight, his grandfather persuaded a friend to

admit Sam to a school so good that his mother, who wrote books and articles about astronomy, was just able to pay the fees. Tearing through his classes, eager for more, he skipped one year and then another. A biology teacher, Mr. Spacek, reeled him in when he reached the upper school, introducing him to the study of heredity. In the empty lab, at the end of the day, he'd enter into Mr. Spacek's fruit-fly experiments as if he were tumbling down a well, concentrating so intently that the voices rising from a baseball game on the field below, or from the herd pounding around the track, shrank to crickets' chirps and then disappeared. From the books that Mr. Spacek loaned him, Sam finally gained the language to shape what he'd been feeling since he could remember. Who am I? Who do I resemble, and who not? What makes me *me*, what makes you *you*; where did we come from, who are we like? What do we inherit, and what not?

Mr. Spacek helped Sam translate his curiosity into hypotheses that might be tested, experiments he might perform. He urged Sam to apply to college a year early, and then got him a scholarship and everything else he needed, including two precious books for the journey up the Hudson River. These, along with the sandwiches Sam's mother had packed him, helped during the bad moment when he confused the motion of the water rushing alongside the train with that of the train itself. Once he arrived at his new refuge, though, he felt fine. The brick and stone buildings were just as handsome as Mr. Spacek had promised, and his room was excellent too, with a big window, two low beds, two desks with lamps and chairs and space for books. Shirts and jackets were already hanging neatly along one half of the closet rod and these, along with a carton of books and a pair of skis, belonged to a wiry boy who introduced himself as Avery Hayes and asked if he might have the bed away from the window. Sam, who'd never had a close friend, right away liked Avery's smile and his calm, thoughtful movements.

"Of course you can have that bed," Sam said. "But are you sure . . . ?"

"Perfectly," said Avery. "I'm sensitive to drafts. If you don't mind, I'll take this desk then, too."

Which left Sam exactly what he wanted, a view out over the quad, past the beeches and benches and flower beds to the long brick building with limestone lintels, which he'd spotted the instant he arrived: the Hall of Science, the reason that he'd come. This was his place, Mr. Spacek had told him, this and no other: because this was the place where Axel Olssen taught.

Mr. Spacek had also arranged for Sam to join Olssen's section of general biology his first semester, and Axel transplanted Sam so smoothly from Mr. Spacek's world into his—soon after the first exam, he hired Sam as a bottle washer, brought him into the lab, and told him to use his first name—that Sam hardly felt the shock. The weeks rocketed by, the work Sam wanted to do crowded by other classes, the regimen of the dining hall, compulsory weekly chapel, and the swimming lessons that were part of the physical fitness requirement. The basement pool was dimly lit, slimy under Sam's feet at the shallow end, where he stood and tried to follow the instructor's motions. He was the only one that year who didn't know how to swim at all, and those first weeks of splashing, coughing, breathing in when he was meant to breathe out, and sinking, perpetually sinking—"You're remarkably *dense*," the instructor said cheerily, trying to support Sam in the water with a hand under his ribs—were humiliating. Thrusting his face back up into the air, Sam lost track of his surroundings and once again was the small, frightened boy who, after his father's death, was sometimes swept away by tantrums. But then, as soon as he crossed the quad and entered the Hall of Science, everything annoying faded away.

Axel was young himself, just a few years out of graduate school, energetic and delightfully informal; he loaded Sam down with his own books, trusting that he could make sense of the material despite being only a freshman. When he discovered Sam's age, he laughed and said genetics was a young man's game—Alfred Sturtevant had been only nineteen, still an undergraduate, when he'd devised the first chromosome map. Calvin Bridges had been an undergraduate too, and a bottle washer, like Sam, when he spotted the first vermilion mutant. Who knew what Sam, the perfect age at the absolutely perfect time, might do? Theirs was a new field, Axel said. A whole new world.

In class, Axel brought new terms and concepts alive with his arms, slicing the air like a conductor, his thick hair sticking up in spikes. They were after more than just the study of vague factors or mysterious unit characters, he said: the gene was not simply an abstract idea; genes were material! Heredity depended on chromosomes, forever splitting and recombining; units of heredity—genes—must be arranged like beads on a string, particles invisible to the eye but visible through their actions, ordered along visible chromosomes. Let the older generation argue about immaterial factors, vitalistic forces, the possibilities of organisms passing on changes caused by will or desire. The truth, Axel emphasized during Sam's first semester, was that the particles of heredity passed from one generation to the next, and could not be influenced by what happened to the body. Every living individual had two parts, one patent, visible to our eyes—the me you see, the tree you touch; that was the somatoplasm—and the other latent, perceptible only by its effect on subsequent generations but continuing forever, part of the immortal stream that was the germ-plasm. Phenotype, genotype (Sam loved repeating those words). Concepts made visible, Axel said happily, through our own flies.

So Sam couldn't swim; so he hated his history class. When he listened to Axel talk about his work, now *their* work, he was entirely alive. If they helped elucidate the way genes were arranged and transmitted, then they'd begin to understand heredity and variation. If they understood that, they'd begin to glimpse the workings of evolution. And if they could understand evolution, then . . .

"You have a pedigree," Axel said one day when Sam was mashing bananas, sprinkling yeast, and measuring agar: by then he was the food maker as well as the bottle washer. "Just like our flies. You were trained by Charlie, and now you're working with me. We were trained by Thomas Morgan, who was trained by William Brooks. Brooks was trained by Agassiz himself, at the summer school for the study of natural history he founded on Penikese Island. One short line: Agassiz, Brooks, Morgan, me, and then you. You're connected to the new biology just as directly as the flies we're breeding in here are connected to the original stocks from Morgan's lab."

Sam didn't share that with Avery, who was as interested in physics as Sam was in biology, but who hadn't yet found the right professor; it would have felt like bragging. But he did love the feel of his own hands linking Mr. Spacek's *Drosophila,* whose ancestors had also come from the fly room at Columbia, to the new generations hatching in the bottles he prepared. Forget the litter, the browning bananas, the morgue filled with bodies drowned in oil. The flies swooned docilely at a whiff of ether, moved easily with a touch from a camel's-hair brush, and then—the variations were marvelous. Eye after eye after eye, all red—and then here were white eyes, and there were pink. Wings all shaped like wings, until one fly produced a truncated set and another a pair curled like eyelashes, each mating yielding surprises, a new generation every ten days: how could anyone think of this as work? Work was waiting for frogs to hatch and pass through their stages until they matured enough to mate. Planting corn and waiting for the seeds to germinate, the stalk to grow, the ear to fill and ripen before one could even begin to guess—*that* was work; he couldn't believe the researchers a few hours away at Cornell had the patience. For him it was always, only, flies. In a clean bottle, a courting male held out one wing to his virgin bride and danced right and then left before embracing her: who wouldn't love *that?* Let others fuss with peas and four-o'clocks, rabbits and guinea pigs: for Sam, the flies were the key to everything.

That first Christmas vacation, he returned to school early at

Axel's request. As the train rumbled north, he looked up from his stack of journals now and then and noticed the Catskills thick with snow, or a crow flying low above the frozen Hudson, but mostly he kept his eyes on his work. The brindled dog at the train station had to bark twice before Sam stopped to pat him, walking on not to his room—the dorms were still closed—but to a small brick house two blocks from campus, where Axel, unmarried then, lived in happy squalor. Clothes on the floor, sheets on the couch (he always had visitors); Sam was welcome to stay, he said, the ten days until the semester started. A minute after Sam dropped his bag, they headed for the lab, which was warm and stuffy despite the bitter cold outside, electric bulbs glowing inside the old bookcases Axel had turned into incubators. Sam found a path through the tumble of plates and coffee cups and reprints and manuscripts, books lying open everywhere, cockroaches investigating the huge stain—molasses?—on the journal that Duncan, whom Sam then knew only as Axel's senior student, had left at his place.

Axel, Duncan, and two other students, both juniors, worked at desks pushed into an island at the center of the room; Sam's place was at the sink, shaking used food from soiled bottles, or at the counter, filling wooden racks with wide-mouthed homeopathic vials. From there he'd watched Duncan mating virgin females in bottles for which Sam had prepared the food, later shaking the etherized offspring onto counting plates, bending over dissecting scopes, shouting happily when he found something unexpected. In November, he'd discovered a new mutant, which Axel had sent to Columbia, and that had made Sam feel—not that he wanted to be Duncan, not even that he wanted to be Duncan's friend (he was shallow, Sam thought even then, and prone to leap to easy conclusions), but that he wanted a chance to work on his own.

He plunged into the clutter, planning to take over Duncan's chair the minute he finished cleaning up. Axel asked if he thought maintaining the stock cultures for the Genetics and Heredity course, even as he was enrolled in it, might be too much.

"I'll be fine," Sam said, bending to his glassware. Everything stank of overripe bananas. "It's no problem at all. I could do more, if Duncan gets too busy . . ."

Axel squashed a fly on the counter and laughed. "You have to sleep sometime," he said. "Although, personally, I think sleep is overrated. Do you want to hear what went on at the meeting?"

"Please," Sam said. "I've been dying for news."

Later—at Woods Hole, in Moscow, every place where, after long days in the lab, he'd end up drinking with fellow geneticists—Sam would try to describe what he felt like hearing Axel summarize the extraordinary paper he'd heard at the international meeting in Toronto. As if he'd sprouted extra eyes, which let him see a new dimension. Or as if his brain had added a new lobe, capable of thinking new thoughts. *It is commonly said that evolution rests upon two foundations—inheritance and variation; but there is a subtle and important error here. Inheritance by itself leads to no change, and variation leads to no permanent change, unless the variations themselves are heritable. Thus it is not inheritance and variation which bring about evolution, but the inheritance of variation.* Surely the name of the man who'd written that—Hermann Muller—deserved a whole separate shelf in Sam's brain. Whenever he recited those crucial lines, others would chime in with more of Muller's essential insights: that in the cell, beyond the obvious structures, there must also be thousands of ultramicroscopic particles influencing the entire cell, determining its structure and function. That these particles, call them genes, were in the chromosomes, and in certain definite positions, and that they could propagate themselves. Magic, they all agreed. Magic!

For ten dazzlingly cold days that winter, before Duncan and the other students returned from their holiday, Axel and Sam talked about Muller's ideas while they worked alone together. Then Duncan returned for the spring semester, Axel showed

Muller's paper to him—and suddenly they were planning experiments while Sam was sterilizing forceps. The whole semester went that way, until Duncan graduated and, for just a little while, got out of Sam's way.

During the day, when trying to move through the mass of people on deck was like being transported through an amoeba, Sam thought often about those early, blissful months in Axel's lab. Here, if Axel wasn't surrounded, he was absent. Reading in his berth, Duncan would say. Or napping, he's exhausted, talk to him at dinner. Each day would end with nothing Sam had meant to say said—and then it was night, when he kept thinking about the night.

The night in the lifeboat, the night on the water, which Axel had shared and which Duncan could never know. The night floating under the clouds and the moon, Sam's boat so flooded that it was in the sea as much as on it, everyone packed together as tightly as bodies in a collective grave. Shoulders pressed to others' shoulders, backs to chests, knees to hips; fifty-seven people who, once they were safely aboard the *City of Flint,* avoided those with whom they'd been so strangely intimate. The woman, for instance, who'd worn Sam's life belt: how was it that they didn't stick together? She had given her chance at life to her son, Sam had given his to her; the gesture might have bound them. Yet she was in one of the bunks near the rear of the ship, nowhere near his cocoon of a hammock, and when he passed her on deck, they nodded politely and kept moving. Each time, he remembered what they'd seen of each other. What that woman—her name was Bessie—had seen of him. Instead of seeking her out, he'd move toward Laurel and Pansy and Maud, who'd turned out to be pleasant company, filled with impressions from their brief time in France and Italy and eager to talk about the news the radio officer relayed.

They kept him company at meals as well, where the questions

he longed to ask Axel—who was beside you, what were you think-ing, what was the part that most frightened you?—dissolved in the perpetual chatter. Duncan and Harold and George invariably settled close to Axel, who then would look at Sam, ruefully, Sam thought, as Sam found a separate place, and pretend to listen politely to the other three.

They were more interesting? They were safer. Harold and George taught at the same little college in Massachusetts, had roomed together at the congress, and, indeed, had come over together with Duncan, yet they gossiped about common acquain-tances and speculated on jobs and funding as if they hadn't just had weeks of each other's company. Duncan chimed in with news about colleagues in California, not just from the institute that his former advisor had established and where he still worked, but from Berkeley and Stanford as well. Even Axel, a fixture now at the college where Sam had first met him, offered modest nuggets gleaned from meetings in New York. Whose lab was expanding, who had lost support. Whose marriage had broken up.

What did any of this have to do with science? Or with the real feeling of what had just happened to them? The meals seemed doubly hard when Sam thought of how much better he'd done recently with Avery. On the inexpensive precongress tour, which he'd taken largely so he could see where Avery worked, they'd been scheduled for a day and a half in Cambridge. Sam had skipped all the other sites to visit Avery's lab at the Cavendish, where he'd admired Avery's new X-ray facility and studied his lab notebooks. Together, they'd happily discussed their most recent projects.

By the time the motor coach left on Sunday, Sam had felt like he knew his old friend again—and it was this, he thought, star-ing glumly into his pea soup during one particularly trying lunch, that had made him optimistic about what might happen with Axel in Edinburgh. So they had not, before the meeting, seen each other in seven years; so their correspondence had shrunk to an occasional exchange of reprints. His warm meeting with Avery had convinced him that he and Axel would also slip back into their old, easy ways.

Through Grasmere and Keswick the following day, on to Edinburgh that afternoon: six hundred geneticists, from more than fifty countries! New work, new ideas; a chance to renew old friendships. He'd been horribly disappointed to find that the Russian geneticists, some of whom he knew from his time in Moscow and Leningrad, had been denied permission to travel. After that, nothing else went the way he'd hoped; the session began to unravel almost as soon it started. Germany and the Soviet Union signed their pact and the German scientists left. Then the delegates from the Netherlands followed the Germans, and the Italians followed them. In ones and twos the British scientists trickled off to join their military units, while the French left all at once.

By Saturday, when Sam gave his talk, the Poles and others from the Continent were also gone, leaving only a spotty crowd of Americans, Canadians, South Africans, Australians, and New Zealanders to listen. Where was it written that they all had to turn against him? That what he said would actually enrage them? Duncan, who spoke later that day, set his own prepared talk aside and instead spent his time refuting every aspect of Sam's presentation. He was so familiar with the last decade of Sam's work—he had read all of Sam's papers, Sam understood then—that he did an excellent job.

Here on the ship, the sound of Duncan's voice sometimes caused Sam such pain that even if Duncan weren't always blocking his way to Axel, he would have wanted to strike him. He'd come around a corner, find Axel and Duncan, catch Axel's eye, see Axel wave—and then Duncan would turn and smile falsely, and he'd keep moving until he ran into Bessie, which would spin him in yet another direction. Then at night, lying like one of a long row of larvae among his canvas-shrouded fellow passengers, he'd return to his night in the boat, when Bessie's knees and shins had pressed uncomfortably into his lower back. With every stroke of the oar he freed himself briefly from that pressure, only to thump back into her bones. He came to hate her legs, then to hate her. But later, when they stopped rowing and waited for the sun to come up, he grew so cold that he sought her legs on purpose. Her shivering shook Sam's body too, and also that of Aaron, her little boy, who was pressed into the hollow between her chest and her bent knees. Aaron's whole right side—shoulder, arm, torso, leg—over the course of those hours also pressed itself against Sam's back. All the adults faced the same way, unable to see each other's faces, sensing their levels of misery through the contact of their wet flesh. Bessie's crying passed from her chest through Aaron's side and into Sam's back, and his groans passed the other way, a wave moving through the boat. Her back had to be pressed into someone else's legs, and that person's back to the next and the next and the next. Each time he went over this, he imagined that Axel was listening and that he in turn would describe his own night.

Meanwhile, the *City of Flint* kept steaming sturdily through the waves, miles passing but far too slowly: how to get through the days? A grim-faced doctor, still waiting for word of his wife and daughter, busied himself by organizing the ship's hospital, stitching up the survivors' wounds, tending to burns and scrapes. He'd been in a boat that overturned and had spent hours floating alone, draped on a bit of rudder. What, Sam wondered, did he think of when he stopped working? A Canadian girl, ten years old, had been struck on the head by a falling beam when the torpedo first hit the *Athenia* and, although she'd been conscious during the night in the lifeboats and her first day on the *City of Flint,* had fallen into a coma; the doctor watched over her closely, and Sam would sometimes sit beside her, reading out loud from a novel Laurel had loaned him.

Eavesdropping at dinner, pretending to listen to Lucinda and

Maud but actually straining to hear Axel responding to Duncan's questions, Sam learned that Axel, when he wasn't resting, passed the hours reading books he'd borrowed from Harold and George. Harold, meanwhile, kept busy with the little daily newspaper he now posted each morning on a bulletin board, around which people gathered to read his notes of the ship's progress and bits of friendly gossip. The college girls put on a fashion show, herding good-humored volunteers along an improvised runway as others voted for the most outlandish costume. On a day when the sea was very smooth, pierced now and then by leaping fish, Sam wrote letters to his mother and to the woman he was seeing back home, neither of whom knew that his changed plans had put him aboard the *Athenia*. The letters, which couldn't be sent until they reached Halifax, were as useless as curled wings on a fly, but time passed as he tried to describe—not the explosions, not the bodies, not his night in the boat. Not what had happened in Edinburgh, nor what Duncan had done, nor his estrangement from Axel. The shapes the clouds made in the sky, then. The porpoises leaping in sets of three and five. The brave little girl in her improvised romper and the kind women, strangers before boarding this ship, who cared for her.

He found a corner where he could wash his face in the morning, and an exercise route—from the open middle deck in front of the smokestack, around the port side of the deckhouse, to the bow, and back down the starboard side—on which, if he rose early enough to beat the crowds, he could pace like a horse in a mine. No matter what he did, or how he arranged his days, he ran into Duncan. When Duncan stopped near the air scoops to light a cigarette, the solid sheet of hair lying over his forehead flapped up and down in the breeze like a lid. Why was he there when Axel, whom Sam so much wanted to see, was always where Sam was not? And when Sam went down below one night to the talent show that Maud and Lucinda had organized, Axel was there, but there with Duncan.

Men sang "Danny Boy" and "Begin the Beguine," children tap-danced, a woman pleated an accordion. Two sailors whacked at fiddles as two more whirled about. Axel came over to suggest that Sam do some little tricks involving toothpicks and gumdrops, which he was good at and used to offer up at parties: two minutes to make a model of a locomotive, a minute—Avery had first taught him this—for a sugar molecule. For a moment, Sam was tempted, remembering how at Woods Hole he'd entertained his companions with models of sea squirts and the polymer backbone of cellulose, but then he looked at Duncan, right by Axel's side and waiting for him to make a fool of himself, and he declined.

Instead, Duncan stepped forward and, in his surprisingly sweet tenor voice, sang a bland version of the song for which, years ago, he used to invent ribald verses, entertaining the students during the summer they'd both spent at Woods Hole. Sam had just finished his junior year at college then; Duncan had been in his second year of graduate school, studying with Axel's teacher, Thomas Morgan. Almost everyone important in their new field was at the biological station that summer, investigating some aspect of genetics or embryology or both. Sam, one of the few undergraduates taking the invertebrate course, paid his tuition by waiting tables at the mess hall and collecting specimens for his teachers. On nights when the moon was in the right phase, he'd bus his tables, drop his apron, and head for the *Cayadetta*'s dock with a long-handled net and a tray of finger bowls. His desire to earn his teachers' approval was as ruthless as the lantern he held over the water, dooming the mating clam worms that spiraled upward.

Afterward, he skipped the gatherings at the ice-cream parlor and the visits to the movie house in Falmouth so that he could work on the project that had seized him. A scientist named Paul Kammerer, who had recently made two American lecture tours and whose sensational work—*VIENNA BIOLOGIST HAILED AS GREATEST OF THE CENTURY. Proves a Darwin Belief,* one newspaper blared—was so controversial that even Sam's mother, who wrote articles for popular-science magazines, had interviewed him, had caught Sam's eye as well. Kammerer claimed to have shown that when a change in the environment of his toads and salamanders caused an adaptive change in them—altered skin color, different reproductive behaviors—these changes could be transmitted to subsequent generations. A kind of heresy, Sam knew—the exact opposite of what he'd seen in the lab for himself. Although he'd breathed in his Quaker grandparents' conviction that the world can be improved, first Mr. Spacek and then Axel had trained him out of his unconscious assumptions that when individuals strengthened and developed their faculties, through vigorous use, they then passed that strengthening along. That the ones they stopped using were lost, and lost for good.

At Woods Hole, though, surrounded by interesting strangers pursuing so many different ideas, the truth had begun to seem more complex again, which made him read Kammerer's claims with real curiosity. Axel had taught him to question everything—didn't that include the beliefs that were quickly becoming conventions in their field? At night, roasting oysters on the beach, he and his classmates talked about Kammerer and speculated on the reasons why some biologists attacked him so furiously. Even those opposed to his conclusions were disturbed by that. They were all flirting with socialism then, some more than flirting; they sympathized when Kammerer complained that no one gave him a fair hearing. With the war just over, no one wanted to hear that inheritance wasn't everything, or that race and class characteristics passed on through generations might be altered.

Tiny, darkly tanned Ellen Eliasberg, a fellow student in Sam's invertebrate course, was moved by Kammerer's passionate statements about the necessity of man passing on what he acquired in the course of his lifetime to his children and his children's children. Sam was caught up by her arguments—and, at the same time, fascinated by the bad temper Duncan's advisor showed whenever anyone mentioned Kammerer's work.

"The leopard *can* change his spots?" he'd say mockingly. "Fathers can pass what they've learned to their sons? Why not just reject every bit of science done in the last century? Why not go right back to Lamarck and his folklore? Cave fishes and deep-sea dwellers lose their eyes because they don't need them in the dark; moles have poorly developed eyes because they're in burrows most of the time; if an organ isn't used, it conveniently disappears and if it's used often—why not point to the giraffe stretching his neck to reach for higher leaves?—it gets bigger. How long has that been believed? And yet Payne bred fruit flies in the dark for sixty-nine generations, without the slightest change in their eyes or behavior. In my own lab, we've seen well over one hundred new types arise spontaneously, with no environmental influence, each breeding true from the start. Overnight—literally, overnight!— eyeless flies have appeared from normal parents, by an obvious change in a single hereditary factor."

Then he'd say that the popular press was being fooled, once again, and foolishly misleading the public (here Sam thought of his mother; had she sorted this out?); he'd say Kammerer was a charlatan and a publicity seeker and perhaps even a fraud. He ranted so wildly that even Duncan looked uneasy, and Sam saw, for the first time, what might happen when the passion required to defend a new set of ideas went too far.

But he wanted to work, simply to work, and he tried to stay focused on that. The old wooden house where he bunked that summer was less than a block from the lab, surrounded by sand and scrubby pines, but during his first weeks he went there only to sleep. Every minute he could steal from his course and his jobs he spent designing an experiment that might prove or disprove what Kammerer contended. Instead of Kammerer's slow-growing salamanders and midwife toads, Sam decided to use his swiftly reproducing flies. And he'd work with their eyes, not only because variations in eye color had been the first and best-documented of the mutations observed in fruit flies but also because eyes and their development had always been central to these discussions.

He used fly cultures he'd kept for Axel, techniques he'd learned in his lab, a procedure he'd seen Duncan do in a different context. With a needle he ground to a very sharp point and then heated, he touched—just touched—the center of the red eye of a lightly etherized female fly; then he touched the other eye and laid the fly on a dry piece of paper, which he put into a little vial. A couple of hours later, he transferred the treated flies to a food bottle. In the few that survived the procedure he watched how the Malpighian tubules, which worked rather like kidneys, turned deep red and stayed that way. So: injury to one organ, the eye, caused what appeared to be a permanent change in another organ: an acquired characteristic.

Later, he mated the treated females to normal males and proceeded as usual. Amid the next generation he found a few mutants—yellow body, narrow eyes, twisted penis—as expected. And also, unexpectedly, seventeen flies, both male and female, with red Malpighian tubules. This was peculiar, and completely interesting: what did it mean? Immediately, he started breeding these to each other. None of their offspring showed the red tubules, but that might mean nothing; the trait was likely recessive, and he had only a small sample.

Duncan and most of the other students had a sense of what he was doing; they wandered in and out of the open labs and they all talked not only while they worked but also during their outings. Still, no one knew the details until the director asked him to give a presentation at one of the season's last Friday-night gatherings. He was nervous when he spoke—undergraduates were rarely asked to speak in front of the whole community—and he referred to earlier work that he hoped might support his own. In particular, a recent symposium that many in his audience had attended and that had examined this crucial question: *could* an injury to one generation cause an effect that was inherited by the next?

Swiftly, he moved through those other researchers' results. One had demonstrated the transmission of acquired eye defects in rabbits, which seemed to have the characteristics of a Mendelian recessive. Others had shown what seemed to be inheritable effects of injury from alcohol, lead, radium, and X-rays. Perhaps, though, this was parallel induction: had a physical agent acted simultaneously on *both* the germ cells and the somatic cells, producing changes independently in each, or had the change induced in the body actually affected the germ cell? Which was the mechanism at work with Sam's flies, and would either case argue for evolution directly guided by the environment? Sam saw Duncan in the audience, listening intently and taking notes, although he didn't ask any questions afterward. Other hands did wave, though, and Sam was pleased with the way he guided the passionate, occasionally contentious, but civil discussion that followed.

In September, when he returned to college and reported all this to Axel, Axel shook his head and said he wished Sam had consulted him before throwing himself at such a controversial issue. He should never, Axel said, have presented this to so many eminent scientists before testing his hypotheses more thoroughly. Then he said that while he didn't yet trust Sam's results, they were intriguing and Sam should push the work forward. He'd supply the flies and the other materials; when the time came, he'd help Sam write up the results. "Although it would have been better," he added, "if you'd done even more while you were still there."

"I should have," Sam admitted.

And would have, he knew, if he hadn't gotten involved with Ellen. Four years Sam's senior, presently working as a biology instructor at Smith, she'd spent the previous year in England, where she'd cut off her hair, befriended several brilliant women, and taken up feminism and eugenics. One opinion she held strongly was that exceptionally intelligent people—"Like you," she said to Sam, during a collecting trip at Quisset, "and me"— should have children together, which would improve the world. Later, she and Sam decanted their specimens side by side, and a few nights after that, when a crowd of students got drunk on the beer two chemists had brewed, they ended up entwined in the dusty wooden attic over the supply room.

The next day, when Sam apologized for what had happened, Ellen calmly claimed it as her own idea and said Sam had only done what she wanted. At the beach, she wore a daring wool-jersey bathing suit that clung to her wiry shape and ended midthigh, the white trim disturbingly like underwear, and when she swam, she looked to Sam, with her close-cropped hair, like one of the elegant spiraling clam worms he collected at night. He had no idea how he felt about her; he was nineteen, and she let him make love to her. Sam couldn't imagine why.

"Because I want to have several children, starting soon," she told him. "And you're such a good specimen. You're tall"—here she tapped one of Sam's fingers—"big-boned and bright"—tap, tap—"hardworking, sturdy, even-tempered."

By then she was working on Sam's second hand, having thrust the first inside her blouse. His hands on her small, pointed breasts, his mouth in the hollow of her throat, her bony feet on his back. He was completely inexperienced when they met; he was astounded. For the last two weeks of his stay at Woods Hole he was with Ellen every night. If I'm pregnant, she said the day they parted, we'll get married. If not—

Not, as it turned out, although they met as often as they could during Sam's last year of college, several times near Sam and twice in Massachusetts, the second time just after Duncan proved him wrong.

What kind of a person would, in utter secrecy, interrupt his own project to replicate a fellow worker's experiments and double-check his results? Duncan published a paper noting that the preliminary results of a young student investigator—here he named Sam—presented orally and informally had sufficiently interested him to push those experiments further. When he did, he found that in flies whose eyes had been burned, the Malpighian tubules indeed turned red, and that a small number of the offspring of those flies also had red tubules.

But he also saw something Sam had failed to see, perhaps because he'd been so absorbed with Ellen. In his early work in Morgan's lab, Duncan had occasionally noticed—or so he wrote; Sam wondered if it wasn't Morgan himself who saw this—larvae feeding on the eyes of dead flies that had fallen on the food at the bottom of the culture bottle; this had colored the intestines of the larvae red. After seeing the initial data (and this did sound like him; he could test a chain of reasoning like a crow pulling at the weak spots in a carcass), Duncan had suddenly wondered if the pigment might be carried through the pupa stage, possibly appearing in the adult fly.

He crushed the eyes of some flies, mixed them with yeast and agar from a culture bottle, and added larvae; their intestines soon became filled with the red food, and a bit later the Malpighian tubules, visible through the larval walls, became deep red. The larvae pupated; adults emerged; their tubules too were red. Variations with different foods showed clearly that some component of the red pigment in the crushed eyes passed from the digestive tract of the larvae into the Malpighian tubules and remained there into the adult stage. Sam's larvae had eaten the damaged eyes of dead flies and that—not a response to the injury itself—had colored their tubules. Sam had found not an acquired characteristic, but simply a transient response to diet. Acquired characteristics were not—could not be, Duncan said—inherited.

Sam was wrong, he'd been proven wrong, but at first that didn't seem so serious—why would people hold his curiosity against him? He was young, he was enthusiastic; he'd seen a big question in Kammerer's work and explored it open-mindedly, trying to follow the data rather than his own preconceptions; he'd shared his findings honestly. Leaving Woods Hole for his last year of college, he'd sensed that others saw him as a wonderfully promising student, welcome anywhere. Six months later, the recent work he'd done in Axel's lab rendered pointless by Duncan's paper, those same people seemed to regard him as a dubious young man who'd overreached himself. Even Axel, after reading the copy Duncan sent specially to him, a little handwritten note—"I'm sorry"—scrawled at the top, groaned and went for a long walk before sitting down with Sam.

"I should have seen that," Axel said when he returned. "If you'd kept in touch with me over the summer, if we'd been talking about your experimental design . . . I should have seen that before Duncan did." Sam couldn't tell whether Axel was more angry at himself for missing it or proud of having taught Duncan so well.

In the wake of that paper, Sam knew he wouldn't be welcome at Columbia, where everyone had assumed he'd follow Axel and Duncan to graduate school. But with Axel's help he found a place in a small program in Wisconsin, run by a sound but middling geneticist. Not one of Morgan's golden boys, like Bridges or Sturtevant; not even someone at the top of the second tier (which was how Axel disparagingly characterized himself), but a man who knew he was lucky to have a lab and the funding for a few graduate students.

Sam spent that last summer in Axel's lab, maintaining the cultures and leaving everything in order for Axel's next helper, wishing, all the time, that he could be discussing new projects with Axel. But Axel, collaborating with a friend in Texas, was seldom there, and Ellen, who might have helped him settle into his new life, instead did the reverse. If she'd gotten pregnant during his last year of college, nothing, Sam knew, could have wedged them apart—but she didn't, and didn't, and when summer came and she still wasn't pregnant, they didn't see each other for several months. In August, she backed out of her offer to drive to Wisconsin with him, and before Thanksgiving she was gone.

For a long time, Sam was able to avoid her. His luck ran out after seven years, at a big meeting in Washington where Duncan received a prestigious award. Sam was moving toward the back of the auditorium, having just heard a talk by a maize geneticist and hoping to escape before Duncan spoke. He ran into Ellen in the middle of the aisle, herding two boys and a girl, all recognizably Duncan's, toward the special seats at the front set aside for the prizewinner's family. She introduced the children awkwardly and asked how Sam was doing.

"Fine," Sam said. "Just finishing my thesis." She and Duncan had married before he'd even started that work. After which Axel, as if inspired by them, had married a mathematician he'd met in Texas, moved to a leafy street twenty minutes from the college, and promptly produced a son.

"We miss you at Woods Hole," she said.

"Handsome boys," he said, avoiding their eyes.

Tugging at her younger son's collar, bending to adjust the skirt on the dark-haired little girl who'd inherited her reedy arms and legs, Ellen said that she and Duncan went back every year, always with the children, who loved it. But nothing had ever been as wonderful as her second summer there. When, Sam knew by then, she'd already left him but he didn't know it. When she and Duncan had both returned and Sam, in the shadow of his big failure, had been unable to join them.

On the lifeboat, before the sun rose, when the night was at its coldest and the waves were tossing them about and when, having long since thrown up everything he'd eaten the previous day, Sam was retching painfully and Bessie's hand was lightly patting the back of his neck, he had thought about his calm hand bringing the needle's point so lightly, so deftly, to each *Drosophila* eye. How the flies' wounds had sometimes stuck to the food, and to each other; how those that lived were weak for several days, some unable to eat. Here on the ship, shaken about like a fly in a test tube, he too was having trouble eating. One evening he learned that while most of the geneticists who'd been on the *Athenia* with him had been picked up by the British destroyers, two were apparently lost. And on the eighth day of the crossing, while he scored patterns in the oatmeal that was one of the few things left to eat, Sam learned that the little girl who'd been in a coma had finally died.

Gloom spread through the ship as each seating heard the news, and later Sam saw Bessie, near the bow, comforting her son, Aaron, who was crying. He and the girl had been friends, Sam thought, or at least known each other the way children even of different ages do when confined together. He couldn't stop himself from walking over to Aaron and squatting down beside him. He rested his hand on Aaron's back, his fingertips moving gently.

"Shh," he said. "It's all right." Which was what he'd said in the boat, when Aaron was so cold and sick that he was crying. Also this was what Bessie had said to Sam. Now she said, "He's taking this very hard."

"Were they close?" Sam asked. The two geneticists who'd drowned, husband and wife, had worked at a small Minnesota college and traveled only rarely to international gatherings. Sam hadn't met them at the congress, but he had on the ship, and he'd envied them when they came down hand in hand to what would be their last dinner. Axel had said, at that same meal, how much he'd been missing his wife and son.

"She took him for walks around the deck, when she was bored," Bessie said, gesturing toward their own crowded railings, so packed with passengers eager for air—they were expecting rain—that strolling was out of the question. "They played make-believe. You know, the way children will: I'll be the mommy and you be the little boy, and I'll get you ready for school . . ."

"She sounds sweet," Sam said. The figures crowding the railings separated, moved together again, bunched, and dispersed, long lines forming only to condense into shorter segments.

"Not always—once she pinched him hard enough to leave a mark."

Aaron shrugged off Sam's hand and pushed himself more firmly into Bessie's legs. "Do you have children?" she asked, smoothing her son's hair.

"I don't," Sam said, and if Duncan and Harold hadn't joined them just then, he might have told Bessie how pained he'd been when he understood that he likely never *would* have any. Ellen, who couldn't get pregnant with him, had gotten pregnant instantly with Duncan; no woman he'd been with since had had so much as a scare. Sometimes, when he'd had too much to drink (throughout Prohibition, he and his friends had always had access to lab ethanol), he used to joke around with a toothpick-and-gumdrop figure he called Mr. Heredity. *Look at me!* he'd have the figure say. *Interested since childhood in how we inherit traits, but I can't reproduce!* But although he laughed as hard as anyone when Mr. Heredity drooped his gumdrop head, later, when he began to grasp the fact that no one would ever have his hair or his blocky nose, his height or his big hands, he felt quite otherwise. The day his heart stopped, the day he got hit by a bus (the day a torpedo sank the ship that was taking him home), everything that had led to his father and mother and converged in him would be extinguished.

But here were his colleagues, bearing down. He managed a smile as they greeted him and, looking at Bessie and Aaron, asked if they could do anything to help. Sam introduced them only by name, without explaining how he knew them.

"We're fine," Bessie said.

Impossible to focus on her and Duncan at the same time. Instead, Sam kept his eyes on the unusually turbulent sky. Great, soft, gray clouds piled one atop the other, pushing each other aside like wrestling dogs.

Bessie said, looking only at him, "Margaret's death made Aaron miss his father more than usual. He keeps thinking something's happened to him, that he won't be there when we get home. Those men we saw in the water . . ." She picked Aaron up and left.

Duncan watched them walk away and then turned back to Sam, eyes bright with curiosity. "You were in the same lifeboat?"

Sam nodded. He'd told Duncan nothing about the night in the boat; what Duncan knew of the torpedo, the flames, the boats in the water, he knew from other survivors, not from him.

"If you ever want to talk," Duncan said, pushing aside his floppy hair, "I'm happy to listen."

After Sam graduated from college, he mostly kept his work to himself. Axel, busy with his new wife and son, also had new students to train and increasingly relied on his connection to Duncan, who was doing very well as part of his advisor's group. Duncan and his colleagues shared fly strains with Axel's lab; Axel and his students collaborated on papers with them, which helped them all. Sam worked alone, steadily and quietly, throughout his years in graduate school, doing nothing without his advisor's explicit approval, choosing a thesis project closer to his advisor's heart than to his own and committing to it entirely. He kept in close touch with Avery, who'd gone to England by then, and Avery helped him modify an X-ray source so he could radiate his *Drosophila* and look for mutations. The experiments he completed were nowhere near as flashy as Muller's work in this area, nor did he and his advisor gather anywhere near as much data— they were working along parallel tracks at first and then, after Muller had yet another big breakthrough, in support of what he'd already shown—but Sam knew it was solid work, a bandage for his dented reputation. By 1930, when he got his degree, he was able, despite the growing effects of the crash, to find a position in Missouri. In between teaching sections of general biology, he worked every spare minute in his own lab, grateful for what he'd been able to salvage and trying not to envy Duncan, who had followed his advisor out to California and had a much better job.

Half his salary he sent to his mother, who, in the wake of both her parents' deaths, had taken in boarders but even so was still struggling to hang on to the Philadelphia house. When he lost his job in 1933, he knew she felt the blow too. Although he wrote to everyone he'd ever met, there were no positions to be had. Axel, who temporarily had to close his own lab, could find him nothing, and Duncan couldn't, or wouldn't, help, despite being the protégé of someone who'd just won a Nobel Prize. When Sam had nothing to lose and was on the verge of going back home, he appealed to the man whose paper had so inspired him during his first year of college, and in whose field he now worked.

He'd written to Muller a few times during graduate school, sending results that confirmed or extended Muller's own and asking about his latest work. At a conference, Muller had tracked Sam down and inspected his most recent data closely; after that, they'd continued to correspond about interesting questions. If a quantum of light could, as Niels Bohr suggested, trigger photosynthesis, was it also the case that an individual ionization caused a mutation? Did chromosome breaks result from radiation's direct or indirect effects? After Muller left Austin in the wake of a scandal involving his support of a Communist-leaning student newspaper, he went to Berlin, where, he wrote to Sam, he was collaborating with a brilliant Russian scientist who shared his interest in using the tools of physics to explore the nature of the gene. The work was intriguing, the company stimulating, but just as he was settling in, Hitler was appointed chancellor and soon his colleagues began to lose their jobs. Muller then accepted his Russian friend's invitation to come help set up a research program and most recently had written to Sam from the Institute of Genetics in Leningrad.

Was it possible, Sam wrote him, that given his background and their shared interests, he could be of some use at the institute? Secretly, he thought they also shared a disgust with what was going on in their country, the mad inequities that seemed to be destroying every good thing. In Russia, Sam thought, science might assume its rightful role, and scientists, instead of being separated into little fiefdoms ruled by petty kings, would work under the shelter of the state, free to follow their best ideas. He was thrilled when Muller, so enthusiastic himself about the Soviet experiment, found money for a position in which Sam was, if not quite an independent investigator, more than a student.

Soon Sam was living in Leningrad, investigating chromosomal rearrangements and learning that many of the apparent point mutations caused by X-ray treatment were actually recombinations of broken fragments. Segments were lost, segments were duplicated; he began to get a sense of what size a gene might be, and how it might function when moved to a new position. What if natural mutations were actually rearrangements of the particles in the chromosomes, rather than changes to the particles themselves? Muller proved to be an excellent guide. Not a teacher, as Axel had been; not really a friend; he was clearly Sam's boss, but he was accessible and kind, and Sam was thrilled to be working with someone he'd admired for so long.

It hardly mattered that, with housing short everywhere, Sam had to sleep in the corners of other scientists' rooms, for a while in a bed behind a curtain in the laboratory, later in a basement hall. Everything was crowded, everyone was improvising; he was glad to be part of the common flow, and even the struggle to find supplies was worth it—such excitement! Such work, for such a purpose. Surrounded by Russians day and night, he learned the language quickly. And when the institute was moved to Moscow, Sam went too, leaving behind several friends and a woman with whom he'd had a brief affair.

Writing to his mother—he tried to write home twice a month—he described the farmers and engineers he met, the German Jews who'd sought refuge in the Soviet Union as the Nazis rose to power, the ardently socialist Englishmen and discontented Americans. He met men who'd soldiered in several wars, including one who'd fought Germans at the beginning of the Great War and then Americans, later, in Archangel, with the Reds. *He showed me the white cotton overcoat he'd worn,* Sam wrote, *which had made him invisible in the snow. He claimed that once, as he'd been scrounging for food in the streets, he'd seen an American soldier*

*leap from the top of a gigantic wooden toboggan run and onto the ice
below. Really, I am living in the most remarkable place.*

That winter, as the snow fell and fell—he was never warm,
no one had enough fuel—Sam thought often of that soldier suspended in the air. Leaping from or leaping toward? For all the
hardships of daily life here, he still felt freer than he had since
his time in Axel's lab, and he moved through Moscow with a
sense he hadn't had in years of everything being interesting.
At the Medico-Genetics Institute he saw hundreds of pairs of
identical twins—how eerie this was, each face doubled!—being
studied like laboratory mice. He visited collective farms, and he
met a geneticist named Elizaveta who'd discovered a remarkable mutant fly a few years before Sam arrived. Walking toward
her bench was like walking into Axel's lab for the first time, the
air dense with the smells of ether and bananas and flies fried on
lightbulbs, the atmosphere of delight. Elizaveta, who had long,
narrow, blue-green eyes below the palest brows, said she knew
that genes controlled development: but were they active all the
time, or did each act only at a particular period of development,
and lie dormant otherwise?

At meetings—so many meetings!—he listened to talks about
the practical applications of genetics to agriculture and the Marx-
ist implications of the theory of the gene. Once, in a dark room
after a day of lectures, he watched a film called *Salamandra,* about
an idealistic scientist who'd demonstrated Lamarckian inheritance in salamanders but then was betrayed by a sinister German who tampered with his specimens to make it look as though
his results had been faked. Denounced, deprived of his job, he
lived in exile until rescued by a farsighted Soviet commissar who
proved his work had been right all along. Partway through, Sam
grasped that this was a transposition of the life and fate of Kammerer, who'd killed himself after a researcher proved that some of
his results had been faked. By then, his own big mistake seemed
very far away.

Working all the time, excited by the new experiments in the

lab, he ignored what was happening out on the streets until, after a while, even he couldn't avoid knowing about the party members being persecuted and executed, those who disagreed with Stalin disappearing. Intellectuals and scientists from different fields began to disappear as well, including geneticists, some of them Sam's own colleagues. The director of the twins study vanished and his institute was dissolved. Elizaveta, more cautious than some, gave her flies to Sam and then slipped away to her grandmother's village. Geneticists had failed, Sam read, to serve the state by providing the collectives with new crops and livestock that could thrive in difficult climates and relieve the food shortages. They were stuck in bourgeois ways of thought. If a society could be transformed in a single generation, if the economy could be completely remade, why couldn't the genetic heritage of crops or, for that matter, of man, be transformed as well?

In this context, Lamarck was a hero; and also Kammerer (Sam could see, now, why he'd been shown that film); and also the horticulturist Ivan Michurin, who'd claimed that through some kind of shock treatment he could transform the heredity of fruit trees, allowing growth farther north. Trofim Lysenko, pushy and uneducated, rose up from nowhere to extend Michurinism beyond what anyone else could have imagined. Lysenko hated fruit flies, he knew no mathematics, he found Mendelian genetics tedious, even his grasp of plant physiology was feeble. How could Sam take him seriously? Lysenko claimed that heredity was nothing so boringly fixed as the Mendelians said, but could be trained by the environment, endlessly improved. At a big meeting Sam attended at the end of 1936, Muller tried to rebuff Lysenko by clearly restating Mendelian genetics and outlining the institute's research programs. Larmarckian inheritance, Muller explained, could not be reconciled with any of the evidence they'd found.

Sam was amazed when some in the audience actually hissed, and more so when, after Lysenko responded by dismissing all of formal genetics, those same people stood and cheered. Genetics was a harmful science, Lysenko said, not a science at all but a bourgeois distortion, a science of saboteurs. Muller and his like were wrecking socialism, preventing all progress, whereas he would now completely refashion heredity! His Russian was failing him, Sam kept thinking; Lysenko couldn't be saying that what should be so, must be so. Yet his friends heard the same thing. Those who doubted him, Lysenko said, were criminal. A theory of heredity, to be correct, must promise not just the power to understand nature but the power to change it.

Muller, after making careful arrangements to protect his colleagues, left the country early in 1937, and Sam followed a few weeks later, first destroying the papers and letters he'd received from his Russian friends. *Of course I understand why you need me to return to the United States,* he carefully wrote to his mother, who'd requested no such thing but could be counted on to understand that his letters were likely being read.

Back in Philadelphia, writing up his last results from the Moscow lab in the small bedroom where he'd slept as a child, the familiar sound of his mother working in the living room complicated by the movements of the two teachers with whom she now shared the house, Sam began another search for work. This time he had better luck, finding a position at a small college near the western edge of Illinois. For a while, as he was trying to set up yet another lab—how many times could a person order glassware, brushes, ether, drying racks, all the bits and pieces needed to do the smallest experiment?—he thought about changing fields entirely. If science in the United States was controlled by a few powerful people, and science in the Soviet Union was nothing but a branch of politics—then what was the point of doing anything? Perhaps he'd do better at farming, or statistics, or auto mechanics.

Soon enough, though, he got caught up in the life of a place that at first had felt to him like nowhere. His better students were curious and eager to learn, and he found—as perhaps Axel had found earlier; Sam longed to talk with him about this but couldn't afford a trip east—that he had to hurl himself at a problem again, simply to give the students something to do. He started a genetics course in addition to his sections of general biology; he bought a little house with two large trees; he met a woman he liked, who planted vegetables in his backyard and taught him how to cook chard. The college gave him an excellent incubator, as well as some other crucial equipment. Through the fly-exchange network he was able to get some useful stock, which in turn put him in touch with many of the researchers trained in Morgan's lab: not only Axel but also Harold and George (that was how he first met them) and, inevitably, Duncan, who immediately mailed to Sam's new address all the papers he'd published while Sam was abroad. Once Sam solved some difficulties with mites and temperature fluctuations, he was back in business and, after hiring a couple of student helpers, began a new set of experiments. For one particular project, he used Elizaveta's flies.

He'd smuggled breeding stock into the country, and when the cultures were established, he turned, with a sense of recovering his younger self, to investigating them. Like some of the curiosities naturalists had noticed and collected for years—crustaceans with legs where jaws or swimmerets should be, plants with petals transformed into stamens—Elizaveta's flies shared the property that one organ in a segmental series had been transformed into another. How were those homeotic mutants produced? And were those variations heritable or caused by damage to the developing embryo? An acquaintance of Axel's had discovered a true-breeding homeotic mutant he called bithorax, in which the little stabilizing structures normally found behind the forewings had been transformed into a second set of wings; Elizaveta had worked with that four-winged mutant, and also with an even odder one called aristapedia, which had legs growing where the antennae should be. Endlessly fascinating, Sam thought, and he began to investigate how a mutation to a single gene could cause such massive effects.

Months passed, a year of hard work passed; thousands of cultures and tens of thousands of flies. In the mutant, he learned, the antennal discs developed early, at the same time as the leg discs, allowing the evocator that normally instructed the leg discs to act on the antennal discs as well. *Evocator:* he loved that word. The chemical substance that acts as a stimulus in the developing embryo. How intriguing, how sensible, really, that the mutant gene didn't build a leglike structure out of thin air. Instead it acted more simply and generally, altering the rate of development so that a whole pattern of growth occurred at a time and place where it ought not to be.

Others were working on this as well, but there was so much to do, along so many branching paths, that Sam had no sense of racing to solve a problem before someone else. Rather, the whole world seemed to shimmer, a delectable feeling he'd first had as a boy, working with Mr. Spacek: the act of throwing himself at one problem, *this* problem, lit up every other aspect of his experience in the world. Legs grew out of a fly's head because of a small change in timing; would his life have been different if his father had died earlier, or later? If he hadn't met Mr. Spacek when he did, or gone to college at sixteen and found Axel willing to teach him. If he hadn't met Avery or Ellen, hadn't met Duncan . . .

In this state of excitement, he'd gone to the congress, where he presented his results and then connected that work with Goldschmidt's, with work on position effects and the possibility that the particles of heredity might move around, with the possibility that maybe all genetic changes were changes in development. Maybe genes weren't particles after all, weren't arranged like beads on a string, but were more like spiderwebs, susceptible to the influence of events in the cytoplasm; maybe they weren't quite as impregnable to outside influence as previously thought? He aimed his ideas at his former Russian colleagues, who should have been there but weren't; at Axel, who was there but had missed all the groundwork; at Muller, who'd found a temporary haven in Edinburgh and who, although distracted by the responsibilities of hosting the congress, still found time to come and listen to him. He sailed past his notes, avoiding the false paths of Kammerer and Lysenko, which, unlike most of his audience, he'd learned for himself, to speculate about the question of timing. When, in the course of development, might a tiny change cause massive later effects? Might inheritance not be far more complex than we'd guessed? When he finished speaking and looked out at the disgruntled faces in the audience—Duncan's face was red, Axel was poking his notepad with a pencil, Muller was gazing at him quizzically—he had a separate thought, which had nothing to do with inheritance. The first big leap he'd taken, with Kammerer's work, had turned out to be wrong. Was it possible that now no one could see the rightness of this second big leap, because of his first mistake?

Two bright white ships, crisp and military-looking with broad red stripes across their bows, came out of the distance to meet them when they were still several hundred miles from Halifax. Sailors from the coast guard cutters transferred food, which they needed badly—oranges! Sam saw, and apples and cheese, potatoes and meat, fresh bread!—along with toothbrushes and hairbrushes, soap, shampoo, donated clothing, more blankets. Two doctors, wanting to examine the wounded to see who might need the alignment of broken bones checked with their portable X-ray machine and who should be transferred to the cutters for care, also came aboard.

For the first time in more than a week, Sam brushed his hair, cleaned his teeth with something other than a finger, and along with everyone else dipped into the new supplies to spruce up for that night's celebration. Officers from the cutters joined them, the captain extracted a case of whiskey from the hold, a few passengers did what they could to decorate the deck while others, beginning to believe now that they'd get home safely, began to relax. All around him, Sam saw groups of people, faces suddenly scrubbed shades lighter, smiling and talking with the friends they'd made on the journey. These women bound to those, these students to those sailors; the college girls—for him, still simply pleasant acquaintances—more closely attached to Duncan and Harold and George than he'd understood.

He felt, for a moment, unusually alone—more so when he saw that Axel, standing only a few feet away as the whiskey was handed around, was barricaded by Duncan and Harold and George. Fanning out from them were Laurel and Pansy and Maud, talking to a young man Sam hadn't met; Lucinda, playing cards with the plant physiologist he'd first seen the day they were rescued; and Bessie and Aaron, sitting on one of the hatches, watching the constellations rise in the sky. Sam went over to Bessie's side as Pansy asked the young man what he planned to do when he got home.

"I'm still in school," he said shyly.

Sam looked up, spotting the stars of Pegasus. He remembered sitting on his father's shoulders, following the line of his arm as he traced out shapes overhead. *Look at the horse, do you see the dolphin? There's a whale . . .* Or did he remember those shapes from other evenings, much later, with his mother?

"I'm an art student," the young man continued. "I was traveling on a fellowship. But now . . ."

"You'll go back when the war is over?" Maud asked.

"What's the point?" he said. "Without my friend."

As Sam continued to pick from the glitter overhead all the constellations he could remember, the student described how he and a dear friend from their school in Boston had split a traveling scholarship meant for one of them so that they could both see Europe. Despite their pinched budget and the signs of war cropping up everywhere, they'd visited Paris, Amsterdam, Verona, Venice, and even Berlin before returning to London, which they'd reached about the same time Sam reached Edinburgh. They too had found their ship home from Glasgow commandeered and later sailings either booked or canceled; they too had boarded the *Athenia* as a last resort. After the torpedo struck, he and his friend had managed to stay together in one of the last and most crowded lifeboats, which was also the most unlucky—the one that had swung too close to the *Knute Nelson* and been crushed by its propellers.

"We dove into the water," the student said, "my friend and I. We dove and then we swam until we found a plank to hang on to. After a while we were picked up by another lifeboat. By then the *Southern Cross* was near us, so we rowed there. And then we got too close to the back of that . . ."

As his voice trailed away, Duncan, who had moved closer, said, "That wasn't the boat . . . ?"

The young man nodded, looking over at Axel and Duncan, then down at the deck, as if embarrassed that others had already heard the story and that some had seen the boat overturned.

"My friend," he said. "My friend—by the time the crew from the *Southern Cross* reached us, he was gone."

How could anyone be so unlucky? Not one but two lifeboats wrecked beneath him, his friend by his side through the torpedoing, through the first lifeboat's destruction, only to be lost. Sam closed his eyes. The ship rolled beneath him, a long, slow movement that made him dizzy. A hand touched his: Axel?

Bessie, Sam saw, when he opened his eyes. "Are you all right?" she asked.

"The whiskey," Sam said faintly.

"Let me get you some water," she said, burrowing through the crowd. Duncan came up on Sam's other side and poked his shoulder. Jovially, stupidly, looking exactly the same as he had all week—the new supplies had meant nothing to him—he said, "Too much to drink?"

Where had Axel gone?

Duncan stopped smiling. "You don't look very well."

"*Now* you worry about me?" Sam said.

An odd look crossed Duncan's face. "What went on at the

congress—that's work. I don't agree with your work; I want it buried. Doesn't mean I want *you* buried. Until you came over the side of this ship, when I thought you might have drowned, I felt—"

"Oh, please," Sam said.

"You're impossible," said Duncan. He pushed past Sam and toward Harold and George. Then, finally, Axel reappeared, his face concerned and his hand stretched toward Sam.

"It's all right," he said quietly. "It's all right. It wasn't as bad as all that."

"What wasn't?" Sam asked stupidly.

"When our boat overturned, under the stern of the *Southern Cross*—I saw you turn pale when that young man was speaking, the one we'd pulled from the water earlier, with his friend. I knew you must be thinking of me, what had happened to me and how much worse it might have been. But it wasn't so terrible, not really. I was in the water for a while but I didn't know I was hurt, I couldn't even feel the gash on my head. And I had an oar to cling to, and it wasn't too long before the crewmen from the *Southern Cross* found me and got me aboard. And then once I got here, and Duncan tracked me down, he arranged everything. You mustn't worry so about me."

How was he only now learning for sure what had happened to Axel? If they'd had time alone together, if they'd been able to talk . . . why hadn't Axel ever come to *him?* That night on the water, he'd scanned every boat they approached for Axel's face. Then, it hadn't mattered that they very seldom saw each other, that since Sam's time in Russia—no, before that, even—since Axel's marriage, perhaps, or since Sam had lost that first job and Axel hadn't been able to help him, they had drifted apart. He'd come to the meeting in Edinburgh hoping to repair this, tracking Axel through the corridors and cocktail parties like a devoted beagle, but although they'd had pleasant moments and caught each other up on the trivia of their lives, they'd never had the one, real, deep conversation Sam had been missing for so many years. And when Duncan attacked him so vigorously, Axel had not defended him. He hadn't supported Duncan—but he had not, in public, stood up for Sam. Instead, afterward, he'd pulled Sam toward a bench beneath a holly tree and questioned him closely about his results. Then he said—Sam felt this simultaneously as a blessing and a dismissal—that the work itself seemed promising. But why, Axel scolded, would he expose it to the world at such an early stage! If he would only stop speculating in public . . .

"That's what happened to you?" Sam said now. "That night in the boat?" It wasn't so much what changed in the environment that altered a living organism; it was the *when*. A question of timing. When in the course of development does the event arrive that initiates the cascade of changes? "That's what happened?" he repeated.

"You knew that," Axel said. "Didn't you? I assumed . . ."

That Duncan had told him, Sam understood. That Duncan had relayed to him whatever Axel, stretched out on his berth, the bandage stuck to his oozing wound, had said. Axel must have told the story of his night on the water to Duncan, who lay on the floor in the place where Sam should have been. Perhaps he'd also relied on Duncan for whatever image he had of Sam's own night; he'd never asked Sam. "Duncan," Sam said feebly.

"I know," Axel said. "Really, I *do* know—he can be so exasperating sometimes, he probably told you more than he should have, he's always too dramatic. And he forgets how attached we are. I don't think it even occurred to him that you might be upset by hearing that something bad happened to me. Any more than he seemed to understand, in Edinburgh, how much he'd hurt me by attacking you."

Sam stared at him blankly. "But Duncan," he said, "the way you are with him . . ."

"I do the best I can," Axel said. "You must have found yourself in similar situations with students. You know how sometimes you have to treat the one you actually feel least close to as the favorite, just so he won't lose confidence entirely?"

"I do," Sam said miserably. Not that he'd ever felt treated as a favorite, but he knew what Axel meant: he'd always acted more kindly toward Sam than he really felt, so that Sam wouldn't be too crushed to go on.

"I've always had to do that with Duncan," Axel said. His bandage, unpleasantly stained, had shifted farther back on his head. "I still do, I find, in certain situations. And here—what could I do? He wanted so badly to take care of me."

"You gave him his start," Sam said, not knowing what he meant.

"It's a good thing I can count on you to understand," Axel said. "You're strong enough to go your own way. That's part of what gets you into such trouble. And part of why your work is so interesting."

The next morning, still a day and a half out from Halifax, Axel and five other passengers were transferred to one of the cutters, which had excellent hospital facilities. The wound on his head wasn't healing properly; the coast guard doctor wanted to debride and resuture it without further delay. Sam, left behind with Duncan and Harold and George, could do nothing but wave goodbye and hope that they'd find each other later.

At the docks, a huge crowd greeted them, Red Cross nurses and immigration officials, family members of some of the survivors, local citizens who wanted to help, reporters from various papers: they were big news. Theirs had been the first ship sunk and theirs the first Canadian and American casualties; when the torpedo struck the *Athenia,* not even half a day had passed since Britain and Germany had gone to war. Nurses moved in to tend to the wounded; volunteers brought coffee and sandwiches; officials herded them into the immigration quarters, where they arranged baths and offered clean clothes. Scores of reporters moved in as well, eager for stories—what had they seen, what had they felt?—and then all the passengers began to talk at once, a hopeless tangle.

How could Sam be surprised when Duncan stepped forward? Of course it was Duncan who, never having set foot on the *Athenia,* still somehow managed to simplify, generalize, organize the scattered impressions. The reporters turned toward him, relaxing, already making notes: so much easier to follow his linear narrative, spangled with brief portraits of the survivors and vivid details of the crossing! He'd listened closely, Sam saw, to accounts of what he hadn't experienced himself. Bits of Axel's story flashed by, along with elements of the art student's, the plant physiologist's, Bessie's, and more. Bessie looked startled, as did some of the others, but what Duncan recounted wasn't untrue; it just didn't match much of what Sam felt, or what he knew to be important. If Duncan were to tell the story of Sam's working life it would, he knew, be similarly skewed—yet who knew him better than Duncan? Who had been with him for as much of the way?

Only Axel, who, leaving the *City of Flint* for the cutter, had held his hand to his stained bandage, looked crossly at the doctor, and said, "Really, I'm *fine.* I don't know why you want to move me like this. I'd rather stay here with my friends." And then had gestured toward Duncan and Sam, on either side of him.

Reading *The O. Henry Prize Stories 2013*

The Jurors on Their Favorites

Our jurors read the twenty O. Henry Prize Stories in a blind manuscript. Each story appears in the same type and format with no attribution of the magazine that published it or the author's name. The jurors don't consult the series editor or one another. Although they write their essays without knowledge of authors' names, the names may be inserted into the essay later for the sake of clarity.   *—LF*

Lauren Groff on "Your Duck Is My Duck" by Deborah Eisenberg

A short story, done right, is a ferocious creature: razor-toothed and bristling and deceptively small for all its power. Think wolverine. Think barracuda. A reader, finding herself alone in a room with a great short story, should feel thrilled, unbalanced, alive.

Such intensity is not for everyone; readers, we are told, have a hard time with short stories, preferring the long slow waltz of novels to the story's grapple and throw. A writer of stories will be told this a hundred times, by publishing houses and book clubs and friends and even family members who are a little bit abashed that they haven't read the writer's own stories. *It's okay,* we say, and shrug, because for the most part we are meek people who have a horror of unwritten confrontations, and only later do we shuffle off to our little word-hovels and weep.

Any fierce lover and defender of the story form should take such statements personally. Frankly, it is not okay. One: the story is not a lesser form. It is merely a smaller form. Two: since when are readers some monolithic block of zombies who have no say in what they like? Maybe readers simply haven't been exposed to the story geniuses rampant on the earth these days, people like George Saunders and Lorrie Moore and Alice Munro and Mavis Gallant and—cripes almighty!—William Trevor.

Or, for that matter, Deborah Eisenberg, whose "Your Duck Is My Duck" was a fever dream from which, a dozen reads later, I have yet to awaken. We judges are given the twenty stories in this anthology to read blind, which means we read the stories without the authors' names attached. But if you love short stories passionately, you read them passionately and in great quantities, and if you read them passionately and in great quantities, you begin to be able to see the individual writer's imprint on her story from her very first words. It was impossible to read "The Summer People," and not know that it was a story by the astounding Kelly Link, or to read "The Particles," and not know that the author was Andrea Barrett, who so often electrifies science in her fiction, or to read "Leaving Maverley," and not understand that the sharp sentences and elegant timeline could only have come from Alice Munro. There were a few among my favorites that I didn't identify immediately, the moving and memorable "The History of Girls," "Two Opinions," and "Pérou," by Ayşe Papatya Bucak, Joan Silber, and Lily Tuck, respectively. When I first read the collection, I simply couldn't choose from among the half-dozen stories that blew my mind. So I put the collection away. I went off to London. I locked the door of my subconscious and let the stories fight it out, a roomful of wolverines, all sleek and snarling and gorgeous.

In the end, "Your Duck Is My Duck" is the one I saw when I opened the door again. It had stayed alive, and, by staying alive, it had changed me. The story bears Eisenberg's signature from the first words, her brittle humor and world-weariness and the astounding grace of her lines. She writes: "Way back—oh, not all that long ago, actually, just a couple of years, but back before I'd gotten a glimpse of the gears and levers and pulleys that dredge the future up from the earth's core to its surface—I was going to a lot of parties." *See what she does!* I want to shout. *See Deborah Eisenberg's brilliance!* Three words in, and our narrator is already contradicting herself; a few more, and we see her oddly self-puncturing bombast; then, boom, the final clause, like the punchline to a joke we won't quite understand until the end of the piece. Already, we've been whipped like a top, and we'll be jittery and teetering, just like the narrator, for the rest of the story.

But what is most thrilling about "Your Duck Is My Duck," what makes it so deeply "Eisenberg-y," is how seductive and light the story feels for most of its gallop. *Okeydoke,* we think at first, *this is a story about self-obsessed rich people,* and for most writers, that would be enough. But Eisenberg is canny and wise, and we come to understand at the end how the story is about so much more, about everything, about the end of an empire and the obscenity of great wealth and millenarian anxieties and the insanity of creating art in the face of the horrors that Eisenberg hints are to come. This is the kind of work that is alive, and that, in turn, sparks other stories to life. This is art. This is the kind of story you want to press into the hands of short-story doubters, because it is its own best defense of its form.

Lauren Groff was born in Cooperstown, New York. She is the author of the novel *The Monsters of Templeton* and the story collection *Delicate Edible Birds.* Her fiction has appeared in *The New Yorker, The Atlantic Monthly,* and *Ploughshares,* among other publications, and has been anthologized in the Pushcart Prize anthology and two editions of *The Best American Short Stories.* Her second novel, *Arcadia,* was published in 2012. She lives in Gainesville, Florida.

Edith Pearlman on "The Summer People" by Kelly Link

I have a taste for the inexplicable and the semisurreal, in literature and in life, and so I warned myself when I began reading these twenty stories (which turned out to be as masterful as expected) to be wary of indulging that taste. And two realistic stories did attract me. One is "Sugarcane" by Derek Palacio, whose protagonist, a doctor in post-Batista Cuba, is obsessed with sugar itself, which represents all that is sweet and rare and addictive and ultimately monotonous. The story is about abstractions like love, loyalty, and deception. It also reveals particulars of life on the island: the annual burning of sugarcane fields to chase out vermin, the saddling and calming of a mule, and a nearly fatal baby delivery, which, like the story containing it, lingers in the memory for a long time.

In "The Visitor" by Asako Serizawa, set in Japan immediately after World War II, there are only two characters—a woman and a demobilized soldier—but the woman's absent son, Yasushi, who fought alongside the visiting soldier, is also achingly present. Yasushi's history seeps into the conversation and reminiscences and gives the story urgency. In seemingly straightforward sentences (with deft side metaphors, allusions, and unexpected adjectives) the story behaves like a scorched flower, slowly dropping its browned florets to reveal the next circle of unpleasant facts or perhaps fabrications or perhaps distortions, always deepening our sense of war's corruption of its warriors. Another memorable tale.

But in the end, despite these worthy temptations, I recognized as my favorite "The Summer People" by Kelly Link. Its setting is an unnamed semirural area of woods, waterfalls, pastures, meadows, and hollows where rich people have summer houses and the local population serves them. The teenaged heroine, Fran, abandoned by her mother, neglected by her father, laid low by the flu and dosing herself with NyQuil, feverishly takes care of summer houses and shops for summer people. She acquires a fascinated sidekick. Two unsupervised adolescents accomplishing adult tasks tickle our interest, especially Fran with her ungrammatical backwoods locutions; her kindness; the intelligence she isn't sure she has. So far, so realistic.

The particular summer people of the title, though, are not rich vacationers—they are a seldom-glimpsed crowd who live all year round in a house in the wooded mountain, where they make wind-up toys and other devices, and also dispense whiskey and medicine. They do need services, though, and they will not release whoever is currently taking care of them and their premises (the caretaker is Fran, just now). BE BOLD, BE BOLD, BUT NOT TOO BOLD, warns a sign within the house.

This is a fairy tale, except that no one is heroic or wise or cruel—not even Fran's alcoholic father and his crooked cronies. There is trickery; there are spooky goings on; there's a pair of magical binoculars. But *be not too bold* could be said by any anxious parent you know, and NyQuil can be bought in your local drugstore. These things anchor the fantastic to the real.

Yes, a fairy tale. It supplies Whys, not Becauses; endings, not wrappings-up; and it dispenses with that sine qua non of realism, motivation. (Conversely, "Sugarcane" lets us in on the doctor's need for sugar, "The Visit" the mother's ambivalent search for truth). But "who knows what makes any of us do what we do?" the poet Amy Clampitt bravely wrote—an insight that writing workshops might keep in mind. Clampitt could have been referring to the characters in "The Summer People." And who knows what made its writer create this tale? To gladden my heart, maybe.

Edith Pearlman's short stories have appeared in many prize anthologies, and in 2011, she was the recipient of the PEN/Malamud Award for excellence in short fiction, honoring her four collections of stories: *Vaquita, Love Among the Greats, How To Fall,* and *Binocular Vision,* which was a finalist for a National Book Award, the Story Prize, and a Los Angeles Times Book

Prize. It received awards from the National Book Critics Circle and the Boston Authors Club, as well as the Edward Lewis Wallant Award given by the University of Hartford. Edith Pearlman lives in Massachusetts.

Jim Shepard on "The Particles" by Andrea Barrett

Although it begins with as flamboyant a narrative hook as you're likely to find—our hero barely able to swim and thrashing about the cold Atlantic alongside a ship that's just been torpedoed—Andrea Barrett's "The Particles" at first seems as unassuming as its main character, the hardworking if moony and mopey Sam. Some of that restraint seems to be generated by the story's expert management of its macro and micro modes: as it processes along, its length making the reader wonder where the short story stops and the novella begins, it unfolds, in turn, the opening of the Second World War, the modern history of genetics, and the dismal and mostly on-hold chronicle of its protagonist's emotional life.

Even as the story never loses sight of the longing and disappointment at the heart of Sam's relationship with his old friend and teacher, Axel, it provides a visceral (and really, epic, if such a term can be applied to the quotidian life of a scientist such as Sam's) sense of his lifelong absorption in science itself. The story renders unforgettably that experience of falling in love with experimental science as if "tumbling down a well," the voices of other kids outside diminishing and then silent. It allows us to feel the exhilaration of concepts made visible. It's marvelous on that moment when the whole world starts to shimmer under the spell of that intensity of curiosity. It even pulls off the nearly impossible feat of seducing us into imagining fruit flies as fascinating. (In that regard, I'm now with Sam. That courting male who holds out his wing and dances right and then left before embracing his bride: "who wouldn't love *that*?")

The story's wonderful too, in its offhanded way, on just where the politicization of science leads us: its account of Trofim Lysenko's dismissal of all of formal genetics at a conference in 1936 in the Soviet Union—"A theory of heredity, to be correct, must promise not just the power to understand nature but the power to change it"—resonates uncomfortably with anyone who's been unfortunate enough to follow the climate-change debate in the United States over the last ten years.

There's something unassuming and appealing, too, in the way in which this world's judgments are apportioned: "In the distance a shape, which might have been the guilty submarine, seemed to shift position." The sufferings of the many are rendered with a distance that seems both compassionate and clear-eyed: "A little string of emptied lifeboats tossed in the swell beside the tanker, the boat closest to the stern still packed with people." And lives are lost almost out at the very edges of our vision: struggling figures, too small to identify, dotting the water in the distance after their lifeboat's been tipped, or an old woman caught in the gap between her lifeboat and a destroyer's hull, a space that disappears when the boats collide.

But for all the suffering around him, the perversity of Sam's inner stubbornness never recedes. Nothing he experiences—his lost love Ellen, his professional failures and humiliations, the Stalinist purges he just evades, or the trauma of the torpedoed *Athenia* itself—has the force of his estrangement from Axel. But of course his primary disappointment is with himself. Much of the story's power comes from its evocation of how, for all of Sam's humility and gratitude for what he *has* been able to experience, life has often seemed to him to have been centered elsewhere: wherever his mentor—and with him, the promise of scientific intimacy, and the white-hot core of genetics—resided. No matter what contrary evidence the story so poignantly provides.

Jim Shepard was born in Bridgeport, Connecticut, and is the author of six novels, including most recently *Project X,* and four story collections, the most recent of which is *You Think That's*

Bad: Stories. His third collection, *Like You'd Understand, Anyway*, was a finalist for a National Book Award and won the Story Prize. *Project X* won the 2005 Library of Congress/Massachusetts Book Award for fiction, as well as an Alex Award from the American Library Association. His short fiction has appeared in, among other magazines, *Harper's, McSweeney's, The Paris Review, The Atlantic Monthly, Esquire, DoubleTake, The New Yorker, Granta, Zoetrope: All-Story,* and *Playboy,* and he was a columnist on film for the magazine *The Believer.* Four of his stories have been chosen for *The Best American Short Stories* and one for a Pushcart Prize. He's won an Artist Fellowship from the Massachusetts Cultural Council and a Guggenheim Fellowship. He teaches at Williams College and lives in Williamstown, Massachusetts.

Writing *The O. Henry Prize Stories 2013*

The Writers on Their Work

Donald Antrim, "He Knew"

This story, like most everything I've written, short or long, began with not much more than a thought, an idea that was not an idea at all, really, but a kind of simple picture of something—in this case, the picture that came to me was of two people, a man and his younger wife, making their way up Madison Avenue on a bright spring day. Right away it becomes apparent that both are compromised, to a degree, by psychiatric issues, and a day spent shopping seems for them to be a pleasure and a distraction from whatever troubles them.

The story, the *writing* of it (as, for me, the writing of any story), progressed slowly, over many months. In "He Knew," narrative movement was guided by the journey up the avenue. Years ago, when I was beginning to write my first novel, I made it a rule that I would move forward in the manuscript without the help of an outline or fixed notions about the story as it developed; the program was to go line by line and page by page, and called for following, adhering to, and extending the accumulating logic of what had been started and written so far. My goal was to have pleasure in the writing, and to make something out of nothing, as it were. And I've come to recognize, as I've worked over years, that, for me, invention and experience tend to exist more or less as subsets of each other. This is absolutely true of "He Knew." Perhaps what I am searching for, ultimately, is something in the quality of the relationship between Stephen and Alice—their love for each other, their compatible incompatibility, their shared history of breakdown, their fate or their destiny—and, I hope, the love that bonds them is enough felt by their author to come through, as well, to a reader.

Donald Antrim was born in Sarasota, Florida. He is the author of three novels, *Elect Mr. Robinson For a Better World, The Hundred Brothers,* and *The Verificationist;* and a memoir, *The Afterlife.* He contributes fiction and nonfiction to *The New Yorker,* and is a past recipient of awards from, among others, the John Simon Guggenheim Memorial Foundation and the National Endowment for the Arts. He lives in Brooklyn, New York.

Tash Aw, "Sail"

The story has its roots in a passing observation: I was in Hong Kong—in Central, the financial district—waiting for a friend in a café. It was lunchtime and the place was full of elegantly dressed men and women, the air rich with a buzzy testosterone-fueled optimism. At the adjacent table there was a man in a suit who looked like any other in the room. But there was something about him that (I thought) suggested that he, like me, was out of place. His shoes were a bit too shiny; his suit and printed silk tie ostentatiously screamed *Success.* He was looking at a brochure for a yacht, constantly putting it back into his briefcase before taking it out again, as if it made him anxious. When he spoke on his mobile phone I noticed he spoke Mandarin with a northern accent. But then my friend arrived and I forgot all about that man and his yacht.

Years later, I was on the Normandy coast, watching sailboats head out to sea; there were a number of them out that day—it was part of a race or a regatta of some sort, I think. And as I stood on the cliffs watching the white sails of the yachts billow and tilt as they ventured out into the Channel, I suddenly remembered that man from Hong Kong. It was the inherent loneliness of these yachts in the vastness of the ocean that recalled that man and his anxieties (or at least the anxieties I had attributed to him). Without knowing it, I had carried him around in my head for years, and when I sat down to recreate his story, the pieces of his life fell into place swiftly, as if I knew him intimately.

Tash Aw was born in Taipei to Malaysian parents and grew up in Kuala Lumpur, Malaysia. *The Harmony Silk Factory* won a Whitbread Award and the Commonwealth Writers' Prize for best first novel, was longlisted for the Man Booker Prize, and has been translated into twenty-three languages. His latest novel is *Five Star Billionaire*. He lives in London.

Andrea Barrett, "The Particles"

In 2008 I started a story called "The Ether of Space," about a middle-aged widow with a passion for astronomy, struggling to integrate the news confirming Einstein's theory of general relativity with older theories about the ether of space. Near the end of the story, her young son, Sam, jumps into the foreground—which made me realize the story's deeper intentions, and also confirmed my desire to explore Sam's character as a grown man. Then I began work on what would become "The Particles." Knowing that Sam, although different from his mother in many ways, would also be drawn to some field of science, I chose genetics because I'm interested in that field's early history. The famous "Fly Room" at Columbia seemed like a natural place for Sam— but as I got to know that world better, positioning him near (rather than exactly *at*) the center of this exciting new field was more intriguing. I wrote eight or nine versions before learning that several scientists attending the 7th International Conference on Genetics in Edinburgh had been aboard the *Athenia,* while others had been on the *City of Flint.*

Pure serendipity; I would have been a fool to resist it (although, for a while, I did). Then I gave in and rewrote and restructured everything. As a result of those choices, the nature of friendship—equal or unequal, passionate or cool, scientific or personal or both, envious or loving (or both)—became crucial to the story.

Andrea Barrett was born in Boston, Massachusetts. She is the author of six novels, most recently *The Air We Breathe,* and three collections of short fiction: *Ship Fever,* which received a National Book Award; *Servants of the Map,* a finalist for the Pulitzer Prize; and *Archangel* (forthcoming). She lives in western Massachusetts and teaches at Williams College.

Ann Beattie, "Anecdotes"

How *did* those pink Uggs come stomping in, how did I write a story that contains the word *Astroturf*? There are many stories hidden in this one that I might have reported, straightforwardly. When writing, though, I get bedazzled by details. Once the necklace was lapis (I had to envision something, but the reader knows it's probably not really lapis, right?), William Butler Yeats's "Lapis Lazuli" began to figure in—especially the poet's tone. I see the little warrior on horseback, at the end of my story, as a lesser version, indeed, of the carved scene Yeats contemplated. In retrospect, I might have had Lucia speak about the poem, or perhaps had her teacher-daughter do so, but I kept it more or less hidden, almost a throwaway: its displacement is all. In the time elapsed, what has the wife thought of the broken necklace sent to her anonymously? Whatever she thought, what does she make of the information she gets much later, which is a lie? I hope the story happens inside the mind of many characters, even if I couldn't fully write those stories.

· · ·

Ann Beattie grew up in Washington, D.C. She has written nine story collections, is a member of the American Academy of Arts and Letters, and in 2011 was the recipient of Bard College's Mary McCarthy Award. She lives in Maine.

L. Annette Binder, "Lay My Head"

This story started with the character of Angela, who—like me—was on her way back to visit Colorado after many years away. I thought about Angela for a long time before starting to write the story, about her return to the place where she grew up and how she knew she wouldn't be leaving again. I'd also been thinking a lot about German fairy tales at the time—the fairy tales my parents told me when I was little—and one in particular kept coming back to me. The story of Lucky Hans, who gradually sets aside all his possessions because he sees them as the burdens they are.

These two threads wove together in unexpected ways when I wrote the story. As the draft progressed, Angela stayed quiet. Normally that would worry me. Your characters need to be active, most people would say. They can't just be still. But this story felt different. Angela was looking at the world and trying to mark it all down, to take it with her, and she had no need for words.

L. Annette Binder was born in Germany and grew up in Colorado Springs. She is a graduate of Harvard College, Harvard Law School, and the Programs in Writing at the University of California, Irvine. Her fiction has been performed on NPR's *Selected Shorts*, and has appeared in the 2013 Pushcart Prize anthology, *One Story, American Short Fiction, The Southern Review,* and elsewhere. Her story collection, *Rise,* was published in 2012. She lives in Boston and New Hampshire.

Ayşe Papatya Bucak, "The History of Girls"

I have a Turkish father and an American mother, and I was born in Turkey, but raised in the United States. As a result, for a long time I hesitated to write about Turkishness, as it's something I've experienced only indirectly. But then I realized I could write about Turkishness in the way that it comes to me, popping up prairie-dog-style into my American life. This happens largely through stories: my mother's memories, my father's metaphors, news items, folktales . . .

A few years ago, the *New York Times* covered an explosion at a girls' school in Eastern Turkey, and initially the cause of the explosion was undetermined. But my mother immediately said, "Of course, it was the gas. It was always the gas." And it turned out she was right. I was struck by the sadness of this—the avoidability. When I began the story, which I always knew would center on the girls in the explosion, I realized I had created a rather difficult scenario to write—my characters were immobile and in the dark; some of them were dead. All they could do was talk to each other. But as is often the way, through writing I figured some things out. In drafting the dialogue, I was reminded of conversations I'd had in the dark as a girl, in the twilight hour of slumber parties when the host's parents have made you climb into your sleeping bags and turn out the lights, but haven't yet come in and yelled at you to stop giggling and go to sleep. Those were some of the most intimate and funny conversations I've ever had. When I thought about my characters' backstory, including the realities of shared life at a boarding school, I realized these girls had been speaking to one another in the dark for years.

Celine's Easternized fairy tale came directly from my father's way of telling stories, which involves an incredible amalgamation of Eastern, Western, ancient, and modern influences. The first-person plural point of view was something I had been wanting to try and that seemed to fit the situation. (One thing I love about teaching is that the close study of other writers and constant focus on craft encourage me to try techniques I might not otherwise.) Originally the story was first-person plural all the way through, but with some help from my two most treasured readers, I realized it needed a stronger sense of progression, which could come from a narrowing in point of view.

Also, I once was terrified by having a hawk's shadow pass over me, as well as by the sight of an unripened potato.

Ayşe Papatya Bucak was born in Istanbul. Her work has been published in *The Iowa Review, Creative Nonfiction,* and elsewhere. She directs the MFA program at Florida Atlantic University and lives in South Florida.

Deborah Eisenberg, "Your Duck Is My Duck"

I was out of context, away from home, in Marfa, Texas, for a good long time, and even the ones inside you who look over your shoulder while you're working and roll their eyes couldn't find me. So I could do anything I felt like doing, and I felt like having a little fun.

It's always impossible for me to remember how a piece of fiction started or developed—for me writing fiction is almost invariably just a very long, very awkward process of discovering that whatever I wrote the day before was an error, being repelled by the error, repeating the steps, and waiting for what's behind all the errors to be disclosed and thicken up into something that has an intent and a shape. And this story was no exception.

In short, I cannot for the life of me remember the specifics of how it grew. I do have various friends—generally struggling artists (something I also consider myself to be)—who sometimes go to stay with wealthy friends of theirs, friends who have spectacular houses in spectacular places. And I suppose I was thinking of them and thinking how happy I was to be on my own in Marfa. And there's something uncanny about a really, really good puppet show—I always envy people who work in media that put at their disposal contrapuntal lines, like music and visuals in addition to words on a flat piece of paper.

Certainly, when I got around to doing what I think of as the post-final draft—that is, to making all the changes I must make after I've thought a particular thing was finished but it turns out I have to confront the question of what the thing is and what it ought to be—I saw that many of my preoccupations and worries were reflected in it: the ravages of climate change, including the growing populations of climate refugees; the worldwide plight of the embattled and looted middle class; the co-optation and trivialization of art; and the relationships—especially in regard to the use of resources—between the middle class, the looters, the artists, and the new wretched of the earth.

Deborah Eisenberg grew up in a suburb of Chicago. She is a MacArthur Fellow and teaches at Columbia University. *The Collected Stories of Deborah Eisenberg* won the PEN/Faulkner Award in 2011. She lives in New York City.

Samar Farah Fitzgerald, "Where Do You Go?"

Usually I begin with an image I'm trying to bring into focus, or a mood I'm straining to pinpoint. But this time the story began more concretely with an anecdote my mother had told me. Several years ago, my parents sold our house in New Jersey and relocated to a nearby townhome. The day after the movers unloaded their belongings, an elderly neighbor queried my mother about cigarette stubs in her driveway. Neither of my parents smoke, so she assumed the butts belonged to the movers, but the old man didn't seem appeased, and my mother felt watched and unwelcomed. Shortly after, a relative paid my parents a visit. At one point the relative stepped out to smoke and was approached by the same neighbor, this time stealthily seeking to bum a cigarette. The accuser turned out to be a moocher, presumably under orders by his wife not to smoke. As I wrote the story over a period of two years, I realized my interest in this little incident had to do with the limits of intimacy—the secrets we keep from the most loving partners and the ultimate experience we must face alone.

But the first draft, which I completed in graduate school, included a loyal re-creation of my mother's telling: old man finds cigarette butts, queries neighbors accusingly, and later exposes himself as a smoker. When I shared the story with my workshop, almost every reader said this element in particular, the sequence of events that "actually happened," felt contrived. In later drafts, I dismantled the anecdote, but by then the setting and characters were more fully formed, including the grumpy Gordon Lippincott. My mother's anecdote had functioned as a kind of scaffolding for my own story. It was an early lesson for me in how reality both can and can't serve fiction.

Samar Farah Fitzgerald was born in Athens, Greece, and grew up in northern New Jersey. She was the recipient of a 2011–2012 Artist Fellowship from the Virginia Commission for the Arts. Her stories have appeared in *The Southern Review, Story Quarterly Online, The Carolina Quarterly, Avery,* and *The L Magazine.* She completed her MFA at the University of Wisconsin, where she received the August Derleth Prize and the Friends of Creative Writing Award. She lives in Staunton, Virginia, and teaches creative writing at James Madison University.

Ruth Prawer Jhabvala, "Aphrodisiac"

The origin of this story was not an incident or a character but a situation—one that has often fascinated me: someone's desire for another turning into an obsession that destroys all of his nobler qualities and higher striving. However, there is nothing of that in Naina and Kishen's early encounter, when she moves into his family home as his brother's young bride. She is high-spirited and playful, and Kishen is enchanted with her and wants to spend all his time in her company, more and more neglecting his earlier ambition of writing the Great Indian Novel.

As the years pass, his obsession grows rather than diminishes, even though she becomes obese with childbirth and suckling the infants clinging to her great breasts. Something primeval enters her personality, physically present in the old servant she has brought from their more backward part of the country. This crone emanates the atmosphere of their desert home and its purdah quarters where previous generations of women lived locked up, honing their secret potions and spells to use against the world. Sensing all this as part of Naina's personality, Kishen's obsession with her is no longer an enchantment but an enchainment, against which he has no strength left to struggle. Instead, as the situation changes and his mother begins to sicken and die, Naina takes on an ever more sinister manifestation: as the goddess of destruction, blood-dripping, death-dealing, Kali herself. Maybe India herself, feared and adored by those who have become enthralled by her. I have to admit that none of this came to me consciously but evolved within the situation of the story, so by the time I had finished writing (as often happens to me at the end of a story) I looked at it and understood: "So that's what it was all about."

Ruth Prawer Jhabvala was born in Germany in 1927 and escaped to England with her parents in 1939. She went to school and college in London, where she met and married the Indian architect C. S. H. Jhabvala. They lived in India from 1951 to 1975. Her first novel was published in 1955. Twelve more novels were published, including *Heat and Dust* and *A Backward Place,* and six collections of short stories. From 1962 on, she wrote most of the screenplays for the films of Merchant Ivory. Jhabvala lived mostly in New York, with frequent return visits to India.

———

While *The O. Henry Prize Stories 2013* was in production, we learned that Ruth Prawer Jhabvala had died on April 3, 2013, in New York. We will miss her stories and her tonic view of mankind. —*Laura Furman*

Nalini Jones, "Tiger"

We were a houseful of allergies when my brother, sister, and I were kids, and when I wrote the earliest version of this story, I'd been thinking about the desperate shape our longing for animals used to take. We could not simply admire the herd of goats we encountered one summer in Rhode Island; we must clearly chase the poor beasts from one end of the field to another in our determination to befriend them. *We loved the goats! Soon the goats would love us!* Surely, if we were patient and spoke in soothing voices—a *Secret Garden*–derived method we trusted entirely—my sister and I could train a goat to stand still while we hoisted our brother onto its back.

Occasional visits to India offered all sorts of other unsuitable animal attachments. We did once fall in love with a family of stray cats, one of many affections that marked us as foreigners.

I've now become so wholly loyal to my dog that simply remembering such devotion to cats was a taxing imaginative exercise—so much so that in the first version of this story I neglected to do very much with the people. The whole narrative was overrun by cats. The editor of my story collection very wisely advised me to put it aside.

A few years later, I picked up the story again because I was thinking about one of its characters, Essie. In the novel I'm writing, her habit of addressing people who aren't there takes a strange turn, and I found I needed to know how all that began. I hadn't intended to rewrite the story; at first I was just revisiting some of the passages to see what they suggested about Essie at that point in her history. It was a consultation, nothing more. But then I began to rework a few pages, trying to learn more about her so that I could carry that new understanding into the pages of the novel. As I kept exploring, the story seemed to rearrange itself, taking on a new shape. And eventually I realized it wasn't part of the novel at all; it was becoming something else entirely.

· · ·

Nalini Jones was born in Rhode Island and grew up in Ohio and New England. She is the author of *What You Call Winter,* a story collection, and her fiction has appeared in *Ontario Review* and *Elle India,* among other publications. Her essays have been anthologized in *AIDS Sutra* and *Freud's Blind Spot.* In 2012, she won a Pushcart Prize and a fellowship from the National Endowment for the Arts. Jones teaches in the graduate writing program at Fairfield University and lives in Connecticut.

Kelly Link, "The Summer People"

I have had a hard time figuring out what to say about "The Summer People." I wrote it during a period in which my two-year-old daughter (born at twenty-four weeks) had recently been released from the hospital for the first time, a period in which we were still living away from home, in order to stay close to her doctors and Boston Children's Hospital. I suppose it makes sense that this is a story about parents and children, about caretakers and about a longing to leave the place where you are. It has all sorts of borrowed things in it: among others, a title from a Shirley Jackson story.

What I thought about, as I was writing, was the overlap between folklore about fairies and stories of alien encounters. I was writing at an intersection of two genres, young adult and steampunk, and I wanted this to be a story in which someone was making beautiful clockwork objects for mysterious purposes. (Another metaphor, I suppose, for fiction in general. The writer Howard Waldrop says that all stories function as metaphors for the act of writing.) Most of my stories come out of various combinations of genres and genre conventions.

Kelly Link is the author of three collections, most recently *Pretty Monsters*. She has edited various anthologies, and with her husband, Gavin J. Grant, she has run Small Beer Press since 2001 and publishes the occasional zine *Lady Churchill's Rosebud Wrist-*

let. She received her MFA from the University of North Carolina at Greensboro, and has taught at Columbia University, Stonecoast, Smith College, and the Clarion Workshops. She lives in Northampton, Massachusetts.

George McCormick, "The Mexican"

This story began with another story: William Kittredge's excellent "Stone Boat." In it he writes, "Orange blossoms had smelled yellow at twilight." When I first read that sentence I identified with its synesthesia, and immediately I began to imagine a world in which such an observation wouldn't simply be "nice," but actually matter.

I read Kittredge's story on a Thursday and by the next morning, writing between classes in an empty blue book a student had left behind, I began "The Mexican." On Saturday I wrote to the story's end, on Sunday I typed it up. Later that week I gave a draft of it to a couple of friends, who read it and offered several cogent suggestions. I made the corrections, and by Thursday—one week after I'd read "Stone Boat"—I had a story of my own. However, what I don't want to convey here is that just because the story came *quickly* that it also came *easily.* It did not. Nothing written with care comes easily.

George McCormick is the author of the story collection *Salton Sea.* His fiction has appeared in *Willow Springs, CutBank*, *Santa Monica Review,* and *Hayden's Ferry Review.* He is a recipient of a Constance Saltonstall Foundation for the Arts individual artist grant, and he works in the Department of English and Foreign Languages at Cameron University. He divides his time between Lawton, Oklahoma, and Cooke City, Montana.

Melinda Moustakis, "They Find the Drowned"

I've spent a lot of time fishing in Alaska with my uncle, Sonny, who tells amazing stories. So I'd always wanted to put a story he told me about a woman who saves a drowning moose on paper in some way. I often combine stories I've heard while fishing on the river with scientific research and the tall-tale aspect of letting fiction stretch, the way a good story stretches over time—how that decent-sized salmon you reeled in one lovely day becomes, in the series of retellings, a monster of a catch in the middle of a blizzard. Usually, this combining process yields a story that is finished within a few months. But not so with "They Find the Drowned." This story is the story that almost wasn't, in many ways, and is the result of a process that took about six years. There were numerous times I thought that this material would remain tucked away in a drawer. I had all of these pieces, these mosaic tiles of words, and it took a process of distilling and rearranging and rewriting to find the right alchemy for this modular story. I knew I had the sequence down when I finally found the title and each piece had its own arc and also fit into the overall narrative. I'd had other stories with similar structures find publication, but "They Find the Drowned" became the last unpublished story in my collection and I had mostly given up on sending it out before it was accepted by *Hobart*. Such a strange journey for a strange story, at least in my experience.

Melinda Moustakis was born in Fairbanks, Alaska, and raised in Bakersfield, California. She received her MA from the University of California, Davis, and her PhD in English and Creative Writing from Western Michigan University. Her debut collection, *Bear Down, Bear North: Alaska Stories,* won the Flannery O'Connor Award and was shortlisted for the William Saroyan International Prize for Writing. Her stories have appeared in *Alaska Quarterly Review, American Short Fiction, The Kenyon Review, New England Review,* and elsewhere. She was named a 2011 "5 Under 35" writer by the National Book Foundation and is a 2012–2013 Hodder Fellow at the Lewis Center for the Arts at Princeton University.

Alice Munro, "Leaving Maverley"

My husband's father was a night cop. He used to get some warm moments from cold nights walking the streets by ducking into the Lyceum Theatre. He was a well-read school dropout (a common thing in those days—lack of funds) and took a dim view of the plots, but had fun.

Also a World War II scandal, a married teacher leaving respectable husband for penniless young vet—somehow I just wound these up and the girl appeared—plenty of dour Christians in that (my) home town, and I went along to see what would happen to them—the preacher getting in, then out—and the two shorn creatures left at the end. Not completely shorn, though, having got along as best they could.

I have been writing stories for sixty years. For quite a while I thought that was a prelude to writing novels (when children and housework eased off). It didn't turn out to be—disappointed publishers in my wake. Then one Canadian publisher, Douglas Gibson, told me to keep writing stories and the word *novel* would never cross his lips. I did, and it didn't, and here I am at this preposterous age having the usual hellish good time, which is how you could describe writing. And so happy to be in it.

Alice Munro grew up in Wingham, Ontario, and attended the University of Western Ontario. She has published thirteen original collections of stories—*Dance of the Happy Shades; Something I've Been Meaning to Tell You; The Beggar Maid; The Moons of Jupiter; The Progress of Love; Friend of My Youth; Open Secrets; The Love of a Good Woman; Hateship, Friendship, Courtship, Loveship, Marriage; Runaway; The View from Castle Rock; Too Much Happiness;* and *Dear Life*—as well as a novel, *Lives of Girls and Women,* and *Selected Stories* collections. During her distinguished career she has been the recipient of many awards and prizes, including three of Canada's Governor General's Literary Awards and two of its Giller Prizes; England's W. H. Smith Book Award; the United

States' National Book Critics Circle Award, Rea Award for the Short Story, and Lannan Literary Award; and the Man Booker International Prize. Her stories have appeared in *The New Yorker, The Atlantic Monthly, The Paris Review,* and other publications, and her collections have been translated into thirteen languages. She lives in Clinton, Ontario, near Lake Huron.

Derek Palacio, "Sugarcane"

I have never been to Cuba. My father was born in Santiago de Cuba in 1950, but his family left the country just a few years later. "Sugarcane" mixes bits from his memory (a distant recollection of my grandfather on horseback, a family-run sugarcane plantation, strong coffee) with disparate facts culled from sporadic research (the economics of sugar production, socialized medicine, a palpable military presence). My father, like the protagonist Armando, is a surgeon, though the character is not in any way based on him. Regardless, I owe my father a debt of gratitude for letting me incorporate parts of his past into my storytelling. This piece, however, was born from a fact before being colored in by inherited memory: I'd read somewhere that during the sugarcane harvest the military would block off the roads and stand guard as the stalks were transported from field to refinery. They worried the crops would be stolen and sold on the ever-expanding black market. The idea that sugar had the potential to become an illicit product in Cuba stayed with me for a long, long time. Eventually there emerged a set of characters (an unmarried doctor, an arrogant son, a plantation manager, a nomadic seamstress) who could participate in that potential criminality and be affected by it, I hope in engaging ways.

Derek Palacio was born in Evanston, Illinois, but mostly grew up in Greenland, New Hampshire. He holds an MFA in Creative Writing from the Ohio State University. "Sugarcane" was his first published story and is part of a collection he is currently working on. His story "A History of Civility" appeared in *Puerto del Sol*. He is the codirector of the Mojave School, a nonprofit creative writing workshop for teenagers in rural Nevada. He lives and teaches in Lewisburg, Pennsylvania.

Jamie Quatro, "Sinkhole"

"Sinkhole" is the only story I've ever written that came to me as a grand-scale, amorphous idea: to write a combination sex/exorcism scene in which neither person realized what was happening to the other. That was all I had. No image or character, not even a fragment of dialogue. It was baffling, because for me the creative process usually works in reverse: a small object or sensory moment—a torn sweater sleeve, the sound of snow tires on ice—will present itself, and will feel lit up with a kind of numinous quality; imbued, somehow, with the potential to extend beyond itself. I'll begin to sketch the image, having only a vague sense of where I'm headed, but trusting—willing myself to trust—that something True will show up along the way. I'll draft and redraft until the story surfaces. The process feels inductive, alchemical, moving outward from the material to the immaterial; meaning distilled from image, spirit from matter.

Yet here was this implausible notion. I couldn't shake it. Individually, the two elements felt like insurmountable challenges. Sex scenes are just plain difficult to write. And exorcism in a short story? Other than Chris Adrian, I couldn't think of anyone who'd attempted it. But to *combine* them? I knew I couldn't pull it off. Could I write about exorcism believably, much less an exorcism during the sex act? Under what circumstances could such a thing happen? How could a *priest*—the only person who can perform the rite—have sex during an exorcism?

Then—as so often happens, if I'm awake to it—a real-life event gave me what I needed. One of the churches in our little mountaintop town hosted an outreach event on the playground of the elementary school, just a few blocks from our house. The entire community was invited. Free ice cream, live bluegrass, dogs welcome! They set up a tent and brought in an actor who played different versions of God (waiter, sheriff, etc.). I wrote the opening scene in "Sinkhole" after taking notes at the event, realizing that this God-actor was somehow involved in the sex/exorcism story, and that my characters would be evangelical Protestants. I wrote the last scene next, revising the Catholic exorcism as a faith-healing. The rest of the story revealed itself from there. Still, it took me two years to finish. At one point I had the main character running with a .380 Colt Mustang duct-taped to his torso. Thank goodness for an early reader who said, "Er, lose the gun and you might have something here."

Jamie Quatro was born in San Diego, California, and grew up in Tucson, Arizona. Her fiction and essays have appeared or are forthcoming in *The Kenyon Review, Tin House, The Oxford American, McSweeney's, The Southern Review, American Short Fiction,* and elsewhere. Her debut story collection, *I Want to Show You More,* was a finalist for the Katherine Anne Porter Prize in Short Fiction. Quatro is the recipient of fellowships from Yaddo and the MacDowell Colony, and holds graduate degrees from the College of William and Mary and the Bennington College Writing Seminars. She lives in Lookout Mountain, Georgia.

Polly Rosenwaike, "White Carnations"

I've never been a great fan of holidays. The imperative to celebrate feels oppressive to me, likely to inspire melancholy rather than good cheer. After writing a sort of anti–Valentine's Day story some years ago, I envisioned a collection of stories that would push against the spirit of a year's worth of holidays, but Mother's Day is the only other Hallmark-sponsored day I've confronted in fiction. "White Carnations" began with a thought jotted down in a notebook about a group of women who come together on Mother's Day to avoid the familial festivities of others. I turned a draft in to my MFA workshop, received the usual amount of smart but paralyzing feedback, and eventually slogged through the overhaul the story needed. When I started writing it, I was luckier than the characters, and my luck has increased. My mother is alive and well. My one-year-old daughter says "mommy" as vehemently as she says "milk" and "cat" and "go." I should enjoy Mother's Day, and yet I'm not prepared to parade around with a corsage pinned to my buttonhole. Though I guess by ending this story with a moment of celebration between two soon-to-be mothers, I'm betraying that I am a bit of a sucker for holidays after all.

Polly Rosenwaike grew up in Philadelphia. Her stories and book reviews have appeared in *Indiana Review, River Styx, ZYZZYVA, San Francisco Chronicle, The New York Times Book Review,* and *The Millions,* among other publications. "White Carnations" is part of a story collection in progress about pregnancy and new motherhood. Rosenwaike lives in Ann Arbor, Michigan, and teaches creative writing at Eastern Michigan University.

Asako Serizawa, "The Visitor"

"The Visitor" is part of a collection of interconnected short stories. Designed to explore the consequences of imperialism and war, the stories are thematically and genealogically linked, with each one providing a perspective that the other stories work to contest and fill out. "The Visitor," which is one mother's story, has two companion pieces—the husband's story and the son's—and they function like panels in a triptych. In this story, the mother assumes all kinds of things about her son (and about her husband, though that only comes to light in the husband's story) and ends up finding out things she had only suspected in the half-light of her consciousness, things she both wants and doesn't want confirmed. The son's story reveals what the mother can never know—what really happened to him—while the husband's story reveals something his wife could never have guessed, which he keeps a secret, even from himself, until the end of his life.

So, from the start, "The Visitor" had specific requirements and specific parameters, and at the conceptual level the process felt a bit like muddling through a maze shadowed by prickly hedges and a dwindling light, which is to say that it felt both restrictive and vastly complicated, with so few possible paths but so many crooked turns confusing the way. When I finally started writing (my way into the story was the image and concept of the photograph), it felt like writing any other story, which is to say a slow, picky process of endless revision. Looking back, it's hard to believe how much discipline this little story took, but I suppose it's fitting. To me, this story is about restraint: the way it can pressure and prey on people's conflicted desires and competing agendas, and ultimately invite the consequences they fear most.

Asako Serizawa was born in Japan. Her childhood was spent in Singapore, Indonesia, and Tokyo. Her stories have appeared in *The Southern Review, Prairie Schooner,* and *The Hudson Review.* She lives in Madison, Wisconsin.

Joan Silber, "Two Opinions"

I'd already written a story about New York anarchists in the 1920s, when the parents in this story were young. I see the beauty and accuracy in anarchism but I'm not really an idealogue by nature, and that not-entirely-comfortable stance probably led to this story. It wasn't hard to invent a daughter who resists her parents' certainties and puts her faith in romantic love. In the beginning, I didn't know how much trouble this tolerance for ambivalence—the habit of holding two opinions—would get her into. As Louise's feelings about her husband became more mixed, I found myself inventing an ambivalent marriage arrangement for her. I see Louise as someone used to people who live out their beliefs. Her friend keeps telling her she's a fool, but she's okay with that. When, in the end, Louise tries to convince us she's fine, I mostly believe her. I often write about the lure of solitude.

Joan Silber was born in New Jersey. She is the author of six works of fiction, including *The Size of the World* (finalist for a Los Angeles Times Book Prize), *Ideas of Heaven* (a finalist for a National Book Award and the Story Prize), and *Household Words* (winner of the PEN/Hemingway Award). "Two Opinions" is part of her latest collection, *Fools*. Silber is also the author of *The Art of Time in Fiction,* a critical study. Her stories have been in two previous *O. Henry* collections (previously *The PEN/O. Henry Prize Stories*), and she's received a Literature Award from the American Academy of Arts and Letters as well as grants from the John Simon Guggenheim Memorial Foundation and the National Endowment for the Arts. She teaches at Sarah Lawrence College and lives in New York City.

Lily Tuck, "Pérou"

I did have a Silver Cross Balmoral navy-blue pram and a nurse named Jeanne. Jeanne, my mother, and I went to Peru at the start of World War II. I was a baby then and I don't remember any of it. However, I have always been fascinated by how Jeanne—a young, simple country girl from Brittany—managed in such a foreign country, so far away from her native France, for five long war years. And why she agreed to leave her family, her home, and go with us—German refugees—in the first place. For me, this remains a mystery, and one I have always wanted to write about, though not necessarily solve. So, I have imagined a story for Jeanne—not a very happy one; the real one, which I do remember, is better. At the end of the war, Jeanne left Peru and went back to France and I lost touch with her. In this story, I try to bring her back.

Lily Tuck was born in Paris. She is the author of five novels: *Interviewing Matisse, or The Woman Who Died Standing Up; The*

Woman Who Walked on Water; Siam, or The Woman Who Shot a Man, a PEN/Faulkner Award finalist; *The News from Paraguay,* winner of a National Book Award in 2004; and *I Married You For Happiness.* She has also published the story collection *Limbo, and Other Places I Have Lived* and a biography, *Woman of Rome: A Life of Elsa Morante.* Her essay "Group Grief" was included in *The Best American Essays 2006.* Tuck's latest work is the collection *The House at Belle Fontaine and Other Stories.* She lives in New York City.

Publications Submitted

Stories published in American and Canadian magazines are eligible for consideration for inclusion in *The O. Henry Prize Stories*. Stories must be written originally in the English language. No translations are considered. Sections of novels are not considered. Editors are asked not to nominate individual stories. Stories may not be submitted by agents or writers.

Editors are invited to submit online fiction for consideration, but such submissions must be sent to the address on the next page in the form of a legible hard copy. The publication's contact information and the date of the story's publication must accompany the submissions.

Because of production deadlines for the 2014 collection, it is essential that stories reach the series editor by July 1, 2013. If a finished magazine is unavailable before the deadline, magazine editors are welcome to submit scheduled stories in proof or manuscript. Publications received after July 1, 2013, will automatically be considered for *The O. Henry Prize Stories 2015*.

Please see our Web site, www.ohenryprizestories.com, for more information about submission to *The O. Henry Prize Stories*.

The address for submission of magazines and hard copy of online fiction is:

Laura Furman, Series Editor, The O. Henry Prize Stories
The University of Texas at Austin
English Department, B5000
1 University Station
Austin, TX 78712

The information listed below was up-to-date when *The O. Henry Prize Stories 2013* went to press. Inclusion in this listing does not constitute endorsement or recommendation by *The O. Henry Prize Stories* or Anchor Books.

580 Split
Mills College
PO Box 9982
Oakland, CA 94613-0982
Stephanie Kreuz, editor
five80split@gmail.com
mills.edu/academics/graduate/eng/
about/580_split.php
annual

A Public Space
323 Dean Street
Brooklyn, New York 11217
Anne McPeak, editor
general@apublicspace.org
apublicspace.org
quarterly

AGNI Magazine
Boston University
236 Bay State Road
Boston, MA 02215
Sven Birkerts, editor
agni@bu.edu
bu.edu/agni
semiannual

Alaska Quarterly Review
University of Alaska Anchorage
3211 Providence Drive
Anchorage, AK 99508
Ronald Spatz, editor
aqr@uaa.alaska.edu
uaa.alaska.edu/aqr
semiannual

Alimentum
PO Box 210028
Nashville, TN 37221
Peter Selgin, editor
editor@alimentumjournal.com
alimentumjournal.com
semiannual

Alligator Juniper
Prescott College
220 Grove Avenue
Prescott, AZ 86301
Skye Anicca, editor
alligatorjuniper@prescott.edu
prescott.edu/alligator_juniper
annual

American Letters & Commentary
Department of English
University of Texas at San Antonio
One UTSA Circle
San Antonio, TX 78249
Anna Rabinowitz, editor
AmerLetters@satx.rr.com
amletters.org
annual

American Literary Review
PO Box 311307
University of North Texas
Denton, TX 76203-1307
Miroslav Penkov and Barbara
   Rodman, editors
americanliteraryreview@gmail
   .com
engl.unt.edu/alr
semiannual

American Short Fiction
PO Box 4152
Austin, TX 78765
Adeena Reitberger and Rebecca
   Markovits, editors
editors@americanshortfiction.org
americanshortfiction.org
triannual

Apalachee Review
PO Box 10469
Tallahassee, FL 32302
Michael Trammell and Jenn
   Bronson, editors
apalacheereview.org
semiannual

Arkansas Review: A Journal of Delta Studies
PO Box 1890
Arkansas State University
State University, AR 72467
Janelle Collins, editor
arkansasreview@astate.edu
altweb.astate.edu/arkreview
triannual

Armchair/Shotgun
377 Flatbush Avenue
Brooklyn, NY 11238-4393
Aaron Reuben, editor
info@armchairshotgun.com
armchairshotgun.wordpress.com
semiannual

Arroyo Literary Review
Department of English, MB 2579
California State University,
   East Bay
25800 Carlos Bee Boulevard
Hayward, CA 94542
Christopher Morgan, editor
arroyoliteraryreview@gmail.com
arroyoliteraryreview.com
annual

Artichoke Haircut
Melissa Streat, editor
artichokehaircut.com
semiannual

At Length
716 West Cornwallis Road
Durham, NC 27707
Jonathan Farmer, editor
editors@atlengthmag.com
atlengthmag.com
bimonthly

Bat City Review
Department of English
The University of Texas at Austin
1 University Station B5000
Austin, TX 78712
Jeff Bruemmer, editor
fiction@batcityreview.com
batcityreview.com
annual

Belles Lettres: A Literary Review
The Center for the Humanities
Washington University in St. Louis
Campus Box 1202
One Brookings Drive
St. Louis, MO 63130-4899
Gerald Early, editor
cenhum@artsci.wustl.edu
cenhum.artsci.wustl.edu/
    publications/belles_lettres
bimonthly

Bellevue Literary Review
NYU Langone Medical Center
Department of Medicine
550 First Avenue, OBV-612
New York, NY 10016
Ronna Wineberg, JD, editor
info@BLReview.org
BLReview.org
semiannual

Black Warrior Review
PO Box 862936
Tuscaloosa, AL 35486
Jake Kinstler, editor
blackwarriorreview@gmail.com
bwr.ua.edu
semiannual

Bluestem
English Department
600 Lincoln Avenue
Eastern Illinois University
Charleston, IL 61920
Olga Abella, editor
editor@bluestemmagazine.com
bluestemmagazine.com
annual

BOMB Magazine
80 Hanson Place
Suite 703
Brooklyn, NY 11217
Betsy Sussler, editor
generalinquiries@bombsite.com
bombsite.com
quarterly

bosque (the magazine)
Lynn C. Miller and Lisa Lenard-
    Cook, editors
admin@abqwriterscoop.com
abqwriterscoop.com
annual

Boston Review
PO Box 425786
Cambridge, MA 02142
Deborah Chasman and Joshua
    Cohen, editors
review@bostonreview.net
bostonreview.net
published six times per year

Boulevard Magazine
6614 Clayton Road, Box 325
Richmond Heights, MO 63117
Richard Burgin, editor
jessicarogen@boulevardmagazine
   .org
boulevardmagazine.org
triannual

**Brain, Child: The Magazine for
   Thinking Mothers**
Publishing Office
341 Newton Turnpike
Wilton, CT 06897
Marcelle Soviero, editor
editorial@brainchildmag.com
brainchildmag.com
quarterly

Cairn: St. Andrews Review
CAIRN Editors
St. Andrews College Press
1700 Dogwood Mile
Laurinburg, NC 28352
press@sapc.edu
sapc.edu/sapress/carin.php

**Calyx: A Journal of Art and
   Literature by Women**
PO Box B
Corvallis, OR 97339
Rebecca Olson, editor
editor@calyxpress.org
calyxpress.org
semiannual

Camera Obscura
c/o Sfumato Press
PO Box 2356
Addison, TX 75001
M. E. Parker, editor
editor@obscurajournal.com
obscurajournal.com
semiannual

Carve Magazine
PO Box 701510
Dallas, TX 75370
Matthew Limpede, editor
managingeditor@carvezine.com
carvezine.com
quarterly

Chicago Review
Taft House
935 East 60th Street
Chicago, IL 60637
Joel Calahan and Michael Hansen,
   editors
chicago-review@uchicago.edu
humanities.uchicago.edu/orgs/
   review
triannual

Cimarron Review
Oklahoma State University
English Department
205 Morrill Hall
Stillwater, OK 74078
Toni Graham, editor
cimarronreview@okstate.edu
cimarronreview.com
quarterly

Colorado Review
9105 Campus Delivery
Department of English
Colorado State University
Fort Collins, CO 80523-9105
Stephanie G'Schwind, editor
creview@colostate.edu
coloradoreview.colostate.edu
triannual

Commentary
561 Seventh Avenue, 16th Floor
New York, NY 10018
John Podhoretz, editor
submissions@commentary
    magazine.com
commentarymagazine.com
monthly

Confrontation Magazine
English Department
LIU Post
Brookville, NY 11548
Jonna G. Semeiks, editor
confrontationmag@gmail.com
confrontationmagazine.org
semiannual

Conjunctions
21 East 10th Street, Apt. 3E
New York, NY 10003
Bradford Morrow, editor
conjunctions@bard.edu
conjunctions.com
semiannual

Crab Orchard Review
Department of English
Faner Hall 2380
Mail Code 4503
Southern Illinois University,
    Carbondale
1000 Faner Drive
Carbondale, IL 62901
Allison Joseph, editor
craborchardreview.siu.edu
semiannual

Crazyhorse
Department of English
College of Charleston
66 George Street
Charleston, SC 29424
Anthony Varallo, editor
crazyhorse@cofc.edu
crazyhorse.cofc.edu
semiannual

Cream City Review
Department of English
University of Wisconsin-
    Milwaukee
PO Box 413
Milwaukee, WI 53201
Mollie Boutell, editor
info@creamcityreview.org
creamcityreview.org
semiannual

CutBank
University of Montana
English Department, LA 133
Missoula, MT 59812
Andrew Martin, editor
editor.cutbank@gmail.com
cutbankonline.org
semiannual

Denver Quarterly
University of Denver
Department of English
2000 East Asbury
Denver, CO 80208
Laird Hunt, editor
denverquarterly.com
quarterly

descant
TCU Box 297270
Fort Worth, TX 76129
Dave Kuhne, editor
descant@tcu.edu
descant.tcu.edu
annual

Ecotone
Department of Creative Writing
University of North Carolina,
    Wilmington
601 South College Road
Wilmington, NC 28403-5938
Nicola Robertis-Theye, editor
info@ecotonejournal.com
ecotonejournal.com
semiannual

enRoute
Spafax Canada
4200, boulevard St-Laurent
Suite 707
Montreal, QC H2W 2R2
Canada
Ilana Weitzman, editor
info@enroutemag.net
enRoutemag.com

Epoch
Cornell University
251 Goldwin Smith Hall
Ithaca, NY 14853-3201
Michael Koch, editor
english.arts.cornell.edu/
    publications/epoch
triannual

Event
Douglas College
PO Box 2503
New Westminster, BC V3L 5B2
Canada
Christine Dewar, editor
event@douglascollege.ca
eventmags.com
triannual

Fairy Tale Review
Department of English
PO Box 210067
University of Arizona
Tucson, AZ 85721-0067
Kate Bernheimer, editor
fairytalereview@gmail.com
digitalcommons.wayne.edu/
    fairytalereview
annual

Fantasy & Science Fiction
PO Box 3447
Hoboken, NJ 07030
Gordon Van Gelder, editor
fsfmag@fandsf.com
sfsite.com/fsf
bimonthly

Fence
Science Library 320
University at Albany
1400 Washington Avenue
Albany, NY 12222
Rebecca Wolff, editor
fence.fencebooks@gmail.com
fenceportal.org
semiannual

Fiction
Department of English
The City College of New York
138th Street and Convent Avenue
New York, NY 10031
Mark Jay Mirsky, editor
fictionmagazine@yahoo.com
fictioninc.com
semiannual

Fifth Wednesday Journal
PO Box 4033
Lisle, IL 60532-9033
Vern Miller, editor
editors@fifthwednesdayjournal
    .org
fifthwednesdayjournal.org
semiannual

Five Points
Georgia State University
PO Box 3999
Atlanta, GA 30302-3999
Megan Sexton, editor
fivepoints@gsu.edu
fivepoints.gsu.edu
triannual

Fugue
200 Brink Hall
University of Idaho
PO Box 441102
Moscow, ID 83844
Alexandra Teague, faculty advisor
fugue@uidaho.edu
fuguejournal.org
semiannual

Gargoyle
3819 North 13th Street
Arlington, VA 22201
Richard Peabody and Lucinda
    Ebersole, editors
gargoyle@gargoylemagazine.com
gargoylemagazine.com
annual

Geist
111 West Hastings Street
Suite 210
Vancouver, BC V6B 1H4
Canada
Barbara Zatyko, editor
editor@geist.com
geist.com
quarterly

Glimmer Train
4763 SW Maplewood Road
PO Box 80430
Portland, OR 97280-1430
Susan Burmeister-Brown and
    Linda B. Swanson-Davies,
    editors
editors@glimmertrain.org
glimmertrain.org
quarterly

Gold Man Review
Heather Cuthbertson, editor
goldmanreview.org
annual

Good Housekeeping
Hearst Corp.
250 West 55th Street
New York, NY 10019
goodhousekeeping.com
monthly

Grain Magazine
PO Box 67
Saskatoon, SK S7K 3K1
Canada
Rilla Friesen, editor
grainmag@sasktel.net
grainmagazine.ca
quarterly

Granta
12 Addison Avenue
London W11 4QR
United Kingdom
editorial@granta.com
granta.com
quarterly

Grey Sparrow Journal
PO Box 211664
St. Paul, MN 55121
Diane Smith, editor
dsdianefuller@gmail.com
greysparrowpress.sharepoint.com

Gulf Coast
Department of English
University of Houston
Houston, TX 77204-3013
Nick Flynn, faculty editor
editors@gulfcoastmag.org
gulfcoastmag.org
semiannual

H.O.W. Journal
405 Broadway, Apt. 4
New York, NY 10013
Alison Weaver and Natasha
    Radojcic, editors
editors@howjournal.com
howjournal.com
semiannual

Hadassah Magazine
50 West 58th Street
New York, NY 10019
Libby Barnea, editor
lbarnea@hadassah.org
hadassahmagazine.org

Harper's Magazine
666 Broadway
11th Floor
New York, NY 10012
Ellen Rosenbush, editor
harpers.org
monthly

Harpur Palate
English Department
Binghamton University
PO Box 6000
Binghamton, NY 13902-6000
harpur.palate@gmail.com
harpurpalate.binghamton.edu
semiannual

Harvard Review
Lamont Library
Harvard University
Cambridge, MA 02138
Nam Le, editor
info@harvardreview.org
hcl.harvard.edu/harvardreview
semiannual

Hawai'i Pacific Review
Hawai'i Pacific University
1164 Bishop Street
Honolulu, HI 96813
Dr. Patrice M. Wilson, editor
pwilson@hpu.edu
hpu.edu/CHSS/English/LitLife/
    HawaiPacificReview/hpr
annual

Hayden's Ferry Review
c/o Virginia G. Piper Center for
    Creative Writing
Arizona State University
PO Box 875002
Tempe, AZ 85287-5002
Beth Staples, editor
HFR@asu.edu
haydensferryreview.org
semiannual

Hemispheres
Pace Communications
1301 Carolina Street
Greensboro, NC 27401
Joe Keohane, editor
editorial@hemispheresmagazine
    .com
hemispheresmagazine.com
monthly

**HGMLQ: Harrington Gay
    Men's Literary Quarterly**
English Department
Thomas Nelson Community
    College
PO Box 9407
Hampton, VA 23670
Thomas Lawrence Long, editor
longt@tncc.edu
quarterly

Hobart: another literary journal
Aaron Burch, editor
aaron@hobartpulp.com
hobartpulp.com
semiannual

Hotel Amerika
Columbia College, English
    Department
600 South Michigan Avenue
Chicago, IL 60605-1996
David Lazar, editor
editors@HotelAmerika.net
hotelamerika.net

**Huizache: The Magazine of
    Latino Literature**
3007 North Ben Wilson Street
Victoria, TX 77901
Diana López, editor
huizache.prose@gmail.com
centrovictoria.net/huizache.html
annual

Hyphen: Asian America
    Unabridged
17 Walter U. Lum Place
San Francisco, CA 94108
Karissa Chen, editor
fiction@hyphenmagazine.com
hyphenmagazine.com
semiannual

Illuminations
Department of English
College of Charleston
26 Glebe Street
Charleston, SC 29424-001
Meg Scott-Copses, editor
scottcopsesm@cofc.edu
cofc.edu/illuminations
annual

Image: A Journal of the Arts &
    Religion
3307 Third Avenue West
Seattle, WA 98119
Mary Kenagy Mitchell, editor
image@imagejournal.org
imagejournal.org
quarterly

Indiana Review
Indiana University
Ballantine Hall 465
1020 East Kirkwood Avenue
Bloomington, IN 47405-7103
inreview@indiana.edu
indianareview.org
semiannual

Iron Horse Literary Review
Texas Tech University
English Department
Mailstop 43091
Lubbock, TX 79409-3091
Lee Martin, editor
ihlr.mail@gmail.com
ironhorsereview.com
published six times a year

Jabberwock Review
Department of English
Mississippi State University
Drawer E
Mississippi State, MS 39762
Michael Kardos, editor
jabberwockreview@english
    .msstate.edu
jabberwock.org.msstate.edu
semiannual

Jelly Bucket
467 Case Annex
521 Lancaster Avenue
Richmond, KY 40475
creativewriting.eku.edu/jelly
    -bucket
editor@jellybucket.org
annual

Juked
220 Atkinson Drive, #B
Tallahasee, FL 32304
J. W. Wang, editor
info@juked.com
juked.com
annual

Kalliope, A Journal of Women's Literature & Art
Penn State University
University Park
State College, PA 16801
Shelia Squillante, faculty advisor
sks172@psu.edu
clubs.psu.edu/up/kalliope/
    submissions.html
annual

Lady Churchill's Rosebud Wristlet
150 Pleasant Street, #306
Easthampton, MA 01027
Kelly Link and Gavin J. Grant,
    editors
info@smallbeerpress.com
smallbeerpress.com/lcrw
semiannual

Lake Effect
School of Humanities and Social
    Sciences
Penn State Erie
4951 College Drive
Erie, PA 16563-1501
George Looney, editor
goll@psu.edu
pserie.psu.edu/academic/hss/
    lakeeffect/index.html
annual

Literary Imagination
Archie Burnett and Saskia
    Hamilton, editors
litimag.oxfordjournals.org
triannual

MAKE: A Chicago Literary Magazine
2822 W. Dickens #3
Chicago, IL 60647
Sarah Dodson, editor
info@makemag.com
makemag.com
semiannual

Mandorla
Department of English
Illinois State University
Campus Box 4240
Normal, IL 61790-4240
Roberto Tejada, editor
litline.org/Mandorla/default.html
annual

MĀNOA
Department of English
University of Hawai'i
1733 Donaghho Road
Honolulu, HI 96822
Frank Stewart, editor
mjournal-l@hawaii.edu
hawaii.edu/mjournal
semiannual

Timothy McSweeney's Quarterly Concern
849 Valencia Street
San Francisco, CA 94110
Dave Eggers, editor
printsubmissions@mcsweeneys
    .net
mcsweeneys.net/books
quarterly

Meridian
University of Virginia
PO Box 400145
Charlottesville, VA 22904-4145
Alexis Schaitkin, editor
meridianfiction@gmail.com
readmeridian.org
semiannual

Michigan Quarterly Review
University of Michigan
0576 Rackham Building
915 East Washington Street
Ann Arbor, MI 48109-1070
Jonathan Freedman, editor
mqr@umich.edu
michiganquarterlyreview.com
quarterly

Midstream: A Quarterly Jewish Review
633 Third Avenue, 21st Floor
New York, NY 10017
Leo Haber, editor
info@midstreamthf.com
midstreamthf.com
bimonthly

n+1
68 Jay Street, Suite 405
Brooklyn, NY 11201
editors@nplusonemag.com
nplusonemag.com
triannual

Narrative
Carol Edgarian and Tom Jenks, editors
narrativemagazine.com
annual

Natural Bridge, A Journal of Contemporary Literature
Department of English
University of Missouri-St. Louis
One University Boulevard
St. Louis, MO 63121
natural@umsl.edu
www.umsl.edu/~natural
semiannual

New England Review
Middlebury College
Middlebury, VT 05753
Stephen Donadio, editor
nereview@middlebury.edu
nereview.com
quarterly

New Letters
University of Missouri-Kansas City
University House
5101 Rockhill Road
Kansas City, MO 64110-2499
Robert Stewart, editor
newletters@umkc.edu
newletters.org
quarterly

New Millennium Writings
PO Box 2463
Room M2
Knoxville, TN 37901
Don Williams, editor
newmillenniumwritings.com
annual

New Ohio Review
English Department
360 Ellis Hall
Ohio University
Athens, OH 45701
Jill Allyn Rosser, editor
noreditors@ohio.edu
ohio.edu/nor
semiannual

New Orleans Review
PO Box 195
Loyola University
New Orleans, LA 70118
Mark Yakich, editor
noreview@loyno.edu
neworleansreview.org
semiannual

Nimrod International Journal
800 South Tucker Drive
The University of Tulsa
Tulsa, OK 74104-3189
Francine Ringold, editor
nimrod@utulsa.edu
utulsa.edu/nimrod
semiannual

Ninth Letter
Department of English
University of Illinois, Urbana-
    Champaign
608 South Wright Street
Urbana, IL 61801
Jodee Stanley, editor
editor@ninthletter.com
ninthletter.com
semiannual

Noon
1324 Lexington Avenue
PMB 298
New York, NY 10128
Diane Williams, editor
noonannual.com
annual

North American Review
University of Northern Iowa
1222 West 27th Street
Cedar Falls, Iowa 50614-0516
Grant Tracey, editor
nar@uni.edu
northamericanreview.org
quarterly

North Carolina Literary Review
Department of English
East Carolina University
Mailstop 555 English
Greenville, NC 27858-4353
Margaret D. Bauer, editor
bauerm@ecu.edu
ecu.edu/nclr
annual

North Dakota Quarterly
276 Centennial Drive Stop 7209
Merrifield Hall Room 15
Grand Forks, ND 58202-7209
Robert W. Lewis, editor
und.ndq@email.und.edu
arts-sciences.und.edu/north
    -dakota-quarterly
quarterly

Notre Dame Review
University of Notre Dame
840 Flanner Hall
Notre Dame, IN 46556
William O'Rourke, editor
english.ndreview.1@nd.edu
ndreview.nd.edu
semiannual

One Story
232 Third Street, #A108
Brooklyn, NY 11215
Hannah Tinti, editor
one-story.com
every three weeks

Open City
270 Lafayette Street
Suite 705
New York, NY 10012
Thomas Beller and Joanna Yas,
    editors
editors@opencity.org
opencity.org
triannual

Opium Magazine
144A Diamond Street
Brooklyn, NY 11222
Todd Zuniga, editor
todd@opiummagazine.com
opiummagazine.com
semiannual

Orchid
PO Box 131457
Ann Arbor, MI 48113-1457
Keith Hood, editor
editors@orchidlit.org
orchidlit.org
semiannual

Orion
187 Main Street
Great Barrington, MA 01230
H. Emerson Blake, editor
orionmagazine.org
bimonthly

Overtime
PO Box 250382
Plano, TX 75025-0382
David LaBounty, editor
info@workerswritejournal.com
workerswritejournal.com/overtime
    .htm
published four to six times a year

Oyster Boy Review
PO Box 1483
Pacifica, CA 94044
Damon Sauve, editor
email_2013@oysterboyreview.com
oysterboyreview.com
quarterly

Painted Bride Quarterly
Drexel University
Department of English and
    Philosophy
3141 Chestnut Street
Philadelphia, PA 19104
Kathleen Volk Miller and Marion
    Wrenn, editors
pbq@drexel.edu
pbq.drexel.edu
quarterly online; annual in print

PaknTreger
The Yiddish Book Center
Harry and Jeanette Weinberg
    Building
1021 West Street
Amherst, MA 01002
pt@bikher.org
yiddishbookcenter.org/pakn-treger
triannual

PEN America
c/o PEN American Center
588 Broadway, Suite 303
New York, NY 10012
M. Mark, editor
journal@pen.org
pen.org/pen-america-journal
annual

Phoebe
MSN 2C5
George Mason University
4400 University Drive
Fairfax, VA 22030
Alexander Henderson, editor
phoebe@gmu.edu
phoebejournal.com
annual

Pilot Pocket Book
PO Box 161, Station B
119 Spadina Avenue
Toronto, ON M5T 2T3
Canada
editor@thepilotproject.ca
thepilotproject.ca
annual

Playboy Magazine
730 Fifth Avenue
New York, NY 10019
Hugh Hefner, editor
sirc@ny.playboy.com
playboy.com.magazine
monthly

Ploughshares
Emerson College
120 Boylston Street
Boston, MA 02116
Ladette Randolph, editor
pshares@emerson.edu
pshares.org
triannual

PMS poememóirstory
HB 217
1530 3rd Avenue South
Birmingham, AL 35294-1260
Kerry Madden, editor
poememoirstory@gmail.com
pms-journal.org
annual

Polyphony HS
The Latin School of Chicago
59 West North Boulevard
Chicago, IL 60610
Elizabeth Keegan, executive
    director
info@polyphonyhs.com
polyphonyhs.com
annual

Potomac Review
Montgomery College
51 Mannakee Street, MT/212
Rockville, MD 20850
Julie Wakeman-Linn, editor
PotomacReviewEditor@
    montgomerycollege.edu
montgomerycollege.edu/
    potomacreview
semiannual

Prairie Fire
423-100 Arthur Street
Winnipeg, MB R3B 1H3
Canada
Andris Taskans, editor
prfire@prairiefire.ca
prairiefire.ca
quarterly

Prairie Schooner
123 Andrews Hall
University of Nebraska-Lincoln
Lincoln, NE 68588-0334
Kwame Dawes, editor
prairieschooner@unl.edu
prairieschooner.unl.edu
quarterly

PRISM international
Creative Writing Program
University of British Columbia
Buchanan E-462
1866 Main Mall
Vancouver, BC V6T 1Z1
Canada
Anna Ling Kaye, editor
prismfiction@gmail.com
prismmagazine.ca
quarterly

Provincetown Arts
650 Commercial Street
Provincetown, MA 02657
Christopher Busa, editor
cbusa@comcast.net
provincetownarts.org
annual

Puerto del Sol
Department of English
New Mexico State University
PO Box 30001, MSC 3E
Las Cruces, NM 88003
Lily Hoang, editor
contact@puertodelsol.org
puertodelsol.org
semiannual

Quarterly West
University of Utah
255 South Central Campus Drive
Department of English
LNCO 3500
Salt Lake City, UT 84112-0494
Daniel Takeshi Krause and
    Jaclyn Watterson, editors
quarterlywest.utah.edu
semiannual

Raritan: A Quarterly Review
31 Mine Street
New Brunswick, NJ 08901
Jackson Lears, editor
rqr@rci.rutgers.edu
raritanquarterly.rutgers.edu
quarterly

Red Rock Review
English Department, J2A
College of Southern Nevada
3200 East Cheyenne Avenue
North Las Vegas, NV 89030
Todd Moffett, editor
redrockreview@csn.edu
sites.csn.edu/english/
    redrockreview/index.htm
semiannual

**Relief: A Christian Literary
    Expression**
60 West Terra Cotta
Suite B, Unit 156
Crystal Lake, IL 60014-3548
Brad Fruhauff, editor
reliefjournal.com
semiannual

River Styx
3547 Olive Street
Suite 107
St. Louis, MO 63103
Richard Newman, editor
bigriver@riverstyx.org
riverstyx.org
triannual

Ruminate
140 North Roosevelt Avenue
Fort Collins, CO 80521
Brianna Van Dyke, editor
ruminatemagazine.org
quarterly

Salamander
Suffolk University
English Department
41 Temple Street
Boston, MA 02114
Jennifer Barber, editor
salamandermag.org
semiannual

Salmagundi
Skidmore College
815 North Broadway
Saratoga Springs, NY 12866
Robert Boyers, editor
salmagun@skidmore.edu
cms.skidmore.edu/salmagundi
quarterly

Santa Monica Review
Santa Monica College
1900 Pico Boulevard
Santa Monica, CA 90405
Andrew Tonkovich, editor
www2.smc.edu/sm_review/
    default.htm
semiannual

Saranac Review
CVH, Department of English
SUNY Plattsburgh
101 Broad Street
Plattsburgh, NY 12901
Elizabeth Cohen, editor
saranacreview@plattsburgh.edu
research.plattsburgh.edu/
    saranacreview
annual

Seven Days
PO Box 1164
Burlington, VT 05402-1164
Pamela Polston and Paula Routly,
    editors
7dvt.com
weekly (fiction published annually)

Slake: Los Angeles
Joe Donnelly and Laurie Ochoa,
    editors
slake@slake.la
slake.la
on indefinite hiatus

Sonora Review
Department of English
University of Arizona
Tucson, AZ 85721
sonorareview2@gmail.com
sonorareview.com
semiannual

Southern Humanities Review
9088 Haley Center
Auburn University
Auburn, AL 36849-5202
Chantel Acevedo, editor
shrengl@auburn.edu
auburn.edu/shr
quarterly

Southern Indiana Review
Orr Center, #2009
University of Southern Indiana
8600 University Boulevard
Evansville, IN 47712
Ron Mitchell, editor
sir@usi.edu
usi.edu/sir
semiannual

Southwest Review
Southern Methodist University
PO Box 750374
Dallas, TX 75275-0374
Willard Spiegelman, editor
swr@smu.edu
smu.edu/southwestreview
quarterly

Spot Literary Magazine
Spot Write Literary Corporation
4729 East Sunrise Drive
Box 254
Tucson, AZ 85718-4535
Susan Hansell, editor
susan.hansell@gmail.com
spotlitmagazine.net
semiannual

St. Anthony Messenger
28 West Liberty Street
Cincinnati, OH 45202
John Feister, editor
magazineeditors@franciscanmedia
    .org
stanthonymessenger.org
monthly

StoryQuarterly
Rutgers University
Department of English
311 North 5th Street
481 Armitage Hall
Camden, NJ 08102
J. T. Barbarese, editor
estory.quarterly@camden.rutgers
    .edu
storyquarterly.camden.rutgers.edu/
    index.php
annual

Subtropics
Department of English
University of Florida
PO Box 112075
4008 Turlington Hall
Gainesville, FL 32611-2075
David Leavitt, editor
subtropics@english.ufl.edu
english.ufl.edu/subtropics
triannual

Swink
Darcy Cooper, editor
swinkmag.com
monthly

Tampa Review
University of Tampa
401 West Kennedy Boulevard
Tampa, FL 33606-1490
Richard Mathews, editor
utpress@ut.edu
tampareview.ut.edu
semiannual

The American Scholar
Phi Beta Kappa Society
1606 New Hampshire Avenue NW
Washington, DC 20009
Sudip Bose, editor
sbose@theamericanscholar.org
theamericanscholar.org
quarterly

The Antioch Review
PO Box 148
Yellow Springs, Ohio 45387
Muriel Keyes, editor
mkeyes@antiochreview.org
antiochreview.org
quarterly

The Asian American Literary Review
1110 Severnview Drive
Crownsville, MD 21032
Lawrence-Minh Bùi Davis and Gerald Maa, editors
prose@aalrmag.org
aalrmag.org
semiannual

The Atlantic Monthly
The Watergate
600 New Hampshire Avenue NW
Washington, DC 20037
C. Michael Curtis, editor
theatlantic.com/magazine
monthly

The Briar Cliff Review
3303 Rebecca Street
Sioux City, IA 51104-2100
Tricia Currans-Sheehan, editor
tricia.currans-sheehan@briarcliff
.edu
briarcliff.edu/bcreview
annual

The Carolina Quarterly
510 Greenlaw Hall, CB# 3520
The University of North Carolina at Chapel Hill
Chapel Hill, NC 27599-3520
Phil Sandick and Lindsay Starck, editors
carolina.quarterly@gmail.com
thecarolinaquarterly.com
triannual

The CEA Critic
University of Northern Colorado
Campus Box 109
501 20th Street
Greeley, CO 80639
Jeri Kraver, Molly Desjardins, and
    Michael Mills, editors
CEA.critic@unco.edu
cea-web.org
semiannual

The Chattahoochee Review
Georgia Perimeter College
555 North Indian Creek Drive
Clarkston, GA 30021
Anna Schachner, editor
gpccr@gpc.edu
chattahoochee-review.org
quarterly

The Cincinnati Review
University of Cincinnati
PO Box 210069
Cincinnati, OH 45221-0069
editors@cincinnatireview.com
cincinnatireview.com
semiannual

The Delmarva Review
PO Box 544
St Michaels, MD 21663
Margot Miller and Harold O.
    Wilson, editors
editor@delmarvareview.com
delmarvareview.com
annual

The Farallon Review
1017 L Street
Number 348
Sacramento, CA 95814
Tim Foley, editor
editor@farallonreview.com
farallonreview.com
annual

The Fiddlehead
Campus House
11 Garland Court
PO Box 4400
University of New Brunswick
Fredericton, NB E3B 5A3
Canada
Ross Leckie, editor
fiddlehd@unb.ca
thefiddlehead.ca
quarterly

The First Line
PO Box 250382
Plano, TX 75025-0382
David LaBounty, editor
david@thefirstline.com
thefirstline.com
quarterly

The Florida Review
Department of English
University of Central Florida
PO Box 161346
Orlando, FL 32816-1346
Jocelyn Bartkevicius, editor
flreview@mail.ucf.edu
floridareview.cah.ucf.edu
semiannual

The Georgia Review
University of Georgia
706A Main Library
320 South Jackson Street
Athens, GA 30602-9009
Stephen Corey, editor
garev@uga.edu
thegeorgiareview.com
quarterly

The Gettysburg Review
Gettysburg College
Gettysburg, PA 17325-1491
Peter Stitt, editor
pstitt@gettysburg.edu
www.gettysburgreview.com
quarterly

The Hudson Review
684 Park Avenue
New York, NY 10065
Paula Deitz, editor
info@hudsonreview.com
hudsonreview.com
quarterly

The Idaho Review
Department of English
Boise State University
1910 University Drive
Boise, ID 83725-1525
Mitch Wieland, editor
idahoreview@boisestate.edu
idahoreview.org
annual

The Iowa Review
The University of Iowa
308 English-Philosophy Building
Iowa City, IA 52242
Lynne Nugent, editor
iowa-review@uiowa.edu
iowareview.org
triannual

The Journal
The Ohio State University
Department of English
164 West 17th Avenue
Columbus, OH 43210
Alex Fabrizio, editor
managingeditor@thejournalmag
.org
thejournalmag.org
quarterly

The Kenyon Review
Finn House
102 West Wiggin Street
Kenyon College
Gambier, OH 43022-9623
kenyonreview@kenyon.edu
kenyonreview.org
quarterly

The Laurel Review
c/o English Department
Northwest Missouri State
    University
800 University Drive
Maryville, MO 64468
John Gallaher and Richard
    Sonnenmoser, editors
TLR@nwmissouri.edu
catpages.nwmissouri.edu/m/tlr
semiannual

The Literary Review
285 Madison Avenue
Madison, NJ 07940
Mina Proctor, editor
editorial@theliteraryreview.org
theliteraryreview.org
quarterly

The Long Story
18 Eaton Street
Lawrence, MA 01843
R. P. Burnham, editor
rpburnham@mac.com
longstorylitmag.com
annual

The Louisville Review
Spalding University
851 South Fourth Street
Louisville, KY 40203
Sena Jeter Naslund, editor
louisvillereview@spalding.edu
louisvillereview.org
semiannual

The Malahat Review
University of Victoria
PO Box 1700
Stn CSC
Victoria, BC V8W 2Y2
Canada
John Barton, editor
malahat@uvic.ca
malahatreview.ca
quarterly

The Massachusetts Review
South College
University of Massachusetts
Amherst, MA 01003
Jim Hicks, editor
massrev@external.umass.edu
massreview.org
quarterly

The Missouri Review
357 McReynolds Hall
University of Missouri
Columbia, Missouri 65211
Speer Morgan, editor
question@moreview.com
missourireview.com
quarterly

The New Renaissance
26 Heath Road, #11
Arlington, MA 02474-3645
Louise T. Reynolds, editor
tnrlitmag@earthlink.net
tnrlitmag.org
semiannual

The New Yorker
4 Times Square
New York, NY 10036
Deborah Treisman, editor
fiction@newyorker.com
newyorker.com
weekly

The Oxford American
201 Donaghey Avenue, Main 107
Conway, AR 72035
Roger D. Hodge, editor
editors@oxfordamerican.org
oxfordamerican.org
quarterly

The Paris Review
62 White Street
New York, NY 10013
Lorin Stein, editor
queries@theparisreview.org
parisreview.org
quarterly

The Pinch
English Department
University of Memphis
Memphis, TN 38152
Kristen Iverson, editor
editor@thepinchjournal.com
thepinchjournal.com
semiannual

The Quotable
Eimile Denizer, Lisa Heins,
    Leslye PJ Reaves, editors
editor@thequotablelit.com
thequotablelit.com
annual

The Republic of Letters
Apartado 29
Cahuita, 70403
Costa Rica
Keith Botsford, editor
nickmatchwell@gmail.com
mag.trolbooks.com
semiannual

The Sewanee Review
The University of the South
735 University Avenue
Sewanee, TN 37383
George Core, editor
sewanee.edu/sewanee_review
quarterly

The South Carolina Review
Center for Electronic and Digital
    Publishing
Clemson University
Strode Tower Room 611
Box 340522
Clemson, South Carolina 29634
Wayne Chapman, editor
cwayne@clemson.edu
clemson.edu/cedp/cudp/scr/
    current.htm
semiannual

The Southern Review
3990 West Lakeshore Drive
Louisiana State University
Baton Rouge, LA 70808
southernreview@lsu.edu
thesouthernreview.org
quarterly

The Sycamore Review
Purdue University
Department of English
500 Oval Drive
West Lafayette, IN 47907
sycamorefiction@purdue.edu
sycamorereview.com
semiannual

The Texas Review
English Department
Sam Houston State University
PO Box 2146
Huntsville, TX 77341-2146
Paul Ruffin, editor
eng_pdr@shsu.edu
shsu.edu/~www_trp/journal/
    current.html
semiannual

The Threepenny Review
PO Box 9131
Berkeley, CA 94709
Wendy Lesser, editor
wlesser@threepennyreview.com
threepennyreview.com
quarterly

The Worcester Review
1 Ekman Street
Worcester, MA 01602
Diane Vanaskie Mulligan, editor
www.theworcesterreview.org
annual

Third Coast
Western Michigan University
English Department
1903 West Michigan Avenue
Kalamazoo, MI 49008-5331
editors@thirdcoastmagazine.com
thirdcoastmagazine.com
semiannual

Tin House
PO Box 10500
Portland, OR 97210
Rob Spillman, editor
info@tinhouse.com
tinhouse.com
quarterly

Trachodon
PO Box 1468
St. Helens, OR 97501
John Carr Walker, editor
editor@trachodon.org
trachodon.org
semiannual

Transition Magazine
104 Mt. Auburn Street, 3R
Cambridge, MA 02138
Tommie Shelby, Vincent Brown,
    and Glenda Carpio, editors
transition@fas.harvard.edu
dubois.fas.harvard.edu/transition
    -magazine
triannual

TriQuarterly
School of Continuing Studies
Northwestern University
339 East Chicago Avenue
Chicago, IL 60611-3008
triquarterly@northwestern.edu
triquarterly.org
semiannual

Unstuck
Matt Williamson, editor
unstuckbooks.org
annual

upstreet
PO Box 105
Richmond, MA 01254-0105
Vivian Dorsel, editor
editor@upstreet-mag.org
upstreet-mag.org
annual

Vermont Literary Review
Department of English
Castleton State College
Castleton, VT 05735
Flo Keyes, editor
vlr@castleton.edu
www.csc.vsc.edu/literaryreview
annual

Washington Square Review
NYU Creative Writing Program
Lillian Vernon Creative Writers
    House
58 West 10th Street
New York, NY 10011
washingtonsquarereview@gmail
    .com
washingtonsquarereview.com
semiannual

**Weber—The Contemporary
    West**
Weber State University
145 University Circle
Ogden, UT 84408
Michael Wutz, editor
mwutz@weber.edu
weber.edu/weberjournal
semiannual

West Branch
Bucknell Hall
Bucknell University
Lewisburg, PA 17837
G. C. Waldrep, editor
westbranch@bucknell.edu
bucknell.edu/westbranch
triannual

Western Humanities Review
University of Utah
English Department
255 South Central Campus Drive
LNCO 3500
Salt Lake City, UT 84112-0494
Barry Weller, editor
whr@mail.hum.utah.edu
hum.utah.edu/whr
semiannual

Willow Springs
501 North Riverpoint Boulevard
Suite 425
Spokane, WA 99202
Samuel Ligon, editor
willowspringsewu@gmail.com
willowsprings.ewu.edu
semiannual

Witness Magazine
Black Mountain Institute
University of Nevada, Las Vegas
Box 455085
Las Vegas, NV 89154-5085
Maile Chapman, editor
witness@unlv.edu
witness.blackmountaininstitute.org
annual

**WLA: War, Literature &
 the Arts**
Department of English and
 Fine Arts
2354 Fairchild Drive
Suite 6D-149
United States Air Force Academy
Colorado Springs, CO 80840
Colonel Kathleen Harrington,
 editor
editor@wlajournal.com
wlajournal.com
annual

Xavier Review
Xavier University of Lousiana
1 Drexel Drive, Box 89
New Orleans, LA 70125
Ralph Adamo, editor
radamo@xula.edu
xula.edu/review
semiannual

Zoetrope: All-Story
916 Kearny Street
San Francisco, CA 94133
Michael Ray, editor
info@all-story.com
all-story.com
quarterly

Zone 3
Austin Peay State University
Box 4565
Clarksville, TN 37044
Barry Kitterman, editor
zone3@apsu.edu
apsu.edu/zone3
semiannual

ZYZZYVA
466 Geary Street, Suite 401
San Francisco, CA 94102
Laura Cogan, editor
editor@zyzzyva.org
zyzzyva.org
quarterly

Permissions

O. Henry Juror Acknowledgments

"Lauren Groff on 'Your Duck Is My Duck' by Deborah Eisenberg," copyright © 2013 by Lauren Groff. Reprinted by agreement of the author.

"Edith Pearlman on 'The Summer People' by Kelly Link," copyright © 2013 by Edith Pearlman. Reprinted by agreement of the author.

"Jim Shepard on 'The Particles' by Andrea Barrett," copyright © 2013 by Jim Shepard. Reprinted by agreement of the author.

Grateful acknowledgment is made to the following for permission to reprint previously published materials:

"He Knew" first appeared in *The New Yorker*. Copyright © 2011 by Donald Antrim. Reprinted by permission of The Wylie Agency.

"Sail" first appeared in *A Public Space*. Copyright © 2011 by Tash Aw. Reprinted by permission of the author.

"The Particles" first appeared in *Tin House*. Copyright © 2012 by Andrea Barrett. From *Archangel* by Andrea Barrett. Copyright © 2013 by Andrea Barrett. Used by permission of W. W. Norton & Company, Inc.

"Anecdotes" first appeared in *Granta*. Copyright © 2012 by Ann Beattie. Reprinted by permission of the author.

"Lay My Head" first appeared in *Fairy Tale Review*. Copyright © 2011 by L. Annette Binder. Reprinted by permission of the author.

"The History of Girls" first appeared in *Witness*. Copyright © 2012 by Ayşe Papatya Bucak. Reprinted by permission of the author.

"Your Duck Is My Duck" first appeared in *Fence*. Copyright © 2011 by Deborah Eisenberg. Reprinted by permission of the author.

"Where Do You Go?" first appeared in *New England Review*. Copyright © 2011 by Samar Farah Fitzgerald. Reprinted by permission of the author.

"Aphrodisiac" first appeared in *The New Yorker*. Copyright © 2011 by Ruth Prawer Jhabvala. Reprinted by permission of the author.

"Tiger" first appeared in *One Story*. Copyright © 2011 by Nalini Jones. Reprinted by permission of the author.

"The Summer People" by Kelly Link was originally published in *Tin House*. Copyright © 2011 by Kelly Link. Reprinted by permission of the author. A slightly different version of "The Summer People" was published in *Steampunk! An Anthology of Fantastically Rich and Strange Stories,* ed. Kelly Link and Gavin J. Grant (Candlewick Press, 2011).

"They Find the Drowned" first appeared in *Hobart: another literary journal.* Copyright © 2011 by Melinda Moustakis. Reprinted by permission of the author.

"Leaving Maverley" first appeared in *The New Yorker*. Copyright © 2011 by Alice Munro. From *Dear Life*. Copyright © 2013 by Alice Munro. Reprinted by permission of Alfred A. Knopf, a division of Random House LLC, and McClelland & Stewart Ltd., a division of Random House of Canada Limited.

"The Mexican" first appeared in *Epoch*. Copyright © 2012 by George McCormick. Reprinted by permission of the author.

"Sugarcane" first appeared in *The Kenyon Review*. Copyright © 2012 by Derek Palacio. Reprinted by permission of the author.

"Sinkhole" first appeared in *Ploughshares*. Copyright © 2012 by Jamie Quatro. From *I Want to Show You More*. Copyright © 2013 by Jamie Quatro. Used by permission of Grove/Atlantic, Inc.

"White Carnations" first appeared in *Prairie Schooner*. Copyright © 2012 by Polly Rosenwaike. Reprinted by permission of the author.

"The Visitor" first appeared in *The Antioch Review*. Copyright © 2011 by Asako Serizawa. Reprinted by permission of the author.

"Two Opinions" first appeared in *Epoch*. Copyright © 2012 by Joan Silber. From *Fools* by Joan Silber. Copyright © 2013 by Joan Silber. Used by permission of W. W. Norton & Company, Inc.

"Pérou" first appeared in *Epoch*. Copyright © 2011 by Lily Tuck. Reprinted by permission of the author. From *The House at Belle Fontaine: Stories* by Lily Tuck. Copyright © 2013 by Lily Tuck. Used by permission of Grove/Atlantic, Inc.